BECOMING LEIDAH

Michelle Grierson

Published by Simon & Schuster

New York London Toronto Sydney New Delhi

SIMON &
SCHUSTER
CANADA

Simon & Schuster Canada
A Division of Simon & Schuster, Inc.
166 King Street East, Suite 300
Toronto, Ontario M5A 1J3

This Simon & Schuster Canada edition April 2021

SIMON & SCHUSTER CANADA and colophon are trademarks of Simon & Schuster, Inc.

For information about special discounts for bulk purchases, please contact Simon & Schuster Special Sales at 1-800-268-3216 or CustomerService@simonandschuster.ca.

Interior design by Carly Loman

Manufactured in the United States of America

10   9   8   7   6   5   4   3   2   1

Library and Archives Canada Cataloguing in Publication
Title: Becoming Leidah / Michelle Grierson.
Names: Grierson, Michelle, author.
Description: Simon & Schuster Canada edition.
Identifiers: Canadiana (print) 20200282743 | Canadiana (ebook) 20200282751 | ISBN 9781982141202 (softcover) | ISBN 9781982141219 (ebook)
Classification: LCC PS8613.R5334 B43 2021 | DDC C813/.6—dc23

ISBN 978-1-9821-4120-2
ISBN 978-1-9821-4121-9 (ebook)

For Anna;
may you find all the lost and stolen pieces

BECOMING
LEIDAH

The First Thread

The storm was a gift from the Norns, though he didn't know it.

The wind—a fluttering of breath from those Sisters of Fate—sent wave after rising wave, rolling at a steady pace from the west. Pushing the trawler away from any hope of land. No longer steering toward the fjords of home, the vessel turned and turned in the endless surge of ocean. The certainty of Norway's shoreline was lost in the ominous squall lines dripping from the heavens. The sky bruised from blue to black, and the sea's hunger widened like a gaping yawn. He knew they were done for.

He yelled to his mate to angle the hull into the wind. But a confused swell of square waves—the dread of every sailor and fisherman—breached across the bow, throwing him to the rails. A strike of lightning met the ocean in fury, igniting the water into two massive walls rising on either side of the boat. White knuckles gripping the railing, the two men steeled themselves. The boat flew weightless in free fall. His hands slipped, and he was airborne. The trawler tipped, crashing into the valley between the swells. He heard the terrible rushing sound of water, sucking hungrily at them. He hit the deck sideways, sliding into the cold.

He scrambled to hold on to something, but it was no use. The gods had acted. The weight of water dragged him under, as if an anchor were tied to his legs. He held his breath as long as he could, but fear made him panic. Punching, kicking, thrashing, he fought against the monstrous current. His fervent prayers, swallowed deep into the throat of the sea.

The gods proved fickle that day, though; the waters flipped and whirled, throwing his limp, weak body up to the surface. Spitting him back out, like rotten meat.

Unconscious, he lay flat in the shallows, belly-up. Alone. Cold water rushed up his trouser legs, reaching with icy fingers as the tide washed in. It pushed him sideways, filling his mouth with salt. Sputtering, he rolled over. Retched, and retched again. Crawled out of the waves, then collapsed onto the beach.

A voice had pulled him from sleep. A woman sang a song in a language he did not recognize, the words lilting and long. Somehow, her syllables of sorrow, of distant places and loves he yearned to know, rushed to caress his skin. *Am I dreaming?* he thought. He opened his eyes, the light blinding him momentarily. Silver-white reflections—like butterflies bobbing up and down in the wake of sunrise—roused him to full consciousness. A clear blue sky was above him. *Where am I?*

He was nauseated, wary, as if he had a night of drink in him. He tried to remember how he had gotten here—at the shoreline of the end of the world, it would seem—but the stranger's voice drowned out his thoughts. The song ebbed and flowed, washing over him, oblivious to any presence, lilting over the sand and dancing on the tides, across the pearls of white foam. His eyes searched the beach, almost expecting a creature to rise up out of the dunes. He had heard of such things: half woman, half bird; singing sailors to death, seducing them to choose a watery grave rather than face a dreary life without the rapture of such a voice.

No creature rose up from the sands. Nor did any woman walk on water, beckoning him into the waves. Rather, her presence became known to him through taste, suddenly bursting inside his mouth. Sweetness and a bit of salt—not of the sea, but of the spicy sweat of fruit—fermented and warm, fleshy and moist. Cloudberry? He wasn't sure. But the flavour was so overwhelming, he sat up, pressing his hand against his lips, sucking tongue against teeth.

It was then that he saw her. Perched on a bed of rock, an island unto herself, a mass of red seaweed and creamy white skin blooming in the shoals. It took him a moment to realize that the only thing she had wrapped around herself was not seaweed but hair, so long and thick it draped down her back, covering everything but her bare feet.

He didn't move. She kept singing, her hands dipping into the water. Pulling up sea-grass, shells, and pebbles, she placed them in front of her. Her clothes lay behind her. Drying out on the rocks, he thought.

He stood quietly, unsteadily.

Her head rotated slowly, as if sensing his presence; his body plunged forward in a graceful dive.

The last wail of her song echoed into the wind. Her thick grey cloak, secured in his grasp.

The rescue boat came before the sun reached its peak. Minutes after her hands had pulled him out of the ocean, after he had folded her safely in his arms. She had welcomed him without words, her song vanishing into the surf. Silently, she lay down, her hair tumbling in thick tentacles over the edges of rock. The array of specimens she had collected—a puzzle she had been piecing together—a bed of chaos and sharpness beneath them.

Her body opened to him in those shoals, a white flower of spice and sweat, receiving him so sweetly, so easily. In the shallows of invisible creatures, he whispered the names of the gods over and over into her copper hair. The waves rocked his body into hers, each thrust binding them together. The delicate puzzle of sea treasures lost in the deep.

What Was

The midwife pulled the blue thing out of her.

Wriggling and quiet, fitting perfectly in the palm of the old crone's hand. Tiny limbs flailing, stretching up and out; the webbing between each finger and toe translucent in the light of the lantern.

"Oh . . . *Gud i himmelen* . . . a caulbearer."

The old crone sucked in a breath, holding the baby at arm's length for the mother to see. Tremors ran up and down Maeva's legs on the birthing stool. She needed to lie down, but the midwife forced her to see. The blue creature squirmed in the woman's grip. The scrunched face hidden under a second skin.

"So it is true, what they say about you," she said to Maeva. "Count your blessings you're married to a fisherman, *jente*." Shaking her head, she laid the newborn at the edge of the bed, rubbing the tiny body to warm it up. The cord between mother and child still pulsing.

The fishwife collapsed sideways onto the straw mattress. The belief—that a caul could protect a sailor from drowning—offered no consolation to her. A child born with such an oddity would surely be seen as an ominous sign. Especially in the remote village of Ørken.

Maeva knew what was coming, all her fears now birthed beside her.

She breathed in the scent of her own insides: blood, feces, vomit. The dark soil that was woman, thick in the air. The earthy scent of juniper branches, burning in the hearth to stave off evil spirits, not enough to mask her own stench. An unexpected contraction gripped her. She curled up in pain, rolling onto her back.

Is there a twin?

The old woman clicked her tongue in acknowledgement, then placed the baby on Maeva's chest. She tucked a clean swatch of cloth, no bigger than a tea towel, over the infant.

Maeva felt a strange tugging inside her pelvis as the midwife moved and fussed with the wiggling creature, the umbilical cord thick as a rope. She peered down at this miniscule animal. Her own hands moved slowly, as if in water, an invisible resistance dragging on her. She held them inches away from the baby, uncertain, hesitant. Afraid.

Will you live?

Helgar wiped her hands on her apron, humming an old Norse melody to the child. It calmed Maeva, enough to allow her arms to settle on her swollen stomach, inches from the baby. The midwife picked up a knife, her palms smeared with blood. She lifted the child's head in one hand. Her gnarled fingers worked efficiently, cutting away the veil on the baby's face in two quick motions.

Tiny nostrils flared, filling with air.

Thank the gods. Maeva exhaled, unaware she had been holding her breath.

Helgar lifted an eyebrow. "Yes, that's it. Breathe. Both of you." She waited for the pulsing of the umbilical cord to stop. Then, in one quick slice, the child was cleaved from her mother.

Maeva was surprised to feel absolutely nothing, this bridge of life suddenly so irrelevant and unnecessary. The child, now a separate being, no longer a part of her.

Helgar slid the birthing stool out of the way, then moved the baby to lie on the blanket inside the cradle.

A wave of nausea overcame Maeva. She closed her eyes. Trying to keep still. Felt hands pressing hard on her belly, the midwife's weight bearing down. She winced and moaned as her womb protested. Maeva opened her eyes in a panic. *Am I going to die?* The next few pushes were almost unbearable as the stout hag leaned her entire body on top of her, lifting off the floor. Finally, in one single violent gush, she felt her insides let go. The afterbirth slid out in glorious, agonizing relief.

It had been a long labour—a week since early contractions buckled her to her knees on the porch; two days since Maeva had sent her husband to hike the mountain pass in the cloak of night to fetch Helgar Tormundsdatter. The old woman followed Pieter to the cabin to find Maeva sweating, cursing, moaning. At this moment, dusk settled like dust on the two exhausted women. It was a calm evening, the wind having died down to a mere whisper in the long grass surrounding the cottage. A distant howl echoed in the valley dwarfed by the silhouette of a mountain. Framed by a purple and green aurora flickering across the sky, Ørkenfjell was an imposing presence. A giant to be feared. But tonight, the inlet of water and rock seemed asleep. Innocent as a babe.

Helgar gestured to the window. "Early in the season to see such colour above the fjord."

Maeva said nothing but understood the midwife's concern. Could almost hear the woman's thoughts. *Sky dancers: the ghosts of the dead. Coming to claim souls.*

The old woman sang to herself, ignoring the howling outside. But the hairs on the back of Maeva's neck stood up at the eerie sound, and she shivered. Helgar turned the oil lamp up. She leaned in closer, inspecting the placenta between the young mother's legs.

Maeva lifted her head to see. Blood and goo. Flesh, but not another baby. *Takk, Freyja.* She dropped her head back onto the mattress.

Helgar inhaled deeply, nodding at the scent. "This is good. Healthy."

Not this time, sky dancers. Maeva sent a prayer upwards, her worry subsiding.

She watched with curiosity as the midwife scooped the remains of her insides into a pan, then scored it with the shape of a cross. Helgar muttered to herself as she did this, making Maeva wonder. *Do you fear me, as the villagers do?*

"We can bury it . . . or burn it. Or chop it up into a stew. Perhaps make a powder for tea. It will do you good."

Maeva shook her head, unable to hide her repulsion.

The old woman shrugged, her attention back on the child. Picking up the baby to examine, she spread the tiny webbed fingers. She rubbed the skin to get the circulation moving, but the blue remained. She frowned. Maeva kept silent, watching as Helgar pinched the webbing. She pressed a little harder, marking it with a fingernail. The child made no sound, felt no pain it seemed. Lifting a diminutive blue foot, as if wanting the old woman to take notice, the baby fanned five webbed toes, each one perfectly round like a tiny pebble. Helgar tried to smile, but Maeva could see the strain in it. The child closed her eyes, content. Without asking— without even a second glance at the mother—Helgar pulled scissors out of her apron pocket and held the newborn's foot tightly in one hand. She began snipping the web with precision.

Maeva tensed, but made no move to stop her. *Perhaps if we catch it early . . .*

The baby yawned.

"Such an entrance into the world," Helgar mused, speaking to the newborn as if she could understand every word. The infant stretched small sausage arms.

Maeva's eyes welled up. *Weeks early, webbed fingers and toes, blue up to the elbows and knees, wearing a mask of skin—*

"And now, hardly any sound. Even when cut." Helgar finished the last slice of skin, placing the scissors in her apron pocket. "A quiet one. Be thankful for this small mercy from God." She placed the child on her mother's chest once more, tucking a blanket around them both, then moved to spread Maeva's legs.

Maeva suffered through fingers probing into her, feeling more blood escape. She leaned toward the bucket beside the headboard, half filled with vomit, and closed her eyes. The repercussions of birthing such a child . . . She knew what would be said, the accusations already taking shape. Her baby was living proof. The village women had been clucking and pecking about her since she arrived last year. It seemed their prayers had been answered. Maeva opened her eyes to look at the little blue thing. *What will stop them now?*

Perhaps Maeva should accuse them of cursing her. Of using magic to sicken her baby inside the womb. That would explain the strangeness of such a child as this. *That would be justice.* She almost smiled, imagining the shock on their prim mouths.

Helgar dipped her wrinkled hands into a bowl of warm water, rinsing the knife and scissors. "Children born under the caul have the second sight. They have powers beyond this world." She grunted. "Not a good thing in this village." She pocketed her knife. "You a Lapp, girl? A northerner? I've seen such things up there, in Finnmark."

Maeva tried not to react. She shook her head. *No, not a Lapp. Not from the north at all. From somewhere else entirely . . .* Saying nothing, she struggled to sit up, holding the baby awkwardly. Her legs were smeared in blood, the hot swamp of creation still oozing out of her.

Helgar reached for a clean cloth and pressed it between Maeva's thighs to catch the bleeding.

"Sit on that straw bale for a few days, at most a week—if you bleed more than that, drink a tankard of hot brandy and pepper. Then send for me."

Maeva's eyes widened.

Helgar waved at her. "Oh, it's all right. You won't die. And neither will she." The old woman picked up the child, gripping her head and bottom, holding her out for Maeva to see. The webbing cut back, the baby almost seemed normal. Except for the discolouration of limbs.

"It's a girl."

Maeva blinked through watery eyes.

"Come now, no time for tears—she's hungry."

Maeva watched as the infant rooted for something to suck on. But she didn't reach for her.

Helgar sighed. "It's not so bad, girl. I will take the caul with me—I'm sure some fisherman will pay a good price. But the child—she's yours."

The accusation was subtle, but Maeva felt it. She frowned. "I would never—"

9

"Stop your worry—I won't tell a soul about her. Or any of this. I was never here."

Maeva teared up even more, her gratitude sincere.

"You mustn't fret—she's perfectly healthy, despite her size. Despite . . ."

Maeva bit back the words. *Being blue.*

"No turning back now. The labour is only the beginning—it's God's way. To prepare us womenfolk for the real work."

In response, a shooting pain seared through Maeva's left breast. The child gurgled again. If only she could sleep for a moment. She closed her eyes, felt the old woman fumbling with the buttons on her nightgown. She shifted on the pillow to allow it. A swollen breast fell out, and the child's mouth latched on with urgency. A throb, then pleasurable relief—a confusing combination—flowed through Maeva. She opened her eyes.

The midwife chuckled. "Now that's a good sign, isn't it?"

Maeva managed a half-hearted smile. She rested her hand next to the girl's tiny head. Her hair was soft, fuzzy, and white. Like down on a baby duckling.

"Pull her close—she won't lose her latch, that one. She's a fighter."

Maeva held her breath, tentatively cradling her arm around her daughter's tiny form. A blue hand fluttered out of the blanket, then floated to rest comfortably on the swell of her bosom. Maeva flinched ever so slightly.

The midwife didn't seem to notice. "What shall I tell him?"

Maeva considered. "Tell him he has a daughter." She paused, then said pointedly, "That's all."

The old woman nodded. "Keep an eye on the bleeding. Drink some yarrow tea, soak yourself in milfoil. A cup of dark ale will help with letdown." She shrugged. "The baby's hands and feet—I did what I could. The web may grow back. The skin needs more warming, perhaps. Pray it fades, *jente.*"

Maeva nodded, knowing it wouldn't. How would she hide such an obvious deformity?

Helgar picked up the birthing stool and the pile of bloody sheets.

"Will you make a stew?" She gestured to the placenta. "Best thing for new mothers. Wards off sickness. And evil."

Maeva swallowed and shook her head, trying to suppress yet another wave of nausea. "But . . . leave the caul."

The woman clucked—in admiration or criticism, Maeva couldn't tell—then dropped the small bundle of skin on the bed. "Suit yourself."

"Takk skal du ha," Maeva said quietly. "My husband has coin for you."

The old woman grunted again and waved her off, taking one last look at the baby bird in her arms. "She'll survive, she's strong. Keep her out of sight for a while, hmm? And swaddle her tightly. Don't forget a bit of silver—a needle or shilling—sewn into the hem. To ward off the *huldre-folk*." Helgar shifted her gaze back to the young mother.

Maeva blinked as though she didn't understand.

She had heard the word before; it was something the church hens called her, behind her back at the market. Half woman, half troll. A suspiciously beautiful girl hiding a tail under her skirts. Though after tonight, the midwife couldn't possibly believe such rumours.

"God natt, Maeva Aldestaed."

The mother watched as the old woman waddled out of the room and then lumbered down the ladder stairs, bags teetering on both shoulders.

Maeva held her breath, listening.

In hushed tones, the news of a daughter was shared.

Wolf

The wolf watched from the edge of the tree line, crouching in the long grass. His animal eye fixed on the cabin.

He was a slave to the scent of blood. The wind thrust the smell upon him, forcing him to follow the signs, breathing it in. Across rivers and forests, mountains and meadows, for days on end, he followed the trace. He didn't sleep or eat. Nothing else mattered.

A wild arc of green light shimmered down toward the cottage, surrounding it in a watery halo. A breeze swayed across the tops of the trees, lifting the celestial skirt of the aurora. A sure sign that the child would arrive tonight. He sniffed the air. The house oozed her distinctive aroma, a scent of something not quite animal, not quite human. The smell of the sea. Inside, a man paced to and fro, pausing every so often at the window, his bearded face lined with worry.

Husband. The word floated up from somewhere deep inside him. His jaw clenched.

Short rasps and moaning from inside the cottage shivered across his fur. Or perhaps it was the trace of a hand stroking the length of his spine. Sometimes he could see her, edges blurred but dancing in his mind. Tonight, he heard her. The call, haunting, as if underwater.

He crawled a little closer, sniffing in every last bit of the tangy aroma. He waited for the man—*husband*—to open the door, or a window. Imagined leaping across the threshold, sinking his teeth into his throat. Shaking him until he bled out. Still and lifeless. Then snatching the child for himself.

He shook his fur instead. He knew he must wait. That to force himself upon her would accomplish nothing. That it would break the rules. He had lived long enough to know that this world—every world—was governed by rules. Laws that reigned over existence, controlling every form of being, human or otherwise. Even in dream time. He knew that to deny these laws, to willfully rebel, was to choose heavy consequences.

The door opened suddenly. An old woman hobbled out into the night. Instinctively, he pulled back on his haunches. Ready to attack. The smell of Maeva was thick on her, wafting from the bundle she carried.

His blood quickened. His muscles contracted, his mouth salivating.

Just before he leaped, a cry erupted from the cottage. It stopped him in his tracks.

An almost human smile spread across his jowls. He waited for the old woman to disappear into the woods.

Then howled back, loud enough for both mother and child to hear.

What Was

She heard the midwife telling Pieter to wait, that mother and baby needed rest, time to acquaint themselves. Then the door opened and slammed, a cool draft sneaking its way into the warm cottage and upstairs.

The baby stiffened, shivering at the rush of cold. She let out a small yowl.

Maeva didn't have much time. She knew her husband; he would not wait long to lay claim to his child, and his wife. Though she could not blame him. She had been in bed for over a month, bleeding intermittently. Pieter had been worried, forcing her to stay still, even threatening to fetch the district doctor. But Maeva knew that such a request would only feed the town gossip; she didn't want more reason for suspicion.

The midwife herself arrived under a crescent moon, on foot. Following Pieter's horse from a distance. A shadow in the night, unnoticed. If anyone understood discretion, it was Helgar Tormundsdatter, the village *klok kvinne*, Ørken's unofficial healer. She was shunned by the church, but she still managed to work steadily, in secret. Surely Helgar knew every man's personal property intimately: Every attic, mud cellar, and barn loft. Every back room and pantry. For that was how she did her work, right under their noses. Maids and mistresses, wives and widows; each had a story that could not be repeated, a story that was somehow attached to Helgar's cures. Confidentiality, an unspoken contract, taken seriously by anyone who called for her, according to Pieter. That was what convinced Maeva she would be safe in the old woman's hands. Despite her being unlicensed and untrained.

The child's mouth pulled at Maeva's nipple, determined to keep feeding. She peered down at this newly born thing. Her hand enveloped the baby almost completely. She watched the eagerness of her suckling with fascination and suspicion—this elfling, both familiar and strange in her animal-like hunger. Her own life suddenly so transformed.

And what of your life, my love?

The question was suddenly there, unbidden and strong.

For a moment, she allowed herself to think of him. Feeling him close, his breath on her cheek, his fingers in her hair . . . The child wailed, unlatching. Instinctively, Maeva began rocking to soothe her. The baby rooted for her breast, then nestled in again. She shifted to lie on her side, placed an arm around her daughter to keep her close and safe, then closed her eyes.

Just a little sleep . . .

The caul. Maeva forced herself awake. Still slightly bloodied, the translucent skin lay beside her, glistening in the candlelit room. Tracing a finger along the spidery pattern of veins, she marvelled at the delicate edges fanning out like a miniature tree. There was still a faint pulse, the hue changing ever so slightly—purple, then pink, darkening to blue—with each beat. The mystery of such a thing, hidden elegantly inside a mere scrap of skin.

But it was no surprise to her; she herself was born under the veil.

She whispered to her daughter. "Not to worry . . . It is how all of our kind enter the world." She fingered the soft papery texture, then lifted the child's webbed hand off her chest. Examining the similarities, the otherworldly luminescence.

She had no choice; she had to hide it.

Maeva pulled the child off her chest, placing her on the bed. She worked quickly, the gurgles of her daughter making her breasts drip. She snipped the caul, her sewing scissors slicing it cleanly in two. Each half into another half, then another and another, until the entire caul was a pile of small pieces, each no bigger than a thumb. She watched the pulsing slow, then die off, soft pink to translucent white. Until all that was left were thin, delicate triangles of dead skin.

Pieter entered the room as she pushed the pile under the bed.

She managed to smile. Standing unsteadily, blood dripped down her legs.

She gestured to the child. On cue, the baby mewed out a small cry.

The new father rushed to his daughter, smitten already.

What Is

The best thing about being small: I can hide in plain sight, without being seen.

The worst thing about being small: I can hide in plain sight, without being seen.

I hid the day I was born, a ghost-girl curling up beside Mamma, while she pushed and squeezed my baby body into the world. I know that sounds like a made-up story, but I remember every bit of it. I was in two places at once. Here and there. I remember floating on the wind, the howl of a lone wolf flying through the trees, pulling me to and fro, inside and outside the cottage, inside and outside Mamma's big belly. She didn't know. She was too scared to see. So scared, she was whiter than the moon. Her red hair sweaty and dark. Like rivers down her back. I brushed it aside, put my ghost hand on her head to calm her. It was hot and damp, and she shook and shook, like a rabbit. I whispered sweet things into her ear, while the old lady caught hold of my baby head and pulled me out. She didn't see the other me either, of course—no one knew I was a ghost in the room.

But I know it happened. I remember being born.

"Enough stories, Leidah. Enough of this nonsense. Go feed the chickens." Mamma shakes her head. She drops the basket of washing on the ground.

I squint up at the summer sun. "It's going to rain."

Mamma squints back at me. "Is it, now? And what makes you think such a thing, with the sun shining high in the sky?"

I shrug. I don't say that the air is sad. That the trees are sad, too. That the sun is never happy enough to last.

I don't bother to tell Mamma that her clothes won't dry today. She won't believe me. I dig my toe into the grass. She reaches into the pile of wet clothes. Shakes out Pappa's trousers with a snap. I peep at her sideways, without actually looking. Bite a fingernail.

"I even remember the blanket you used to wrap me up in. It was red with patches. How would I know that if I wasn't there, Mamma?"

Her eyes roll up to the clear blue sky. Her hand waves in the air, at bugs I can't see.

"You were there, child—you wouldn't be standing in front of me today if it were otherwise. But to remember any of this, as a mere babe— let alone be two places at once—it's . . . it's simply not possible." She pins the pants to the line, hanging between two trees. "It's a good story, I will admit." She reaches to pull my fingers away from my mouth. "Such a bad habit."

I bite my lip instead. I watch a caterpillar crawl across the grass toward my foot and wiggle my toes, feeling the webby bits stretch and pull.

"Then how do I know other things, Mamma? Things about that day? How do I know about the old lady?" I bend down to watch the caterpillar squirm through the grass, moving my toes a little closer. "Sometimes I see her walking. But she doesn't have any feet." I stop and think. "I guess it's more like floating than walking. The old lady never touches the ground."

She holds Pappa's shirt by the sleeves. The collar falls forward, like it's bowing its head. Like she's about to dance with a man who isn't there.

I wonder at the thing that might convince her. It comes out so quiet, I hardly hear it myself. "I couldn't see that night. Something covered my eyes. Then the old woman cut it away. I saw everything after that."

Her arms drop the shirt. The invisible man, gone.

"I heard things, too . . . A wolf. Howling."

She rubs her forehead. She must have a headache. The only thing I can see is her mouth. Lips pressed hard.

"Enough. Nonsense." She points to the barn. "Chickens. Now."

I jump a little at each word, standing up. Marching up the steps onto the porch, stomping as loudly as I can, I ignore the pointed finger and the hungry chickens. I stop and spin around, feeling taller on the porch.

"I know things, Mamma."

Her eyes get really small.

"You can't tell me I don't." I open the door before she can say another word. "I remember it better than you."

Slam. The door bangs behind me.

I close my eyes and wait. Nothing happens, but I can feel her, all tight and jittery on the other side of the door.

"Just do as she tells you, Lei-lee. Be a good girl, ja?" Pappa says.

I huff toward the fire, where he is sitting, and he pulls me onto his knee, the rock of the chair soothing me, back and forth, back and forth.

After I stop huffing, I shove my thumb between my teeth, biting and sucking back tears.

Sometimes, I hate her.

"It is good for us to hold our tongues, child," he says. "It keeps us out of trouble."

He smirks, his scruffy black beard covering his mouth. One eyebrow up, the other down. Then, like magic, there is a toy in his hand.

I grin. It's a doll—my *dukke*—the one Mamma made me before I was born. She used to have red yarn for hair, and a pretty apron. But now, she's naked, with no face. I grab at her, putting her under my chin. Then I bite at the web of skin in between my fingers. "But you believe me, right, Pappa? I was there, you know."

Both eyebrows go up. "Of course you were, child. It was a day none of us could forget. Even the wind remembers. It roared around the house for days before you came, and then, nothing." He snaps his fingers, leaning in to whisper in my ear. "I remember listening to the quiet, thinking, *This child must be special, to make even the wind stop its shouting.*"

I giggle. He smiles and pulls me close. I snuggle into him, nuzzling his beard to my cheek, feeling better already. He tells me of his pacing. Eight steps across the floor of the cottage, one for each month of my growing, his feet pacing one way, then back again, five, six, maybe seven hours of walking, each step a prayer for my safe coming.

"I wished you into being, even before you were the size of a pin inside Mamma's belly."

I stop biting my finger. "I was never that small, was I?"

"Of course you were! And I sang songs of the sea into Mor's belly, making up rhymes with different names—Jens for a boy, Clara for a girl—testing them out on my tongue with different voices. Sometimes lullabies, sometimes shouts: 'Jens, you dropped the eggs!' 'Clara, how could you ruin your Sunday dress?' It drove Mor mad, those songs, those voices. All that practice."

Pappa's brown eyes shine. We watch the fire dance and spit in the hearth.

I frown. "But I'm not a Clara or a Jens, Pappa."

"*Nei, jente.* You are Leidah. *My* Lei-lee."

I nod, smug. I let the doll sit on my lap and squeeze Pappa's hands.

"Careful, now. These old fingers ache sometimes."

I let go. "Because of all the fish you catch?"

Pappa wiggles them. "Because of all the fish. And don't forget about the sea monsters."

We hear Mamma climb the porch steps. He stops rocking.

I don't ask why I am Leidah and not Clara. My hands curl inside Pappa's. His fingers are red and swollen. Mine are blue, and thin like sticks. The web between each finger almost see-through.

Definitely not a Clara's hands. Or a Jens's. These hands are Leidah's hands. Small and ugly. Like my name, though I don't tell Pappa. It starts pretty, but ends in a hard thud. *Lie-duh.* Leidah, the girl who has to hide her ugly hands and feet; whose mor has to cut and hide a little ugly piece of her, every week. Leidah, who, one day, will have so much of her ugliness cut away, there will be nothing left. Only ugly blue bones.

"Why did I come out blue, Far?"

He shifts me to his other knee. "Because you're special, child . . . It is God's gift of specialness."

I roll my eyes. "Mor doesn't think so."

Pappa makes a face.

"Lei-lee, don't be so easily fooled. Your mor thinks you are special. But she wants you to be able to do ordinary things. So she makes sure you can do everything other children can."

I scrunch up my nose. "Like washing and cooking."

He laughs. "And feeding the chickens. Which you haven't done today?"

I ignore the question. "Then why can't I go into town? Go to school, like the other children?"

We hear Mamma stomping her feet on the mat; then she opens the door. "Because your mor thinks it's best." He kisses my forehead, shifting me off his lap. "Go on, now—go collect some eggs so Mor and Far can talk, ja?"

"Ja. First I need to get my apron."

I hold on to my *dukke*. Pappa pushes me to the ladder stairs. I climb with her under my arm. Then I sneak to sit against the railing. I hug my legs into my chest, sitting the dolly on top of my knees, hiding most of my face. *Maybe they won't see me, right,* dukke? My heart beats so loud, I am sure Far can hear it all the way downstairs. I peer over the landing, my forehead almost between the bars. He stands, hands on hips. I hear the door shut, and then the creak of the chair. I can see him at the fire. He picks up the poker.

"What is it?" Mamma asks.

"I spoke with Pastor Knudsen yesterday. In the village."

The laundry basket drops to the floor. "Oh? About what?"

He waits, and then says, "Leidah attending church."

My mother spins to face him. Her long braid swinging down her back like a rope. "We tried that, remember? Once was enough. It's not something any of us want to repeat."

"But she's older now—people change, Mae."

"People do not change. If you send our child into that—that—hell again, she will suffer. We all will—and it will be your fault. Can you live with that?"

"The Ørken church is anything but hell, Mae. Don't be sacrilegious."

Mamma laughs. "I would have to be religious to commit such a sin." She takes the poker from him, shoving it into the heat. "They eat people alive."

Pappa makes a face.

"Why now, Pieter? What's happened?"

"There's a new shipmaster from Stavanger at the harbour. He's hiring for the winter—"

"No one hires through the winter."

"The pay is good, Mae. I need the work."

Mamma stops stirring the fire.

"They need more men on the boats . . . To follow the herd up the coast to their feeding ground."

She turns, holding the poker like a sword. But says nothing.

"They need men who know the western coastline, who know the weather . . . And we both know only Christians will be hired." Far pulls the poker from her hands and sets it beside the fire. "This will never change. Not in this town. Men pray to a single God and bow their heads on Sundays, even if they whisper Odhinn's name to the wind. If I want steady work, I must do the same."

Mor hugs herself.

He puts his hands on her shoulders. "We need the money. We need our daughter to eat through the winter. And you—how else will we fatten you up to have another child?"

She pulls away.

"Maeva, please. We only feed the gossip by hiding her. Hiding you." He pulls her to him, lifting her chin.

"I want to keep her safe."

"As do I. But it's been seven years since her birth. Surely the danger is no longer what it once was. It's time, Mae . . . Please."

A clap of thunder makes all of us jump.

Mamma runs to the door. "The clothes!"

I go to the bedroom window, watching them. They rush about the yard, pulling shirts and sheets off the line. The sky opens up as soon as they reach the porch. I hear them laugh. The rain shushes down, telling all of us to hush. I walk away from the window and hug dolly.

They don't feel the sadness in the air.

They don't feel the danger coming, riding in on the wind.

What Was

After the storm, the rain had pounded for hours, finally slowing to a light drizzle, then shaped into a foggy mist. The air, so damp it showered them in slickness. The fury of wind had subsided, the waves surprisingly calm. As if no tragedy had occurred.

The blond man jumped off the trawler and onto the pier. He grabbed the massive rope, securing the bowline to the dock. The other man—the darker, bearded one; the one Maeva couldn't quite look at in the eye—whistled once from the back of the boat. She stole a sideways glance at his hands, moving deftly, weaving the rope around a cleat. Round and round, he pulled and tightened, until the sway of the boat almost stopped. She experienced a sudden flash of those same hands gripping her hips back on the island . . . She leaned over the side of the railing, her stomach queasy. Swallowing a taste of sea-water, she sank to the deck floor, huddling under the blanket he had given her.

Even though the wind had died down, the bite of the coming winter was sharp. The mist suddenly vanished; in its place, weightless white fluff fell around Maeva. *The first snow.* Underwater, she had always felt warm, but here, exposed to the frigid elements, she shivered. She tried not to panic. Her breath came in short rasps. Her only thought, looping into a tangled knot in her mind: *How will I get back?*

It was her own fault. Her sisters had warned her not to take so many risks.

The burly man called from the pier. "She's as secure as she can get. *Takk.*"

Maeva understood the words enough to wonder, was he referring to the boat or her?

The bearded man moved to the helm, stood with his hands on his hips in front of her, with a confidence that spoke of conceit, a man used to adoration. "I should be the one thanking you. It was quite a rescue." Though he spoke to his friend, his eyes fixated on her huddled body.

Her eyes darted away, to the sea. Searching for some sign of rescue herself. Perhaps her sisters had seen what had happened. Perhaps they were biding their time, waiting for the right moment? Her mind, beginning to fray at the edges.

Where are you, my love, when I need you the most?

"I don't even want to think about what could have happened if I hadn't gone after you." The blond man boarded the trawler, his tone serious. "Though it seems like you still managed to bring in quite a catch."

The two stood side by side, staring at her.

Maeva sensed the animal in them. She shifted away, pulling the blanket tighter, tucking her legs completely into herself. Trying to shrink. Wishing she could dive back into the water. But now, she was weak, vulnerable. She wouldn't get far. Not in this cold.

She leaned her head against the side of the boat, hitting something.

"Careful," the blond man said.

She craned her neck as he reached above her. She stared, having only seen such a thing at a distance. The stuff of cautionary tales, told by her sisters to frighten her, from the time she was a toddler. The long-handled pickaxe had a blunt edge, for bludgeoning. The other end, a spiked hook.

For gutting an animal from gullet to groin.

Her breath quickened. The men didn't notice.

The blond man scratched at reddish stubble on his chin. He gestured to the village up the hill. "I will head Innesbørg off at the pass. Someone will have to tell the wife." He paused, then murmured, "Widow, I mean."

The other one took his wool cap off. "I will do it. She shouldn't hear it from anyone else." His voice cracked.

The blond man nodded, but said nothing.

Maeva tried to quiet her fear, focusing on the words of the two men. She wondered at the cause of the wreck: Did he go out with a crew, despite gales the size of a cyclone?

"Go ahead, Hans. Say it." His voice was low, trembling. "You warned me. I didn't heed the warning. Antum is gone because of my stubborn ways." He put his cap back on, pulling it down low over his brow.

Hans opened his mouth to speak, then shut it.

They both stared at the horizon. Silent, lost in thought.

Maeva took the opportunity to crawl away from the railing, toward the helm. She could reach the galley if she was fast enough; perhaps their grief could be her escape. She stood and moved across the slippery deck in three strides, holding the blanket around her shoulders with one hand, the other hand at the ready, to take back what was hers. Her eyes were frantic, quickly landing on the treasure under the wheel. She lunged, fingers stretched to snatch it.

All of a sudden, his face was in front of her, his lips almost touching her forehead. Her hand shrank back.

He didn't seem to understand her actions. "You must be cold. Hans, we need to find some clothing for—for . . . *Hva heter du?*" he asked her.

Hans shook his head. "We already tried speaking to her, Pieter. She's clearly not from here. She won't understand the common tongue."

Maeva didn't correct him.

"Let me try," Pieter said. He dropped Maeva's treasure into a fish barrel, then pivoted around. He grasped her shoulder. She jerked out of his grip. His eyes registered surprise, hurt. She ignored him anyway, steadied her gaze on the barrel.

His hand patted his chest. "Pieter. Pieter Aldestaed." He moved his finger to touch her, then pulled back. Hovered it above her heart. "And you are . . . ?"

She waited, not wanting him to know how much she comprehended.

Somehow, their not knowing her name kept the two men at a distance. He repeated his name again, hitting himself more urgently. Maeva stared blankly at him.

Hans pointed to the village. "I'll go tell the magistrate; hopefully we can find some clothing for her." He shook his head at Pieter. "Good luck. I think you're going to need it."

Pieter nodded, then called after him. "Don't tell him everything. Remember what we agreed."

What had they agreed? Maeva wondered. She realized that if she didn't speak up at some point, she might never go home.

"Maeva." She whispered her name, so low he had to lean in.

"*Hva?* Say it again." His eyes gleamed with success.

She cleared her throat and said it louder. "*Is mise Maeva . . . Tha mi airson a dhol dhachaigh.*"

"I don't understand—tell me again."

Maeva said it one more time, with force. *I want to go home.*

"Nei. I still don't know what you're saying."

"I should hope not, Pieter Aldestaed. Sounds like nonsense to me," a woman's voice interrupted from below, on the dock. "Now where's my husband?"

Pieter's face crumbled at the question. In an instant, he became a small boy, caught doing something terrible. He searched Maeva's eyes—for help or sympathy, she wasn't sure. As if she could save him from drowning. As if she were his lifeboat.

She balled up her hands into fists.

The woman persisted. "Where is Antum? Most likely drunk, I'm sure. I've waited a fortnight, and I shan't wait any longer. And who the devil is up there with you?"

Pieter touched Maeva's wrist, ignoring her flinch, then spun to the ladder to climb off the boat. Before he did, he closed the lid on the barrel, securing the metal latch with a click.

Maeva cursed silently. She waited for him to descend, then pulled at the latch, trying to be as quiet as possible. It didn't budge. She snuck past the barrel, staying out of sight to peer over the edge of the railing.

A middle-aged woman in a black wool cloak and bonnet stood with arms crossed, her face pinched into a scowl.

"*Hilsener, Fru Vebjørnsdatter. Jeg beklager . . .*"

Maeva watched the dark-haired man struggle to find the right words. The shape of letters that would grind this woman to dust. Shrink her into half of what she used to be: a wife without a husband.

Maeva was fascinated at the change, the animal in him gone. Replaced by something gentle, careful. Almost loving.

His words floated in the salty air. Hovering, then sinking into soft flesh.

Maeva could feel the woman's heart reshaping itself. Shrinking, dying.

Time suspended—disbelief, denial lengthening each second—until he repeated the words, again and again. The horrible news, finally solidifying into a violent truth.

The widow tilted her head, beginning to tremble, shattering into ugly fragmented sobs, her legs buckling. Pieter caught her easily, holding her tightly in his arms. She keened uncontrollably, sharp gusts of breath expelling from her contorted mouth.

Maeva didn't move. Uncomfortable, awkward.

Pieter's eyes, full of guilt.

He absorbed all of it, the earthquake of grief crashing through his solid frame. Minutes passed. The entire time, he held Maeva in his gaze.

She couldn't tear herself away, feeling his desperate need for her to be his witness. Confused by her captor's tenderness, Maeva wondered, *Who will be my witness?*

The widow stepped back abruptly. Wiping her eyes with a handkerchief from her apron, she straightened her skirt and bonnet, a surprising calm overcoming her. The storm of woe replaced with curmudgeonly determination. It was then that she looked up.

Maeva wanted to smile, but her mouth wouldn't cooperate.

The widow glowered, scrutinizing every unkempt detail. Maeva reached a hand up to tame her dishevelled mass of red curls. Tugging at the blanket to hide herself, she was startled by the shame she felt; never before had she been embarrassed by her own flesh. Then, finally, the widow crossed her arms, as if a judgement or decision had been made. Ice-blue eyes, more bitter than the winter wind, pierced into Maeva.

Pulling herself up to her full height, Maeva met the woman's gaze directly.

There was a slight retraction of the widow's head. Her nose lifted upwards, her face pinching into sourness, as if smelling something afoul in the air.

Pieter cleared his throat.

Birgit sniffed. *"What* is this?"

Pieter stepped toward Maeva. He turned to the widow, with Maeva above him at the railing. The words tumbled out. "We rescued her. She's my . . . Maeva."

Maeva's eyes widened.

"My"?

The widow's face mirrored hers, both women taken aback by the declaration. The claim of ownership.

Pieter peered up at Maeva, seeming uncertain how much she comprehended. But Maeva understood perfectly. Somehow, two complete strangers—a fisherman and his catch of the day—were now bound together in his estimation.

It was at that moment Hans marched toward the trawler with an even bigger man at his side. Presumably the town magistrate. The man's face mottled from exertion or too much drink. He stopped a few feet away. There was an awkward silence; all of the figures homed in on a single focal point.

Like wolves, they watched Maeva with varying degrees of ravenousness.

Pieter held his hand up. "Magistrate Innesbørg, allow me to introduce you. This is Maeva . . . My bride-to-be."

Maeva felt the blood drain from her legs. *Oh God, no.*

The widow gasped in shock.

Innesbørg grunted. Scanned her up and down as if she were, indeed, a caught fish. Then stopped to stare at her naked feet, just above his eye level on the deck.

Somehow, this made Maeva feel even more violated. She backed up, curling her toes. She struggled to remain composed, but she couldn't hide her horror. The realization that she was trapped. And she wouldn't be going home any time soon.

You aren't coming for me . . .

Salty bile collected in her throat. She couldn't contain it any longer. She ran to the railing and spewed onto the pier. Inches from the widow's feet.

The First Knot

Helgar Tormundsdatter shuffled past the local inn with stealth. Her thumb and finger worried away at the black stone—the one she always carried, shaped like a hammer—inside her cloak pocket. Ahead, the tall wooden spire of the church stabbed the sky. She put her head down, ignoring the draw of laughter and ale. It had been the middle of the night when she was summoned to Maeva's side, the village fast asleep. Much easier than the dinner hour, she thought. She must make it past the church, to the mountain path home, without being seen. The delivery of the Aldestaed baby a secret best kept from prying eyes.

The inn and the church—one bright red, the other black as pitch—stood at opposite ends of the village, like soldiers at war. Recruiting was a daily struggle: villagers swaying between states of drunkenness and piety, sometimes simultaneously, much to the chagrin of the pastor. Ørken's inhabitants—all two hundred and thirty-three of them, plus one more as of tonight—born and bred for the sea, living their entire lives around the will of the tides, the whims of wind and season; this made worship an act of fervour on Sundays. But the changeable weather, the uncertainty of a good haul of fish, made most lose themselves in drink every other day of the week, praying to the gods, a private nightly ritual.

Tonight, the small pub was bursting at the seams. A ship of fishermen from Bergen had arrived hours ago, thirsty for more than just drink after such a long stint at sea. Helgar could sense it, could hear it in the volume and intensity, the gales of laughter and shouts echoing out into the night. Most were too drunk to notice an old spinster passing by. Too young to want an old crone in their bed. Still, Helgar was careful to keep her hood pulled around her face; the ways of men were unpredictable.

The aroma of roasted chicken made her mouth water. She hadn't eaten much since yesterday. A pint of something—anything—would certainly be a deserved reward for such a birthing. But she couldn't risk being stopped. Couldn't risk questions about whose blood had stained her skirt and hands. *Thor's hammer, do your work. Protect me.* The threat of discovery—and the mob of drunken men—forced her to keep moving, the weight of the small birthing stool heavier with each step. The weight of what she had witnessed tonight even heavier.

What child deserved such deformity? Could this truly be the Christian God's handiwork? She had lied to the mother about seeing such things in Finnmark. She had never been that far north. But there were always rumours, strange tales about those Lapp women. *Huldrefolk. Havfruer. Hekser.* Fairy folk, mermaids, and witches. Though she had seen odd things right here in Ørken: a baby born blind, another missing a toe. God's punishment of sin, most would say. But Helgar had never seen a caulbearer, or a webbed child. She had never seen hands and feet the colour of a stormy sea. Bluer than moonlight. *Unless it was dead.*

This small babe—not much bigger than a herring—suckled as though she were six months old. Helgar chewed her lip, thinking of the caul. Born to anyone else, it might have been seen as a *seierslue*, a victory cap. God's blessing of good fortune. But on anything born from Maeva Aldestaed, it would surely be seen as the devil's mark. Strangers were never welcome in Ørken unless they brought wealth or work for the village. Maeva Aldestaed did neither. And the infant? No chance of the *huldrefolk* stealing such a deformed thing.

Helgar feared for the child. She knew what it was like to be an outsider. Though she was the daughter of one of the town's respected shipmasters, that hadn't been enough. Her mother died in childbirth, leaving Tormund Arnessen to raise a daughter on his own. Everyone loved her at first. They certainly loved her father; he was wealthy and made sure to hire new workers every season. But as time passed and Helgar grew into a woman, it became apparent that she was nothing like her father: She was stubborn, unpleasant. A loner. Uninterested in duty or Christian worship. Uninterested in marriage, despite several boys asking for her hand. She knew they only wanted to marry the family money, so she refused every offer. Then her father became ill. He died of pneumonia, and she was left to fend for herself.

Helgar grieved, to be sure. Secretly, she also felt relief. Her father's death meant she was left to her own company. No one forcing her to go to church. No one chastising her for collecting medical textbooks. No one pushing her to become someone's wife. Though the protection of her father—something she had taken for granted—disappeared the minute he stopped breathing.

Instantly, people's suspicions of her were brought to light. Most avoided her gaze on the street. Until they had a sick child, or a broken bone, and the district doctor was a day's ride away. Then, desperation knocked at her door, even in the dead of night. She always answered, because, despite what her neighbours believed, she truly did have what they would call a Christian heart. Though such generosity came with a price: she was arrested a number of times, charged with practicing midwifery without a license. A bit of coin and a few nights in a cell fixed that. Since then, a new pastor had come to town: Lars Knudsen, a short, thin waif of a man with a smile bigger than his feet. Turning a blind eye to most things, he seemed content as long as donations flowed into the church coffers.

Helgar paused on the street and glanced around to ensure no one was watching before opening her sack to check on the eggs Pieter Aldestaed had insisted on giving her. Her black book—a journal of recipes and cures passed down from her grandmother—lay flat overtop her tools, protecting the eggs from being crushed.

Eggs, she scoffed. Her own yard was overrun by hens. It was the last thing she needed. She should have refused. But she was no fool when it came to payment; an exchange of services or food was always a better reimbursement than coin. Rabbits, the occasional duck or lamb. Deer meat, but only if it had been smoked. Carpentry work, chopped firewood, especially if her back needed a rest. All necessary items, "gifts" from grateful neighbours. But not money. Money implied status, implied official title and esteem, the same as any professional physic. Any she received, she immediately gave to the church with a wink and a handshake. Being a woman, she knew her place.

Pieter Aldestaed had tried to pay her with coin tonight. How could she take money, especially for such a birth? From a man about to lose everything?

She scolded herself. Perhaps it would be all right. Perhaps the townsfolk would never discover what lived on the periphery of their village and their awareness, right under their noses. Helgar certainly wouldn't tell. She wondered if Maeva Aldestaed even knew what she had birthed.

"Fru Tormundsdatter!" a man's voice bellowed from down the road. Helgar tensed. She kept walking, pretending not to hear. The wind kicked up a tornado of dust, forcing her to slow.

"*Stopp, vent!* Helgar—*vær så snill*, it's my wife!"

Helgar stopped rubbing the stone in her pocket. She pivoted to see a winded Nils Innesbørg running at full speed—which was rather slow for his stout body—from the direction of the harbour. She lifted the stool on her back, tossing her cloak over her shoulder to hide it. He caught up to her, red-faced, his fat belly heaving. He leaned over, hands on knees.

"What could be so urgent at this hour, Herr Innesbørg?"

Helgar had been to his house two times this month—entering through the back door, the maid shuffling her inside in secret—each time to reassure the lady of the house that digestive cramps were not signs of early labour. Innesbørg was Ørken's *sorenskriveren*, the town magistrate. The very man who had arrested her for illegal medical practices two years ago.

"The baby's coming I'm sure of it." It came out as a single gush of words.

Helgar sighed. "I doubt that—it's too early. Besides, it's no concern of mine. Your wife needs Doctor Jakobsen, not an old spinster like me."

"Jakobsen is two villages away, tending a broken leg on a horse. And there's no time to fetch someone from Bergen." He took a breath. "Her waters have come."

She nodded, trying to hide her concern. Another early birth, on the same night? What were the chances? *Though the moon will soon be full.*

"Are you asking me to deliver your wife?"

Nils Innesbørg rubbed his neck, clearly disturbed by the question, by the predicament he found himself in, desperate and at the mercy of the likes of her, a *kvaksalver.* A quack.

"Nei, I am not. This is a simple request, neighbour to neighbour, to attend her bedside. To calm her nerves . . . until the physic arrives." He cleared his throat. *"Vær så snill."*

Helgar tried to suppress a smile, the word *please* so satisfying. Never did she think she would hear such a plea—twice, no less—from the man who had jailed her.

She considered the implications of such a request. If she helped but the child came too early, both mother and baby could die. And Innesbørg would surely have her arrested and convicted, most likely hanged, for something only God could answer for. Then again, if she refused to attend, he would never forgive her for walking away from him in his wife's hour of need. And if she managed to deliver the woman successfully, the Innesbørg household would be indebted to her should any indelicate situations arise in the future.

She didn't care about gifts or wealth; she didn't need them. Her father died without a son to bequeath his lands to. Though the state seized all his property, they did not—could not—seize the gold he had hidden for decades under the boathouse. Not so easy to excavate, but well worth the week of midnight swims. She had learned to pretend, to live as a poor spinster in a small shack on the edge of town, despite the treasure under the floorboards. What did she need of fine clothing, fancy furniture, and the like? Only to die and have the state seize that, too? The guise of poverty was a small price to pay for freedom.

She chuckled to herself, imagining china place settings on her tiny kitchen slab. Nei, what she needed was far more valuable. She needed impunity.

"Will you help, Fru Tormundsdatter?" He shifted from foot to foot. A cold ocean breeze swirled around them, the rustle of leaves on the ground a promise of winter.

Helgar pulled the birthing stool off her back. *No need to hide it now.* "Consider it a favour, from me to you."

He scowled, then nodded once. "You come prepared, I see. Another birth?"

Helgar shook her head without hesitation. "I had a feeling about tonight."

He opened his mouth as if to speak, but then shut it.

"Lead the way, Magistrate."

What Was

Pieter had poured the last pot of boiling water into the rain barrel. It sat in the centre of the cabin, taking up far too much room, but he didn't care. It was well worth the effort of dragging it inside if it achieved what he hoped. At first he thought it was the shipwreck—hers, not his—that caused her to tremble every time he placed a hand on her body. He tried being gentle, hoping the angel he met on the rocks that fateful day would return with time, with a little coaxing and kindness. Instead, this poor girl had become increasingly distant and sad. Silent tears and trembling at his every advance. She wandered around the cabin, lost in its four walls, tentatively picking up spoons and cups as if they might bite, as if she had never seen such common objects. The cuckoo clock under the ladder stairs became a particular fascination; she watched the acorn weights make their slow descent toward the floor, startled every hour by the wooden bird's predictable alarm. So much so, Pieter was forced to switch off the birdsong to calm her.

He had begun teaching her words—*pot, chair, table*—hoping she would say them back to him. But the only word he managed to squeeze out of her was her name. Did she even understand him? He didn't know.

He wondered what she had left behind, whom she had lost. Grief slept between them at night, yawning and wide.

He watched her out of the corner of his eye. The fire in the hearth crackled and flickered; the clock ticked. Steam from the melted snow he had collected in daylight washed over his face as he leaned over the barrel. He sighed, then closed his eyes, waving his hands to draw more of the warmth toward him. It was a welcome change from the fields of ice outside, and the bitter temperature of nightfall. From the frigidity of his companion.

Maeva sat on his rocking chair, motionless. White knuckles gripping the wood.

He dipped a hand in to test the water. *"For varmt,"* he said, shaking his hand to demonstrate. "Too hot."

She glanced up at him, then back to the floor.

Two weeks of utter silence, he thought. He shook the water off his hand, vexed.

He gestured again to the barrel and pretended to wash himself. *"Det er et bad . . .* A bath."

She shifted uncomfortably.

He tried again. "Bathing. For Sunday." He twirled in a circle, pretending to have a long skirt, then pointed at his mother's dress, which he had hung from the rafters. "The wedding. You and me. Marriage." He pretended to be a bride, batting his lashes and holding imaginary flowers. He performed a curtsy, his burly torso bowing clumsily.

Her eyes narrowed at his antics. But he caught a glimmer of a smile, almost imperceptible, threatening to break at the corner of her mouth. Encouraged, Pieter spun again in his imaginary gown, but tripped on his own feet. He caught the side of the barrel, almost tumbling right into it and near toppled it, but then recovered awkwardly. Maeva let out a clipped giggle, her hand flying to her mouth. Pieter grinned, then bowed again.

"Tusen takk, young lady. One of my many talents."

Shyly, she pulled her hands under her chin.

He clapped. Pointed his finger to the bath. *"Er du klar?* Ready?"

She shook her head, then pointed back at him.

He opened his eyes wide with surprise. "Me first? What, do I smell that terrible?"

A loud snort erupted out of her, and he laughed wholeheartedly. The moment was a surge of something new, a sudden rush. Their eyes met. Hers sparkled, but not from tears this time. He pushed a bit more, realizing she must understand more than he thought.

"I will go first. But only if you help me get rid of my smell?" He held up the lye and tilted his head to one side, pinching his nose.

The smile faded, her eyes finding the floor again. She wrapped her arms around herself, sullen. Stubborn. *Damn it.* He tossed the soap, then waved nonchalantly. "Don't worry, I'll wash myself. No woman should have to suffer such an odour."

He disrobed, leaving his clothes in a heap. He could feel her eyes on him. Stepping on a stool, he climbed into the tub, groaning involuntarily at the delicious heat. The water level rose, and he leaned his head back, closing his eyes. *Steady and gentle. No pressure.*

He licked sweat off his lip; the heat was almost too much, but he was determined. To lure her in by ignoring her. And there was just enough room, a tub made for two.

After a few minutes, he felt the water ripple around him. Keeping his eyes half closed, he waited with a fisherman's patience. Her foot grazed his leg. He didn't dare move. Neither did she.

Submerged up to her nose, her green eyes drank him in.

Her copper hair, the seaweed that had ensnared him that first time, floating around her shoulders. *Caught. Which one of us is fishing here?* He bit back a grin of satisfaction.

She sank down fully, curling into a ball under the water. Her hair spread across the entire surface of the barrel, hiding her naked body. He shifted to give her more space, but it was so tight, she was almost on top of his feet. Gently, he swirled his fingers to part the tentacles of hair. Bubbles danced up to tickle his thighs. A minute passed, then another. He started to fret.

Was she drowning herself? The prospect of marriage, unbearable?

He plunged his arms down to the bottom of the barrel. She wiggled away and up, bursting to the surface in a rush of spittle and breath. Pushing her hair off her face frantically, her skin glistening. He rubbed his hands through his own slick black hair.

"Christ, Maeva. You scared me."

She stared at him, expressionless. Then lowered her face into the water once again.

The stream of spit caught him by surprise, right between the eyes.

What Is

Maeva watches her daughter from the cottage window, unseen, amused by the display outside. She can't help but smile at the girl, white hair sticking out every which way from two long braids—*I barely tamed that hair an hour ago*—apron stained with berry juice and dirt and grass. Pockets perpetually sprouting wildflowers, stones, and seeds, spilling every particle of dust to the ground, as the child hangs upside down from a tree branch. A well-worn toy—the *dukke* she had sewn for Leidah years ago—forgotten in grass still damp from the rainstorm.

Underneath the hanging girl, an entourage of barn kittens leap and pounce, tumbling on top of one another to sniff at the pile of pocket stuff on the dirt. Two hens run in circles, following the waterfall of seed. Leidah suddenly stretches her arms long, holding her hands out toward the ground. To Maeva's surprise, the animals freeze at the gesture. Then Leidah flips herself over and lands on her feet. Tipping her chin to the sky, she crows like a rooster. So convincingly, a rooster calls back from inside the barn.

Where did you learn such things, child? Certainly not from me. Maeva shakes her head in wonder. She envies her daughter's sense of abandon, her absolute joy of play, feet pounding, dancing, skipping through life, not a care in the world. *The way I used to be.* A small pool of regret spreads inside her chest. *The wild is in our blood. Despite these walls. Despite my best efforts.* She surveys her hands—rough and dry—holding a needle and thread. *When did my life become this?* Agitated, she pokes the needle into the fabric, sets it aside. She can't quite place what she is feeling—defiance? determination?—but all of a sudden, she has the urge to go outside again.

The chores can wait, Maeva reasons. *What harm could a little playtime do?* But then she sees her husband exit the barn, calling to their daughter. Resigned, she plunks herself back into the chair.

The work will pile up. Easier to do it now.

She pulls her attention back to the sewing task at hand, vaguely aware of a ticking coming from the clock under the ladder. A sound that used to annoy her; now, calming. Time has been sneaky over the years, worming its way past, unnoticed. One moment, Maeva was a girl; the next, she birthed one. She never imagined how much a baby—or time—could shape and change her. It is as if Maeva's life is divided into two distinct parts. Everything before Leidah, so distant now. Everything after, so pressing. Urgent in a quiet, ordinary kind of way. Teaching the girl to clean and wash and cook and sew. To be like every other little girl. Becoming ordinary, the best kind of protection for Leidah, even if she never leaves the cottage.

Maeva has learned to find comfort in routine. The minutes measured by predictability, by stitch and stain and spoon. But lately, she can feel her body decaying, slowing down as time speeds up. Making her pine for the life she used to have. For who she used to be.

Swimming under the moon. Singing with my sisters. Diving with him.

A flutter rises up from her pelvis. An old familiar wanting, a feeling she hasn't had in years. How fierce her love was back then! How much she yearned and agonized—the risks she took—to steal a moment with him.

Unbidden, her mother's voice fills her head, the warning before she died surprisingly clear: *This love? It's nothing. It will toss you about, take what it wants, then throw you back like an undertow. Wait until you become a mother. That is love. With more ferocity than any man or storm or sea.* Maeva remembers rolling her eyes, dismissive and doubtful.

But she was right. The child births the mother. The moment Leidah came into the world, Maeva became someone else: a nameless, devoted servant whose heart broke at every whimper and cry. The fragment of love she had known before—as sister, daughter, lover—faded and shrunken in comparison. Her memories of him hazy. Evaporating like mist.

And yet . . . here I am thinking of you.

She wonders if he ever thinks of her. Wherever he is, after all this time. What risks might she take if he suddenly returned? A warmth flushes across her cheek, down her neck.

From outside, Leidah claps her hands at the parade of kittens and hens, twirling in a circle. Magically, the wild spectacle follows her command and rushes to her. She runs at top speed to her father at the barn, knocking over the water bucket she was supposed to bring inside, chased by a cacophony of feathers and fur and clucking. Pieter grins, easily picking his daughter up with one arm, carrying her sideways. Maeva cringes as Pieter tips her right-side up, Leidah's head barely missing the door-frame. The girl squeals with glee. The entire procession disappears into the barn.

Stillness and quiet press in. The only sound, the clock; a soft, relentless click keeping her on task. She picks up the quilt, moving away from the window. The flash of heat and memory replaced by another kind of wistful yearning. *You are growing up.* Maeva holds the quilt out to examine it. *So many patches. So many years gone by.* Painfully, she's aware that Leidah no longer runs to her with such joy. Too many chores, too many lessons. *Perhaps I am too hard on you.* But someone has to keep watch, keep them all safe. Even if that means keeping Leidah away from other children. Keeping her away from the village. Keeping the truth hidden. *Even from Pieter.*

She drops her arms, letting the quilt crumple. He comes and goes like the tides, never home long enough to ask or even register the change in his wife. *Or perhaps he doesn't care.* Maeva sighs, placing the blanket onto the kitchen table. No matter. She feels it; *something* is shifting, swimming around inside her body like a hungry fish. Making her thirsty, restless. Her feet, always moving: tapping, fidgeting, kicking in her sleep. Even her hands won't stop; withered and aching, they sew long into the night. Sometimes, she wakes with yarn wrapped around her fingers.

Rubbing at a dry patch on her wrist, she sits down at the table to examine it. Tiny white circles on her forearm flake at the slightest irritation, erupting like a miniature snowstorm. *Perhaps butter will help*, she tells herself. But somehow, she knows there is no remedy for this. Piling the sloughed flakes of dry skin into a small mound, she collects them, then drops them into her apron pocket. *For later.* She opens the quilt across the flat surface to examine the work, a welcome distraction from the itching.

But her thoughts tick away inside her. The dance of needle and thread not enough to divert her. The choice that must be made, a single thread weaving its way into everything she touches.

Who will you run to, child, when time runs out?

What Was

Pieter listened to the quiet footsteps leaving the cabin in the middle of the night. He rolled over, planting his feet on the floor.

Not again.

It had been months since the wedding. Weeks of acclimatizing. Of adjusting. Of careful navigation. Reading his wife daily, sometimes hourly, as he would read the skies before venturing out on a fishing trip. A seemingly calm and sunny day could darken in an instant, a storm clouding over, thunder booming inside her.

It might be something he said or didn't say, a misunderstanding that grew between them in the slow hours between dusk and dawn, somehow swinging the world upside down right under his nose. The next morning bearing an icy wind, a cool distance, as if his mere presence were the problem.

Perhaps it is. His mind picked at the day's events. Which particular moment had changed the weather, to blow in such a wind? Could it have been simply his return from a fishing expedition? Was she angry at the days he spent away from her?

Or does she want me to stay away longer?

He sighed. He didn't know. He never knew what made his wife retreat.

Climbing down the ladder, he noticed the hour: a minute past three o'clock. Then he saw the empty hook on the wall, her cloak missing. *Christ.* He had no choice but to follow, her naivety at what might be lurking in the woods—wolf, moose, bear—incredibly frustrating.

He grabbed his own cloak, wrapping the fox fur around his shoulders. He pulled on his boots, then stepped out into the greenish light of almost dawn. His breath formed clouds of steam. The smell of spring— the promise of green, of sun—missing from the barren trees and snow-covered fields. Soon, though, the equinox thaw would come, an easier season for them both. She could go to market, he reasoned. She could talk with the womenfolk, perhaps find some kinship.

Unbidden, an image of long black curls flashed across his mind.

No, he told himself. *I'm married now.*

The footprints in the snow forced him back to the present. The trail veered into the woods. Toward the path that eventually led to the waterfall. Apprehension washed over him: What if it wasn't only restlessness that awakened his wife in the middle of the night? What if she was . . . searching? He tried to shake the ridiculous notion out of his mind. Still, he quickened his pace, easily tracking her footsteps into the forest. Immediately, the light changed; the darkness caught him off guard. He stopped to allow his eyes to adjust.

As he'd suspected, the prints led away from the path, farther into the bush. Pieter counted in his head how many times he had heard her get up in the past two weeks, how many times he had fallen back asleep. How many times had he ignored the signs? How could he have been so blind? So stupid?

Love.

Madness and ecstasy, a fury that pounded against all reason and doubt, love had rattled him senseless. He was smitten, beyond the point of no return, beyond anything he had ever experienced. The way she held her head, tilted ever so slightly, when she didn't quite understand his words. He adored the small escape of giggles, her hands covering her mouth as if it were sinful to laugh at him tripping over his own feet or singing loudly in the tub. He especially loved her in that damn rain barrel—*thank you,*

Freyja, for such an inspiration—the only place he witnessed a change in her, a softening that allowed him to steal a little closer. To smell and touch and taste her. To absorb her with all of his being, for a few moments of profound release.

Water changed her somehow. She became the woman he *wanted* her to be. The woman he imagined she was, under all the sharp looks, the petulant silences, the bristled retreats.

He believed she was starting to adapt, to even like the life they were building. He prayed she might even begin to love *how* he loved her. That somehow his love would be big enough for both of them.

He hiked past the clearing until he reached the rocky, ice-covered cliff. His foot slipped, but he caught himself. He squatted down low, hiding in the drifts, peering over the edge.

She was there, kneeling in the snow. Motionless. *Not searching.*

His relief allowed him to take the scene in: like a painting, everything was frozen. Even the waterfall was caught in suspended time, shards of icicles sharp, dangerous in their impending gravity. He watched her, fascinated by her stillness. The extreme contrast of colour—a blueish cast, glazing everything except her hair, the fiery red mane like an open wound on the icy landscape.

It was then that he heard it. A quiet whimper. He whirled around to see if a wounded animal was behind him. But no, it was her, his new wife. She was crying.

He struggled to comprehend. He'd thought she had moved past the grief, the source of which she never divulged to him. She'd had days upon days of dry eyes recently—or so he had assumed. Was it him? Was he the cause of such misery? He considered the possibility: Hadn't he provided clothing, a warm bed, a place to call home? Hadn't he cared for her, bringing home fish and wool and needle and thread—whatever else she asked for?

What else does a woman need, for God's sake?

He was perplexed. He wanted to forbid her from leaving his side, but he had enough sense to know that such a demand would encourage the opposite. No, he must be clever in his handling of her.

Perhaps all she needed was his steadiness, his consistent adoration. His solidity as a husband, a provider. Eventually, she would see how much she needed him. Eventually, she would want him as much as he wanted her. She would want their love to grow. She would want a family.

Yes, that's it.

He teared up at the thought of a child. Yes, that was the answer. A baby. He would continue doing everything he had been doing, and more; she would be loved at every turn, in every moment. Each chore, he would be right there beside her. Celebrating her, encouraging her. Showing her how much he loved her. How *right* they were for each other, how right this life was for her.

Love's miracle would beget a child.

He slid back from the cliff edge with stealth. Pleased at his new plan, satisfied with the simplicity of it.

Let her wander . . . Soon, she won't be able to leave my side.

Waiting

She waited for Pieter at the edge of the mountain pass. At the tree line, where they met in secret, their love hidden from prying eyes.

She watched the first snowfall. Snowflakes flying, landing, melting in her long black hair. She had left it loose for him, the way he liked it best.

❧

She waited. Until the sun dipped below the craggy cliff.

She waited and waited. Until the realization hit her.

He has forgotten me.

What Is

Mamma is moving around in the dark. Like she does every night. Footsteps so light I can barely hear them, then a nightgown swish on the ladder.

I sit up, hugging my *dukke*. I count the ticks and tocks of the clock. *En, to, tre, fire, fem* . . . When I get to eleven, the front door bumps closed. I am up and down the ladder, with dolly under my arm. Into the night we go before we change our minds.

I hold my breath on the porch. I don't want her to go. I peer up at the sky, wishing for more rain. The cold wind nips at my bare skin, end of summer already. I squeeze my shoulders up around my neck, shivering, squinting in the purple light. I guess the sun doesn't want to go to bed, like Mamma. Maybe the rain will put us all back to sleep.

Her white nightgown floats across the field—she's almost at the edge of the long grass already. I tiptoe down the steps. The cold dew makes my toes curl. I wish I had put boots on. But I don't want to lose the trace of her.

My feet squish into warm mucky pebbles. Probably chicken poo. I don't care. I run into the night. The grass tickles up my arms— *swishswishswish*—swiping across my face. And the doll's, even though she has no face. I can't see anything other than the sky above me. No stars, no moon. I try hard not to think of all the crawly things on the ground.

Bugs. Worms. Snakes. Wolves. *Snakes.*

I run faster and faster, my feet hurting from sharp bits in the grass. But I don't stop. I run and run and run. Before I know it, I'm across the field. Mamma is a few steps ahead. She stops at the trees, listening. I duck just in time, hold my breath, shrink to the size of my doll, and make myself still, like a tree root underground. Mor glances back. My heart is so loud in my head, I'm sure she can hear it. I am my own ticking clock—

Boom-boom-boom—hide me! Please, God.

I squeeze my eyes up tight; God hears me better when I close my eyes. At least, that's what Pappa says. I wait, squeezing harder and harder until my eyeballs move to the back of my brain. I hear her breathing in the cold. Then she's gone. I open one eye. I remember to thank God—*and please, if it's not too much trouble, keep Pappa asleep*—before my other eye pops open. Then I run like a fox. Into the trees I go, my mother's shadow. That's me, a puff of air at the edge of her.

Mamma pushes branches away, ducking, fighting against the trees, noisy as a bear. I don't need to fight. The trees are my friends, and I am the wind. I flow through anything and everything. Only the leaves feel me, nodding hallo as I sneak by.

Mamma stops at a clearing. I hide behind the nearest tree trunk and lean out to let *dukke* take a peek. My mother is on the ground, digging at the foot of an old tree. She has a spade in her hands. She stabs at the earth, her white nightgown dragging in the mud. Her hands are like animals, digging and searching . . . for what? What could possibly be in the ground that she needs so much? Maybe she is planting something? A night garden? I lean out a little farther. A pile of earth grows beside her; then a shower of dirt flies at me. By accident, I hope. I duck behind the tree again. The smell of rain is in the wind; my skin buzzes and hums. The purple light is fading to pink beyond the trees. The sun is waking up, without ever going to bed. *Like Mamma.*

She doesn't have much time before Pappa wakes up, too.

Above me, a branch shakes. I freeze. So does Mamma. A crow watches us, hidden by the arms of the willow. We must have woken it up. The bird flaps its wings. Black feathers, black branches, black shadows. Black eye.

I have to pee. So does *dukke*. I wiggle and cross my legs, dropping the doll.

Mamma whispers to herself, *"En fugl, Maeva.* Only a stupid bird." The crow squawks. She ignores it, pushing the spade into the dirt again.

Hallo, crow. Don't mind Mor. She's just tired.

The crow doesn't answer. But the wind does, talking to the branches and leaves, telling stories between all the black and green shadows. I can feel so many secrets in the air. I hear the warning of the wind, but Mamma isn't listening. The sky spits on my nose. I guess the rain wants to tell me a story, too.

My mother curses at the hole. "Bastard. Lying bastard."

I have never heard her use such words. Words I would never think of saying. I close my eyes again. *Please, God, forgive Mor.* Then I open them, worried that God might not know Mamma anymore. She is a muddy dog, digging for a bone in the earth. The sky spits at her, and she wipes her face with her gown. Then curses again.

The crow caws even louder.

I open my mouth to the rain, tasting dirt, salt. The moss on the bark eats up all sound except for the words coming out of Mor. She prays and curses, curses and prays. Calling on the moon, the rain, the earth, the sea. Freyja. Frigg. The Virgin Mary. Jesus.

"Drite. Where is it? Jesus, where have you hidden it? Damn you to hell, Pieter Aldestaed."

She stops digging and stands up slowly. Her shoulders, shaking. She throws the shovel aside.

A funny feeling starts to bubble in my belly. Pappa? What could he have hidden that would make her cry?

She mutters, "Goddamn you, too . . . Odhinn." Her voice is shaky. The crow flies away, all feathers and flaps. Mamma snorts. "That's right, leave. You're no help anyway."

I don't blame you, crow. I wish I could fly away, too.

I crawl backwards, dragging my doll in the dirt, needing to pee badly.

Rain gets louder, shouting its story on my back. Telling me to run. I dig my toes into the damp earth and tiptoe away.

The forest is shining. All clean and new. I cling to moss, peering over my shoulder every few steps. My nightgown sticks to me. I stick to the earth, my toes spread wide. I am a toad, hopping to hide. I am a dragonfly, buzzing and humming above the puddles. *Buzz-hum-buzz.*

I reach the edge of the trees. The cottage is across the field. I gulp a big breath, one that will get me through long grass and slimy and sharp things, and then I bolt. Out of the trees and into the open. My legs are hot and tingly, my feet on fire, but I don't care. I run even harder. The rain beats against my face so much it hurts.

I fall up the porch steps, my shins smashing hard against the wood. I drop *dukke* and curl into a ball.

"Bastard in hell!" Rolling my legs to my chest, I curse in whispers, testing the words that came out of Mamma. "Goddamn you, Oh-din." Oh, it feels good. Better than good. And God probably doesn't mind so much. He can't hear me anyway, since only one eye is closed, so it doesn't count. I wipe my face on my sleeve.

Beyond my arm, I see her: my mother, floating across the field. It takes me a second to figure out that I need to hide. She is shining in the dark, a wood nymph in a dirty dress. Her hair tangled with twigs and leaves. Her gown torn. Her skin glowing in the moonlight. And her feet hidden. She is floating, flying through wildflowers and rain.

Behind her, barely there, I see the old lady, the one I always see but no one else does. She floats behind Mamma, all white shadow and mist. She must be wet, too, but she doesn't seem like she minds.

Mamma doesn't see the old lady or me.

I crawl and spin in a circle, but there is nowhere to go.

Then I see the wood-box.

I sneak over to it and open the lid. Piles upon piles of logs. No space for a girl to hide. Mary Mor and Jeezus! The rocking chair is the only other thing on the porch, but it won't hide me for long.

I can see the floating white dress beyond the steps through the railing. My heart is pounding like the rain. She is close, so close, and if I get caught,

I don't know what she will do. I don't want her to be angry with me. But why doesn't she stay in bed, stay home, where she's supposed to be?

She steps onto the porch.

I hug myself. *Goddamn it, Oh-din! Hide me.*

She stops. Listens.

Thunder cracks in the sky.

And poof. I feel a rush of rain—my blood, swirly-whirly, down and down, into the bottom of me. Dirt inside my bones, the dance of wind and water, the wild in all things big and small, up and down, head to toe. It hits my hands and feet at the same time. I become everything and nothing at once.

Butterflies and bats and wind and wildflowers and tree bark and laughing and words, crowsandmilkandwolvesandhowlingandsealsandwhaleswavescloudsstarsmoonsun. Spacespacesomuchspacethereisonlyspace . . . I taste the huge black sky in one single second, everything and nothing on my tongue sliding down my throat and hollowing out from deep inside my belly until every part of me is empty. I can hear the crunching and munching of every living thing. Bugs inside the woodpile, gnawing at me to leave this world. Join them and hide, hide, hide—

My mother bends down to pick up something. *No. Dukke!* She frowns. "Leidah?"

Her whisper is almost lost in the downpour. She is frozen, staring at the open box.

I watch her through wood splinters. Through cobwebs.

I am dust.

I am the damp.

She mutters to herself about being too tired, seeing things that aren't there, and then she walks toward me, looking right through me, the doll in her hand. Closes the box. The sound of her feet fading to nothing in the sleepy house.

⁕

I wake up freezing. It takes me a moment to remember where I am. My head is pressed between logs, splinters in my cheek. I push open the lid of the wood-box and jump out, shuddering the bugs and dust off, feeling spider-webs sticky all over. My neck hurts. I rub it and stare out at the field. Rain has stopped its story, leaving everything sparkly. Except for me; I am a wet and dirty grub crawling out of the night. I have no idea what happened, and I don't have time to figure it out. Pappa will be up soon, if he isn't already. I wipe my muddy feet on the mat before slowly opening the front door. I listen, waiting for my father's footsteps, or my mother calling out for me. Like she did last night. Had she seen me?

Nothing makes a sound but the old clock. *Tick, tick, tick.* I creep up the ladder like a spider. Before I reach the top rung, the tiny bird pops out of the door of the clock house. Even though it makes no song, it still scares me silly. I wait for a sound from Mamma or Pappa, but no one is awake. I tiptoe past their bedroom, into my own, shutting the door behind me.

I pull up my nightie and squat on my pee pot, just in time.

I close my eyes, so glad to be home.

Takk, Oh-din.

Crow

The raven perches on the top of the chimney, watching the scene below. The rain falls steadily now, but he doesn't care, his slick black feathers repelling the water easily. He must see if she has found it—what she has been seeking since before her daughter was born. It has eluded both of them for far too long.

Sometimes, her spirit wanders into his dreams, searching. He can feel she is unaware of it, that it is merely cosmic entertainment for the Sisters of Fate. Urd, that decrepit old biddy, has woven a tale of tragedy for both of them. But Skuld—the veiled one—unravels the web of the other two Sisters. *What will be will save us all.* It means that someday, somewhere, they will both wake up in their true forms. He can wait for this. Wait for her to fulfil her duty as wife, as mother. Wait for her skin to weather, her breasts to sag and dry up. He welcomes time passing. It is all an illusion, a convincing trick of the eye. He knows what she is underneath.

He wishes he could help her. Has searched high and low, wearing the face of many: a rooting pig, a rabbit, even a chicken. But he has found nothing. The Sisters are clever; they guard secrets well. And the husband is completely oblivious to the bitch-hags of fate who help him.

Out of the blue, the tiny sprite bounds out of the forest, as if being chased by a predator. All legs, a scrawny white-haired elfling. He stretches his head. His crow-eye, wide and focused. To his surprise, his jealousy has abated. He likes watching her; she has a playful curiosity, like a mischievous pup, that has kept him coming back, beyond his need to watch Maeva. Seven years have passed, and lately, he watches the girl more than her mother.

Soon, this child will show signs of who she actually is. Her mother watches for it, he can see. He waits for this day, waits for Maeva's power to ooze out of the girl. That's when the tides will change in his favour, he is certain. For how can Maeva possibly stay if her daughter becomes so strange she's impossible to hide? Surely she will run. Leave this place, leave the husband. And he will be waiting.

For now, he simply watches; waiting for grass to grow, for a tree to lose its leaves. The changes are slow and subtle. The girl is smaller than a goat kid, frail and thin; her large head and big round eyes odd on such a tiny frame. Her humanness barely there, her beauty disturbing.

Like her mother.

He flies to the edge of the thatched roof. The girl falls onto the porch, then curses, loud enough for him to hear his own name. *In the tongue of Old Norse*, he marvels. He cackles at such a tiny mouse roaring like a bear.

Maeva is not far behind. He feels her before he sees her, the air vibrating. Behind her, barely noticeable, is the old woman. Faded, almost invisible.

He flies across the field, swooping dangerously close, his wing-tip mere inches from Maeva's cheek. He breathes her in; her sweat, a perfume he would bathe in.

She ducks at the surprise of him, her arms instinctively flying up, protecting her face. The old woman spills into mist and circles Maeva, hiding her.

He lands on a pine tree, disappearing from view. It is enough time for the child to have found a hiding spot. Her mother will never be the wiser. A little rebelliousness, a good thing in his estimation; a sign of strength. He clicks his beak. With one final caw, he lights to the skies as the sun peeks through the valley of the mountain.

The old woman watches him from the porch.

The child, nowhere to be seen.

What Was

Pieter slept soundly beside her, his arm slung across her hip.

Maeva tossed and turned. The ache of what used to be—everything she had hoped for, a few months before—squeezed out by the new presence in her belly. *Love is cruel*, she decided. *I don't want it anymore.*

She tried her best to anticipate the rhythms of her new husband, to adjust to his routines. His humanness. His need for a roof. For edges and corners and hard surfaces. For wood and knives and ale and fire. His need to capture and gut living creatures, to traverse the world on the back of a horse or at the helm of a boat. On top of water. On top of field and mountain. On top of everything, skimming the surface. Such solidity, so foreign to her. She felt how clumsy she had become, weighed down by objects and walls and furniture. Suffocated by the press of chores, the need to fulfil wifely duties. A husband's needs and wants and desires, a new and awkward world for her.

Maeva constantly felt the intrusion of his presence, eating away at any space she managed to carve between them. She couldn't even breathe without his concern swallowing her whole. She often escaped while he slept, needing fresh air, the stars, open space. Time to think. Refusing to give up the bits of solitude she stole in the quiet of night.

I will not—I do not—see you.

She felt herself slipping away. The baby had moved in; there wasn't much room for her anymore. Her mind had become mushy, forgetful. Important details had packed up and left: the curve of *his* mouth, the sound of her name on his tongue. She sat outside for hours in the cold, trying to remember details of what used to be. The tears slowed on her cheeks, her whole body numbing to ice. Everything around her white. Lifeless. Begging for green.

She had never expected to become a wife. Or a mother. Worrying about the baby—*Who will you take after? Will you be healthy?*—had become the cause of many sleepless nights. She had learned to sew with speed, each stitch allowing her more time, the guise of an acceptable domestic escape into stuffed toys and trinkets, blankets and bibs.

Pieter praised her clumsy work.

"So sweet, Mae. A bear?"

She shook her head at the sad oval shape, nubs for hands and feet. "Nei . . . It's supposed to be a doll."

"Oh. Of course it is . . . Some hair might help."

None of the toys came out quite right; each one had something missing or strange. One eye or no eyes, mismatched ears, a tail instead of a leg. But she didn't care. *The baby won't know the difference*, she reasoned. Anything to distract her from worry. *And him.*

The noise of that damn clock didn't help; it often kept her awake, despite Pieter disconnecting the hourly trill of the cuckoo. The ticking was still loud to her ears, a reminder of how slowly time passed in this place. Sometimes she found herself lost in the space between one second and the next. Her mind dulled in the drone and clunk of this life. So unlike the beat of waves, the dancing pulse that still thrummed inside her blood, stretching across time. Calling her home.

Pieter rolled over, snoring loudly. Somewhat akin to waves, if she closed her eyes and imagined. In and out, crashing with a slight sucking noise.

Over and over, night after night, water beckoned. The rain barrel that sat beside the fire hearth—a sweet, albeit self-serving invention of Pieter's— such a sad, poor substitute. A reminder of what she had been missing.

His enthusiasm, sometimes endearing, but not enough. Never enough.

What Is

It is Sunday. Pappa calls from down below. The smell of sausages and eggs sneak into my nose. I leap out of bed and put on my nightdress as fast as I can. I jump to the ladder, my belly rumbling so much it makes my feet fly. From the third rung, I let go and land hard on my bottom. Pappa calls again from the hearth.

"Someone is up. It must be my little *kanin*."

I grin and start hopping, my hands like paws. I sniff with my nose, peeking around a chair. Pappa sees me and smiles.

"Mae, it is our little *kanin*, and I'll bet she is hungry!"

I nod and hop up to the table, sniffing. The food smells so good, my mouth waters. I jump and perch on the edge of the chair, my knees up to my throat, my nightgown falling like fur over them. I wiggle my whiskers. Pappa throws his head back and laughs, flipping an egg in the pan. I sneak a piece of sausage and chew it up with small, fast bites, like a rabbit. Mor places a plate in front of me and smacks my hand.

"*Jeg er sulten, Mamma!*"

"You can wait for everyone to sit, Leidah—you're not starving, child."

"Mae, let her eat—the next batch is almost ready—and she needs her food to grow big and strong, don't you, my little *kanin?*"

I nod and sneak another piece of sausage. I am small for an almost eight-year-old. Half the size I should be, so Pappa says when he thinks I am asleep. He compares me to other children he sees in town, children who have rosy cheeks and round bellies, who go to school and learn their letters and play with other girls and boys.

"They seem so healthy, Maeva," he says. "How much a child can grow in one season." He doesn't say *unlike Leidah*. But I hear it anyway. I know he doesn't mean to be mean. It's his way to get Mamma to take me to the doctor. Maybe even let me go to school. It never works. She always waves him away, like she's swatting flies.

"Leidah is growing perfectly fine, Pieter," she says.

I don't know if that's true. I have had the same clothes for three years. That's a lot of seconds—too many to count—of not growing.

"Sit properly if you're going to keep eating," Mor says, "and put your feet on the floor."

I pout and pull my nightgown out of the way, the game spoiled. My mother is about to lift a mug, then stops. I peer up at her, wondering what else I have done wrong, but it isn't anger I see. She looks shocked, wide eyes staring at the chair. I look down and freeze, too.

Last night is all over my legs and feet. God, how could I have forgotten? I cover my toes with my hands, which only makes the dirt stand out more. *Mary Mor and Jeezus. Bastard in hell.* She continues to glare at my feet. I stare at my plate and wait for the scolding, holding myself very still.

Far doesn't notice. He whistles over the fire while Mor glares down at me.

"Well, my little *kanin*, are you ready to go into town?"

I mumble an answer and hug myself tighter.

"I think Leidah should stay home, Pieter—her colour is off."

"Oh? Let me see, Lei-lee—are you sick, child?"

"I . . ."

"She seems fine to me, Mae. Besides, a little fresh air will do her some good, right, Lei-lee?"

"Ja, Pappa."

"I don't think so, Pieter—she has dark circles under her eyes. Didn't you sleep, girl?"

I want to shout out, *You didn't either!* But I don't. I shake my head no. Pappa stops cooking and comes over to me. He sits, pulling me onto his knee.

"Bad dreams? Oh, Lei-lee, why didn't you wake me up? You know I will always chase the monsters away. Let me see those eyes. You are a little pale. Maybe your mother is right."

"Nei, Pappa, *vær så snill*—I want to go with you!"

"You can go to church next week," Mor says. "The gods—God—can wait, I'm sure. Besides, we have plenty to do for harvest—"

"I thought you said she was sick, Mae. She's not staying home to do chores," he says, all quiet.

Mor presses her lips into a hard line.

Pappa does the same. Lifts me off his lap. I sink to the floor and hug the leg of the wooden chair. I don't want to be told to go outside; I don't want to be left behind. I don't know how to explain last night, what I saw Mor doing or how I somehow disappeared, waking up in the wood-box. I'd much rather go to church than face Mor's questions or think about what happened on the porch.

I look up at Pappa, who looks at Mor, who looks at both of us. Pappa's head is sideways, like he's trying to see a ship far off at sea. I wonder which way the wind will blow.

My mother stirs and shakes the pan on the fire. The sizzle and smell of meat makes my stomach growl again. We would have to eat fast to make it in time for the morning service. I scratch at the chair leg with my fingernail, making small lines, counting each one in my head.

Pappa finally talks as I scratch twenty-three. "Go get dressed, Leidah—we're leaving after breakfast."

Mor is scratching, too: that itch on her arm that never seems to go away. I tiptoe past her, then rush upstairs, leaving Pappa staring at her.

❧

It happened once before, Pappa standing up to Mamma about church. I was five. I remember pressing my ear to the wall, listening to their whispers in the dark.

"We should go, Mae. It will be good for Leidah to see other children, to hear stories of Jesus."

"Stories, yes—exactly, Pieter."

"Oh, Maeva, what's the harm now? Besides, it will convince the right people that we are a common God-fearing family who go to church every Sunday, who put their trousers on one leg at a time, like everyone else."

"We are not God-fearing or normal, despite what you want everyone to believe. Besides, it is *not* the ones wearing trousers that I fear most. You know what they are like, Pieter. Remember what happened at the baptism. What happened to . . ." Her words, all shaky. "I'm only doing what you asked. I'm keeping our daughter out of harm's way."

"We are going, and that's the end of it. Would you rather me not work, and we eat only eggs for the winter?"

"Nei."

"How else to convince the shipmasters I am a good hire, that the rumours about Leidah are unfounded?"

"But they aren't unfounded, are they? How much longer do you think we will be able to hide?"

Those words—*God, rumours, hide*—snuck along the floor, under the warm covers, under my skin. Rolling over and over, inside my head, keeping me awake. I didn't know what church was, or who this God person was, but I knew I had to go and meet him. I didn't even know we were hiding, but if we were, I knew it had to be because of me.

I wanted to be like everyone else. I wanted to meet other children. I had only heard of them from Far's tales, little boys and girls waving at the tall ships from the docks. He said they were like me, and when I asked, "Are they blue, too?" he closed his eyes and held my hands inside his big, rough palms. I waited and waited with my fingers pressed inside his, my heart thumping at the idea that other little girls had blue hands. Somehow, it seemed only right and fair that this God person, who was supposed to have made everything, including me, wouldn't make a mistake, that he wouldn't leave me alone in the world. The other blue children were out there; I simply had to work hard to find them.

My world tipped sideways, as if my head were halfway into the sea, one eye above the water and one eye below, an entire other world—the way things truly are—hidden but always there, waiting to be seen. I held my breath, closed one eye. Then switched, blinking left, then right, watching Far's head move with each eye twitch. It made him seem like he was rocking, back and forth, back and forth, faster and faster, like a boat in a storm. Then I shut both eyes tight. *Please, please, please, God.*

When Far finally opened his eyes, they were watery. The blue children sank into the deep, along with all the things we didn't talk about. I saw those blue girls diving, down and down, into my belly until there was barely a ripple, a small burp. Maybe it wasn't so important, this other world. Maybe it wasn't real. I didn't need those girls so long as my father held on to me. He smiled and rubbed my hair. I leaned into his chest, and Mor clapped hard. Bedtime, she said.

I don't know how he finally convinced her, but he did.

I was so excited at being allowed to go to church, the entire week leading up to that Sunday, I couldn't sit still. I bounced up and down trying to make time go faster, flying from room to room, dipping and diving at my mother, question after question spilling out of me—*What do I wear? What's praying? Why do people do that? What if you don't pray? Does God hear our thoughts? What will the other children be like? Will they like me? Will God be there? Do you think God will like me, Mamma?* Going to church meant Mamma sewing me a new dress. It meant meeting other little girls, and no chores for the entire day. It meant a long wagon ride and maybe even seeing the big ships that Pappa worked on. I loved being with Pappa, and it meant hours and hours of that.

Mamma finally stopped when I followed her outside and tugged at her arm, spilling the bucket of water she was carrying. My questions about God hanging in the air. I dug my bare toes into the grass and put my hands behind my back, like I was sorry. She pulled my hands toward her. I thought she was going to squeeze them hard, squeeze me quiet. But she didn't. She lifted my hands to her creamy face and placed them on her soft cheeks. Sunshine behind her head, her copper hair glowing with light. Mor was an *engel*, the kind that Far told me about, shiny and golden. She smiled at me, the sweetest gentlest smile, her eyes sad.

"Oh, Lei-lee. Of course God will like you."

And then she surprised me Sunday morning with a gift: a fancy pair of cream gloves, the fingers wide with new stitches, all neat and even, fitting my webbed fingers so perfectly, they felt like a new skin. I jumped up and down, waving my hands like butterflies.

Mamma laughed, and then went into the bedroom. Pappa had to help me fasten my pale frock that she had made that week. She didn't have any new fabric, so she cut up an old quilt that was falling apart. The apron had a braided ribbon along the hem, a ruffled bit of lace on the sleeves and collar, with a long full skirt. The lace was from an old coverlet, but it was much prettier on my new apron. I became a flower in it, and I twirled until Pappa told me to stop, we didn't have time for dancing.

Far took a long time with all the tiny buttonholes under his thick fingers. I had to pretend I was a tree so I could stand being very still. I fidgeted with my doll while he grunted at me to stop moving, all the while both of us wondering where Mor was.

"But why doesn't Mor want to come?" I asked Far. I was sad that she didn't want to come with us; I was hurt that she didn't even want to see me dressed up like a grown-up lady, let alone help me with the buttons she herself had sewn on.

He finished the last button and patted me on the back.

"It's time, Lei-lee," Pappa said, setting my doll on the bed, ignoring my question. I followed him outside to where the horse and wagon were waiting, freshly scrubbed for church. He sighed, drumming his fingers against the wood.

"Aren't we going to be late, Pappa?" He nodded, lifting me into the back. Then he bowed. As if I were a rich lady, and he were my driver.

"Where to, dear lady?" he asked, tipping his hat.

I giggled. "Church, please."

That's when Mamma stepped out of the cottage.

Both Pappa and I gawked; she never dressed up, always was in a stained apron and worn-out frock, her hair in two messy braids, wearing Pappa's big black boots to trek through the fields and muck out the barn. But that morning, she was as clean and fresh as a water lily, as if she had risen out of a mountain spring, her skin all dewy and soft. The green frock she was wearing made her face glow, setting off her hair, curls of fire down her back. She climbed into the seat beside Far, as if these were her everyday clothes and going to town were an everyday thing.

Both Pappa and I stared and stared until she said, "Enough, Pieter—we'll be late." Pappa snapped the horse forward, grinning at the road in front of us and stealing looks at Mamma the whole way into Ørken. I was so happy I thought I'd burst. We—all of us, even our old grey mare—were going on an adventure to meet God. To find the blue children.

When the horse pulled to the end of the street in Ørken, the church service had already started. I scrambled out of the seat, catching my apron on a nail. My mother grabbed my elbow, telling me to slow down. But I needed to get inside—maybe I'd meet a real friend! I looked up in wonder; I had never seen such a building. It was all black, with a long face, high windows for eyes, and black double doors that were shut tight, like a mouth.

We could hear people singing, barely hitting the high notes. I wondered if God's ears hurt like mine did. I started to hum, even though I didn't know the tune, but it seemed that the people inside didn't know it either. Mor whispered, "Shh, Leidah!" and Far took my hand. I marched up the wide wooden steps, quiet on the outside, jumping on the inside.

We snuck into the church as if we didn't want God knowing we were there, but the heavy doors closed with a loud *thud*. It was a sound that made everyone turn.

Row upon row, everyone smushed together on thin long benches, their skin white and pasty. All the same, sweating in their wool, about to be cooked for God. But God wasn't there. There wasn't any space for him. Or the blue girls.

The singing stopped. I held on to Far's hand and hid behind him, so happy for the gloves Mor had made, for my father's tallness. I wanted to show them I was like any other little girl, dressed in my flower apron, wanting to make friends and say hallo to God. I peered around Pappa's leg and saw everyone's hands, pale and bare. A brown-haired girl in a brown frock stood in the aisle. She didn't even look at my face. Her eyes were stuck on my gloved hands.

Everyone else had eyes on my mother. I didn't blame them; she was pretty as a linzer pastry and they were hard stale bread, each one tightly bunned and bound up from head to toe. Mamma's green dress hugged her chest tightly, her long neck stretching like a swan's.

She pushed me forward into the last bench. My father took off his hat, and his eyes found the floor. I wasn't sure what we had done to be sorry about, but I copied him anyway. I stared at my shoes the whole time, my face hot, probably as red as my mother's hair.

My mother kept her head raised, as if she were up to her neck in water and was determined not to drown. Just like a water lily. Even when it was time to pray and we were supposed to stare at the floor, she looked up at the ceiling. It seemed more right to me, because God was supposed to be in the sky anyway, but I wasn't a water lily, more like a drooping daisy, and so I kept my head down. Even the nice man at the front—the one in black—noticed Mamma, stopping every so often and clearing his throat. He smiled right at me when he asked everyone to bow their heads. I shoved my chin hard into my chest, but then peeked up at Mor. She lifted her chin even higher. Other people noticed, too, even though they kept their heads down. The nice man talked about sin and suffering, and something called humility. He talked about lots of ladies—Eve, Mary Magdalene, Jezebel—and how the world had lost its way because of them. But if we loved Jesus, we could find our way home. I didn't understand any of it, but Mamma had a small smile on her face. I wasn't sure what was so funny, but I was glad she was enjoying it.

The ride home was quiet, my mother sitting in the back with me. Mor peered out the side of the wagon, her face flat. I wanted to talk about all the new words I had heard, like *sin* and *abso-lution*. I wanted to ask why everyone prayed to the ground when God lived upstairs. I wanted to ask her what Eve did that was so bad. But it didn't seem like she wanted to talk. Or listen. So I counted cows and sheep.

When we got home, Far climbed down to help me, but he didn't bow like before. He kept his eyes on the horse as Mor stepped down. She leaned into his ear and said something I couldn't hear. He didn't seem to hear it either, patting the horse over and over again as she walked away into the cottage.

It was the first and last time we would see her in green. The last time she would ever walk through the Ørken church doors.

⚬⊗⚬

I shake dried mud off my nightgown, rubbing my dirty feet on the braided rug. It doesn't seem to help. My toenails are caked. I wipe them with my nightgown. Behind me, the door closes.

"Don't even think of putting those feet into clean stockings."

I stand and face Mor, ready for my punishment. She doesn't look at me, kneeling down with a wash-cloth and bowl of water. I sit down on the bed. She doesn't say anything. Begins to wash my feet. I want to ask her how she got clean so fast, after a night of digging in the mud like a dog, but I don't.

She rubs my skin raw, not using much water on the rag. It hurts, but not talking hurts even more.

"Other foot," she says. I lift my leg. I can feel tears growing in my eyes. *"Jeg beklager, Mamma."* She holds her hand up to stop the words and keeps washing, as if she is trying to wash away my skin. The tears start falling down my cheeks, landing on the back of her head. She doesn't feel them. She grabs both of my feet, pushing me to lie back on the bed for my weekly check-up. Her fingers open my toes, roughly stretching the web wide, as if they weren't attached to me. She reaches inside her apron and pulls out her tiny sewing scissors.

"But, Mamma, Pappa is waiting. We'll be late." Her eyes—cold stones—glare into mine. I bite my lip and close my eyes.

She holds my foot over the bowl of water and begins to cut the web. I feel a bit of heat as the scissors slice. I never used to feel a thing, but Mor says that the heat is a good sign, that I'm growing up, that the web is changing into lady-skin. I open one eye and watch the drips of red swirl into the water like smoke. "Hold still," she says. I spot a bug on the ceiling. I count each snip of the scissors. *En . . . to . . . tre . . .*

Far calls from downstairs, "Hurry up, little *kanin*—hop to it or we'll be late!"

I cringe at my bloody feet. I won't be hopping much today. The final slice next to the baby toe is always the worst, because it's mostly skin with the tiniest bit of web. I bite the insides of my cheeks, hoping Mor doesn't cut into the skin part. She holds the cloth over my toe, stopping up the blood. My nose starts to run, and before I have a chance to wipe the snot on my sleeve, she hands me the towel.

"*Takk.*" I wipe and hand it back to her. She drops my left foot into the icy bowl of water, pulling my other foot into her lap. She stops to scratch the dry patch on her arm. It must be sore. I watch a flake of skin fall off her elbow, onto my leg.

"Does your arm hurt?" I ask, hoping she'll talk to me.

She waves my words away, picking up the scissors again. The quick *snip snip snip* sounds almost happy, her hands working fast, as if she is cutting a sewing pattern she knows by heart. She collects the pieces of web on a towel, saving them in a jar; she has kept every piece ever cut from me, from the time I was a baby. Once, I got up the courage to ask why, and she laughed. "Someday we will stitch them all back together, of course." I laughed, too, but inside I didn't. I wondered if she wanted to make another baby—a better me—out of all that skin.

I hold my breath waiting for that last cut on my little toe.

The scissor catches the inside and I yelp, pulling my foot to my chest.

"Sorry, child." Mor's tone changes, her eyes no longer stones. "We'll put some spider-webs on it, ja?"

Spider-webs are like magic; they always make everything better, Mor says. I watch her collect a cobweb from the corner of my room. *Sorry for stealing your home, spider.* She balls the silk up in her fingers. I lift my toe and let her press it into the cut. We wait a bit; then she puts my right foot into the bowl. The cold water feels good. I sit up, and we both watch my feet wiggling like fish in a red sea. Pappa calls again. Mor taps my leg, and I lift my feet out, dripping onto the towel. She holds both of them on her lap, patting and tapping, soft and tender-like. I close my eyes. She sinks them to the floor, then reaches for my hands.

"Nei, Mamma, please—they will bleed right through my gloves."

She stops and then nods, knowing I am right. Standing, she wipes the scissors on her apron. They leave a rusty mark, shaped like a wing. She opens the wardrobe in the corner of the room. I have two good aprons. She pulls out the pale grey one. It is September, still warm enough for cotton and bare legs. I try not to pout; I hate it. It would be pretty on a dark-haired girl, but not on me. Pappa says that I am like a silver fairy, all wisps and wishes. I know it's not true; when I look in the water at myself, a plain girl stares back at me. Snowflake hair, face whiter than the whitest white.

I stand slowly, leaning on my heels. Mor slips off my dirty nightgown and tosses it onto the bed. She shapes the apron skirt into a large pouf so I can shimmy into it, pushing my head through. Her fingers crawl up my spine like spiders, pulling the laces of the apron tight. Then she turns me around and finally looks at me—a good long look. I search her face, hoping to see forgiveness. Hoping the cobweb worked its magic, making everything better, including her. I want to talk about last night, but I'm too scared.

I look deep into her eyes and see myself. The girl is so small, like a baby bird opening and closing its mouth. Mor doesn't offer a thing, not even a worm of a word.

"Mamma, I'm sorry . . . I didn't mean to be bad. I . . . I only wanted to be with you."

She says nothing, pointing at my feet.

"No stockings today," she says.

She leaves me like that, bleeding on the rug.

The Second Knot

She leaned over the black book on the floor, in the flicker of candlelight. Her long black hair was loose and free; her naked body, an offering to the night. A circle of salt surrounded her. Her dagger glowed as she carved invisible symbols in the air, marking the four directions with the tip: the cross of Odhinn. Whispering to Freyja, she invoked the goddess, her wrist spiraling the shapes into being, a magical drawing down of energy onto the parchment.

A small flutter moved inside her. *The first kick.* She marvelled at it, placed her hands on her belly. *On the new moon.* The perfect time to pray for protection. For the life growing inside her.

She dipped her quill into the ink. Though she had not written the first half of the book, she was determined to add her mark. An inheritance of remedies, recipes. *Spells.* Her breath caught in her throat, the word still too charged to say out loud. Yet what else to call such a collection, passed down from hand to hand, generations of women doing exactly as she was doing: recording secret knowledge in the cover of darkness.

Her fingers gently held the pen. She looped the letters of her prayer:

Protection of a baby though labour,
H.T.

Would he approve of such a prayer, given that his heart now belonged to someone else? She imagined how different things might be had he stayed onshore that terrible day. The day his boat was stolen by the sea and he washed up on a distant island. Into the arms of *her*.

How happy they could have been, had the Sisters allowed it. That storm, so unexpected it must have been sent by the gods. Even the charm she had given him—a simple bit of twine tied into knots, binding and harnessing the power of coastal winds—proved useless in the face of such a tempest.

Was it you, Skuld, who snipped my time with Pieter short?

Or was it her, that devil-haired witch?

She opened her eyes, sniffing back a tear. Wiping her nose with an ink-stained hand, she dipped her pen again. What good would crying do now? It was done. The baby growing inside her, the best part of their secret love. And once she revealed the news to him, he would have to act.

Please, let me have this, Sisters, she prayed silently. *Let me have his child.*

What Was

Pieter kneeled before her, leaning his head on her protruding belly. He whispered loud enough for her to hear.

"Are you praying to the *gods*?" Maeva was incredulous. "Shouldn't you be praying to Jesus?" Though she hadn't ventured to church since winter had blown in—since that first time, at their wedding—Pieter had skied into town three times. Claiming that the entire congregation asked about her welfare and the baby's. His enthusiasm almost convinced Maeva that the villagers were capable of such goodwill.

He pulled away, cupping his hands around her round bump. "I'm simply putting prayers into the wind. It's not my business who listens." He bent to kiss her stomach.

She shook her head, bowled over at the transformation in her husband. And herself.

She had never expected to revel in his attention. He had always watched her, but this felt different somehow. His face almost beatific, his praise constant. It was as if he were drunk, every insignificant action worthy of worship in his eyes. Collecting eggs from the hens. Milking the cow. Carrying water from the well. Even shoveling manure seemed to inspire joyous contemplation in him—the natural cycle of life, the wonder of seeds growing in the dank earth, reason enough to celebrate the miracle of gestation.

"Careful," she warned. "People may suspect you've gone mad."

He stood, holding her in his arms. "And I will blame you for my madness. I am mad with love, and I don't care who knows it." He leaned in to kiss her, his lips hovering for permission. She tilted her head to accommodate, finding it hard to resist his fervour.

Lately, she found herself wanting more of him, more of this affection. She basked in the glow of his adoration, which seemed to feed his light even more. Dreams of her old life had finally subsided. Releasing her, fading in intensity. New dreams, new concerns—a new life—had flooded in, on the wave of her growing belly.

"Er du klar for markedsdag, min kone?"

She nodded, surprised at the excitement and trepidation she felt for market day. *"Ja, jeg er klar, ektemann."*

Pleased at her pronunciation, he spun her in a whoop of joy. "I love it when you say 'husband.' Say it again."

She rolled her eyes. "Husband, husband, husband. There. Now, can we go, please?"

His smile stretched as wide as his face. "Ja, wife." He patted her belly one last time. "We can go."

She hummed a lullaby as she settled into the seat of the wagon.

"I love it when you sing," he urged her. "Sing for me."

So she did, all the way to market.

⚬⚭⚬

Pieter guided the horse and wagon to a fence-post next to the red tavern, then climbed down to tie off the harness. Maeva observed the pier, where rows upon rows of vendors were setting up their wares. She had never witnessed such a bustling throng of people.

"Everyone in town must be here," she marvelled.

Pieter grinned at her. "And the next three villages, at least. It's Sankthansaften. Jonsok. A time for celebration."

She bent her head to hide her eyes. *Midsummer. Of course.* Memories of her sisters, of their own rituals of honouring the sun, flashed in her mind.

He paused, then asked, "You know it? I mean, you celebrated such a thing?"

More images washed over her: Huge bonfires, dancing, feasting, laughter. Flirtation and coupling. Mock weddings. The many times she snuck away to meet *him* in the water, while her sisters danced with young men on the mainland.

Maeva nodded but said nothing.

He sighed, then snatched his satchel from the wagon.

She sensed his quiet frustration. This sudden change in him happened whenever he asked about her past. Her recent habit to appease, to cajole him out of his unexpected mood swings and keep the peace, was absent in her today. She refused to surrender this last piece of herself; she had to keep something that was hers. Revealing more about the life she had left behind—the people she missed—was simply too much. Too private. Too painful. *They are mine, and mine alone.*

That old feeling—of being consumed by Pieter—pressed in on her. *How quickly things shifted. It must be me. The baby.*

Pieter studied her. Her loose hair hanging well past her hips in curly disarray. "Perhaps you should wear your bonnet today?"

"I forgot it at the cabin. It's too hot for such a thing anyway." She was surprised at herself, the lie tumbling out before she could stop it.

His brow furrowed. He hesitated, then wrapped one of her red curls around his finger. Her head tilted to the side as he tugged at her hair, a little too forcefully. "A braid, then. To help you stay cool."

⌒∞⌒

She held his arm tightly. She could feel his pride expanding larger than her belly—a new wife on his arm, showing fishermen and villagers how happy he was. Each person smiling at Pieter, their friendliness wavering as they took in Maeva, who towered over most of the locals. She reached for her braid, the tip of it swaying like a horse's mane, and twined the end of it around her fingers, doing her best to smile and pronounce salutations correctly.

"*God morgen . . . Hvilken nydelig ull . . . Uh, hva—hvor mye?*"

Pieter's eyes gleamed at her somewhat successful attempts to make conversation. Her nervousness making the pitch and shape of the words like birdsong. He didn't seem to notice the hardness in people's eyes, or the pinched expressions. Their clipped responses revealing more than words ever could.

"Mor, why did God give that lady such oddly coloured hair?"

Maeva turned to see a young girl, about twelve years old, pulling at her mother's arm at the next stall. The woman shushed the girl, her attention on the lobsters for sale. But the child persisted. The mother lifted her head, then paused as she registered Maeva.

"I'm sure I don't know, Unna." Her coolness seemed familiar. "Perhaps God has a sense of humour."

Then Maeva recognized her from the day she had arrived in Ørken: the woman who had lost her husband at sea on that terrible day, because of the storm. *Because of Pieter.*

Birgit nodded ever so slightly. "*God morgen, Pieter Aldestaed.*" She eyed Maeva's stomach. "I see you've been busy over the winter months." Her daughter held on to her mother's arm, peering up at Maeva with curiosity.

Pieter laughed good-heartedly. Oblivious to the bite in the widow's words. "That we have. You remember Maeva, my wife? She's due sometime at the end of the harvest."

Birgit nodded, the smile almost a sneer. "*Gratulerer og velsignelser.*"

Maeva tried to hide the fact that she didn't quite understand, but Pieter noticed.

"It's so nice to have blessings bestowed on us, isn't it, Mae? *Tusen takk, Fru Vebjørnsdatter.*"

The widow tilted her head, then gestured up the hill. "With a child on the way, you will have need of wool, ja? I have heard that the Finn girl is selling today. Reindeer hides, sailor's knots, yarn, all at a good price. In celebration of Sankthansaften."

Pieter's smile faltered. "I'm sure my wife can weave something just as fine."

The young girl pulled at her mother, bored of the small talk. "I'm hungry, Mamma."

Birgit shushed the child, then lifted her chin. "I don't doubt your wife's skills. Though a new mother might appreciate some help. Some relief of the many chores she will have in the coming months, however small, would be welcome, I'm sure."

Pieter cleared his throat.

"*God dag, Pieter.*" Birgit stared at Maeva, mouth and eyes pinched. The exclusion in her goodbye pointed. Then her back was to them, toward the lobsters, with her daughter still staring.

Maeva hated to admit it, but she knew the widow was right.

"I think we should at least have a peek at the Finn girl's stall. Perhaps she has some coloured thread and wool I could use."

For a moment, Pieter looked flustered. Then he recovered, nodding. "Of course, my dear. Whatever my wife wishes. But you look flushed— perhaps sit by the dock while I hike up the hill? I won't be long."

She wanted to protest, to insist on choosing herself. But the chance to sit next to the waves, alone, was too heavenly to resist. She watched him march up the hill, his head down.

⚬✖⚬

Maeva shivered and rubbed her arms, feeling a chill underneath the warmth of the day. She moved through the crowd toward a bench by the dock, the lighthouse in full view. People jostled her by accident, then, seeing her, stepped around her carefully, as if she were a mud puddle or a diseased animal.

Perhaps I'm imagining it. She tried smiling, but that only made things worse. They avoided her even more, quickly pushing their children past her. The absence of Pieter—her shield—making her keenly aware of how alone she was.

She stopped at a stall with racks of *torrfisk*. Her mouth watered; her stomach rumbled. There would have been a time when the smell of such a thing made her queasy. But she was past the point of morning sickness and well into the stage of being hungry all the time. She dug for a coin inside her apron.

"May I have one piece, please?" Behind the rack, an older man with a heavy black beard continued to hang fish. She repeated the request, wondering if her pronunciation was wrong. Still, the man ignored her. She tried a third time, a little louder, when someone grasped her elbow.

"You heard the lady, one—nei, make it two. *Vær så snill.*" A blond man winked at her, dropping her arm to pay for both pieces. He handed her the fish and grinned.

She managed to stutter a response. *"Takk, Herr Bjørnsen."* His name, a familiar one from Pieter's stories. His face, a little too familiar. From the day he rescued them.

He steered her away from the crowd, to the bench by the water. She allowed it, to show her gratitude for the snack, despite wanting solitude. Despite her uncertainty that she could trust him.

The smell of salt, the spray of foam in the air, hit her hard. She was overwhelmed by the tantalizing crash of waves, the spill and retreat of water on the rocks. She closed her eyes, reveling in a moment of bliss.

"Missing home, I suspect?" Hans studied her, then the sea, his reddish stubble highlighting ruddy, sunburned cheeks. "I know that feeling. When I'm not out on the boat, I pine for water, too."

Grateful for his accurate assessment, the common ground they seemed to share, she smiled slightly. She was pleasantly surprised at the burly man's apparent sensitivity. Somehow, his own admission of yearning didn't feel like an intrusion. More like an unspoken secret, a bridge of intimacy between strangers.

He continued. "It's been a long winter. Must have been hard, holed up in that small shack . . . Especially with a man like Pieter."

Her eyes widened at his nerve.

His face broke into a smirk, teasing. "I mean, he must be insufferable at times. Teaching you new words at every moment, as if he invented them."

She paused, then nodded. "Yes. I mean, nei, he's been . . . It's been . . ." She stopped herself. How had it been, honestly? What word could encompass all she had gone through, all that she felt about this place? This new life, her new husband, a child on the way?

He filled in the gap. "Overwhelming."

She said nothing, her confirmation obvious.

He took a bite of fish, chewed it loudly. He pointed to the market. "I know Pieter wants the best for you, and your child. But you should know . . . Sometimes, he's snow-blind." He faced her, his eyes grave.

She cocked her head.

"He only sees the light, doesn't see anything beyond it."

"Ah," she said, still not fully understanding.

"The villagers. They don't like new people. It's fear, you see. They're afraid of what's out there." He waved a hand dismissively at the sky. "Afraid they may have thwarted the gods by their new faith. Afraid the new God might be wrathful. Either way, their souls, eternally damned: by the Christian devil's fire or the eternal ice of Niflheim."

Maeva struggled to chew the hardened fish.

He picked at a thread on his trousers. "You must be familiar with such things, where you come from." He probed a bloated finger into the snag, scratching at the hole in the wool. "The belief in the old gods is waning everywhere."

Not for me. She heard a murmur under the crash of surf. *Odhinn* . . . Heat spread across her cheeks.

He took another bite of fish, talking through the mouthful. "That's why they don't like you."

Maeva gulped. "Pardon me?"

Hans held up his hands, the stockfish stiff. "Nei, I didn't mean that. I meant . . . You remind them of what they used to believe in. Before Christians decided that *everything* is full of sin. That the devil invented anything pleasurable." He sneered. "Guilt is just desire. Dressed up in a wolf suit."

"But today is Midsummer. How can everyone be celebrating such a thing, given this new faith? Aren't they—aren't you—calling yourself Christian?"

"Only when it suits." He extended a hand for her to shake. "But mostly, I call myself Hans."

Her hand flew to her mouth. Hans stared at her with seriousness, then abruptly chortled, slapping his knee. A full-bellied guffaw leaped out of her throat, the sound of which made Hans laugh even louder. It felt so good to let go, to make noise, to feel alive, that she let out another whoop. Soon, the two of them were bent over, unable to stop themselves.

"Glad to see people are enjoying the celebration."

Maeva stopped giggling, the mood broken. She peered up to find a sweating scowled face, souring in front of them. *The magistrate.*

"I see Midsummer has managed to empty your pockets." The man pointed to a rope with three knots tied to Hans's belt.

Hans grinned. "How can a fisherman resist such a promise as controlling the winds, eh, Innesbørg?"

The man grunted. "A sailor's knot. Ridiculous superstitious charm. Waste of good money."

"Agreed. I should have spent a bit more coin. For a few more knots. Then I could be rid of foul weather *and* people." Hans's eyes sparkled mischievously.

Innesbørg ignored him. "Fru Aldestaed . . . Maeva, isn't it?"

Hans chewed as he spoke. "A fine Christian name, wouldn't you agree, Magistrate?" Hans smirked and winked at Maeva, and Maeva smiled half-heartedly, the previous ease gone. She distracted herself by taking another bite of fish.

The magistrate appeared confused, then frowned. "Shouldn't you be out on your boat, hunting squid or seal? At the very least helping to skin the meat for the town feast, Herr Bjørnsen?"

Maeva almost choked on her fish.

Hans narrowed his eyes. "Today's my day off. Little bout of *spekk-finger.*" He held a hand up, the first finger red and swollen. "Consequence of the job."

"I'm sure a little women's work will do the trick," Innesbørg quipped.

"I'm sure your wife would appreciate your expertise, Herr Innesbørg."

The two men stared long and hard at each other.

Maeva folded her fidgeting hands onto her belly, gripping the stock-fish, suddenly feeling the need to get away from both of them.

Hans stood and bowed gallantly. "It's good to see you again, Fru Aldestaed. See you at church sometime." He winked, then tipped his hat at the magistrate.

Innesbørg's jaw tensed, watching him go. Then, without invitation, he stretched himself onto the bench, his knee casually touching Maeva's skirts, his hands on his own protruding stomach.

She shifted her legs uncomfortably. Scanned the hill, hoping to see Pieter.

The magistrate tapped his fingers. Looked her up and down.

Maeva kept her eyes fixed on the yellowed fish in her hand, at the dried-up folds of stiffened skin. Then, beyond her hand, she couldn't help but notice his boots.

Seal hide.

Maeva's hand tensed around the hard fish. She could feel the tender fibres cracking under her grip.

"My wife, Maren, is with child . . ." He floated the words out there, unfinished.

Maeva blinked. "How lovely. Perhaps our children can play together."

He stared at her, as if she had spoken in a foreign tongue. Finally, he said, "I doubt it." His tone was gruff. He didn't offer any words of explanation, but Maeva understood.

Then she felt a butterfly flutter inside her belly and forgot the red-faced man beside her. Forgot Hans, forgot the villagers, forgot the market.

She sat up in awe at the dance inside.

An old woman wearing a flower wreath stopped in front of them, her eyes almost as silver as her unruly hair. She pointed a finger at Maeva's belly. "A magical time, to be sure."

Maeva nodded and smiled, happy to receive some kind words from a stranger.

Innesbørg grunted, unimpressed by such maternal wonder. "Magic has nothing to do with it. Move along, Fru Tormundsdatter."

The old woman pressed her lips together, hiding amusement. "'Tis true. All the blame can be laid at the feet of ordinary men. At least that's what your lovely wife has told me, the last time we spoke."

Maeva suppressed a smile, impressed by the cheek on the woman.

"*God dag, Nils, Fru Aldestaed.*" She bowed her head and left without any further introduction.

Maeva watched people step away and around the woman, almost as if she carried the plague. *Like they treat me.*

Innesbørg rolled his eyes. Maeva waited for him to explain who the woman was, but he moved to stand, brushing his leg into hers again. Pausing awkwardly, his upper lip wet with sweat, he stared at her hair.

Maeva flipped her braid to hide it behind her back. She scanned the hill again. Pieter was marching back at a fast pace. *Just in time.*

Innesbørg followed her gaze, then snorted phlegm down his throat. Without a goodbye, he disappeared into the throng of people.

Pieter was breathless by the time he reached her. She grabbed his hand, grateful for his presence, to be out of the magistrate's grip. She wanted to blurt out so many questions but couldn't seem to form the words. Later, she told herself. When they were at home in private. Instead, she pointed to the bag in his hand. "Well, what did you purchase?"

He was distracted, searching the hill.

"What? Oh . . . of course. Here." He passed her the satchel. Took the *torrfisk* from her hand and bit off a piece.

She opened the satchel. Inside, there were spools upon spools of silken thread, perfectly spun for the smallest of stitches.

All of it blood red.

The Third Knot

She placed the spools into a sack. The shock of seeing him inside her tent—after weeks upon weeks of waiting for him—making her visibly tremble.

His excuses, too many to count.

Such a winter this year . . .

I've been helping my wife navigate her new duties . . . Everything is so foreign to her.

I'm not sure if you've heard? She is with child.

Through it all, she kept a convincing smile. Ached to rush into his arms.

To slap the joy off his smug face.

Instead, she made her hands busy, gathering the threads.

Making sure the incantation she whispered was so quiet, even the wind couldn't hear it.

What Is

Pappa carries me across the doorway, setting me down in the rocking chair by the fire. He has to duck under the herbs hanging from the rafters, some of the leaves falling into my hair. It smells so good, I don't mind. Pappa brushes them away, then lifts my leg in his hand. Mamma glances up from her embroidery but doesn't say anything. I hold out each boot, wincing as Pappa unlaces it. He peels the heel of the first one away. A piece of dried, crusted blood pulls at the skin between two toes. Fresh blood drips on his fingers.

The morning at church became a daylong adventure: standing, sitting, kneeling, skipping, running on the pier. I held on to Far's hand, an ordinary girl, with ordinary feet. The effort of being so ordinary ripping the healing web open, again and again.

Pappa coos as he lifts my foot, "Oh, my little *kanin*, why didn't you tell Far you were bleeding?"

"I was having too much fun. I loved the part where we all sang about Jee-zus."

Mor raises an eyebrow. "Sounds like she's perfectly fine, Pieter."

"Look at her feet, Mae." He holds up the wet brown shoes, the tips dark, like I had stomped through a puddle.

She waves the needle at the corners of the rafters. "Gather some cobwebs. Make a paste for the wound."

"I'm fine, it was just a lot of walking."

"You are not fine, child—your boots are a mess. Christ."

I flinch, knowing it's bad to say Jesus's name like that.

"It's the Lord's day, Pieter." Mor pulls a red thread tight and pokes the needle through the frame.

"You don't have to remind me, Mae."

"Maybe you shouldn't have walked her so much, showing her off like a new horse for all to see." She stops to glare at him. "I take it the congregation embraced you with open arms?"

"As a matter of fact, it was fine. Absolutely uneventful."

He forgets to mention everyone's owl eyes on me. No one smiled or talked to us at all.

"Except for the fact that she was bleeding through her shoes."

"You could have stayed home."

"How was I to know you cut her feet this morning?"

"I cut her feet every week, husband." She squints at the stitches. "If you were home more, you'd know this."

"But why this Sunday? When you knew I was taking her to church? Surely you could have waited until after."

"And cut her before bedtime, to bleed through the bedding?" She stabs the fabric. "Fine, next time, *you* do the cutting, at your convenience."

"Nei, I won't do that."

"Why not? It's a little blood, for God's sake, and if it isn't done, she may not be able to walk properly. Or hold a spoon. Is that what you want?" The needle stops. She whispers to herself. "It's enough dealing with one child; I cannot deal with two."

Pappa lowers my foot gently, but I can hear him grinding his teeth.

"Yes, two children would be unthinkable, wouldn't it?"

She pushes her chin forward, her eyes sharper than the needle. "Go outside, Leidah."

"But, Mor, my feet hurt."

"Leidah, listen to your mother." Far snaps out the words.

I try hard not to cry at the change in him, the bite in his words. I look from one to the other through tears. They stab at each other with their eyes. I am invisible.

I slam the door, slump on the wood-box, waiting. Listening.

"I am not going to talk about this, Pieter."

"Talk? Oh, nei, I agree, the time has come to do away with talking. I'm ready for something else."

"Good, then. While you figure it out, our daughter's feet need tending."

"Maeva, stop it."

"Stop what? Taking care of our daughter?"

"Is that what you call it?"

"You're the one who insisted on church, despite my warning."

"I want her to live a normal life. Don't you want that for her, for us? *Beklager*, Maeva, but I happen to love my family—I want the best for them."

"And I don't?" She gets really quiet. "How dare you."

"It's been seven years—seven long, lonely years . . . Have a little mercy. Some forgiveness, damn it." His words are shaky.

"I have done what I agreed to. I have taken care of you, I have given you a daughter. Now it's your turn, husband. Where's your mercy?"

"Has it been that terrible, Mae? Am I such a brute? I want what any man wants: a son. *Our* son. A brother for Leidah, another child for us to love."

"You say you love me—that you love our daughter—then you keep what's mine. What you *stole*."

"You gave it to me. Willingly, as I recall."

"I did no such thing." Her voice is sharp. "You want me to keep my promise? Then keep yours, goddamn it."

"Not until you give me a son."

I stumble off the porch, tears spilling.

I cry because my feet hurt.

I cry because Mor hates me sometimes.

I cry because she is sad.

I cry because Mor doesn't love Far. Or at least, not like he loves her.

I cry because I am not enough. I am not a boy.

I am not even a proper girl like the ones at church, a girl with dainty fingers and toes. I am a bleeding mess. I can't even hold a spoon right.

I run behind the cottage, the sun burning through the trees. Every blade of grass and tiny rock splitting the skin between my toes even more. But I don't care. I run past the barn to the well, ready to throw myself in. Maybe then Mor will love me; maybe then Far will wish for his girl back and forget about having a boy.

I reach the well and climb up the stones, tossing my legs over the ledge, letting my toes hang above the deep black hole. A chilly draft breathes up to meet me.

What would happen if I just let go? Would I keep falling and falling?

I wipe my nose on my sleeve and pick a pebble off the ledge. It is small and round, the size of a cat's eye. I let it hang at the edge of my palm, tipping it, playing with the idea of falling forever. Never feeling the ground or my feet again.

I flip my palm over quickly and wait for the tiny sound of a splash. *En, to, tre . . .* Ten seconds go by. No splash. I think twice about throwing myself in.

I wait and wait. Wondering when they will stop arguing. Wondering when someone will remember I'm gone.

The splash of the pebble never comes.

A grey furry spider crawls up the side of the well, then stops just before reaching my finger.

Maybe you can weave me a new house, spider. Let me live with you.

I watch as the spider begins to spin a silver web across the stones. I think about stealing the web to heal my bleeding feet. But it doesn't seem fair, so I don't.

The light sinks below the trees. I sit perfectly still, in case she comes. She needs to know I don't care about anything, especially her. I will not go inside, ever.

I think about the other girls I saw at church today. Wonder if any of them would ever want to be friends with the ugly blue girl. None of them smiled at me. So probably not.

Footsteps swish-swish in the long grass. I hope it's Pappa.

It's not.

I want her to wrap herself around me and scoop me up so I can push her away. Then maybe she would hold on forever, keep me safe, never letting go, not letting me fall. She would hug me and wipe my tears, saying she hated cutting me as much as I hated being cut. Laughing and crying, she would tell me I'm her girl, that she would never replace me, especially not with a boy. And after a while, I would give in, tell her I forgive her. We would walk hand in hand back to the cottage, and Pappa would say he was sorry, too.

She sighs, a tired sigh. She holds my doll in her hand, waiting for me to take it. I don't. She sets it on the ledge. Her arms hang at her sides. I swallow fresh tears down my throat. There is no bottom, no limit to the well inside me. I remind myself that I am mad at her. I wait for her to speak. To reach out. To do something. Anything.

She sits beside me, staring into the well, a towel on her lap.

I watch out of the corner of my eye as she reaches for the bucket, throwing it over the side. It clang-clangs against the wall, then splashes into the water. I peer over the ledge, trying to find the bucket in the dark hole. I grab dolly, even though I'm angry. The bucket floats up out of the dark, appearing like a ghost as my mother's hands work the rope. She unhooks it, then places it on the grass. Then lifts me off the ledge. Her touch so quick, it's gone before I even feel it.

I hold my next breath, wishing I could melt into her skin. If I threw myself in, would she dive in after me? Probably not.

"Have I ever told you the story of the well of Urd?" she asks.

I shake my head.

"It is an old one, much older than anyone in the village, older than anyone lying in that rotting church cemetery. Older than the church, even. Older than the trees. Older than this well."

She pours the water into a smaller bucket. She taps my knees, and I slip my feet in. The water wakes me up; it is deliciously cold, soothing the cuts. I am quiet, hoping she will begin the story. But she doesn't. She hums, waiting for the water to do its work. She bends down, picking at the grass and tearing each blade into little pieces. Not saying a word.

"Can you tell it to me, Mor?"

She pauses, then nods. "At bedtime, child."

I try to hide my excitement by sloshing my legs around, pretending I am crushing grapes. Last week, Mor told me about how wine is made, people squishing tiny balls of fruit under their toes. How strange to drink toe-jam. I almost forget being sad and mad. But not quite.

And then she says something. So quietly I barely hear her.

"This is the last time, child." Her words, big and heavy. "Pappa wants it so."

I stop my grape-stomping. The last time? What does she mean? She holds the towel out, and I step out of the water, waiting for her to explain. She doesn't. But then I know, by the way she dries my feet ever so gently with the towel.

No more cutting.

She hums our lullaby—the one she has sung to me since I was a baby—all the way back to the cabin. I join in, and we sound like one person.

I follow her onto the porch, each step hurting more than the last. I imagine my feet growing into flippers, huge fins. So blue and big, not even Pappa's black boots could hide them.

A Bedtime Tale

B efore time knew itself, before the earth knew how to spin, there was a Great Tree at the centre of everything. No one knows how this Tree came to be, only that from it all life was born. In its mighty limbs, the Nine Worlds were held, each one clinging to a separate branch, precariously hanging in the balance of all that is."

Leidah sits up on her elbows. "What's 'pre-car-ee-us-ly' mean?"

Maeva fluffs her daughter's pillow, then snaps her fingers for her to lie down. "It means dangerous. Uncertain."

Leidah settles back into the pillow, wrinkling her nose.

Maeva is perched on the edge of the bed. The single candle on the nightstand flickers, casting shadows across her face. "At the top of the Tree lived a great eagle. At the bottom, a fearsome dragon. The two hated and spewed poison at each other, using a mischievous squirrel to carry messages up and down the trunk of the Tree."

" 'Mischievous.' " Leidah grins. "I know what that means."

"Each of the Nine Worlds felt the warring of these beasts keenly, assuming the terrible earthquakes and hurricanes that ravaged their lands were caused by the conflict—"

"What's 'ravaged'?"

Maeva sighs and leans on her arm. "What do you think it means?"

The girl considers for a moment, her eyes on the rafters. "It's when the wind's angry at everything." She looks back at her mother. "It rips up everything. The wind doesn't mean to, it's just so damn angry, it can't help it."

Maeva tries to hide her amusement. "Don't say 'damn.' And yes, when the land is ravaged, it means exactly that. It has other meanings, too, but in this case—"

"Like what?"

"Well . . . when someone ruins something—someone—beyond repair. Destruction so complete, there's no hope."

"But why would someone do that?"

Maeva smooths the blanket distractedly, tucking Leidah's *dukke* beside her. "It's . . . complicated. It's not what the word means in this case anyway. Shall I keep going?"

Leidah nods, then yawns.

"Secretly, sitting inside the heart of the Tree, were three scheming Sisters who were the true cause of all the changeable weather. Most knew them as the Norns—"

"What were their names?"

"Their names were less important than their duties: they were the guardians of the sacred well of destiny, the waters that kept the mighty Tree and all of the Nine Worlds alive."

The child begins to close her eyes, drowsiness taking over.

"These Sisters were older than any god, and bowed down to neither man nor beast. They controlled all that was, all that is, and all that ever will be. They carved the destiny of everything into the bark and leaves of the Tree, pouring sacred water down its trunk and onto its roots. Water so pure, it bleached anything it touched to alabaster, carving the bark with long silver trenches that recorded time itself."

Leidah murmurs, "What's alabaster?"

"A shade of white found in marble, a smooth type of rock."

Leidah rolls to her side, snuggling into her doll. "Just say 'white,' then." Her words, slow and sleepy.

Maeva holds back a smile. "The Sisters could see and hear everything through the reflections in the well, even the buzz of a wasp's wings in a thunderstorm. And Wind was their faithful servant, singing the secrets of the worlds. They knew everything there was to know about every living creature, in every world: the nightmares of men, the secret desires of women, the dreams of giants, the passions of the gods. They witnessed it all, sitting at the edge of the well, weaving intricate patterns into each of the Nine Worlds."

Maeva waits, but there is only a quiet exhale from the girl, and the familiar ticking downstairs. She leans toward her daughter, lowering her voice to a whisper. "The eldest Sister spun the red thread of what had come before. The middle Sister held that thread, weaving what was becoming with every passing second. The third Sister—the veiled one, the one without eyes—wielded the sharpest scissors, unravelling and cutting what needed to come to an end. All of this happened simultaneously, time overlapping itself."

She pauses, then blows out the candle. Makes one last adjustment to secure the covers snugly around her daughter. The girl's elfin blue hand curled like a baby bird under her chin. *This has never changed, from the time you were born.* For a moment, she allows herself to remember Leidah as a baby. When time stretched itself wide and long, and her daughter was attached to her at every moment. Being able to hold her close, keep her safe, made the world—the danger—seem more manageable somehow. She stands, but Leidah whimpers in her sleep.

Carefully, Maeva lies down beside the sleeping child, wrapping her arms around Leidah, whose little hands clutch the worn stuffed doll. She smiles at the comfort such a misshapen toy has brought. Despite its ugliness. *Despite your pappa's certainty that no child would play with such a sad thing.* She thinks of Pieter trying to hide his disappointment in her lack of domestic skill; she appreciated his restraint, but it was still a bumpy start to their marriage. *But what did he expect?* Unbidden, she remembers his face the first time they met: the arrogant smirk, the determined brow, the unkempt beard . . . Uneasy, she stares into the dark.

The wool itches against her dry skin; she resists the urge to scratch.

Putting her forehead next to Leidah's, she breathes in the grassy scent of her. She has a vague memory of snuggling like this with her own mother, the tips of their noses barely brushing as she floated asleep. *Will you remember this, child?* Maeva closes her eyes. How she wishes she could stop the world from turning, stop Leidah from growing up. *Freeze everything, as it is now.* Having to explain it all to her daughter, to prepare her for what's coming, a cruel necessity. *Soon. But not yet.*

Leidah rolls over, her breath softening into a deep sleep. Carefully, Maeva sits up. She shifts to the edge of the bed and sees the doll on the floor. She picks it up and begins to tuck it back in when she notices something strange. On the pillow, beside Leidah's cheek—where Maeva's own face had been—a pile of dry flakes. She pinches a bit between thumb and finger to examine, disturbed. Scooping the remainder into her hand, she stands up slowly. Her other hand rubs behind her ear. Tiny pieces slough off onto her fingertips.

She tiptoes out of the room, cupping the fragments of skin and the raggedy doll. She carries everything to the sewing room and sits on the stool. A feeling of dread overwhelms her as she opens her hand. Translucent curls that could easily pass as sea salt, as snow—a sure sign that time is running out. *I am falling apart.*

She brushes them onto the small table, placing the toy beside the pile. Its head is almost flat, the stuffing barely there from years of love and comfort. *And neglect*, Maeva thinks, having found the forgotten doll in the dirt more than once. Threading her sharpest needle, she flips the *dukke* on its side. Using the point of the needle, she tears away at her clumsy old stitches, creating a new hole. She stuffs the dried-out flakes in between the fabric, making sure every last one is inside. Then, she pulls the thread tight, sewing up the hole. She holds it out to examine.

Perhaps Pieter was right. A little hair would help.

She sews well into the night, affixing individual strands of red yarn. Her mind, spinning more and more questions.

What will become of her? Of Pieter?

What will become of Leidah, when her world is ravaged beyond repair?

What Was

After the holiday celebrations, Pieter decided to take another day off from the boats. He told himself that he needed the rest, but truthfully, he couldn't bear to be away from Maeva, leaving her to her own devices, with too much time on her hands. He couldn't stand not knowing what she was doing, the possibility that she might fall into old habits—wander away from the cabin—too much for him.

He hung the witch's knot inside the barn, on the hook for harnesses. Superstitious, perhaps. A braided rope of nine knots, each one a spell that bound, protected, controlled. Wind, weather, people. *What's the harm in having a little assurance?*

Hidden in plain sight, such a mundane object wouldn't be questioned. *Tusen takk, old friend.*

Odhinn

He stretched his feathers, flying up and up, searching for the right island.

After he had left her that last time, he slipped in and out of himself, testing which disguise to use. He knew it had to be his most clever. The Sisters were too astute for his usual chicanery.

He flapped his wings, then soared into the sky. The shape of an eagle, useful for fast travel across worlds, but only temporary. Not convincing enough to hide his true identity.

After drifting on the wind for hours, he finally saw it. Or, rather, sensed it, his feathers rising, his gut churning. The absence of anything that resembled civilization a sure sign.

One of a hundred green mountainous isles, it bobbed in the middle of nowhere. Its similarity to all the other islands, a grand ruse that had worked for eons to keep it hidden and protected. Inhabited only by sea terns, puffins, and white gannets pitching themselves off cliff edges, diving for food. Diving for mates. Not a human, demon, or god in sight.

Yes, this was the right place.

Legend told of a bridge—the channel to the centre of the Great Tree, where the Norns weave—that resembled a modest cave. White water dripped across the threshold, a milky river sliding down its face, hiding what was inside.

The glamour of bird shit. A clever camouflage.

He floated on an updraft, flying toward the opening in the rock face.

A snowstorm of feathers suddenly enveloped him. Beaks and claws and wings beat at him, attacking his disguise so viciously, he had no choice. He pushed out of the eagle skin and leaped away from the horde of birds, springing into the sky. Into nothingness.

Instead of transforming into another creature, he hovered in between. Dangling on the mouth of wind. He rumbled with pleasure, at his own cleverness, born out of accident and indecision: he had become pure air.

Without effort, he whooshed past the threshold into the cave, into the bark of the Great Tree, winding cleverly under and over and through a maze of roots and rough stone, past every trick and trap the Sisters had set. He delighted at the speed at which he travelled, catching himself just in time, before his enthusiasm revealed the disguise. Slowing impulse to a mere draft, sucking into himself, he reached the very heart of the Norns' lair. The Great Hall of Time.

The beat of a drum—*or the cadence of a heart?*—echoed through him.

The Sisters sat at a grand spinning wheel that filled the entire chamber. Around the perimeter, a moat of silver. A river that gurgled and danced as the wheel spiraled its web.

He floated in and around the three women. Brushing against Urd's withered hands, he watched as she spun and spun an endless red thread, the spool rotating round and round. He blew past her to land at Verdandi's feet, her toes digging and looping into the huge tapestry. The pattern of red threads danced between her adept feet, growing miraculously across the floor. The veiled one, Skuld, sat in the centre, meditating. Suddenly, she stabbed her scissors into the sea of red, snipping a hole into a beautiful series of knots. Then she waited as the pattern redefined itself. The waters of the well bubbled and churned in response, a new fate taking hold of some poor wretch somewhere in one of the Nine Worlds.

All at the mercy of Skuld.

He wondered how, in all the worlds, the Norns came to be the guardians of time. The gate-keepers of everything, weaving such cosmic consequence for even the tiniest of creatures. The mightiest of demons. The strongest of gods.

Including me.

He tasted a bitterness rising at the back of his throat.

Why shouldn't I have such powers?

He almost vibrated in glee, though, when he thought of the things he would do if his plan worked. How everything could change: what was, what is, what will be . . . Skuld's scissors controlling it all. He could even create a different past, a life where she had been at his side all along.

What would that be like?

Cause and effect, creation and consequence. The life he *had* lived—the worlds he had built, the people he loved—gone in one quick snip, ephemeral as air, disappearing into the overlap of *what used to be* and *what will be*.

In both admiration and fear, he couldn't resist getting closer. He puffed up a small tornado of dust and leaves, hoping to make the Sisters pause, if only for a moment.

Long enough for Skuld to put down those damn scissors.

Instead, the three women moved to the mouth of the moat, where the well waters flowed from the trunk of the Tree. They began to chant in a language he didn't understand. Determined not to be ignored, he became a whirlwind, rippling across the water, billowing their skirts upwards.

Still, they ignored him. Finally, he exhaled so hard, the water flooded over the edge of the well. Instantly, the puddle on the floor became white, seeping into the dark earth. The Sisters cracked and snapped their bones, bending to witness a vision in the well.

He couldn't help himself; he had to see what his presence had caused.

In the water, he saw a small boat, rocking endlessly on a tumultuous sea.

He saw Maeva, waiting for him on the rocks. Naked, vulnerable.

Urd wrapped the red thread around her thumb, placing her hand into the water. He felt a tugging inside his own heart, a violent wrenching that left him breathless. Skuld cackled, then raised the scissors.

Somehow, he knew he must act. That to stay hidden would put Maeva in danger.

He spiraled out of the wind's vortex, spinning into his own masculine form.

"Who dares to enter the hall, disturbing our work?" Skuld dropped her scissors.

Verdandi sniffed the air, repulsed. "It is the arrogant one, the god who seeks from Asgard. We know what you seek, and for that, you must pay a price."

He stepped forward, his toes sinking into the puddle of white water. Though he meant to say Maeva's name out loud, other words tumbled out of him. "I want the power of the well. I want to shape destiny. I want to know what will become."

The three Sisters snorted, then spoke in unison. "Do you think you are so clever in your pathetic disguise? That we don't know your desires even before you have them? All that you seek, all that you wish, all that you regret, all of what you are . . . born from *our* threads."

Swiftly, the waters of the well clouded over, and a new reflection formed. A dark-haired man washing up on shore.

The eldest Sister, Urd, yanked on the thread wrapped around her thumb. Skuld opened her scissors wide, the metal gleaming.

"She is *what was* . . . but not *what is* in your world. You want to be what she will choose."

He nodded, unable to take his eyes away from the man in the water.

The third Sister grinned under the veil. Out of her mouth, a thousand spiders spilled. Their hairy legs danced, spinning a cocoon of silver threads, around and around his feet, spiraling up his body even before he could protest.

"Your true form shall remain here until it is time for reunion. We'll allow your spirit to roam, but only in beastly form. Until then, we want your eye."

At that, the veiled Sister thrust the metal shears into his right eyeball.

Immediately, he was assaulted by a merciless rush of pain from head to heart. Blood spurted into the well as he buckled over. His ribcage snapped, splitting down the centre. He couldn't see. But he knew what he had done. What his failure to meet Maeva at the shoreline had caused.

He could *feel* Maeva. Her heartbreak was excruciating; it was wondrous—for truly, finally, they had become one: her body, his spirit, tangled in love and agony.

Bereft, abandoned, she waited for him.

Where are you, my love? Why have you left me?

He wailed, his cries echoing Maeva's thoughts, accusations cutting him to his core.

Seven years, a lifetime, an eternity without you.

The Sisters ignored his keening—as if he were a child in the midst of a temper tantrum—the new pattern emerging in the tapestry more captivating.

Skuld lifted her veil, then popped his right eyeball into her own hollow socket. She pocketed the scissors.

He managed to groan, his entire body now encapsulated in a cocoon. "Surely I have suffered enough. What will you give me for such a gift of vision?"

The eldest Sister considered. "Seems to me that it is *she* who suffers."

Verdandi spread her toes across the weaving. "One sip is fair, I suppose."

His satisfaction, his wish for wisdom—to be a master of destiny—eclipsed by Maeva's turmoil. The consequences of his plan beyond comprehension.

As the water passed over his lips, his remaining eye witnessed one last change in the reflection of the water, the final skewer of his heart impaling him, over and over, for years to come:

Maeva's belly, swelling with life.

The Fourth Knot

S he opened the book on her growing stomach, tracing her fingers on the letters, inked by the women of her family, now long dead.

To hide in plain sight:

Place a reflective piece of glass or other mirror in a bowl of water under a full moon. In the morning, bury the mirror face down in the ground for three days. Mix three drops of your own blood into the water. On the fourth day, dig up the mirror, then drink the water. Put the mirror in your pocket, and pray to Jesus; you will go unnoticed until evening.

She placed the needle beside the pages. Perhaps it could work. Lurking in the woods and spying on the Aldestaed cabin, not something she wanted to do. But she had to. Didn't she?

The need to see his new wife, almost unbearable.

The market gossip dripped like poison into her ears. Villagers rushed to spread the news of a foreign bride, her hair red as fire. Her skin pale as snow. Some of the women grinning like cats as they mewed about how stunning this stranger actually was.

Otherworldly, they crooned. *Like Freyja herself. Full and round with child, like the moon.*

She feigned disinterest. Sold her wares with a nod and a smile, like any other day.

But underneath, the words stung, like a thousand pinpricks into her heart.

She turned her attention back to the book.

To induce labour:

Gather three leeches from a stagnant pond or riverbed. Place one leech into the mouth, until fully engorged. Then, allow the other two leeches to drain the first leech dry, in turns.

Finally, the fattest leech must be held in the hand of the pregnant woman until labour occurs.

She paused. Where could she gather leeches?
She read on, to the last spell.

To attract good fortune or true love:

Catch a dove in a metal cage, on the setting sun of a Thursday. Allow it to beat itself against the metal, until all hope of escape in the bird is gone. Then slice open its chest and steal its heart. Drain the blood. Place the heart under your pillow for three nights, before a waxing moon. On the first evening, recite a prayer to Frigg. On the second evening, drink the blood from a copper cup, imagining what or who you wish to attract. On the third evening, cut a piece of the heart away, and cook it in a stew. Save the stew, and eat it on the eve of the full moon.

It was Thursday. The fishermen had shipped out on Wednesday— Odhinn's day—for good fortune and a good haul. Pieter would surely return by Saturday.

Which meant his wife would be alone.

She bit her upper lip in thought, then read the last line of the spell:

To ensure proper binding, weave a feather from the dead bird into a wishing rope. Place the rope on the back of a bedroom door. This will keep any man from fleeing into the arms of another.

She fingered the feather in her pocket.

What Is

An almost full moon wakes me. I rub my eyes and sit up. It is dark, but the milky silver light spills across my bed, across the floor to the landing. All the way to Mor's tiny sewing room. *She's awake?*

I kick the covers aside. My feet still hurt, so I place them lightly. I hobble my way along in the dark, following the moonlight on the beams of wood. Pappa's snoring is so loud behind the bedroom door, I know he can't hear anything. I stop at the sewing room, kneeling down to peer through the crack in the door. One eye, fixed.

Inside, a candle dances. Mamma's dark shape is hunched over like a bear. She sweeps a bit of cloth sideways, lifting her head up, then down again, whispering to herself. Pulling a thread through to the other side. *Schlip.* What is she making in the middle of the night? Soft pink shapes. Almost a quilt, but not. Like no blanket I have ever seen. I push my eye farther into the crack, smushing my cheek. The door rattles.

Her arm freezes. The needle stops. Instantly, her shadow fills the room, a mountain on the wall.

"Leidah?"

I hold my breath. *No hiding in the wood-box this time.* My fingers start tingling.

Before I even have time to pull my eye away, the door opens. My mother's face, like the moon in the dark hallway. She squints and takes a step toward me. "Lei-lee?"

I want to tell her I've had a nightmare about the Sisters, that I can't sleep with all this whispering and worrying from her—*and what are you sewing in the dark, Mamma?* I try to move my lips, but I have no mouth. My tongue is gone; my nose is gone. I don't have a face anymore.

It has happened again.

I am lying on my back, flatter than bread. My mother's bare feet slap against my skin, across my belly, my chest. She digs her heel in, at my throat that isn't there. I can see her head turning toward her bedroom. Snores crawl under the closed door. The door to my room is open, but she can't see my bed from where she stands, can't see that my bed is empty. She nods to herself: everything as it should be. Her foot grinds into my chin. The door to the sewing room closes behind her.

I struggle to sit up. I wiggle my hips and jiggle my legs. It is no use. I am stuck, pressed flat into the grain of wood under me.

But it's not under me. *It is me.*

I have become the floor.

I know it's true, even as I tell myself I am dreaming, that I am still in bed under the covers. My blood whirls inside the wood knots, spinning and rushing, sucking me down and down. The nicks of boot prints stomp and kick at my bones, like a bruise. I feel the clunk of one board to the next, like bumps of a wheel over stone. And then I am all of it, every knot, grain, and sliver, running down the hall, whooshing like a river, ever so fast, over the edge and down a waterfall, rushing from room to room. I pour myself under and over and through, feeling objects brush against me as I pass by. Bookshelves, bedposts, Pappa's slippers, a fallen dressing gown, the stubby ends of an old chair. A mouse hiding inside a hole in the wall. Mor's needle bobbing up and down.

How is this possible?

I am so wide, I can see both Mor and Far at the same time, even though they are in different rooms, one wide awake, the other fast asleep. I feel my father's breath easily, sinking through the bed into me, while

Mor's breath fights against me, against the floor. In and out, each breath swimming away, away, at the speed of her needle, up up up in out in out outoutout—*let me out, get me out, I want out.*

That's what Mamma is thinking, and I hear it, loud and clear. I strain my ears against the wood to get back into my own body. Nothing happens. I try again, but this time push hard with my arms that aren't there. Nothing at all. I stop and sink, letting go, giving myself into the floor.

Seven, soon to be eight . . . it's time, time's up, time to go.

The needle is singing, as sure as stitches on a seam. I am inside the thread, inside her head. Mamma is ticking—*onetwothreefourfivesix—*

Seven. Seven what? And why is it time to go?

Don't leave me, Mamma. I beg her feet, her knees, her hips, her chest, her heart, my begging spreading like a big squid into the very skin of her.

It's then that I feel it.

Something is happening to Mamma. Something neither Pappa nor I have noticed.

She is becoming dust.

She is dryer than the wood I have become, her skin flaking, her eyes peeling, her hair shedding. She is drying out, drying up. My mother is becoming sand, changing to powder under that milk-white skin, pieces of her about to curl up and fall away.

I twist inside the floor, wringing every last drop of wetness out of me, pushing it into her.

Drink me. Take me, take me, takemewithyou.

The thread tugs tight, then stops. I pull back, but it's too late.

⁂

Maeva pauses. *Are you here, girl?* But no, that can't be true. *You're asleep. Aren't you?* She drops to the floor and whispers, "Out, Leidah, out!"

She slaps the wood three times. In a whoosh, Maeva feels an invisible push against her back, a slight wind that rushes past her toward the wall. She whirls around. In an instant, Leidah is there, in the corner. Choking and spitting, curled into a heap of confusion.

Oh God, child. She embraces her daughter, rubbing her back. "Lei-lee, how can this be? Why? . . . I'm here, it's all right. Yes, that's it, big breaths."

She rocks the trembling girl, holding her close, unsure of what else to do.

"I am so sorry, child."

"For what, Mamma? What's happening to me?"

She tries to speak, but a sob betrays her. *I don't know . . . This is my fault.* An avalanche of guilt suffocates her, the strong resolve to hide the truth from both her husband and child crumbling to rubble.

Leidah clings to her, short rasps into her mother's neck. "Mamma, I'm scared—"

Then, she is gone. Maeva's arms hover in the air, holding nothing.

Nei, child! She begins to tap everything, calling the girl's name in a tender way, as if she were coaxing a kitten out of hiding. *Stay with me, Leidah.*

She feels a sharp pinprick, on the side of her temple. *Yes, good girl!*

Maeva picks up the needle sticking out of the quilt, speaking to it. "Listen to me carefully, Lei-lee—you must let go of your fear and jump out of the metal."

Nothing happens. She places the needle on the floor. Bends down on all fours. "Pretend you are on the edge of a cliff, staring down at Ørkenfjord. Focus on the waves—into the eye of the needle, Lei-lee. Now, fall."

Within seconds—a mere blink—Leidah appears, holding her head as though she has clunked it on the floor. Maeva gasps at the shock of her.

Leidah lunges into her mother's arms, hanging on for dear life. "Don't let me go again," she whispers.

It's the sweetest plea Maeva has ever heard. "I won't." She kisses her daughter over and over. "But you have to promise to keep this a secret. You can't tell Pappa."

"I don't even know what to tell—"

"Promise me! You must never tell. Ever."

She pulls Leidah away from her chest, fingers digging into the little arms. Leidah nods, then frowns, her eyes like moons. She takes in the quilt that surrounds them, spreading from table to floor: a pink sea, with oddly shaped patches, see-through and paper thin. Red stitches, marching like ants across the landscape.

"What are you making, Mamma?"

The words catch in Maeva's throat. *A safety net* . . . She lifts a section of the quilt, finding the worn-out doll underneath. She holds up the faceless *dukke*, hoping to distract the child.

"Her hair grew back! *Takk, Mamma.*"

Maeva sinks into her daughter's hug. *My precious, magical child.*

The quilt, an infinite ocean surrounding them.

Mouse

His head is pressed against wood, watching from a sliver in the wall. His mouse eye sees the child disappear into the floor.

She *becomes*.

She is something else. Not human.

He begins to tremble, his tiny squeaks heard by no one.

His cage of rodent bones loosens. Across worlds and across time, the waters of the well pour down the Great Tree. Inside the Sisters' cocoon, his true form awakens.

It has begun.

The Fifth Knot

Pieter had left that morning to go fishing, before the sun was up. She watched him mount his horse, then trot down the lane. She had to control the urge to surprise him on the road—wanting so badly to touch him, kiss him, confront him—but she forced herself to stay hidden. She simply had to see Maeva Aldestaed for herself. Watching and waiting for signs of life from the cabin, she crept to the front door. Quietly, she placed the glass jar on the porch, then retreated to hide in the trees. In the distance, the September wind blew across the grassy fields, carrying the aroma of cow dung. *How perfect*, she thought. Then, the door opened. She crouched in the grass under a canopy of low branches, squatting like a toad. She had faith in the spell. But just in case.

She watched as his pregnant wife almost tripped over the jar, and then frowned as she noticed it. She couldn't help the twinge of jealousy rising up as she took her in for the first time. Red hair like fire. High cheekbones, full lips. Wide-set eyes. *Too wide*, she thought, shifting onto the backs of her heels. *And much too tall.*

The woman scanned the field, seemingly for a sign, evidence of who might have placed the jar there.

No one out here. Go on, pick it up.

She bent down carefully, her stomach so big she had to lean sideways. She managed to grab the jar, standing slowly and awkwardly. Holding it up to the light with one hand, she pulled it closer to her face. Her other hand cupped her round belly protectively.

Inside the jar, a single gigantic leech was stuck to the glass. Fat, fully engorged with blood.

Almost as fat as you, she mused silently. Then, she whispered a curse into the wind to bind and close the spell.

Immediately, Pieter's wife buckled over, dropping the jar. The glass shattered, the piercing sound echoing across the field. The woman stumbled and fell to her knees, onto the shards.

Not so pretty now, she thought.

What Was

Pieter kept his head down, pulling in the latest catch of salmon off the small trawler. Crews worked silently around him, their usual joviality vanishing as soon as he arrived. *Strange*, he thought. He inhaled the aroma of brine, a welcome freshness to the fetid mood of the men, and wiped his brow, the noonday sun warmer than usual.

"Aldestaed! You have returned." Pieter glanced up to see Hans standing before him. "Are the rumours true? Is there a new addition to the family?" Hans kept his voice low, holding out a bandaged hand.

Pieter's eyebrows raised. "Cut yourself?"

"Seal finger." Hans shrugged, then switched hands. "Enough about me—are we celebrating or not?"

Pieter hesitated, then shook it, grateful for the sincerity in Hans's tone.

"*Takk skal du ha*. We haven't told anyone yet, but yes. After a long labour, we have a girl." He said it quietly, not wanting the other men to hear.

Hans smiled. "A beauty like her mother, I'm sure."

Pieter grinned. "That she is. She's absolutely perfect. But I am partial to my own kin." He pushed the baby's blue skin out of his mind. *It will fade.*

"That's all right—a father should be." Hans laughed through crooked teeth. "I can't wait to meet the new little member of the family."

Pieter bent over to dump the net of fish into the barrels on the pier, hiding his unease.

Hans leaned forward to help, holding the edge of the net. His face serious. "You are blessed, Aldestaed. Not everyone has such blessings."

Pieter kept his eyes on the barrel. *Would you say such things if you saw her?* A few wayward fish escaped onto the pier, slapping their bodies against the dock, desperate for water. "What do you mean?" He bent down and chucked the fish back into the barrel.

Hans peered over his shoulder. He leaned in closer.

"Nils Innesbørg—his wife, Maren. Went into early labour five nights ago . . . She died this morning."

Pieter gasped. Five nights ago: the same night his daughter was born. "And the child?"

"Died last night." His eyes met Pieter's. "I am telling you this as a friend: don't count your blessings too loudly. Where there is grief, there's anger. Especially with someone so high up. Blame will be laid at someone's doorstep. I pray it isn't yours."

"I don't understand. Why in the world would anyone ever blame an innocent child for the death of another?"

Hans rested a hand on Pieter's shoulder. "Not your baby, Pieter. Maeva. And the *heks* that delivered both women."

Her name escaped his lips before Pieter could stop it, despite his promise to keep the midwife a secret. "Helgar Tormundsdatter? But she's a harmless old biddy."

Hans held up his hands in surrender. "I agree—old and mad. And ugly. But some may ask: Why did your child live, and the other die?"

"How in the world can anyone know such a thing? It is God's will who lives and dies. It's arrogance and folly to think we can ever know the gods'—God's—plan."

Hans said nothing, but his eyes said everything.

Pieter sighed. "Just say it, Hans. I know you're holding back."

"It's Maeva . . . I am glad for your happiness. Hell, I would have married her myself that day if you hadn't found her first."

Pieter blushed, remembering how he'd tried to cover Maeva's naked body as Hans's boat arrived, and Maeva sinking into the water to hide herself. Thank the gods it was Hans, a man he had been friends with since he was a boy, and not someone else. Maeva surely would have been taken by the Ørken magistrate to be shipped off somewhere, for someone else to deal with. Hans understood, as soon as he laid eyes on the pearl-white skin and copper hair. Those green eyes. Maeva was perfection incarnate. Pieter's lust became love well before they set foot on the Ørken shoreline.

"She's not one of us, Pieter. The day your ship crashed was the day you met her. It was also the day a man drowned. In this town, that means there will always be suspicion around her."

"Unwarranted, and unfair. That kind of judgement is based on fear— if they only got to know her, they'd see." He stared into the barrel of fish, feeling his eyes well up. *She's a little different, that's all.*

Hans clapped his back. "Perhaps you are right. But they won't get to know her if she stays hidden in that cabin. You must register the child." Pieter began to protest, but Hans held his hand up. "It's the law now—the baptism must occur within eight days of birth—and Pastor Knudsen has already been asking after you, preparing for the certainty of a church service for you. I know you aren't much of a Christian—" Pieter reddened. "Truth be told, neither am I. But you must bring the baby in—it's the only way to stop the rumours about both your wife and daughter."

Pieter knew his friend was right. It was his wife he had to convince. *What will they think when they see our baby?* His shoulders sank.

"One can only hope and pray that all will be well, once the baptism is over." Hans paused.

Pieter gathered the empty net, not speaking.

Hans cleared his throat. "What's her name anyway?"

Pieter's eyes lit up. "Leidah."

Hans laughed, understanding immediately. "Thank you, my friend. A better name could not be found." He shook Pieter's hand one last time. "I will keep the news quiet, until you are ready. In the meantime, watch your back. And Maeva's. For Leidah's sake."

Pieter watched his friend walk away. Hans boarded his trawler, a medium-sized beauty with flaking and faded red letters, *L-E-I-D-A-H*, near indecipherable on its side. Pieter smiled to himself, thankful for that fateful day when the *Leidah* rescued him. And Mae.

His smile faded. Hans's last words, echoing. The warning, uncomfortable.

The men bustled around him—still silent—pulling loads of lobster off the next trawler. He watched as the net released onto the deck of the boat a mass of red claws and shiny backs, gushing like a river. Leaving only two, dangling, caught on the rope.

What Is

I dream of drowning. Of my mother. Her body becoming the ocean.

Pappa is there, rowing the two of us inside a glass boat, toward a shore that never gets any closer. He stares where the sky meets the sea, his eyes moving back and forth, searching for Mamma. Black waves lap against the side of the boat. A few fish swim close, then are gone. And then, there, under the glass bottom of the boat, I see my mother, her round eyes.

"Far! Mor is drowning! She's here, under the boat. We have to save her!"

He begins to laugh and cry at the same time. "Why? The sea can't drown."

I pull at his arms and point. "But Mor needs us!"

"Mor? What about us, girl? Who will save us?"

"From what, Pappa?"

"The sea . . ."

I wake up, all shivers and sweat. The bedcovers, sopping wet.

Did I pee?

I sit up quickly. Patting the blanket, I smell my hand. No. I pull the wet blanket out from under my hip, kicking it away. A sharp sting shoots through both feet. Already the web is growing back, knitting the skin together. I wonder if I will be able to walk without Mor cutting my toes apart anymore. I wiggle my feet, trying to stretch the skin, but it's no use. My toes want to stay a family.

I stand up. My nightgown feels cold and damp. A puddle is under my feet. I kneel down, wondering where it's coming from. *Drip, drip, drip.* I can hear the plop of water all around me, but I can't find where it starts. The drops roll off my fingertips and down my legs. The longer I stand, the more I can feel water running off me. The puddle under me becomes a small pond, growing bigger and bigger.

I hop back into bed, hoping the water will be plugged up by the straw mattress.

Mamma's head peeks in—"Good girl, Lei-lee; stay there until I call you"—and then she is gone. I hear my father's heavy footsteps downstairs. The front door slams. The sound of her skirt swishes into the room.

"Come, child, we don't have much time."

Dripping and squishing, I climb down the ladder stairs after her to the fire in the hearth. I rub my hands together and kneel into the flames, so close she pulls me back. She covers me with a dry blanket. She sits in Pappa's old rocking chair, her arms and feet crossed. I hold my hands out to the heat, glancing up at her every once in a while. She is watching me, as if I am a new guest, a stranger. I pull the blanket tight around my shoulders. The crackle of fire talks to the tick of the clock.

"Well?"

Her body is tight, as if she's about to burst; her eyes all sparkly, like stars in the night.

I don't know where to begin, or what to tell her. I bite a fingernail, waiting for the words to come.

"You had a dream." She pulls my hand away from my mouth.

She must be magic to know such a thing. "It was nothing . . . a nightmare."

"A nightmare about what?"

"Pappa and . . . a boat."

"And what, child? Was I in the dream? Did you dream of the sea?"

I stare at her, startled. She *is* magic. She stands and begins pacing, talking to herself. Scratching at the patch on her arm.

"September, beginning of September, that means there's only six weeks left . . . But why so soon? It can't be time yet, I need more time to find it . . . To teach you."

"Mamma?"

"Shh, Leidah, let Mor think." She starts rubbing her other arm. "Think, Maeva, think, where would he hide it? Where in God's name is it?"

I watch her, afraid she's gone mad. I stand up, letting the blanket fall off my shoulders.

"Nei, child, you haven't dried out yet. Stay put until I tell you!"

I fall to my knees. She wraps the blanket around me again, rubbing my arms and back. I want to enjoy this, but can't.

"What is it, Mamma? What's happening?"

"Oh, Lei-lee . . . where to begin?"

"It's me, isn't it? Something's wrong. Am I sick?" I start to cry.

"No tears, girl. You mustn't cry, you'll float away." She tries to laugh, but then stops, her own tears eating up her words. "You are fine, child."

"Then why am I leaking? Why am I not myself sometimes?"

"I'm not sure. But you aren't sick."

I breathe out a big sigh. "But what about you? Something's not right—I can feel it. Whatever it is, I can help."

"*Nei, tulla.* The only person who can help me is your far—and he won't lift a finger."

I think of the other night. The digging in the dirt. "I'm small. I can crawl into places you can't. I can find it. Whatever it is."

She freezes, her fingers digging into my shoulders. Looking into my eyes, as if seeing me for the first time. She takes my hands, checking the skin on my arms closely, then lifts my braids to check inside my ears, the back of my neck. Finally, she lets out a sigh and pulls me into her, hard. My heart jumps to meet her. I try to breathe without moving, her chest smothering my nose and mouth until finally, I need to pull away, gasping for air. She laughs, messing the top of my hair. *Everything will be fine.*

Then her eyes are serious again. She lifts my chin.

"There is so much I haven't told you . . . so much I don't know myself. But if you want to help, you must never tell Pappa."

"But maybe Pappa could help us find it."

Her eyes flash. "Never. Do you hear me? He is the one who hid it, Leidah. He would never want me to find it. But I must find it, I *have* to find it, do you understand?"

"I think so."

"Do you still want to help me?"

I stop to think. Pappa would be upset at both of us for keeping secrets. But I don't want Mamma to be sad. "I want to help you."

She grins and claps her hands together. And then the front door slams shut.

"Help Mamma do what, little *kanin*?"

Pappa is standing in the doorway, a leather harness in one hand.

Mamma quickly pulls the blanket over my arms and shifts me toward the fire.

"She's going to learn how to use the loom, Pieter. First, a simple braid ribbon, that's all. What brings you back so soon?"

She moves about in a flurry, as if Pappa has interrupted her chores, and how dare he interrupt our daily chores? She reaches into a basket for an egg, then cracks it with one hand into a skillet. Places the pan into the fire while her other hand pours water out of the kettle. Her fingers shake a little.

"Broken bloody harness, as soon as I hit the bend for Ørken." He stops in front of the table and drops something small onto a plate. Mor turns at the sound of tinkling.

"What's that?"

"I found it on the porch—a seashell." He puts his hands on his hips. "You haven't been to the beach, have you?"

She walks over to the table and picks it up, her face white. "Of course not. But how . . ." She rubs a finger along its smooth pink edge, over and over, as if it were alive, lost in thought.

He frowns, then speaks to me. "Embroidery, huh, little one?"

"Weaving, Pappa."

"Do you think she can hold the threads, Mae? I mean, if you aren't cutting her fingers anymore."

She pockets the shell. "Leidah will be fine, won't you, child? Now go upstairs and get dressed—the chickens are waiting."

I rush out of the room, glad for Mor's quick thinking. I climb the steps two at a time and slide into my bedroom, forgetting about the puddle on the floor. My bare feet hit the water—*swoosh, splash, crash*—and I am upside down.

Pappa is above me before I can even yell ouch. He almost slips himself and catches the bedpost, but he loses his footing anyway and ends up beside me.

"What in the world—there's water all over the bloody floor!"

I giggle at his funny face, all scrunched up.

He glares at me. "It's no laughing matter, girl—what the devil happened in here?"

I don't know how to answer, since truly, I didn't *do* anything. How could I tell Far that I had a dream about water and woke up in a puddle? How could I tell him that I seem to be jumping in and out of myself, at the strangest times, and that I'm afraid I won't remember how to get back?

"Well?"

"I didn't do anything, Pappa. Honest."

I shrug and roll my legs around in the water. His arm reaches out to stop me from splashing, then his face gets hard. I follow his eyes to the empty chamber pot under the bed.

"Maeva! Bring a towel, and be quick about it."

What did I do, Pappa?

"Why didn't you tell me that you had an accident? Oh, Lei-lee. The last thing I need today, to be stinking like goddamn piss on a new job. Mae, I'm already late!"

I bite my lips. Pappa never used to say words like that to me.

Mor rushes in with two towels in hand. She helps Pappa up and pushes me out of the way, mopping and moaning. I'm about to stomp my foot, but Mor catches my eye and winks. I bite my lip to stop the giggles from spilling out. Mamma and I have a secret—no, two, maybe three big secrets from last night and this morning—and I might burst. I don't want to think about what Pappa might say if he knew we were keeping things from him. What he might say if he knew how much Mamma was drying out.

Pappa looks from me to Mor, and then to me again. He shakes his head and strides away into the other bedroom. Crashes about like a bear.

"A man needs a reliable horse and a clean set of trousers—is that so much to ask, Lord? To venture out into the world to take care of all those damn trivialities that seem so damn important."

I freeze and wait for Pappa to stop. His words go on and on, his feet stomping. Then he calls to me, "Lei-lee, it's not your fault." Somehow, I don't believe him. I look at Mor with big eyes, to see if she is as surprised by Far's grumbling as I am.

She has stopped cleaning. Closes her eyes and drops her head as Pappa says, "Damn it," one more time. He marches back into my bedroom, red-faced.

Mor nudges me. "Leidah, do you have anything to say to your pappa?" *I didn't do anything!*

Her one eyebrow goes up, and she flicks her head in Pappa's direction.

"Sorry, Pappa, for making you all wet. It was an accident."

"Aww, my little *kanin*, it's not you. Pappa is just late. Now get to the barn for Mamma, hmm?"

I nod. He kisses the top of my forehead, and then spins on his heels.

"When will you be back?" Mor asks.

He passes by her without a glance.

I watch him climb down the ladder, his footsteps echoing through the cottage. Finally, he yells, *"Jeg vet ikke."* The door slams, and the cottage is quiet. Mor stands perfectly still, like a stone. *I don't know.*

Three small words that seem to mean a lot to Mamma.

All of a sudden, two wet towels hit the wall with a *thwap*. She wipes her hands on her skirt.

I hide a snort behind my hand. Mamma glares at me sternly. Then, like sunlight bursting through a cloud, a grin. We try to stop ourselves, but I fall over, squealing, and she splashes me with water. I splash back.

She stops then, grabbing my hands. "All right, Lei-lee, we have much to do, don't we? So much has changed, in the blink of an eye."

I nod, even though I don't know what she means.

She reaches into her apron pocket and pulls out the seashell Pappa found on the porch. "First things first: we swim."

"Swim?"

"Ja. Swim."

"But I don't know how to swim. I thought we were going to search for the lost thing—and Pappa doesn't like us going to the beach anyway, and he's already mad, at both you and me—"

"Exactly—two very good reasons why we need to go swimming." She holds out her palm, the tiny shell, a perfect swirl of pink.

I am about to take it but then stop. *How could swimming possibly help us find the lost thing?*

"Leidah, do you want to help Mor or not?"

I nod. She plunks the shell into my hand.

"Then you must learn how to swim. I can't imagine Pappa hiding it under water, but it's the one place I haven't searched. And, well, you'll be eight years old in little over a month, won't you? And every eight-year-old should know how to swim."

I roll the pink shell between my fingers. "But what if I can't, Mamma? What if I sink? What if I drown?"

She laughs, a clean, clear tinkly sound, like water spilling over rock. Then pulls me to my feet and picks up the wet towels lying on the floor. "Oh, Leidah. The sea can't drown."

I am wide-eyed. *The dream.* "What does that mean, Mamma?"

"What, child?"

"What you said. Am I the sea?"

"It's just an expression. My mother used to say it."

"I've heard it before."

Mamma stops and stares at me. "Your dream?"

I nod, watching her skin go ghosty.

"Then we mustn't waste any more time."

What Was

Helgar slumped against the rough stone wall in the tiny cell, holding her small black stone. She was exhausted. And nauseated by the foul stench. Though she had been here for three nights only, the odours of history—piss and shit and damp decay—were thick in the air, the ghost perfumes of people long gone from this place. Perhaps her own stink was about to join them.

She hated Nils Innesbørg. The traitor.

He had showed up at her door, hours after his newborn died, determined to make an arrest in front of witnesses. The pastor and two farmhands—stable-boys too young to even drive the witch cart—stood behind him, in case of escape. As if an old woman could ever fight off such a crew. Lars Knudsen carried a Bible, fingers fidgeting with the simple wooden cross around his neck. He couldn't meet her eyes. He wasn't smiling, for once in his life. That's when she knew she was in trouble.

The only window in the cell—too high for her to reach—was a sad hole in the wall, no bigger than her hand. The patch of grey sky barely there. Every once in a while, a gull cried. Wind blew in from the north, bringing the frosty bite of Finnmark. She was glad of it. It reminded her that life continued elsewhere, outside of Ørken's small existence. It didn't matter whether she lived or died. She had lived long enough. She didn't need more of this world. Though it was nice to smell the sea every so often.

A key-ring jingled in the lock. Helgar moved her hand quickly, hiding the black stone in her boot. The heavy wooden door creaked open. She shielded her eyes against the light, her wrists chafing against the iron cuffs. *Iron, to weaken a witch.*

The guard—Innesbørg's nephew, Olaf—gave her a sneer of disgust. He was stocky and sweaty, like his uncle.

"You have a visitor."

Helgar narrowed her eyes. They were allowing visitors? *Who in the world would come see me?*

Olaf pushed a tray with his foot across to her: a hard bun and grey-brown gruel.

"My uncle says we have to feed you until the trial."

Helgar nodded, understanding. The food would stop the minute she was found guilty. Then she would most likely be shipped to Bergen to waste away in a prison. Or worse: hanged from a noose, right here in the village square.

She ignored the tray. Olaf sneered again and stepped aside.

Maeva Aldestaed stood in the doorway. Even more fiery than Helgar remembered. Her cloak billowing from an enlarged chest, her belly still swollen.

"You have five minutes. Don't waste it." Olaf slammed the door, turning the key in the lock.

Helgar took the guard's advice. She struggled to stand, her bones stiff from sitting all night.

"What in God's name are you doing here? Are you daft?"

The girl blinked. Took in the sparse surroundings. A bit of straw to lie on. A bucket to piss in. And a smaller pan of water, with a rusty ladle.

The old woman welcomed her with a flourish of arms. "Almost as good as home. Except the food is worse." She kicked the spoon out of the gruel. It clattered beside Maeva's foot. She didn't move. "You come without the child. Is something wrong?" Helgar's voice was gruff, abrupt.

Maeva shook her head. "She is with Pieter. She is fine . . . I told him I had to come, and he agreed." The old woman snorted, but Maeva continued. "You must know why I'm here, Fru Tormundsdatter. This is my fault. I can set you free."

Helgar lifted her bound hands. The chain rattled. "You aren't the reason I'm in here. Don't you dare utter my name. It will get us both killed." She lowered her voice on the last word.

Maeva paced in the small cell. She managed three steps before she had to turn and start again. "I know. But if I come forward, say you birthed my child safely, without complication—"

"Nei. Don't speak of it, ever. That will seal both of our fates."

Maeva's eyebrows pinched together. "But you are in jail for malpractice."

"Illegal practice. Malpractice is only for doctors with licenses. Innesbørg is a cheat and a liar—he begged me to deliver his wife. Promised he would never throw me in jail again if I agreed." She smiled, revealing cracked teeth. "Yet here I am. Three times, a charm."

The previous arrest, Helgar had spent a few nights in jail. Thankfully, the man who accused her—a particularly fervent pastor who believed women shouldn't be relieved of God's gift of suffering in childbirth—died in his sleep the night before she went to trial. She slipped the magistrate a bit of coin, not wanting to gamble on the case being thrown out due to lack of evidence. Her accuser, despite being dead, had friends. The bribe worked; she avoided being falsely convicted. Death had knocked at the right time. *On the right door.*

Maeva cocked her head, confused. "But you are in here because— both Maren and the baby—they . . ."

Helgar sighed. "Ja. They died. Sometimes, birth brings death—it is God's business. Not mine."

"But if I tell them how you birthed my Leidah, how healthy she is . . ." Her words slowed.

Helgar waited for the realization to land on the young mother: her baby's oddities, not exactly what would be deemed healthy by anyone in the village.

"If you breathe a word of my involvement, they will surely accuse you. And once they see the child, see her colouring, it will confirm it . . . Hanged, like that." Helgar snapped her fingers. "Leidah, hmm? An odd choice. Not Norwegian. Icelandic or Finnish, perhaps? The name of a Viking? Or maybe a sorceress?"

Maeva lifted her chin. Irritated by the obvious prying into her ancestry. "My husband chose the name. Not that it should matter. I am no witch, nor do I come from one." Her voice sounded small, the tight quarters closing in.

"Did I say such a thing? But I will admit, I am curious—what are you, if not a witch?"

Maeva leaned her back against the wall, fingers spread wide against the stone, silent.

Helgar shrugged. "It is none of my business. But I have seen things— things you'd best keep hidden, girl."

"Are you threatening me?"

Helgar snorted. "I am protecting both of us—and that odd baby of yours. She's not of this world, that's for certain." Maeva's cheeks reddened. "All it will take for them to hang me is to find out that I touched you on the same night my hands touched Maren. The fact is, one lived, the other died. Conclusion: Innesbørg would find the two of us guilty."

Helgar paused for it to sink in further. "Illegal midwifery is one thing." She shuffled to stand in front of Maeva, forcing her to look down. "Sorcery is quite another."

"I told you, I am not a witch. I swear to the gods." Maeva threw her arms to the sky, her voice louder than it should be.

Helgar shushed her, pulling her hands down and eyeing the cell door in alarm. Satisfied the guard hadn't heard, she dropped her grip. Quietly, she asked, "But will you swear to the one God?"

"Nei. I will not."

Helgar clapped her hands. "And there we have it, Magistrate Innesbørg, Pastor Knudsen. I rest my case." She bowed dramatically for effect, then grabbed her back. "Damn bones."

Maeva watched the old woman struggle, slide down the wall to sit.

"What about you? Do you swear to the one God?" Her green eyes flickered. Her tone, sharp.

Helgar chuckled. "Not so daft after all. I will swear to whatever is necessary, child. What do I care? Religion is not my concern."

"I knew it. You don't bow to the Christian God any more than you bow to Freyja . . . Or Odhinn."

Helgar smiled, enjoying the banter. "Ah, but that is where you are wrong. They are all one and the same. It is the folly of men to believe one is different from the other, or more right." She reached for the stale bun, ripping it in half. She held a piece out, offering it to the woman. Maeva refused, then slid down the wall to sit beside her.

"The question is not which god. God is God. Male, female, spirit, animal—all of it, part of God. The more pressing questions are: What man is in front of me? What story must I tell in order to appease the ignorant?"

Maeva's mouth fell open, shocked. Helgar winked.

The young woman smiled reluctantly, then snorted in agreement. "But what of the lie? Will it not anger the gods—God—this lack of loyalty? This unwillingness to declare the truth?"

"What truth? Do you think God cares for man's petty dramas? For who has more or less faith? God has other concerns, I'm sure. That baby is God's work—no more or less special than any other child." The old woman patted the young mother's hand. "Protect yourself. Protect that child. Hide her from this terrible world and the terrible men who do terrible things." She reached into her boot. Pulling out the black stone, shaped like Thor's hammer, she held it out to the young woman. "Here. Take it."

Maeva's eyes welled up.

Helgar shoved the stone into Maeva's hand, closing her fingers around it. "A little help never hurts us womenfolk. Keep this close . . . Go on, it's not that bad. Deny me, and I will deny you. Then, maybe, we'll survive this."

"But you could be convicted." Maeva's voice quivered. Her hand made a fist around the stone.

"If the gods are kind, I will be sent to jail." She patted her own thighs. "Not so bad for an old girl like me."

Maeva swallowed. "And if they are not so kind?"

The old woman cackled. "If they are *truly* kind, I will hang by the neck and croak immediately. And then I will haunt Nils Innesbørg till the day he dies."

Maeva smiled through tears. The keys rattled in the lock, and Olaf pulled the door open.

"Time's up, *heks*."

Helgar tilted her head, unsure which woman it was meant for.

"I wouldn't touch this hag if I were you," Olaf jeered. "She'll kill that baby inside you, quick as a wink."

Surprise flushed across Maeva's face. Her hand moved to her side, the stone hidden; she stood with effort, straightening her long skirts. Making sure her swollen belly was noticeable, cupping the roundness above and below.

"I will pray for you, Helgar." Maeva peered into the old woman's face.

Helgar met her gaze. "God bless you, girl. And the child on its way."

A flicker between the two women, unseen by the guard.

Maeva Aldestaed lifted her chin high, then walked through the doorway. Without even a glance back.

Olaf scowled at the midwife. "Guess that one got away, huh? Too bad for you."

Helgar smirked. The boy had just handed Maeva's salvation to her. "*Ja, gutt*—I'll be dead before that one arrives."

A Snipped Thread

She heard of the midwife's arrest, the market talk that Pieter's baby had been born. *Unbaptized. An abomination of God*, the women whispered. She closed the flap of her stall, shutting out the gossip. *Takk, Skuld. You heard my prayers, finally.* Bitterly, she threw the last word upwards, without a care for consequences. Immediately, a flood of grief washed over her. Her own tragedy still fresh and raw; though it had been several months, she couldn't stop crying. The terrible day in April, when her body—along with the midwife, and Skuld—betrayed her.

The day she became a sea of red.

Skirts, mattress, floor, all dripping with blood.

The midwife had tried to hide her alarm. But she could see through the old hag's attempts to calm her with empty words and camomile tea.

"It will be all right, lie back now. Drink the tea—the whole cup, now. That's it, good girl."

She gulped it down in seconds, then another contraction hit. She turtled into a small ball, but Helgar pulled at her legs to shove another towel under her, as if such a thing could stop the flood of life oozing out of her womb. She felt another gush pour out, and then the hard, heavy pressure of a head.

She pleaded with the gods. "It's too soon, he can't come yet. Stop it, please."

"There's no turning back time, child. He—or she—is coming, ready or not. Now push."

Then, the horrible pain of bearing down, the heavy pull of the earth taking over her entire body, forcing her to expel the baby months early. On the wave of the last contraction, she sank into the pain, allowing it to open her completely. In a trance, she saw her love trying to swim above the currents to reach her. But something kept pulling him under. She breathed in and out, in and out, willing her own lungs to fill his. Vaguely aware of where she was: the midwife's one-room cottage, on the old woman's bed. She had come in the middle of the night, her skirts soaked by the time she reached the mountain path. But who else could she turn to? Certainly no one in the village. Her baby, a secret from everyone, even the father of her child.

The Sisters are taking their payment. Magic is never free.

Her mind played tricks on her, singing out curses, along with the spells she cast, over and over. That terrible night, she heard the ocean crashing, the wind gulping the father of her child up. Helgar muttered her own prayers—to Freyja, to Mary—holding a crystal on a red thread above her belly. The quartz danced this way and that. She felt herself splitting in half, the last push, a torturous relief, one that brought an even worse kind of pain.

She didn't need Helgar to tell her what she already knew.

The name bloomed on her lips, even before she laid eyes on the baby, before she knew it was a boy.

She held the dead body to her heart, whispering his name like an incantation. Like a curse.

Pieter.

What Was

They arrived after sunrise.

Maeva knew they would come; she dreamt of armies, throngs of angry men, carrying torches and rope. And Helgar's neck wrapped in a noose.

She moved in the dark, not even waiting for the baby to wake for a third feeding. Her shuffling roused Pieter from sleep, but only for a moment. She picked up the child from the cradle, opening her nightshirt. Pieter fell back asleep almost instantly. Somehow she was comforted by this, a routine already taking hold.

But the dream . . . The image of men carrying torches gripped her. She tried to calm herself further, encouraging the milk to flow. Closing her eyes to concentrate, she conjured the faces of her sisters. The sea. Her home, before this place. Before she ever met Pieter.

She thought of *him*.

The relief of let-down was immediate.

The child suckled hungrily. Maeva thanked the gods before pushing him from her mind to focus on the urgency of the task at hand. She tried not to be disturbed at how fuzzy her thoughts had become, those familiar faces now blurred, watery. The edges, vaporish. *The consequence of time, that's all. And motherhood*, she told herself. Every inch of her was being consumed by the baby, and, surprisingly, she didn't mind at all. She pulled the sleepy child off her breast after mere minutes. Kissing the child's cheek, she unwrapped the blanket, changing the wet wool between the baby's thighs. Then, swaddling her tightly in a long thin cloth, Maeva held the child close to her chest, inhaling the sweet scent of milk and skin. She reached into her apron pocket for the black stone that Helgar had given her. Kissed it for luck, then slipped it into the bottom of the swaddling cloth. *For protection.*

Without making a sound, without waking her husband, she tiptoed down the ladder, out the front door, and across the field, to the barn. It was a chilly, overcast morning, the clouds dark and low, hiding most of the mountain to the east. Maeva bounced the baby and hummed a tune, soothing her back to sleep. Opening the barn door, she pushed aside the huge pile of hay waiting to be baled. The trapdoor in the middle of the floor was small, but mother and child slid through easily. Down the ladder, to where the barn cats made their beds. She found the wooden crate, the one with a secure lid; apples were inside, treats for the horses. She threw out several mushy fruits, tossing them onto the floor of the mare's stall. *You deserve it, old girl.* Then, she placed the swaddled baby inside.

Leidah was fed, warm, and content as a lamb. Asleep already. A white curl peeked out from under her woolen cap.

"Sweet dreams, Lei-lee. Until I come for you." It was the second time she had used the nickname, coined by her husband within the first hour of life. It suited the small fairy child. She whispered into the darkness, invoking a prayer. "Hlin, Syn, Sigrun. Thor." She hesitated. "And you, too, Odhinn. Protect this child. Keep her hidden and safe."

She sang the last line of the lullaby, ever so quietly, like sweet birdsong into the child's dreams. Closing the lid, she waited for any noise or fussing.

All was quiet. A barn cat wrapped around her leg, startling her. She pushed it away with her foot, then made her way above ground.

Maeva slid into bed beside Pieter as the sun broke through the clouds.

The first knock startled both of them. Pieter rolled over. The two were frozen for a moment, staring into each other's eyes.

The second knock was a hard fist pounding on the door.

Maeva sat up, grabbing her robe. Pieter stood, his naked chest exposed.

"Pieter Aldestaed!" A loud yell from below.

Pieter grabbed a sweater from the floor and pulled it over his head, rushing to the window. Maeva peeked from behind. A small band of people stood on the path to the porch. Horses were tied to the fence-post. She could see the pastor's grey cloak. The black hat of the magistrate.

Pieter took a breath. Then opened the window, calm as could be. "Can I help you, gentlemen?"

Nils Innesbørg yelled up. "Official business, Aldestaed. We need to ask your wife a few questions."

Pieter sounded surprised. "At this hour? Surely this could wait until I have eaten my first meal."

Innesbørg marched out a little farther from the cabin, craning his neck. "Business like this can't wait. Don't make a grieving widower stand outside." His face, red and sweaty, clouded over. Pieter nodded, then closed the window.

Maeva raised her eyebrows. *"Er du klar?"* She wondered if he remembered; he had asked her that, in the tub, almost a year ago, when she barely spoke the language. So much had changed since then. The weight of that simple question, now full of gravity.

Pieter didn't answer. Peering past her, he pointed to the wad of wool, wet with urine. She picked it up quickly, shoving it behind the headboard.

"And our daughter?" His calm demeanor betrayed by the slight waver in his voice.

"She is well hidden. Protected."

He nodded once, brow furrowing. He didn't need to ask how Maeva could have known this was coming; she had powers he would never understand. *Thank the gods.*

"And Hans? Will he—"

"He won't say a thing."

Maeva wasn't so sure, but she held her misgivings. She stepped forward, kissing Pieter hard on the mouth. She pulled back and looked him directly in the eye. "This will work. Trust me."

He squeezed her shoulders. "With my life." He descended the ladder slowly, giving her time.

She moved to the cradle and the small chest holding all of the newborn's woolens. Gathering the dirty ones off the shelf, along with the clean wool, Maeva shoved them with the others, behind the headboard. The hay bale sat in the corner of the room, bloody from a week of sitting. She flipped it over, breathing a sigh of relief at the sight: clean. Scouting for more evidence, she heard Pieter open the door. Her hands flew to her belly, pressing the fabric of her gown flat. Still swollen, but perhaps not enough to convince them. Surely Innesbørg wouldn't examine her so carefully? She moved to the landing. Men's voices floated upwards.

"Pieter Aldestaed."

"*God morgen*, Magistrate. Please let me offer my condolences."

Maeva inhaled sharply, wishing Pieter had remained silent. She watched Nils Innesbørg's reaction. Abruptly, he took off his hat. Then stood beside the pastor, who was clearly uncomfortable, fiddling with the cross around his neck. Two boys flanked him, gangly and awkward. It was then that another man stepped into view, wearing black like the others. He turned, as if aware that someone was watching him. *Jakobsen. The district doctor.* Instinctively, Maeva covered her stomach with her hands.

"*Takk skal du ha, Aldestaed.* Sad events have come to pass. I would hate to think you and your wife may be the cause."

Pieter sounded defensive. "But how is that possible, Herr Innesbørg? I have been at the harbour as usual. And my poor wife has been holed up in this cabin, preparing for the birth of our child."

Maeva waited. All three visitors shifted uncomfortably, perplexed.

The pastor spoke softly, clearing his throat. "Forgive the intrusion, but the news of a baby being born has spread all over the village. I trust that if this were the case, I would have seen you on Sunday, for the baptism"— he shrugged his shoulders apologetically—"but the magistrate felt it necessary to investigate today. Given the circumstances of tragedy in his home, I felt compelled to accompany him."

"Pastor, you would be the first to know—beyond Maeva and me, of course—if our little girl—or boy—had arrived. But as you can see, there is no baby. Any day now, I'm sure." He addressed the doctor. "We may be in need of you soon."

Jakobsen, small in stature, took off his hat, as if about to speak.

Innesbørg beat him to it. "We need to question your wife. Where is she?"

Maeva tiptoed quietly back to bed, sliding the covers up.

"She's upstairs resting. She's had some bleeding, you see."

Smart husband. She had been bleeding on and off again for weeks— since she collapsed that day on the porch—and after the birth, it had con- tinued to flow. If they demanded an examination, surely they would find blood, but now, they would expect it.

"Bleeding before the birth? Rather concerning, for both mother and child." The doctor unwittingly filled in the gaps. Pieter agreed.

"Yes, so we have been told. Our neighbour, Fru Tormundsdatter, offered some advice—she told my wife to stay in bed, until the baby is ready." There was an awkward pause. Then, "We were told you were busy in the next village, so we had to make do with a neighbour helping out."

Maeva heard Innesbørg grunt, his voice angry. "Do not speak the name of that *heks*."

Pieter was quick to apologize. "Please—I do not mean any offense. My wife will offer you our condolences. Maeva?" He called up to her. To warn her.

Innesbørg shushed him. "I will go to her bedside, man. If she bleeds, she should not be out of bed. No need for further tragedy."

Maeva sat up and fixed the blankets nervously, expecting only the magistrate. But all three men hastily followed Pieter up the ladder. Her husband's twitching eyes betrayed him, darting to meet hers in concern. She reached her hand out and he took it, perching on the edge of the mat- tress. She felt a slight tremor in his fingers, but it would be undetectable to anyone else. She smoothed her long braid with her other hand, praying that Innesbørg was still taken by her red hair.

"*God morgen*, Pastor Knudsen, Herr Innesbørg, Doctor Jakobsen—this is quite an unexpected gathering. What brings you?" *Sugar and sweetness*, she thought.

Pieter interrupted. "Herr Innesbørg is here to ask us about our child."

Maeva smiled prettily, resting her hand on her round bump. "I have questions, too—but the baby isn't answering."

The pastor laughed, seemingly grateful for the levity.

Innesbørg's eyes narrowed at her. "Rumour has it that you already birthed that child a week ago. Hans Bjørnsen confirmed it."

Oh, no. I knew it. The hurt on Pieter's face was hard for Maeva to watch.

Knudsen interrupted, "He didn't say the baby had come. If I recall correctly, he said he didn't know—"

"And the womenfolk are claiming that you must have been delivered by that—that—*heks*." Innesbørg gritted his teeth on the last word.

Maeva did her best to appear shocked. Pieter squeezed her hand.

"It is true, she did visit, but only once. Just to ensure my bleeding would stop."

Innesbørg stepped toward her, leaning in with his hawk-like nose. "That is illegal practice, woman—she is not a licensed professional."

Pieter shook his head, holding both hands up in defense. "We made no payment, only asked for advice. She came to the house with a remedy—"

Innesbørg pounced. "What remedy? A chant or spell of some sort? Did she perform magic to stop your bleeding? Did she consult a black book, perhaps?"

Maeva knew better than to mention Helgar's handbook, a practical compendium of remedies and advice, passed down by someone in her family, no doubt. Deemed to be devilry and witchcraft, if not in the hands of a man of God.

She pulled the coverlet farther up her chest. "Nei, she did not. Unless you consider yarrow tea and a bit of gossip magic." The magistrate scowled. "And as you can see, I am still bedridden with child." Maeva's hands curved around her belly, the blanket forming a perfectly round shape.

Pieter continued. "The bleeding has almost stopped. And Mae has taken to cleaning everything in the house—when she feels well enough—a sign that her time is near, so I've been told by other husbands."

Innesbørg's jaw hardened. Maeva couldn't tell if it was sorrow or irritation that had overtaken him. He spoke quietly, with menace. "We will have to examine her, Pieter. You understand. We must be sure."

Everyone froze. Maeva felt her breath catch. Her skin crawled at the thought. Pieter's eyes searched hers, helpless.

The pastor interrupted with a kindly tone. "Wait downstairs, Pieter. This is a private matter between God and the law."

Maeva could barely contain the urge to grab Pieter's hand. *We are doomed.* Her eyes pleaded with him, unable to hide her fear.

He stood. "Allow me to stay, gentlemen—please. My wife shouldn't have to suffer such indignities alone."

Innesbørg looked from Maeva to Pieter, then Maeva again. He waved in agreement, grudgingly.

She pushed down her fear, even though she felt as if a bird were fluttering inside her ribcage. Pieter pulled back the coverlet, then peered at his wife, before shifting her nightdress. She nodded, then pushed down the tears she could feel threatening. Unbuttoning her shift with trembling fingers, she folded it back to reveal her fleshy stomach. Her spine grew hot, her hands clammy. She was suddenly feverish and thirsty, the walls closing in.

Knudsen coughed. Innesbørg moved closer, sitting on the edge of the bed. Maeva spied a stain of blood on the coverlet. *Oh God, no.* Her finger rubbed at it.

"I am sorry for the bleeding—the tea Helgar gave me seems slow in its effects."

Innesbørg muttered, "Of course it is—the old bitch knows nothing."

The pastor frowned at the language.

Jakobsen's eyebrows pinched. "Has the child been moving? Are you sure the child is . . ."

Pieter placed his hand on hers and squeezed. He nodded eagerly. "Ja, we are sure. The baby is a kicker—"

Maeva interrupted. "Though I have not felt anything this morning. I hope that is a good sign—it's rather tight in there now, not much room to kick." She gave a half-hearted smile, hoping Pieter understood to be quiet.

"Shouldn't be much longer now." Pieter moved his hand to her belly. The doctor leaned forward, but Innesbørg blocked him with his burly torso. Maeva pushed her bump outwards, making the skin tighten. She tried not to recoil at Innesbørg's intrusion, his large hand knocking Pieter out of the way, then pressing against her stomach with force. *Just breathe, Maeva. Count something—the beams in the ceiling. Onetwothreefour—*

The magistrate moved his hand suddenly, mere inches above her pubic bone. Maeva froze.

Why does this feel so . . . Her mind struggled to focus, a familiar panic building inside her chest. Something was trying to surface, but she couldn't reel it in. Her tailbone started to ache. She felt strange, as if her body were separating from her; she was about to float into the ceiling. She concentrated on the names for things in the room—*seng, teppe, vindu, himmel*—trying to ignore the odour of men and sweat invading her lungs.

Pieter fixed his eyes on her stomach. Knudsen fiddled with the cross around his neck.

Finally, Innesbørg pulled his hand away, rubbing his beard distractedly. "The old witch must have hexed her. I feel nothing." Pastor Knudsen's fingers released the cross.

Maeva felt her body settle on the mattress.

Doctor Jakobsen stepped forward, pushing past Innesbørg to sit on the bed. "Perhaps we should refrain from such accusations until a medical professional weighs in?" He winked at Maeva, a hint of amusement in his eyes. "I don't think we need an entire gallery peering in at Fru Aldestaed. Gentlemen, will all of you wait downstairs while I have a look? Perhaps Pieter has some ale to dampen suspicions and comfort those in need."

Innesbørg scowled, but said nothing.

Relieved, Lars Knudsen nodded to her. "Excuse us, dear lady. I trust Herr Jakobsen is quite capable. Blessings to you and your child, Maeva."

The use of her first name sparked a flicker of guilt at the lie she had woven. She managed a smile, despite wanting to plead for Pieter to stay.

The doctor waited until all of the men were downstairs. Then he reached for her hand. She tried not to flinch.

He patted her hand, then took off his spectacles to clean them on his sleeve. "Nothing to fear, I won't put you through any more. This unfortunate visit is simply a repercussion of tragedy and the beginnings of grief. None of it has anything to do with you, or your unborn child. Of that, I am certain."

Maeva's head fell back on the pillow, involuntarily. She couldn't hide her relief; she tried to mask it as fatigue. The doctor—fortyish, with the slightest hint of grey starting at his temples—observed his surroundings. The sparsely furnished bedroom. A wardrobe, a small nightstand with an oil lamp. An empty cradle hanging from the rafters beside the bed, a simple rope system to rock the baby and save much-needed floor space. Jakobsen's fingers traced the delicate carvings—seashells and fish—a miniscule model echoing the carvings in the bedposts that Pieter had made months ago, as a wedding present. The doctor's eyes stopped on the hay bale. As he stepped toward it, voices floated up to them, from outside.

"Ja, in the barn. There is a keg brewed from last summer. Come, it is quite a good batch."

Pieter's words sank in quickly. *The barn.* Maeva bit her lip.

The doctor smiled. "I will leave you to it. Please send for me, should the need arise."

She nodded in earnest, sitting up.

Jakobsen affixed his spectacles. "I find myself quite thirsty all of a sudden. *God dag, Fru Aldestaed.*" He left her breathless on the bed.

Pieter led them to the back of the barn. The barrel sat in the corner. He pulled a tankard off the wall, hanging by a nail.

"It's a bit light, but I'm sure you will find it passable." He pulled the spigot, filling the tankard halfway. He handed it to Innesbørg, knowing whose temper needed the most cooling. The magistrate muttered, *"Skål,"* then took a swig. The man nodded his approval, then gulped the rest down.

Pieter held a cup for the pastor. "Drink?"

Knudsen hesitated. "I'm not sure my constitution will agree, so early in the morning."

Innesbørg scoffed. "Surely God will allow a man to slake his thirst—especially when doing his work, stamping out evil and sin." He held the tankard out for a refill. Pieter didn't argue, filling it again.

"You misunderstand me, Magistrate—God isn't in protest, my stomach is." The pastor laughed half-heartedly, his smile faltering. He cocked his head to one side. "Did you hear that?"

All three men listened. A wandering hen clucked, pecking at the straw near the door. Then, under the small conversations of wind, trees, and animals, they heard it: a quiet mewling.

Pieter's hand froze in mid-air. Innesbørg grabbed the tankard, walking a few steps toward the sound.

"Ja, I hear it." He spilled ale on the straw. "Do you hear it, Aldestaed?" His eyes flashed with accusation.

Pieter shrugged. "Sounds like a kitten to me. Our barn cats had babies a couple months ago." He smiled easily. "Would you like to take one home? Maeva would be very grateful—they are starting to outnumber the chickens."

Innesbørg stared him down. Knudsen tapped his cross, wondering what to do.

The door slid open, startling everyone. Jakobsen gestured to the keg. "Any left for me, Pieter?" He slid the door shut, pausing for only a second to notice the harnesses hung on the back of the door. He fingered a rope, tied with several knots and feathers. His eyebrows pinched together in thought.

Innesbørg's attention homed in on the sounds below. He dropped the tankard. Three long strides, and he was at the trapdoor. His foot kicked the straw away, revealing the metal handle. Leaning down, he pulled hard.

The whimpering grew louder.

In one fast motion, Innesbørg slid down the ladder before Pieter could stop him.

The three men stood awkwardly, waiting.

Pieter's hand was wrapped around the spigot. Jakobsen didn't ask again.

Then, Innesbørg's head popped up. "You weren't lying, huh, Aldestaed?"

Pieter held his breath.

Innesbørg guffawed. "You're overrun, man." Two grey kittens leaped from the large man's hands, running to hide behind the keg.

Pieter grinned.

Inside, the cradle suddenly swayed with weight.

Maeva gasped, shocked at what she found.

Leidah, gurgling quietly.

Inside her tiny blue hand, Helgar's black stone.

What Is

It is midday by the time we reach the beach. Gulls dip and dive in the sunlight. It is warm, hot even, the shine of the water hitting our cheeks, baking us to pinky red right away. I hop over the maze of stones that leads to the water, then take off my shoes to squish my toes into the warm sand. I run to the shoreline, the cuts on my feet tender. The salt stings at first, but the cold water numbs the pain. Mamma stands on top of a dark grey boulder, looking out at the blue-green waves.

It almost feels like a fun, end-of-summer day. And yet I know it's not. There's a tightness in Mamma's eyes pulling at the edges of her hair, an extra wrinkle scrunching up her forehead. I can feel her jitters—of being at the beach, of Pappa finding out—which makes me jumpy, too. I thrash and splash my arms and legs over and over, getting soaked to the bone. Mamma doesn't care. Her eyes eat up the sky and sea, searching for something I cannot see.

"What is it, Mamma? What's out there?"

She ignores me, steps into the water, shoes and all. I stop splashing and watch what she's watching, out in the deeper blue, squinting against the shimmer of the sun.

"Should I take off my dress, Mor?"

"Hmm? Ja, Lei-lee. Put it on the shore, then come back in the water."

I pull my apron over my head and ever so carefully lay it out on a sand-bed to dry. It's almost like a real girl, a wet, sandy sister lazing about in the dirt. I drop to my knees and shovel a mound of sand to where her head should be, shaping a round face with two finger pokes for eyes.

"I shall call you Hildy, dear sister, and you shall be my twin." I stick my finger in, where her mouth should be, and force a smile into the sand.

I rush over to Mamma and tug on her arm. "Mor, see—I made a sister. Her name's Hildy."

Her eyes flash. "Where did you hear that name?"

"Nowhere. I made it up." I shove bits of seaweed around the sandy head. "Doesn't she have beautiful hair, Mamma?"

She ignores me, her whole body stiff.

It is then that I see it. A dark grey shape—a head—bobbing on the waves. She gasps, falling to her knees, the waves crashing against her. I watch as the grey shape swims closer. Mor starts crawling, then dives out into the blue. The shape gets even closer.

"What is it, Mamma? What could it be?"

She answers me, but it's nonsense, words I don't understand. She claws her way through the waves, out to the dark shadow, making strange sounds. The grey shape calls back with a slow long wail.

"Mamma . . . Mamma!"

Her arms flap like a bird, stretching out to touch the beast in the water. A grey-and-black seal, bigger than both of us.

Then together, they both sink.

"Nei!"

I fall into the water, my legs tumbling behind me, water gushing into my mouth. I cough and spit. My feet scramble to find solid ground, but there is no bottom anymore, no up or down. I feel the waves pull me, and my head bobs one last time before I am eaten. I hold my breath and open my eyes wide, but the salt hurts so bad that I close them again. I pray to God, feeling the world tip over again and again. When the water squeezes the last bubble out of me, I am gone. Legs and lungs mushed into the push-pull of wave after wave.

I let go.

There is no need for breath. No need for a mouth, eyes, hands, feet.

I am big and small. A single drop of rain inside one big wave.

I am foam, the sun's rays kissing me into a spray of bubbles.

I am the air, floating on the wish of wind and water.

I am the current, the pull of downdowndown, the darkness of the sea's belly, the meeting of earth and sea, rubbingpressingpushinggrinding, the dance of the sea slapping, smacking, beating, retreating from the earth . . .

And then, I can feel her. *Mor.*

She rolls beneath me, tumbling in the deep, tangled inside the paws of the grey monster. I become the empty spaces in between the two of them, rolling and wrestling in the current. The beast is strong; it will not let my mother go. I push harder between them, trying to save her. But she closes the gap by wrapping her legs around the monster, which shrinks me back into nothingness.

I will save you.

I feel the cool skin of the animal pressing against her, the rocking of the waves, push-pulling. No matter how hard I try, I can't get them apart. They beat against each other, and I graze against belly and back, flesh and fur, hair and whisker, teeth, cheek, thigh, tongue teethcheekthigh . . .

My body is here, in a single whoosh, like a gulping of water, like a spitting up. I change so quickly, it almost chokes me.

I am drowning.

"Mor!"

I am under again, but this time it is me: white seaweed hair, fists and feet punching and kicking, choking. All legs and arms, bubbles, grasping, gulping. I feel her fingers grabbing my arm, my waist. She pulls me, and I shoot up from the dark blue-green.

My fingers slide along the skin of the black seal, the black paws. Black eye . . .

Hallo, seal.

Mor pulls us away.

She swims on her back, keeping our heads above water. One arm holding me tight, so tight I can barely breathe, but somehow, I don't care.

The waves throw us up on shore. She falls flat on her back, pushing me past her so that I fall forward, eating a mouthful of sand. I gag, spitting up sea-water. I feel her hand clap my back a few times; with one more heave of salt water, I fall onto my back, the clear blue sky above me. The sea licks our legs, the sand sticky on our skin.

I gasp for air. The same air that my mother breathes. Wanting so badly to know what—or who—was out there on the waves. Wanting to know why she wouldn't let me save her.

I bite my lips and wait.

"Enough swimming for today." She tries to smile, but it's upside down.

"But, Mamma?"

"Ja, child?"

"What was that thing? How come . . . When you saw that—that—animal, it was like you forgot about me."

I hold my breath. I am so still. A single grain of sand, a speck in the water.

"Nei. I could never forget."

"But what were you doing, Mamma?"

"I was remembering."

Remembering what? Who? When? But she rolls over and starts wringing the water from her dress. I watch as she stands and takes one last look at the sea. Whispering a strange word she said before.

"*Shoormal.*"

"What does that mean, Mor?"

"Nothing, child. Nothing. Mor is talking nonsense."

"But you never talk nonsense, Mamma."

The wind lifts her stray copper locks, and she tucks them behind her ear. She reaches for my hand.

"I used to. Before Pappa."

I curl my fingers around her thumb, and we begin to walk away from the water. I want to hear more, to climb inside the "before Pappa" smile, to know Mamma when she was full of nonsense.

She stops, looks toward the sea one last time, closing her eyes as if she tasted the most delicious tart. And then one last whisper slips out of that wide mouth, slow and sad, into the sea.

"Tha gaol agam ort . . ."

I close my eyes and open my lips, almost tasting the letters on the salt spray.

Who knew that nonsense actually had its own words? The sound of which I know somehow. My blood and skin, singing to meet it.

Seal

He smells her watching from the shoreline, inhales her musk as he surfaces. Her humanness, no longer the dominant scent. The change is coming; of that, he is certain.

The bitch-hags kept his eye; a small price to pay for such a gift as *seidr*—the art of seeing, of divination. Sensing all times layered overtop one another, a patchwork, with only one eye in his head—an irony not lost on him. Despite their calculating coldness, the Sisters do indeed like to laugh.

All of us at their mercy.

So convinced of the illusion the Sisters have spun—that time moves in a single line, and only in one direction—even Maeva has almost forgotten the truth. But he can smell her anguish, her longing—mirroring his own—for time to quicken and slow simultaneously, yearning for him in every moment. Her dreams are his dreams, the two of them meeting at the shoreline between worlds. *Shoormal.* Where sand meets sea. Where they have always found each other. Where they have promised to meet, one last time, when all of it is done. When the knots of fate unravel.

He sends her messages constantly. Gifts of cloudberries on her doorstep, lupine blooms strewn on windowsills, sea-glass and pebbles arranged just so, leading away from the cottage into the woods. At first, she didn't seem to take much notice, assuming the child had placed them. But lately, he has seen her stopping to pick up each one, wondering. Knowing deep down, he is sure, who has left such gifts in her path.

Today, he left a solitary seashell, carrying it in his squirrel mouth.

The smell of the sea, an invitation.

What Was

Pieter's plan was a good one. Though Maeva didn't want to cooperate, she knew she must.

It was Sunday. Baptismal day. A week after Leidah mysteriously appeared inside her cradle, when she should have been inside the wood-box, safe from kittens and rotten apples and the prying eyes of men. Where she barely escaped discovery by Nils Innesbørg. The fateful day when all of them—especially Helgar Tormundsdatter—would have suffered further investigation. Possibly even a trial. Conviction.

Maeva couldn't help being suspicious. The news of the birth had travelled so quickly into the ears of dangerous men. *Was it you, Hans?* Pieter was adamant that his friend would never knowingly put him or his family in harm's way. But who else would have betrayed them? Certainly not the midwife.

No matter. The child saved them all. At least for the time being.

How could you have known? Maeva watched the baby with curiosity, waiting for something magical to occur. Leidah shoved a blue fist into her rosebud mouth. Maeva cooed at her. The girl was destined to be special, no doubt of that; she had to figure out how to contain it, whatever "it" might be. For how could a mother ever begin to explain such mystery, even to her own husband? Leidah was a secret best kept, even from Pieter.

Sometimes such children had tails.

Sometimes they were covered, head to toe, in soft fur.

Sometimes their faces were stained blue, the kiss of the sea.

Maeva caressed the baby's soft cheeks, then lightly tickled her tiny nose. It was much harder to hide this kind of magic, but still, she should count her blessings. Perhaps blue hands and feet were manageable, considering the alternative.

She checked the soft woolen mittens that were secured to the baby's sleeves. She had sewed them the night before, after hearing Pieter's plan to bring the child in for baptism. Knowing he was right didn't make her feel any better. She was afraid for the baby. Afraid for herself. But sooner or later, the pastor would come again to see the baby. Sooner or later, Leidah's blue skin would be noticed by someone. Perhaps the best way to stave off curiosity was to hide her in plain sight. Make her unremarkable, like everyone else.

They would weave a story for the villagers about the labour coming just hours after the village men departed. No time to fetch the doctor, or a neighbour. No time for Pieter to do anything but attend his labouring wife. Surely a husband would not be faulted for that? It was a believable story; the child so small, she could have arrived into the world only hours ago.

Leidah blinked her blue-green eyes. Focusing intently, as if she could read her mother's thoughts.

"What do you know, little one?"

The baby gurgled and clasped tiny caterpillar fingers around her mother's thumb.

"Much more than any of us, I'm sure."

Maeva kissed her child's fingers, feeling a wave of love take her. She tucked the tiny hand inside the arms of her baptismal dress, its red embroidered hem sewn shut. Checked the edges one last time: all secure. No chance for even a sliver of blue to peek through. She felt for Helgar's stone at the bottom of the gown. *May the gods protect you.*

She paused, then dared to murmur his name. "Odhinn. You've failed me before. Don't fail me now."

The room was quiet except for the urgent scratching of a mouse in the wall.

Don't fail her.

She picked the baby up, tucking her into the sling of fabric. Leidah let out a small cry.

"I agree, Lei-lee. I don't want to go either, but we don't have a choice."

She sang the first bit of the familiar lullaby to her daughter. The baby stopped to listen, then echoed a single note back, as though she knew the tune.

Maeva nuzzled her nose into Leidah's. *"Tha gaol agam ort.* I love you, little pup, I love you." She sang the phrase over and over. She tucked her shawl and bonnet under her chin, flipping her braids back. With a sigh of resignation, she marched out the front door.

The winter chill caught her off guard. The landscape brown, lifeless.

Her husband eyed her with concern, insisting on helping her into the wagon. She allowed it, feeling overwhelmed by what was ahead. She snuggled Leidah close to protect her from the wind. Pieter pulled his hat down, settling in beside her, then snapped the reins. The horse moved quickly, snorting in the cold. Neither of them spoke, the weight of the day—the story they would have to tell—large and heavy between them.

As they pulled onto the narrow road to Ørken, she noticed a moving shape in the woods. It followed at a distance, hiding among the trees, then all of a sudden appearing farther up ahead.

A wolf.

Odd to see such an animal, without a pack, in the early morning. For a second, it bounded out of the woods, then disappeared, its fur mangled, ribcage protruding. Maeva tucked her shawl protectively over the baby. She was about to alert her husband, whose eyes were fixed on the road in front of them, when the animal popped up in the meadow beside them. He cocked his head, then lay down, rolling over to expose his belly.

"Huh," Maeva marvelled.

The wolf rolled over, his jowls grinning.

Pieter didn't take his eyes off the road. "*Hva*—what is it?" He held the reins loosely in his hands but didn't slow the pace.

"There's a wolf, there—" She pointed to the ridge of dry grass, now empty, then frowned. "It was there a moment ago, I'm certain of it."

Pieter's mouth curled to one side. "Doubtful at this hour. Probably the Karlsens' hound."

Maeva nodded, unconvinced. A shiver passed through her. She felt woozy.

"You don't seem well." Pieter put a hand to her forehead. "Perhaps you shouldn't go. I could tell them that you're exhausted, that the baby can't travel—"

"Nei, let's get this over with. Then they will leave us alone. I don't want to entertain another houseful of snooping men."

Pieter snapped the reins in agreement.

The horse trotted them past the meadow. Maeva turned her head in time to see the wolf spring up one last time, almost camouflaged in the grass. It tilted its head, watching them pass.

Pastor Knudsen greeted them silently, with a nod from the altar. He was mid-sentence, giving a sermon about grief and the wisdom of God's plan, his small frame lost in black robes, dwarfed by an imposing cross hanging above the altar. Maeva had almost forgotten what the interior of the church was like, having been in it only once—at her own wedding ceremony—less than a year before. She had been so nervous, keeping her eyes on the floor the whole time, uncomfortable in Pieter's mother's wedding dress, which barely covered her shoes. The villagers seemed willing to ignore this at first, so curious—even pleased—to witness such a surprise marriage, especially Pieter's, as he was a bachelor and the sole surviving Aldestaed in Ørken. He showed up unannounced on a Sunday, with a red-haired beauty on his arm, a stunning silent creature from somewhere unknowable. Was she a Lapp? A Finn? Or perhaps a Scot—a Highlander? The fiery mane certainly a sign of foreign shores. It didn't help that she didn't speak—only to Pieter, in short, garbled whispers—the initial village excitement spoiling like sour cream, within a week.

Maeva learned the word *huldra* even before she learned *hallo*. It was one of the many whispers that chased her, even in dreams. She learned quickly to avoid the village. Avoid neighbours. Avoid the market. Avoid church. Which had sealed her fate as the scapegoat for all manner of ills: Snowstorms, stable fires, sparse crops, empty nets. Illnesses. Even shipwrecks. *Didn't Pieter Aldestaed meet her before his boat sank? Or was it after? Suspicious either way* . . . The gossip, never-ending. The consequences, far-reaching in the small district.

The Aldestaeds stood side by side at the back of the church. Pieter pushed his back against the closing door to soften the noise. But all eyes had already turned to them; murmurs and whispers floated through the congregation. Then silence. Maeva stepped in front of Pieter, keeping her gaze on the pastor, who extended his arms wide, gesturing to the large wooden cross above him. It was a good distraction; Maeva slipped into the last empty pew on the women's side, holding Leidah close, should she cry out. She tried to catch Pieter's eyes, feeling adrift.

Pieter moved to the men's side but didn't sit, keeping to the corner. A few more fishermen than usual—most likely another crew from Bergen—occupied the last row. A blond man in the second-to-last pew craned his head: Hans. He raised an eyebrow to Pieter, who nodded his head proudly at his wife and child. Hans showed his approval with a wink, then turned his attention back to the pastor.

Knudsen clapped his hands.

"And now, it is time to welcome new members into the fold, a most pleasurable duty of ministry." He held his arm out, pointing to the back of the church. There was another round of murmuring. A flush of heat overcame Maeva, who shifted nervously, rocking the baby even though the child was fast asleep.

"What exciting and blessed times are these, praise God." He beckoned the new family forward. "Let us all witness the blessed event, the baptism of this child of God."

Pieter moved to his wife, wrapping an arm around her. She stood, forcing her feet to step forward. They shuffled down the centre aisle, passing Nils Innesbørg, who stared straight ahead, avoiding their gaze. The sermon on grief and the necessity of loss, a difficult one. Maeva tried to ignore the inexplicable wash of guilt she felt.

"I am very glad to see you here, in the name of Jesus. And with our newest convert." The pastor reached out to Leidah, who curled into her mother, eyes still closed. "God's blessings on you."

Maeva didn't know what to say. Pieter squeezed her elbow.

The pastor addressed the congregation. "This is a joyous occasion, coming on the heels of so much tragedy. God's ways are mysterious and not to be questioned. Let us welcome any blessings that God chooses for us." Maeva heard a cough, then silence. "I ask for someone who will attest to this birth. To stand for this child as a witness, guide, and protector."

Both parents held their breath. Pieter's family had died years before, in the terrible famine that claimed over a quarter of the farmers in the district. Before marrying Maeva, he might have had any number of villagers to stand for him, for his child. But months had passed; things had shifted. Friendships, changeable as the weather.

Pieter dared to look back at the congregation. Maeva darted her eyes just long enough to take in her husband's imploring expression. *Oh, Pieter.* She wanted to shake every last one of them.

"I will stand, Pastor."

Everyone turned toward the back of the room. Hans Bjørnsen grinned, making a mock salute. His broad figure, large and confident.

Pieter's relief was so great, his eyes teared up. *"Tusen takk,* old friend."

Maeva moved the baby to her other arm, filled with even more unease. How could she trust this man, after all that had happened, to become a guardian for her daughter? *Will he accept Leidah for what she is?* Maeva's mind jumped into the future. She saw them suffering through forced visits with Hans, the two of them scrambling to hide their daughter's skin in their own home, always wondering if Hans would be tempted into crafting a good story for his fellow fishermen. Leidah, in constant threat . . . *By the gods, no.* She tried to get Pieter to read her silent protest, but it was no use.

The pastor cleared his throat. "Ah, yes, thank you, Herr Bjørnsen. And is there anyone else? A good and kind heart, a Christian woman who is willing to be godmother to . . . to . . ."

She whispered, "Leidah—her name is Leidah."

His mouth shut momentarily, his openness wavering. "*Leidah* . . . daughter of Pieter Aldestaed?"

The women stared back. Implacable. In the third row, Birgit Vebjørnsdatter scowled and leaned to her daughter, whispering loud enough for Maeva to hear, "Should be named Clara, for Pieter's mother. That poor woman must be rolling over in her grave."

"Like Maren Innesbørg. And her baby. Right, Mor?" The words, abrasive in the hushed church.

Maeva bit her cheek. Another rush of heat to her cheeks.

Hans spoke loudly. "My sister, Kjerste Bjørnsdatter, will stand."

The pastor cleared his throat again. "Splendid. And is she here?"

Hans shook his head. "But she will return from our cousin's farmstead in a fortnight. I will have her sign the registry then." Pieter nodded his gratitude, then made a silent plea to the pastor to move on.

Pastor Knudsen muttered to himself, "A bit unorthodox, but I suppose it will have to do." He addressed the women. "I trust that you have sent blessings and well wishes to Maeva, with *sengemat, fløtegrøt, kjæring suppe*?" It was a perk of new motherhood—a basic expectation—to be fed by the neighbourhood women in the first week of a baby's birth.

Maeva bit her cheek. The women said nothing.

He continued, seemingly oblivious. "Let us pray for this child to be welcomed into the loving arms of God, welcomed into the ministry of serving Jesus Christ, our Lord and Saviour, for the rest of her days on earth, rewarded in the afterlife. This baptism of Leidah Pietersdatter, given to us by the grace of God and his mercy. Washing away all sin, endowing her with Christ's forgiveness and removing all stain from her skin . . ."

Leidah squirmed.

"All who are baptized, ye are 'clothed in Christ, heirs according to the promise.' Galatians 3:27."

Maeva's finger worried against the hem of Leidah's sewn sleeve. In unison, the people of Ørken church bowed their heads and closed their eyes, listening to the pastor's words.

Maeva kept her head up. A bead of sweat fell from her temple, onto the baby's cheek. Leidah scrunched up her face, stretching awake. Under Maeva's skirts, a trickle trailed down one leg. She crossed her legs, knowing immediately it must be blood. *Open your eyes, Pieter.*

Leidah began to fuss. Maeva jiggled her, whispering "Shhh," but the child ignored her and began to howl.

Pastor Knudsen continued praying, a little louder to be heard over the crying. Pieter still did not open his eyes. Maeva swayed side to side as Leidah wailed even louder. Finally, the pastor said, "Amen." Pieter opened his eyes. Maeva was burning up, the skin of her hands a pale yellow-green.

"Bring the child forth, to be cleansed by the holy waters of God."

Maeva stepped forward, her legs shaking. Pieter was quick to support her, putting an arm around both mother and crying child.

"Do you, Leidah Pietersdatter, renounce all form of devilry and idolatry, in the name of the Father, the Son, and the Holy Spirit?"

Maeva glanced at Pieter, confused. *How could a baby even be asked this?*

Pieter answered loudly. "She does."

Maeva opened her mouth, then clamped down. *Does she?*

The pastor dipped a chalice into the baptismal font behind him. He continued, holding the cup above his head. "And do you, Pieter and Maeva, parents of Leidah Pietersdatter, promise to renounce all forms of devilry, witchcraft, magic, and idolatry, keeping yourselves whole and clean, as stewards of this newly born soul unto God?"

Maeva cuddled Leidah, who was now inconsolable, into her shoulder. *What if I said—*

Pieter answered again. "We do."

No.

The pastor stepped forward, the cup of water in front of him. He dipped his fingers into it.

"Please open the child's gown."

Maeva looked at Pieter in alarm. He nodded at her to open the silver clasps. Her fingers fumbled and shook as she opened the first one.

The pastor dripped water onto the child's pink chest and face. She wriggled and squirmed.

"I baptize you, Leidah Pietersdatter, in the name of all that is holy, by the grace of God, in this place of Ørken, on this day, the second of November. Born on . . ." He whispered to Pieter. "What day was the birth?"

Maeva watched her husband's eyes shift, his confident demeanor now gone. The baby let out a stubborn yelp. *That's it, Lei-lee, shout—*

Then, a miniscule blue fist, free from its sleeve, waved in the air. Maeva heard a gasp. She looked up to see Hans, his mouth agape in wonder.

She quickly tucked the blue hand back inside the sleeve, fastening the clasps.

Knudsen cleared his throat, repeating a little louder, "The date of birth?"

Maeva felt more blood drain from her. "October . . ." Her knees gave way.

Pieter caught the baby as she fainted to the floor.

⤜❧⤏

Maeva awakened to Pieter's worried face above her. She sat up quickly, realizing that the entire congregation was on their feet, leaning forward to see, though it didn't feel to be out of concern. She had become a spectacle, despite every effort to appear as conforming and ordinary as anyone in Ørken. Pastor Knudsen kneeled beside her, the wooden cross around his neck bumping against her cheek.

Maeva struggled to stand, embarrassed by all the attention. She pushed a wayward curl back under her bonnet.

"Are you all right, my dear?" The pastor's blue eyes regarded her with concern. He held her arm to help.

Maeva nodded quickly, reaching to Pieter, to take Leidah back into her arms.

"Ja, ja. I'm fine." *I need air.*

The pastor dropped his chin, his eyes still questioning. Pieter placed

171

an arm around her, protecting them both from the prying eyes of worshippers.

Inexplicable anger—at her husband—washed over her. She stuttered nervously, "I—I am a bit weak—and a little overheated—from all the excitement."

Pieter added, "The carriage ride here, perhaps too soon."

This seemed to spark the pastor into action. "Ah, yes. The registry. Perhaps not a good time to complete the registration of birth?"

Maeva forced a smile. "Nei, nei. Please, it has been a long journey, I do not want it to be in vain."

The pastor addressed the women of the congregation. "Our young mother needs some fresh air. Is there someone who will take Fru Aldestaed outside for a moment while we sign and date the registry?"

Maeva focused on the baby, feeling exposed and rejected. After what seemed like minutes passing, though was probably only seconds, Birgit Vebjørnsdatter nudged her daughter. Unna stood, reluctant, twirling the ends of her two braids.

Knudsen clapped his hands. "Good. *Takk skal du ha*, young Unna."

Maeva held Leidah close, rocking side to side gently, mostly to comfort herself and settle her frustration. She couldn't believe she'd fainted at such a time. If she weren't so worried—*so angry*—Maeva might have laughed aloud at the baby shaking a blue fist at the whole lot of them. She wondered who actually had witnessed it; Hans must have, for she was certain that he had gasped. *But perhaps he was reacting to my fainting. Please, Freyja, let that be the case.* She marveled at Leidah, who was once again content and sleeping, blue hands safely tucked away.

Unna watched her with suspicion, as if examining a foreign species, standing at a distance, her feet planted on the bottom steps of the church entrance. Though the morning sun shone high in a clear blue sky, winter was definitely on its way. Maeva put her back to the sun, shielding the baby from the harsh light and the cold. Unna didn't move.

After several minutes of silence, the girl blurted out, "Can I hold her?"

Maeva was so stunned, she couldn't think of a good reason to refuse. She slowly passed Leidah to the girl, all the while wanting to snatch her daughter back and run into the woods to hide.

Unna examined the baby closely, holding her up to eye level. "She's so small."

Maeva breathed a sigh of relief. "Yes, newborns are very small."

"My mother says you had the baby weeks ago."

Maeva shook her head to stop her mouth from spewing vitriol, so adamantly she almost believed the lie.

"She also said you couldn't have her baptized."

"Why not?"

Unna shrugged, then began to jiggle the baby on her shoulder. Leidah started to wriggle. "She said the minute Pastor put holy water on her skin, she would burn up."

Maeva felt heat rising up her cheeks, but this time, she wouldn't faint. *How dare you.* She managed to suppress the urge to snap back an answer— to chide the girl's rudeness; instead, she took Leidah back into the safety of her own arms, giving the girl a slight push.

"You can go inside, Unna. I'm much better now, thank you." Maeva produced a false smile, wishing Pieter would hurry up.

The girl didn't move. She was transfixed on the woods.

Maeva turned. She managed to catch sight of the tail of a grey wolf, raised majestically as the beast wandered into the trees.

Unna turned to her, watching warily. Her face changed slowly: her eyes narrowed, then widened. Abruptly, she climbed the steps two at a time, throwing the heavy door open.

Maeva ignored her. A shiver travelled from shoulder to throat and up to her right temple, to rest in her hair. As if someone had trailed a fingertip along her skin. Her breath caught.

Her eyes rested on the closed doors of the church as she debated what to do. She glanced back to the shadowy forest. *I wonder . . .* She shifted the baby to her other arm, then moved down the steps, taking each one slowly. Then hurried to follow the beast.

She stopped short of the tree line, the branches conspiring to hide what was beyond the road: the emboldened animal sitting calmly, as if posing for her. Maeva's grip on the baby tightened, but she made no move to leave.

The one-eyed wolf stared back at her hungrily. Maeva felt caught. Hypnotized. Seconds passed. Neither moved, holding each other frozen in an intense stand-off, until finally, Leidah yawned. Maeva almost giggled. About to apologize and explain the ways of babies to a wild creature.

She muttered to herself, "I'm going mad. You are a wolf—you can't possibly be . . ."

Yours.

Maeva drew back, the possessive word penetrating brazenly into her mind. The wolf settled onto his belly, languid, confident. Stretched his neck long. Surely she didn't see a hint of a grin on those jowls? Her stomach flipped. A warmth spreading between her thighs.

It must be lack of sleep. It can't be. Not in this world . . .

The wolf tilted his head, an almost human gesture.

Is it you?

Behind her, Maeva heard the church doors open. She spun around to see the congregation spill out.

When she turned back, the wolf was gone.

The Sixth Knot

It was after sunrise. A black bird landed on the ledge of the cell window, pecking at the bars and waking the old woman. Helgar opened one eye to glare at the bird. Its head cocked sideways, gazing back at her. Then, the crow tipped its beak upwards, warbling a throaty hallo.

Helgar groaned. "Tell Odhinn it is too early for messages. Go find a tree to light on and leave an old woman in peace."

The bird answered with several more pecks at the metal, squeezing between the bars, first inside, then outside. Flaunting its freedom.

"*Takk*, winged one, but escape is impossible—I am not as wily as you."

The crow hopped to the floor inside the cell, flapping its black feathers.

Helgar shifted to sitting, slowly and carefully. Prayed for death to take her old body away. "Anytime is a good time, Skuld. Snip the thread and be done with me. I am ready."

Keys jingled in the lock. The bird stopped to listen, then abruptly flew up to the window with a caw. Helgar struggled to stand. The door opened, bringing a gust of fresh air.

"No such luck, Fru Tormundsdatter. I would like nothing more than to watch life ebb away from your body." The magistrate hooked a ring of keys on his belt. "But we still have business to discuss—due process requires questions to be answered. Perhaps you should pray to God and not Skuld?"

Helgar smoothed her frizzy silver hair. Standing as tall as she could— which wasn't very tall at all—she felt the chain around her wrists rattle. Her eyes met Innesbørg's barrel chest. He closed the cell door. She smiled to herself. *As if I could escape iron shackles. But such a thought must worry him; otherwise why close it?* She decided to play with him, to amuse herself.

"I am happy to oblige any question, Herr Innesbørg, even at this hour. As you know, I am a very skilled healer."

He snarled, "You are no such thing, *heks*. If you were, you would have saved my wife and boy . . ." His voice broke. He shifted his eyes to the window. Helgar followed his gaze. The crow pecked under a wing. He glowered at the bird, his eyes narrowing.

She rested against the wall. "True. I am just an old woman. A neighbour that came to your wife's bedside, *at your request*. I cannot explain what happened that night. Nor the mysteries of life. Only God knows such things."

Innesbørg snorted. "God and not Skuld, now? How convenient. How fickle of you." He leaned in closer, his breath sour with ale. "My fault in this is my pure desperation, nothing more. It is you who let my wife bleed dry." He stopped, flushed and trembling. "No matter, justice will be served. For you and that red-haired devil woman."

Helgar straightened at the mention of Maeva. Her tone changed. "Grief is a vicious thing; it can make us say and do terrible things. Blame can only be laid at the feet of God."

Innesbørg struggled to stay calm. "What a good Christian you are, voicing such sentiments to the man whose life you have destroyed."

Helgar rolled her tongue to the roof of her mouth, refusing to argue.

"Women like you should never be allowed into a village. Women like you . . ." He stopped, sputtering, his finger wagging at her. "Should rot away in a cave, away from good, God-fearing people."

"I fear God as much as you do, Nils." She said his name quietly. An attempt to bring him back to his senses.

It had the opposite effect. "Fru Tormundsdatter, you are charged with illegal midwifery, pending a trial. Manslaughter in the second degree, for illegal medical practice leading to harm and death, once we solidify the evidence, which is why I'm here." He walked to the window. The crow cawed at him, lighting to the sky. He shooed it away, then sneered. "Friend of yours?"

Helgar didn't flinch. "I don't have friends."

"What about Maeva Aldestaed?"

"That woman has fewer friends than even me."

Innesbørg scowled, unable to deny it. "Perhaps I need to send word to officials in Bergen. To help me with the investigation. They would surely need to interview all of the womenfolk."

She closed her eyes at the threat. *Maeva—and the child—will be doomed.* She opened her eyes, determined.

The silence grew. Innesbørg eyed the window. Then her. He picked at dirt under his thumbnail.

"Confession cleanses the soul, Fru Tormundsdatter."

"I confess to nothing because I have nothing to confess."

Innesbørg flicked the dirt in her direction. "Refusing to confess to witchcraft is obstruction of justice—not to mention a denial of God. I'm here to glean the facts, yet you refuse me—the victim and widower— some kind of explanation." He stopped, his gaze direct. "Am I not owed this, at the very least, Helgar?"

She cursed him in her head, then nodded solemnly. "Of course. I can't even begin to understand the loss you have suffered." She cringed, realizing he had trapped her with sympathy and guilt. "But I did everything I could. She wouldn't stop bleeding. I would never feel malice toward anyone—especially Maren."

"Then tell me what I need to know, if you wish to alleviate my grief. At the very least, give me this bit of solace, woman."

She watched him as if he were the one caged, wiggling to weasel out of her confession. Finally, she gave up, nodding acquiescence.

Innesbørg pounced. "There has been talk among the womenfolk. Of that book you consult. For healing?"

Helgar heard the crow somewhere off in the distance, cawing. *What woman hasn't consulted a black book?* She sighed, defeated.

"Ja, I have such a book."

Innesbørg leaned in, waited for her to continue.

"But it is only a record of things I observe—a simple journal, to keep track of ailments and symptoms. Cures that seem to work, passed down over the years."

He smiled then, almost genuinely. "I need that book. For the trial—it's the one thing that could set you free, Helgar. Perhaps even save the village from more tragedy."

She felt the jaws of a trap tightening around her throat.

"I understand—but I don't have it. Unfortunately, the last time I saw it was the night of the birth . . ." Her words faded to silence. *Search high and low, Magistrate. That book will never see the light of day.*

He wiped sweat from his brow, protesting, "Do you mean to imply that it was with you, at my place of residence? That somehow you lost the *svartebok?*"

Helgar fought the smirk spreading across her thin lips; the irony of such an item, one that could seal her fate, lost in his own house . . . It was almost laughable. The image of Innesbørg tearing apart his entire house made her want to laugh and cry at the same time. But she refrained. Simply shrugged.

"I would be more worried about its whereabouts. But it seems I won't be needing it anytime soon, given my change of surroundings."

The beefy man leaped toward her, his blotched purple scowl inches from hers. His sweat, almost as foul as his breath. "Don't worry, neighbour. I'll find it for you."

She held her own breath but didn't flinch.

He spun on his heels. The cell door slammed shut, then was locked.

Helgar sank in exhaustion.

It is up to you now, Skuld. Have mercy. Let it be done.

What Is

Maeva moves in a daze of memory, unable to calm her mind—her thoughts, a confused tempest of both worry and euphoria; her body, not even registering how cold she is. She feels a slight squeeze on her fingers. Leidah, pulling on her. Maeva's eyes are fixed on the road, fixed on the shock of what has occurred. The sudden, unmistakable appearance of him—his spirit in animal form—making her legs weak, making her heart weep with joy and bitterness. So much unspoken between them, her insides were screaming.

Where have you been? Why have you come now, after all this time? How dare you show up. I don't need you anymore. I have a husband, I have a child . . .

God, I have missed you.

Abruptly, she drops Leidah's hand and rubs her eyes, trying to hide the tears. The guilt—her desire—a sudden ambush. How easily she fell into him. How quickly she forgot, the life she has built all these years vanishing in an instant. Her daughter. Her husband. This world, gone. *Unforgivable*, she chides herself, even as a flood of persistent yearning and realization crashes into her. *I still love you.*

Leidah stops walking. Maeva shakes her daughter's elbow. "Hurry up, girl. We need to get home."

The child jerks away. "I don't want to go home. And you don't either."

Maeva stares at her, incredulous at the child's nerve. Her astuteness.

"Oh, Lei-lee. Forget today. You are a child and it was wrong for me to . . ." Her voice falters. "You are too little; there's so much you can't possibly understand."

"I'm old enough to know everything. And I can keep a secret, I promise."

Maeva doesn't answer, thinking about the consequences of Pieter finding out. The encounter in the water, with her daughter as witness . . . *Never again.* She crosses her arms and shakes her head vehemently, guilt hardening her. "Absolutely not."

Leidah plops to the ground. Starts to kick and flail at nothing, pounding the air and the road with her fists, fingernails digging into the skin of the road.

Hate me if you must, child. I hate me, too. How can she tell the truth when she can barely admit it to herself? *I can't stay . . .* She scowls at herself. Fighting an unbridled urge to scratch at the dry scaly patches on her arm, to run back to the water. To scream at him.

Take me with you!

She balls her fingers into fists. Forces every muscle to focus on Leidah, exhaustion already beginning to calm the child's tantrum. A minute passes, then another. The frustrated grunts and kicks slowing, quieting.

Maeva waits for complete stillness. "Are you quite finished?"

Leidah glares at her mother, her cheek and hair in the dirt. She rolls on her back, feet raised, ready to kick her away. "Nei. Not until you tell me everything. Not until you tell me about that thing in the water."

Maeva steps in front of her, surprised at Leidah's petulance. The girl's tone, accusatory. She bends down, grabbing the child's ankles. "I am going to start walking. And I'm not coming back. You can either follow me or stay here, lying on the road for a horse to trample." She pushes the girl's boots to the ground, then stands up, brushing her damp dress off to hide her trembling. "If you continue this crying, you will melt right into the ground."

"Good. Then maybe you'll miss me." Though the words are angry, a tear rolls down Leidah's cheek.

I miss you already, girl . . . Maeva fights to keep her voice steady. Softens her tone, her façade breaking. "I almost lost you once today—in the ocean. You were slipping away from me. You have a rare gift, Lei-lee. One I wasn't expecting to be so strong. So strong that it may become a curse if you don't learn to control it. And you won't learn anything lying on the road."

Leidah sits up, hair dishevelled, face stained with dirt.

"Now stand up. I have much to tell you. And it seems as though I don't have much choice."

"There once was a time when all things could speak. When all things could *become*. This was the time before the separation of worlds, when *what was* depended on *what is*."

"But that's backwards. Time only moves forward, Mamma. Everyone knows that."

Maeva squeezes the girl's hand. *"Now* it seems to move like that. But before, time was a labyrinth. It could move any which way, whenever it pleased."

Leidah tilts her head to one side and closes one eye.

"Do you remember those Sisters I told you about? The ones that sit inside the Great Tree? Those Sisters could weave time into whatever shape they wanted. They could stitch a quilt together piece by piece and unravel it, all at the same time."

The child stops walking. "But that makes no sense. That would mean that the future was—"

"Already written, yes. One Sister spun the yarn, the second wove a story with the threads, and the last one snipped at the pattern. Until all that was left was a tangled mess, to begin again."

"Seems like a lot of work for no good reason. Why not start with the mess in the first place?"

Indeed. Maeva marvels at her daughter's insight. "Not knowing how it will turn out—whether our lives might actually change for the better—

this keeps us going. To begin again, to have another chance. That is the glimmer of hope inside all the chaos and knots." *It's my only prayer*, she thinks. *For us both.*

She leads Leidah off the road, into the trees, following the trail to where she was digging the other night. The aroma of lilac and mint in the air. She takes big strides into fireweed and cloudberry, ignoring the sting of nettles.

"It was a time when everything hung off the Great Tree like ripe fruit, waiting to be plucked," she says. "A time when gods and humans and mysterious beings all lived side by side. A time of magic, when people danced with the fairies and swam with sea creatures."

Leidah squeals. "Like you did today?"

She pauses, weighing out how much to confess to such a small child. "Yes, I suppose so. As you can imagine, all that fruit was very tempting. Sometimes, humans fell in love with a god. And once in a while, a god fell in love with a magical creature."

All of a sudden, the forest is silent. The insects stop buzzing. The trees listen. Sunlight streams through the lace of the leaves. Leidah stretches her fingers out, trying to catch it in her hands.

"When this happened, the Sisters lost control. The pattern spun itself without their help."

"But why, Mamma?"

Maeva reaches out her hand, stretching it underneath Leidah's, to frame her daughter's blue fingers. The light dances across their skin. "Because magic—true mystery—can't be controlled. It just *is*. So, you can imagine what the Sisters did."

Leidah thinks for a moment. "They stole the fruit off the tree? Like Adam and Eve?"

Maeva smiles, folding their hands together. "Not quite. That story isn't as old as this one. The Sisters separated everyone into different realms, like little pockets of time, each one invisible to the other. No longer could a human see a god, or a god talk to a human. Oh, they all tried—with prayers and drums, runes and songs—but contact became next to impossible. These pockets became the Nine Worlds, with all creatures bound by the laws of these worlds. And magic disappeared—or seemed to disappear—from the human world."

Leidah drops her hand. "But that's so sad. Isn't there any way to bring it back?"

"There are always secret ways. Remember the part about gods and beasts and humans falling in love? Well, their children are still here. And their children's children."

"And their children's children's children?"

Maeva holds her daughter's elfin face between her palms. "Exactly. And these children hold the secret to magic. The secret to crossing over. To another world."

Light flickers across the child's face, and she blinks. The sunbeam skips and leaps, dancing in the grass. Leidah pulls away and points at the shifting shadows. "Look, Mamma. Magic!" She runs past her mother, quick as a fox, chasing the light toward the other side of the clearing.

Maeva shouts an alarm, and the girl slides to a stop, just in time.

She is at Leidah's side in an instant, gripping her shoulders.

The cliff.

She pulls the girl back, peering over the edge. *Oh . . . how the light changes things.* The last time she was here, it was the middle of the night. And she had been preoccupied, digging, searching in the dirt. She had forgotten how heavenly the water was.

Sunbeams spill onto the waterfall, like jewels diving into the clear blue pond edged in yellow and orange and white lilies, and huge flat rocks. Maeva can feel her skin aching for moisture, a deep thirst in her mouth.

"So pretty. Can we go see?" Leidah's face is full of wonder. *And hope.*

Maeva pulls her daughter into her belly, her white-blond head barely reaching her hip. "First, tell me how it happens," she says. "The magic. How do you . . . become something? Something other than yourself?"

Leidah hugs her mother tight. "It's not magic. It's only me being me."

"Nei, child. It *is* magic, *and* it's you. *You* are magic."

Leidah laughs. "That's not true."

"Believe me, Lei-lee, it is. Don't worry, I can help you manage this—this gift. Do you know before it happens?"

"Nei, it just kind of . . . happens."

"There's no warning sign? No feeling inside your body?"

Leidah closes her eyes. "There is a humming in my head . . . and in my fingers and toes."

"Good, good. And what else? What's in your mind before the change?"

"I'm scared, and then . . . I want to disappear. I want to be invisible."

"And then? You actually do it—you disappear? You jump? Into whatever is closest?"

"I guess. I don't know. I don't plan it, honest I don't. I never know what I will become."

Maeva bends down. Her daughter's blue-green eyes, so full of truth and innocence, Maeva can't speak for a moment. Leidah blinks. Bites a nail.

"Listen to me, child. You must learn to control this—this *becoming*. You must practice. Start by willing yourself into another thing. See if you can stay inside it. Practice this until you master it. Otherwise . . . well, I don't want to think about what could happen." She pulls Leidah's hand away from her mouth.

"What, Mamma?"

"You're not a baby anymore, so I'm going to tell you the truth." She takes a deep breath. "You could disappear into one of those pockets I told you about. Get stuck inside something and be trapped. No one would know where . . . I wouldn't be able to . . . How would anyone know where—or what—you had become? You would be lost, in another world. Possibly forever."

Leidah's mouth opens wide. "Lost?"

"Ja. Like today. It was careless of me, plain and simple. To leave you alone on shore. My mind was playing tricks on me. I was remembering and forgetting at the same time . . ." She stops, struggling to explain. *I don't even know myself.* "You must learn to swim, Leidah. Water is dangerous. It's a gateway—it can lead to the other worlds, if you know how. I should never have been so thoughtless—so forgetful—not teaching you the most important thing, maybe the only necessary thing, before I have to . . ." Her voice falters. "I don't want to lose you." She stops, her head racing with all the things she must tell her daughter.

The sea is my home. I have to go.

"I don't want to be lost, Mor. And I don't want to lose you either." Leidah squints, hesitates. "I . . . I've missed you. It feels like you went away for a long time."

"I know. I'm sorry. I want to say, I've been here all along"—Maeva tries to smile, but the tears are already visible, the shame welling in her throat—"but I don't think that's quite true."

"Where did you go?"

"I got lost in *what was*, Lei-lee. And what *could be* . . . But I'm here now." She smooths Leidah's braids onto the girl's back. Kisses her hand. "We're together, you and me. Always, no matter what."

Leidah grins. "I know. My heart knows it, too. And it's so happy, it's jumping up and down!" She throws her arms around her mother's neck, almost knocking both of them over.

Maeva recovers, standing with her daughter in her arms. Her heart breaks. *Forgive me, child . . . How I will miss this.*

Leidah snuggles close. "So, what do we do now? How will we find it?"

"Find what, Lei-lee?"

"The thing that Pappa hid. How will we find it if I can't swim?"

Maeva puts her down gently, then faces the edge of the cliff and the pool of water below. She clasps Leidah's small fingers.

"We'll find it, child. And don't worry, you're going to learn to swim. Right now."

❦

She leads the girl to a hidden stone staircase, overgrown with weeds. She points to the stones spiraling down to the water's edge below. "This place is old—ancient. There is so much power here. Do you feel it, girl?"

Leidah holds out her hands and wiggles her fingers.

"Your magic—your gift—will be stronger than usual. Be prepared—it might be overwhelming. I need you to go behind the falls, all right, child? It will be slippery—hold on to the troll moss once we get there."

She steps out of her skirts and apron. Tosses them over the edge. They spin and tumble, landing on a branch sticking out from the water's edge. Standing in her cottons, she steps in front of Leidah.

"What's that, Mor? On your back?"

Maeva feels tiny fingers rubbing the mark on her tailbone. She pulls away, covering the spot with her hand. "Nothing. An old scar."

"It's the shape of a star," Leidah marvels. "I wish I had the sky on my back, like you, Mamma."

Every muscle tenses inside Maeva. The sudden smell of sweat, stale breath, rotting fish, and algae fills her nostrils. Her mind is assaulted by another time and place, memories crashing and bobbing against her. She feels dizzy and hot, her head splitting in two.

Leidah reaches for her hand. "Don't go away again. Please, Mamma. Stay."

She focuses on the warmth of her daughter's hand, on her own breath. *This moment, right here. The sunlight on my face. The rush of the waterfall. The smell of mint. Leidah's warm hand in mine.*

Steadily, the earth rights itself under her feet. She takes a deep breath, letting the air cool her lungs. *Grass, earth, flowers. You.* The rot of dead things receding. A hole—one she didn't even know was there—knitting itself back together. Filaments reattaching, like a seam gathering into itself.

My precious, strange, magical girl . . . You are my home.

Her body finally lets go, the incessant worry flaking into inconsequential pieces that float away in a gust of wind. The way forward, so clear in its direction

Of course.

"Wherever I go from now on, you're coming with me," she says to her daughter. *No matter what. No matter who tries to stop us.*

Leidah squeezes her hand. "Promise?"

Maeva squeezes back. "Promise." She motions to the cliff. "Now. Are you ready? Time to be brave."

Leidah peers over the edge. The long drop into the pool, so far away. She backs away, her face full of fear. "Can't we use the steps?"

Maeva shakes her head. *Come on, child. You can do this. We can do this together.*

With a dramatic sigh, Leidah squares her shoulders. *I know we can, Mamma.*

Maeva's jaw drops. The words, unspoken but so clear, as if Leidah had said them aloud.

Don't let go. Leidah clasps her mother's hand tighter, unfazed by the new way they are communicating.

In awe, Maeva smiles. *Never.*

Then, with a loud whoop, mother and daughter jump off the cliff.

They fly like one giant bird, arms spread like wings. Leidah's shout is quickly consumed by the splash into the pool. Maeva feels immediate relief; no more itching, no more peeling and flakes. Only wetness. Bursting through the surface, she takes a huge gulp of air, pulling Leidah above the water. *Yes. This is what I need. What we both need.*

⊱✖⊰

They swim behind the waterfall, Leidah riding on her mother's back, squealing the entire time. The rush of the water is loud, and Maeva has to shout for Leidah to understand to climb onto the rock bed. Leidah grabs the lip of a boulder and easily hops out. Maeva struggles to heave herself onto the slick stone, and Leidah reaches down to help pull her up. Both of them stand together, peering inside the cave.

The long, thin fissure in the centre of the rocks has always been a curiosity to Maeva. The boulders shaped like two hands praying; the gap between palms, a dark question. *What are you hiding?* A den too small for her long limbs to fit inside, making it a perfect hiding spot. *Until now.*

With one arm, she hoists Leidah up by the waist, pushing under her bottom with her other hand. Her arms tremble, but not from the weight of the small girl. *It's in there, I can feel it.*

Leidah grabs hold, scrambling to find purchase with her feet. She catches on the rock and gasps. "I'm too big."

"I doubt that very much, little fairy." Maeva lifts a little more, enough for Leidah to lean her torso fully into the opening. *Sisters, please guide her to what's mine.*

Unexpectedly, Leidah howls. Maeva panics, yanking her out in one fierce movement. She puts her down, then kneels to examine the girl. Leidah lifts her slip to expose a raw scrape on her hip. Maeva sucks in her breath. "Oh, Lei-lee—you're bleeding. I think it's time to stop."

"I didn't cry out because I'm hurt. I cried because—because there's . . ."

"What is it?"

"I felt something. Inside the cave."

Oh, please, could it be? "What did you feel?"

"Something kind of smooth . . . with whiskers."

Leidah drops the hem of her slip and, in a single jump, forces her arms back into the gap. Maeva grabs her, supporting her firmly, impressed by her determination. This time, she squeezes through the rock with ease, her legs disappearing with a flicker. Within seconds, a rubbery mask flies out of the cave at Maeva. She catches it, flabbergasted.

"Well, Mor—is it the thing? Is it what you've been looking for?"

You are my saviour, girl. Yes! Maeva slides down the rock. She clutches the prize in her hand. Laughing. Crying. *Now we can go home, child! Our true home . . .*

She barely hears the little voice, still shouting, as she suddenly realizes something is wrong. *No, it can't be.* The voice shouts out again.

"Ja, good girl, Lei-lee! Now search for the rest of it. It must be close by."

"The rest?" There is a pause. "But there is no more—that's all there is."

"Nei, there must be more, this is just the head. Feel around, you will know when you touch it."

She whispers to herself, "You split it in half. Clever husband."

Leidah's eyes pop up, barely at the height of the opening. She shakes her head.

"Check the cracks in the rock, girl." *That bastard.* She hears Leidah sniffling. "No time for tears. He must have hidden it somewhere else." *There's still time*, she tells herself.

Blue hands reach through the opening. Maeva pulls at Leidah's wrists, but the angle is awkward. "Jump, Leidah. I can't lift you from there."

"I can't."

"You must." She hears Leidah's panic, the girl scrambling and scratching, an animal, caged. Trapped.

"I'm stuck. I can't get out!"

Maeva shushes her, face pressed into the hole. The waterfall sounds even louder. "Try something for me?" She slaps the rock. "You feel this wall? I want you to concentrate, focus all your thoughts on this rock, as if your life depended on it. Can you do that?"

"Ja, Mamma, I can do that."

"I want you to focus so hard on the stone you become it. Do you understand me?"

"I . . . I don't think so."

"It's about willpower. Leidah, you can choose what you become. You have to will it. Offer yourself to the rock."

"But if I give myself to the rock, what will the rock give to me?"

"Yes, exactly. Good girl. It is an exchange—like a conversation—a give-and-take. The rock creates a space for you to crawl into."

"But I don't want to get lost—you said not to get lost—I don't want to disappear."

Maeva's tone is urgent. "Trust me. This magic is inside you; it runs deep, and all you have to do is allow it."

"Who gave it to me? Elves, trolls? Witches?"

"That's not important."

"Did you give it to me?"

Maeva pauses. *Time to tell the truth.* "Yes, I suppose it is from me. But I could also say it is from the spirits of the land. Or the gods." Then quietly, "Or your father."

"Pappa? I've never seen him do anything like this. And I've never seen you do it either."

Maeva smacks the rock again. "Leidah, listen to me! Stop doubting and asking questions. If you believe you can do it, you will become. Think only of the rock. Nothing else, ja?" Maeva closes her eyes. Tuning into the rush of the water, she opens herself up, allowing all of her senses to relax. Then, she can sense it: the hum and shape of Leidah's mind, tumbling and twisting.

Rock, rock, rock . . . hard, sharp, smooth, dark . . . damp, cool, wet . . .
puddle, pool, waterfall, hush shush rush rain ripples currents sinking down
down down down falling . . . do rocksfallyessssssshhhhsssssssshhhhhuuu-
uuushhhhsssshiftingscrapingdriftingspirallingsinkingsoftnessswirlingblue-
girldiving—

Then, quiet. No more words. Only the noise of the water. "Leidah?
Lei-lee? Are you there?" She slaps the rock, saying her daughter's name
over and over. Somehow, she feels Leidah leaving, then disappearing completely, as if caught in an undertow. *Oh God. The water.*

Maeva dives into the pool, frantic.

She follows the darkness to the very bottom of the pond, her eyes
open, her arms grasping, searching. The guilt of everything Maeva has
done—the secrets, the lies, the shame, the truth of who and what Leidah
is, all the time lost—dragging her body down and down, sinking like a
stone. Her mouth full of bubbles, opening and closing, a fish gasping for
air. Her lungs tighten, bursting with need. *What have you become?*

Her arms flail and splash. A strong current swirls under her, shooting
her body upwards, into the light. Gasping, she breaks the surface. She
floats on her back, sculling the water away, gulping for air.

Directly above her, in the blue sky, is Leidah.

I must be hallucinating . . .

She is suspended in the air, like a dragonfly above the pond, a huge
grin on her face. Shouting with glee, flapping her arms, she calls to her
mother below.

"Mamma—I can fly!"

Maeva can't believe her eyes. Leidah hovers, then takes a step, her blue
feet almost the same hue as the pond. As soon as her toe touches the surface, the reverie pops; she falls with a splash.

Maeva doesn't waste time. She dives down, but Leidah is already sinking. She propels herself easily, grabbing her daughter around the waist.
Underneath her legs, Maeva feels the same push as before—*an invisible
hand?*—and they get thrown onto a big rock in the shallows. Gasping,
she drags the animal mask out of the water and thumps it down beside
Leidah. Its eye holes stare back at both of them.

Maeva pushes wet hair away from Leidah's forehead. "You did it—you saved us. Saved us from drowning."

Leidah is incredulous. "I did? How?"

"You shot us right out of the water." She smiles, her nose leaning in to touch the girl's.

"That's when I became the wind. Before that, I was the bubbles. And the muck. Even a fish, I think."

"You see. You *can* become anything you set your mind on. You walked on water, Lei-lee! I've only known one other person who could do that."

"Who, Mamma?"

No more secrets, she decides.

"Your father."

Fish

He swims the depths of her. Feels the power of that tiny elfling expanding, stretching far beyond her mother. An earthquake tremors across his fins.

Is she . . . becoming me?

He opens his gills, absorbing the beautiful, disturbing truth of such a magical creature as she.

This is no human child.

She was not conceived from any man.

No bearded husband.

This girl is mine.

What Was

The crowd of women spilled out of the church, then circled tightly away from Maeva, waiting for the menfolk to untie the horses and wagons. Maeva huddled under the willow tree in front of the church. The sun was hidden now by heavy grey clouds, threatening snow. She prayed for a storm. For Pieter to feel her urgency to escape this place and the women who stood guard.

Unna spoke loudly enough for her to hear. "I held it. But something didn't feel quite right."

The girl's mother piped in. "Of course not. Thank God you were on holy ground."

The others nodded and murmured. Maeva could feel their eyes boring into her. She jiggled her daughter, pretending not to notice.

"I'm surprised she can even set foot inside without consequence."

"The consequence will come later, I'm sure. The devil works in mysterious ways. But God will always strike at that which must be purged from us. Amen."

The rest of the women muttered an "Amen." The crowd moved as one closer to her. Birgit pushed Unna forward. Maeva stepped back, hugging Leidah close.

"Fru Aldestaed? My mother and I would like to extend some neigh-bourly hospitality, with a bit of *sengemat*, as Pastor Knudsen suggested. We will call on you soon."

Maeva tried not to react, though her stomach churned at the thought. "*Tusen takk*, but I am quite fine. Fru Tormundsdatter ensured I was prop-erly stocked with food."

The entire throng gasped at the name of the old midwife. Maeva cringed at her own stupidity.

Birgit marched toward her, hissing, "How dare you mention that witch's name on holy ground."

Maeva looked over her shoulder, willing her husband to appear, to wit-ness the scene that was unfolding. She spotted him laughing with Hans, the two men patting their mare's mane, oblivious. *Please, Pieter. I need you!*

Birgit took another step. Maeva could feel her breath. "How dare you refuse our kindness? But what can we expect from a Lapp? Ungrateful heathens, all of you."

Maeva didn't dare say a word.

The widow leaned dangerously close to Leidah. "We know the truth about you, and this *thing* you hold in your arms." She pointed a crooked finger and wagged it in Maeva's face. "How a good man like Pieter could end up with you, only God knows. Or perhaps you *do* know. You arrived the day my Antum was taken by the sea. A strange coincidence, don't you think?"

Maeva began to protest the ridiculous accusation, but Unna chirped in, "He should have married that other girl, right, Mamma? What was her name again?"

Maeva frowned. *What other girl?*

Birgit smiled and tilted her head. "Hilde, if I recall. From the north. Truly, not much better than you—a Lapp or a Finn, I can never tell the dif-ference, you're all the same—selling her self-respect along with her cheap thread and trinkets. But she stopped coming to market when you showed up. Curious, isn't it?" Her eyes narrowed, honing in. "You may have be-witched Pieter Aldestaed, even our pastor, by batting those lashes. But you cannot bewitch God. Or Magistrate Innesbørg."

Finally, Pieter spotted her, the smile on his face fading as he registered the crowd closing in on his wife and daughter.

" 'What the wicked fears will come upon him, but the desire of the righteous will be granted.' Proverbs 10:24," Birgit pronounced with indignation.

Maeva lifted her chin. "But I say to you that everyone who is angry shall be guilty before the court . . . Whoever says 'you fool' shall be guilty enough to go into a fiery hell." She stretched taller, casting a shadow over the older woman.

Pastor Knudsen appeared at the top of the steps of the church. "*God dag*, ladies. My heart is warmed by the sight of such fellowship. Fru Aldestaed, we wish you and Leidah blessings and good health." He focused solely on Birgit. "Don't we, Fru Vebjørnsdatter?"

She responded by striding past Maeva in silence, holding on to her own daughter. The other women followed a few steps behind, sheep in her flock.

Maeva exhaled, her legs shaking. Pieter held her gaze as he moved through the throng. She muttered a "Thank you" to the pastor, burrowing into the safety of her husband's arms. He led her to the wagon, and lifted both her and Leidah up onto the seat. As the horse began to trot forward, Maeva heard the crowd erupt.

Unna screamed. The young girl raised her arm for all to see. The skin was bright red, blisters so large even Maeva could see them from the moving wagon. Pieter snapped the whip, and the horse trotted on.

Lars Knudsen scrambled to keep the peace amidst the flurry of women alighting on the girl.

"She's cursed! Her skin has been burned!"

"As if the devil himself has touched her!"

"Or the devil's wife."

Maeva turned her back on the flock, the words of Birgit Vebjørnsdatter ringing in her ears.

What the wicked fears will come upon them.

What Is

The sun dives like a fish into a pool of purple sky. An owl hoots somewhere outside. There is no wind today, no stories rushing through the trees. Even the bugs are still. The clunky noise of my spoon, too loud.

I chew my kelp slowly, counting each bite to keep my mind busy. Careful not to watch Mamma too much. Careful not to even glance at Pappa and spill the secrets of the day in a single gush. Mamma sits by the fire, a quilt wrapped tightly around herself. She is freezing, unable to warm up from our adventure in the afternoon. I know I can't tell Far what happened—how would I explain it?—but I am bursting. I can feel the words climbing up the back of my throat, ready to jump off the edge of my lips—*Mamma and I went swimming and I found a thing inside a cave and we almost drowned but I saved us by changing into wind*—but I gulp my milk instead, glad for something to fill my mouth. Pappa eyes Mamma, then me. He sips his tea, his fingers gripping the mug as if it might suddenly jump away from him.

"Can you walk on water, Pappa?"

His face wrinkles up. "Only Jesus can do such things, child."

I wonder why Mamma told me he could. I want to say, *I can do it, too,* only I don't.

I wiggle in my seat, feeling dampness under my skirt. "Can I be done?"

"Nei. Finish eating. How will you grow if you don't eat?"

"I'm done growing."

Pappa's mouth curls up on one side. "I don't think so, Lei-lee. Someday you will be taller than Mor, taller than me. But only if you eat your fish. And drink your milk."

I know he's lying. I push the last two pieces of fish around on the plate, using my fork like a paddle. They are so sad. No water to float them out to sea. I reach for the water jug, my arm accidentally knocking my cup over.

"Oh, Leidah . . . It's fine, a little spilled milk, nothing to fret over—go get a cloth." Pappa lifts my fork and starts rescuing the potatoes from drowning.

I stand up, milk dripping off the table and my apron. I grab the towel from the rain tub and start sopping up the milk.

"Do I have to eat my dinner? It's soggy now."

"And whose fault is that? Hmm?" His face folds into a frown.

"I know, Pappa. But I'm not hungry." I pick up my cup. "I'm still thirsty, though."

He reaches over and tousles my hair. "Oh, Lei-lee, you can have more milk. But first, wipe the seat. There's a puddle! And under your feet, little one—did you spill the entire jug?"

I pick my foot up to check the floor. Sure enough, there is a puddle. I quickly put my hands under my bottom, feeling where the dampness started. My skirt is soaked. I bite my lip and peer at Mamma, hoping she can save me. Hoping Pappa doesn't see that it isn't milk under me.

"What is it? Let me see, child. What in the world?"

His eyebrows go up and down, and then meet in the middle of his forehead.

"Did you have another accident, like this morning?"

Not knowing what to say, I grab my empty cup and pretend to drink.

Pappa rubs his beard. "Maeva? Mae!"

She stares into space.

"Mae, Leidah's had an accident again. Did you hear me?"

He doesn't see that my mother needs saving, not me.

"Mamma isn't feeling well, Pappa."

"What?" He stares at Mamma. "Are you ill?" He reaches out, feels her forehead, pulls his hand away.

"Does she have a fever?"

He shakes his head, marches toward the door, grabbing his coat and hat, moving faster than the wind.

I rush after him. "Pappa? Where are you going?"

"Take care of your mother, Lei-lee, until I get back."

"From where?"

He calls over his shoulder before the door slams. "Jakobsen's."

Mamma jumps to her feet, the quilt falling to the floor. Her eyes meet mine. *The doctor.* Without saying a word, we both drop to our knees and, using the quilt, sop up all the water that is leaking from my skin. But the more I move, the more water pours out of me—from my feet, my hands, my back—even my belly is sweating.

"What is it, Mor? Why am I sweating so?"

"It's not sweat, girl."

I stop mopping and press against my dress. A flood of water seeps out. *Bastard in hell.* "Mamma. Am I melting?"

She stops. I want her to laugh and say, *Melting? What a silly thing to say!* Instead she takes my hand, looking at the map of lines on my palm. Her fingers are freezing.

"I always knew it would come, but I thought the sea would claim me, not you."

"Mamma, please—no nonsense—you're scaring me."

She drops my hand and grabs my face. Her skin so rough, it scratches my cheeks.

"I won't let you disappear, child. We'll figure this out, ja?" Her forehead is full of lines, like deep ruts on a road, the skin peeling and dry. Her lips, chapped and bloodied.

"Your hands are cold, Mamma."

"I know, child, I know—no time to worry about such a small trifle— we must clean up and get you in bed before the doctor gets here."

"But it's not bedtime—I don't want to go to sleep."

"Leidah, don't argue—you must get into bed so we can soak up all the water or put a pot under you or something, ja?"

I nod. Soon, Pappa will figure out that I am leaking—or melting—and if he does, Mamma might be in trouble. For what, I don't know exactly. But somehow, he will blame her. I reach toward her, but she spins me around.

"Go into your room and change into your woolens. Climb into bed and stay there. I will get some blankets. For now, that will have to do."

I climb the ladder, my wet feet slipping as I run to my room. I strip down, leaving my clothes in a heap. My skin is so hot to the touch. I smush my belly. Drops of water slide along it. I wipe them away, but new ones appear, until they are running down my legs like rain. A puddle grows at my feet. I pull on my woolens, feeling the roughness against my wet skin. Mor comes with the blankets, tucking them under my bottom. I can feel her mind buzzing. She tucks my hair behind my ear, her fingers like ice.

Pappa arrives as I am falling asleep—I can hear the front door creak open. I can feel that the bed is full of water. I stay perfectly still, uncertain what to do. Mamma whispers from the next room. She can hear my thoughts, like she could at the waterfall.

"There is nothing to do, Leidah. Lie down and wait."

I lean back on the pillow. The sound of dripping makes me have to pee.

Downstairs, Far is playing host.

"*Vil du ta deg en drink?*"

"Nei, Pieter, I never drink on the job. Dulls the senses."

"Of course, of course. Shall we?"

I hear feet on the ladder. I pretend to be asleep.

"Maeva, my dear? The doctor is here."

"*God kveld, Fru Aldestaed.*"

"*God dag, Doctor Jakobsen.*"

"*Hvordan står det til?*"

"*Bare bra, takk—*"

"You are not fine, Mae—she's not fine, Doctor."

"Thank you, Pieter. I can handle the patient from here. Now, let's have a look."

I want to get out of bed, but I don't. I barely breathe, listening.

"Uh-hmm. Breathe in and out. Stick out your tongue. Hmmm. *Ja vel.*"

"What is it, Doctor?"

"Can you leave us for a moment, Pieter? You understand, it will only be a moment."

I hear Far's footsteps. I shut my eyes, hoping he doesn't check on me. But then, I feel a hand on my forehead. I snore ever so slightly, but it doesn't fool him. He clicks his tongue.

"You are burning up, Leidah—are you feeling sick, too?"

I shake my head no, more heat racing across my cheeks. He sits on the bed, and then jumps up. Water gushes out from it.

"What in the devil? Leidah, sit still, don't panic. Pappa needs to . . . Oh, Christ. Doctor Jakobsen!"

The doctor rushes into the room, shirtsleeves rolled up, round glasses slipping down his pointy nose. He's a gnome next to my father, eyes shifting from side to side, as if something may attack him. So this is who my mother is afraid of? He doesn't seem scary. Pappa lights the candle on the side table and holds it up to my face. I blink. I smile. Pappa frowns. Then he holds the candle low, peering under the bed.

"What is it, Pieter, what's gotten you so . . . What the devil?"

I watch as the two men crouch down to see the large puddle, growing before their eyes. Doctor Jakobsen takes off his glasses, leaning even closer. He sniffs the air, then puts a finger into the water. Tastes it and raises his eyebrows.

"Oh my. I wonder how . . ."

"Our daughter seems to be having trouble holding her bladder lately—perhaps an infection of some sort."

"Nei, Pieter. It's not urine. This will sound strange, but it appears to be salt water."

"That's impossible—where would it come from? Sea-water doesn't just appear."

"Is there a leak somewhere? The roof, perhaps?"

I curl up my knees and lie on my side, holding my legs tightly, as the men search everywhere. The roof, the walls, the bed—everywhere except where it actually is coming from.

I listen for Mor in the next room, but she is quiet. I am on my own.

I wait while they try to think it out—faulty roof, an open window, a prank by a naughty child—"Leidah would never do anything of the sort, I assure you," says Far. Finally, the doctor holds his hands out, like rain is about to fall from the rafters. He asks me to sit up so he can examine me. I shake my head slowly, knowing the minute I move, more water will flood out.

"Leidah, do as the doctor asks. Be a good girl, ja?"

I sit up. Water rushes out of either side of the mattress. The doctor gently pulls me forward. Another gush. He touches my leg. A squishy wet spot oozes out of my thigh.

"Something is very much . . . out of the ordinary."

My father clasps his hands in front of his chin.

"Temperature is high, colouring is off. Why, she seems to be—I mean, her hands. Oh. Oh my."

Doctor Jakobsen stops for a moment. Brings my fingers even closer to him. I hate being seen. I want to ball my fingers into a fist so badly to hide the blue, and the web. But I don't. Doctor Jakobsen looks at my father, his face all mouth and eyes. Pappa nods once. The strangeness of his daughter, the secret that is me, in that single nod. *I'm sorry, Pappa.*

"Let me see your hands, Pieter." Pappa seems surprised, but he holds his hands out. The doctor slides his glasses down his nose and squints. "Hmm. A bit of *spekk*-finger here, on the ring finger, but nothing too serious. You've been out sealing recently?"

Far pulls his hands back, crossing his arms, his face like a closed door. "Never. Not my trade anymore. It's only a bit of swelling from working the nets."

"Camphor oil should do the trick." The doctor takes off his glasses, then smiles at me. "Can you spread your fingers for me? Huh. Fascinating. I've heard rumours, of course, but I didn't believe them. There is a condition known as syndactyly, but it's quite rare. How long has she—it—the hands been this way?"

"Since birth."

"But something could have been done to stop the fingers from fusing together. Why didn't you consult me?"

"Her mother. She . . . didn't think it necessary to involve doctors when Leidah was born."

Jakobsen stops and stands upright. "Ah. I understand. If I recall, that was a particularly challenging time in the village, for everyone."

Because of me?

"Thankfully, the world has progressed a little more since then. Science has become the reigning voice of reason. I can thank God for that." He chuckles. Pappa's mouth pulls at the corner, but he doesn't smile.

Far sits down on the window ledge. I rush to his side, slipping through the puddle before I hug him. He picks me up on his lap.

"Oh, my little *kanin*, it's fine. Shh, no need to cry now."

"I don't know what to say, Pieter. Quite frankly, I am dumbfounded."

"It's a birth defect, Doctor—one that hasn't caused her any pain."

Defect?

"Nei, nei, not her hands. Confounding, to be sure, but not what I am concerned about. Clearly, she is a healthy girl—though a bit small for her age. How old are you, child?"

"She is seven."

"Almost eight, Pappa!"

I wiggle out of his arms to stand as straight as I can. Stretching my chin up to the ceiling. Water drips down my neck, tickling me. I quickly wipe it away, tiptoe tall.

"Eight years old! Well, we can't have an almost eight-year-old leaking everywhere, can we?" The doctor tweaks my nose, then puts his glasses back on. "I am perplexed by all this—this—water, if that is indeed what it is. In all my years, I have never . . . Perhaps it's some other rare condition, though I've never heard of anything of the sort."

"Like what?"

"Something caused by the defect. Of course, I can't be certain. Unless . . ."

"Unless?"

"It can only mean excessive perspiration of some sort, cause unknown, though certainly glandular in origin. I don't think it's serious, but then again, dehydration may be a real concern."

"But that can't be possible—I mean, the amount of water is—well, it simply can't be sweat."

"I can't speak to that until she is properly examined. And I certainly can't treat her without a diagnosis. Now, your wife . . . that's another matter."

Pappa's face changes. "Why?"

"It seems to be what we call hypothermia—the only diagnosis that matches her symptoms. Her temperature is quite low, she can't stop shivering, her skin is almost blue." He looks over at me, at my hands, and clears his throat. "If I hadn't seen Leidah's colouring, I'd say she has cyanosis. But perhaps this is hereditary. At any rate, her pulse is slow, her breath laboured. There's also some hallucinating, it would seem."

"Hallucinating?"

Doctor Jakobsen pushes his glasses up to sit on his head, his thumb and finger pinching the skin between his eyes. "I hesitate to mention it, but hallucinations are common in cases of hypothermia, so it seems to fit."

Pappa crosses his arms.

"She has been mumbling, in and out of sleep. Some strange . . . accusations, for lack of a better word."

"Accusations? Of what?"

"Not what, Pieter. Who."

Pappa swallows. I copy him, knowing it must have something to do with him.

"What has she been saying?" Far asks.

"Perhaps it was just remnants of a dream. But she seems to think you have stolen something from her."

"What? What does she claim I have stolen from her?"

"She woke up insisting you've taken some kind of inheritance, a family heirloom? When I pressed her for details, she burst into manic sobbing, then fell back asleep almost immediately. Or perhaps she was asleep all along, in the throes of a nonsensical dream."

I giggle, wanting him to see how silly this all is.

The doctor smiles. "Who can know a woman's mind? Certainly not her husband, Pieter. I myself gave up years ago, and my wife thanks me for it." He shakes his head. "Though I am concerned there might be a more serious problem with Maeva's level of . . . ah, instability. Perhaps warranting further examination."

"And Leidah? Would she have to—"

I grab Pappa's hand. *Nei, nei, nei!*

"Yes, I think that would be wise. But no need to worry yet until I have sent the proper letters to the appropriate people."

Pappa sinks against the window ledge. I wipe my nose on his sleeve, water dripping off my lip. *Pappa, don't let them take us!*

"Unfortunately, it would mean admitting both of them for a longer stretch of time somewhere—perhaps a fortnight or two, possibly in different facilities. Maybe even longer. In the meantime, Maeva's medical condition is worrisome. Has she recently been submerged in cold water? For a long period of time? It's the only explanation I can think of—she would have had to be submerged for hours for such a condition to develop. Though, given Leidah's state, perhaps there's a connection."

My mother calls from the other room. Pappa nods for me to go. The doctor begins to clean his glasses on a handkerchief. I run out of the room as he lists off what must be done: warm blankets, head and neck covered, heated stones under the armpits . . .

"What is it, Mamma?"

She reaches out for my hand. Her skin is even colder, a shade of blue almost the same as mine. My fingers are so happy to be wrapped in hers. We are both blue—twins. *Like sisters, aren't we, Mor?* I sing the words in my head.

Her voice sounds old and tired. "You must hide what we found today."

"Hide it? Where?"

"I don't know, child. Somewhere Far won't think of."

"Maybe in the sewing room? He doesn't go in there."

"Nei, child, that is too easy . . . Then again you could be right. Hiding it in plain sight may be our only option." Her voice drops to a whisper.

"Should anything happen to me—anything at all—if Pappa takes me away—"

"Mamma, you're scaring me."

"Listen to me. If something happens, you must find the quilt I have been making for you. The see-through pink one—"

"What's all this talk about?"

I jump at Pappa's words. Mamma closes her eyes. He walks over to me, taking my hand.

"Lei-lee, the doctor wants to examine you—it won't hurt—a routine check-up. Your first one! I will be right here taking care of your mother." He studies Mamma's face. She ignores him, rolls her head to one side, keeping her eyes shut. Pappa gently pushes me toward the door.

"I will take good care of her, little *kanin*, don't worry."

I wait a long time for sleep to come, bundled in layers of blankets to soak up the water. The doctor is gone; he said he needed an expert to tell him what to do. I'm not sure if that means there is something horribly wrong with me, or if I am, as he put it, a "fascinating case." He wants to write to a hospital clinic, to see if there have been any other cases like me. I don't like being a "case," and I told him that. He laughed, calling me a brilliant mind. Pappa agreed that his girl was indeed special.

Special. A case. A special case. I roll over. I don't want to be special anymore. Especially if it means being sent away.

I kick the blankets off. The night is quiet, but I hear shuffling from the next room. Whispers, short and tight. Then footsteps.

Pappa leaves the bedroom, a candle in his hand, shadows jumping on the wall ahead of him. I sneak to the ladder, forgetting about the leaking for a moment. He fetches things from downstairs: a mug of tea, a hot stone wrapped in a towel. I tiptoe back to my bed, pulling the covers up. Watching as he walks by my door. He drops the stone onto the floor, and curses. Mamma calls to him, asking if he is hurt. He doesn't answer, shutting the door to their room.

Wait . . . Am I still leaking? I pull back the covers to see. I feel down my legs; my woolens are damp, but don't seem any wetter. Which means the water has stopped. I sit up, excited to show both of them. To tell Pappa that I'm not a special case anymore.

Then I hear hissing in the dark. "I deserve some answers, Mae. What in God's name were you thinking?"

"Not now, Pieter. It's late. I'm not up to an interrogation."

"Interrogation? A husband doesn't deserve to know what his wife is doing behind his back? I told you years ago, no more trips to the water. And to bring Leidah! What have you done to our girl?"

"For pity's sake, I've done nothing. The water has been leaking out of her for a week. You simply failed to notice."

"So you take her to the waterfall? Did you not consider that it might make it worse?"

"She needs to learn how to swim. That's all we were doing."

"You can't expect me to believe that."

"Please, Pieter, stop. You'll wake Leidah."

"Just tell me. Was it worth it?"

"Whatever are you talking about?"

"You know exactly what I mean. What did you tell Doctor Jakobsen?" Mamma doesn't answer. "He told me what you said. I can't even begin to understand what you were thinking, what would possess you to say such things, to do such things as you did today, when you know damn well I am only trying to protect you, protect our daughter. And now we must suffer a doctor's intrusion."

"At your request! I did not ask for that."

"Nei, you did not . . . But your condition forced my hand."

"Condition? What condition? I am *not* hysterical."

"I meant the hypothermia, but hysterical is a good diagnosis . . . Jakobsen thinks you both need to be examined. Committed to a hospital."

"And what do you think, husband?"

"I don't know what to think . . . I don't know what to do with you anymore, Mae."

"I ask only one thing. If you love me—"

209

"You know I have loved you from the moment I first saw you. I told you the day I married you that I will love you until the end of our days—"

"The end is here, Pieter. I'm telling you now, you must believe me or—"

"Or what? You'll disappear? Shrivel up and die? That is a bedtime story, a tale for children."

"It has more truth in it than any story about Jesus you feed her."

"Except that Jesus is *real*. Jesus gives her hope—"

Mamma laughs. "Hope? Hope in what?"

"Acceptance. Love. Hope that she *can be* like everyone else, in God's eyes."

"Rubbish. Leidah is *not* like anyone else, nor will she ever be accepted by this town. Whether you choose to see it or not, your wife and child are anything but ordinary."

"My God, woman, don't I know that!"

"Then open your eyes to what's in front of you. This magic is strong; it is not something to be toyed with. It is more real than you can possibly know. You are married to living proof of the old ways, husband. I may have lost myself—for your sake, to be your wife—but I haven't forgotten what you have stolen. Jesus, Pieter, how could *you* forget what I am?"

"I have forgotten nothing. You don't know what's real anymore. There is only what's here, right now. You, me, Leidah. We will grow old together and die in this house, content—"

"Christ, Pieter! Can't you see? I am drying up; I am a withered, rotting apple—"

"You are just tired, worry getting the better of you."

"*Nei!*"

The small word, like a clap of thunder. I pull the covers over my head.

"It is happening. For Leidah's sake, please."

"Don't. You will not drag our daughter into this."

"She is seeping water like a sponge! Do you not see that it's connected? By God, Pieter, if you love me—if you love our daughter—you will do what's right and return what is mine."

"I can't."

"You mean you *won't*. But if you don't, you will lose us both."

"Is that a threat?"

"You said yourself that Jakobsen wants to take her. Take us both. Is that what you prefer? To have us locked up like animals? Is that better than—"

"You leaving?" His voice cracks. "Why can't you admit it? You have wanted to leave since the day I rescued you. You thought I didn't know? For God's sake! All these years, even when you seemed content, I knew it, underneath. Do you think I can't see how absent you are? How much you've left already? How you yearn for your old life?"

"Love has grown between us over the years. You must feel that."

"Ja, Mae, I do."

Silence. No one says a word. I pull the blanket off my head, listening. *Is it over? Can we sleep now?*

"But love is not enough to keep you here, is it?"

"It's enough to save us. Save our daughter. I'm sick, Pieter. Why don't you believe me when I tell you the cure for all of this?"

"Because it's not true."

"The truth doesn't care if you believe in it. I am asking—nei, begging—for you to save me. I never expected Leidah to become so . . . For the pull of the old ways to be so strong. I thought she'd take after you—I prayed she would—I wished with all my heart for her to be like every other child."

"She's a little different, yes—like her mother. But underneath, she's no different from anyone—like her father." His voice is soft. "She's a perfect combination of her parents."

"The gods have struck you blind."

"You are the delusional one, for Christ's sake. Jakobsen's diagnosis explains everything. A hospital stay would do you—all of us—some good."

I hear the door slam. Pappa's footsteps, loud on the ladder.

Then, the clock: *ticktickticktick*. Almost as though time is running away, too.

And Mamma, crying herself to sleep.

A Dream

Maeva's tears don't stop. Even in dreams.

A shriek from outside. She rushes down the ladder, still weak but moving with a mother's speed. She knows when her daughter needs her, the call unmistakable. She throws open the door. A snowstorm—in September—blows in, a white flurried demon.

She sees Pieter in the squall, running out of the barn, pitchfork in hand.

Leidah is barefoot, on the last step of the porch, pointing at the yard.

Then, the oddest sight: a fat black snake slithering across a field of fresh white snow. Without a second thought, she jumps off the last step to scoop up her daughter. Pieter throws the pitchfork. The weapon spins end over end in circles, except it's no longer a pitchfork; it is something else, sharp and dangerous, stained with old blood. It hits its mark, the hook splitting the snake down its middle. Red guts spill onto pristine white.

Leidah starts to sob.

Pieter pulls the metal out of the ground. Shakes off the pink flesh and picks up the dead reptile. "There, there, my little *kanin*. It's dead. No need to cry," he croons, holding the carcass out for her to see.

Leidah snivels, then puts her face into her mother's neck, whispering, "But he was our friend. Right, Mamma?"

Maeva wakes up crying, unsettled and shaken. She shudders, realizing what the pitchfork had become the moment it left Pieter's hand.

A hakapik.

What Is

Morning wakes up without any sound, not even birds chirping. I can't even hear the tick-tock of the clock. Out my window, a grey fog hides the sky. I roll over to face the wall; I want to hide, too. Forget everything from the last few days. Especially the doctor's examination, Pappa's sadness, Mamma's crying. The strange thing hiding inside my wardrobe. I curl up into a ball under the covers and pretend to sleep.

Pappa's heavy footsteps are loud.

"Wake up, little *kanin*—you are coming with me today."

I mumble from under the blankets. *"Hvor,* Far?"

"To town. Put on your nice apron."

I throw the quilts off and let out a small whoop. Another trip to Ørken, so soon after church?

Mor calls from the next room. "Into town, Pieter? What could you possibly need?"

He winks at me and leans around the door.

"I need to collect my pay. The shipmaster is in town for one day only, so I have no choice. Your fever has broken, your colour is almost back. You need rest, Mae, and you don't need us underfoot. Sleep. We'll be back before sunset."

"But, Pieter, I don't think Leidah should be outside, given her condition."

"'Condition'?" He steps into the bedroom, where I can't see him. "Are you agreeing with Doctor Jakobsen now?"

"Fine, never mind, go."

Pappa walks into my room, winking at me again. I pull open my wardrobe to find only my grey apron. Then I remember: my other dress is hanging on the clothesline, still damp from the swimming lesson two days ago. I quickly pat my thighs, my hips. Dry. *Phew.* I reach for the grey dress.

"Nei, Leidah—we aren't going to church, child."

Pappa moves toward the wardrobe. The thing—Mamma's secret—is at the bottom of it. I shut the door quickly and hold the dress in front of me.

"But my other one is wet, Pappa."

Far frowns. "But surely you have more than that."

Mor calls out, annoyed. "We can't afford such luxuries, husband. She can wear her barn clothes. No need to impress, it isn't a day of worship."

He slides his tongue along his teeth, as if trying to remove a piece of meat.

"Perhaps it's time for a little luxury." He holds my shoulders, his eyes shiny. "Why don't we stop at the market? You can pick out some fabric for Mamma to sew you a new dress, a birthday dress. What do you say, little *kanin?*"

I clasp my hands together in delight. "Can we?"

Mor stumbles into the room, holding on to the wall. "Pieter, no. I will weave some new material. You know we can't afford it—don't get her hopes up."

"The money I am owed from Selzenberg for the salmon I caught last week—it sold for a good price—there should be a little extra."

"That extra is to satisfy our bellies, not throw away on frivolities."

She rests her head against the door-frame, closing her eyes for a moment. Her hair falls in a tangle of knots, barely hiding the blue of her skin. I swallow hard, wondering how she could have aged so much overnight. She peers at me through the veil of hair. I bite my lip, trying not to feel it, but a knowing is inside me, clinging to the back of my throat: Mamma is sick. Very, very sick. Pappa doesn't see it. I drop the dress onto the bed and sit down, feeling too heavy to move. Mamma shouldn't be out of bed.

"Fine, Pieter. Go and buy the fabric. I will sew her a birthday dress."

"Nei, Mamma—I don't need a new dress."

"Hush, child—it will be your birthday in less than a fortnight—your father is right. It's the perfect time for a little luxury."

She tries to smile. I push down the joy creeping up inside me; though it doesn't feel right, I want that new dress. I shove a finger inside my mouth to stop myself from squealing.

Pappa leans down to pick up the grey dress, his hand on the wardrobe door. Mamma's eyes go big. *Oh, no.* He stands with his back to the dead thing inside.

"That settles it, then. To Ørken we go."

Mor sighs after he leaves the room. *Thank the gods. Right, Mamma?*

On market day, the pier is a stewpot: sweaty bodies bumping against one another in the warm sun, with so many smells. Vendors calling back and forth, shouting out their wares—"Catch of the day like no other, still swimming it's so fresh!"—while people push forward for a better view, for the best price. Children and dogs play chase between stalls. I hold tight to my *dukke*, and to Pappa's hand, ignoring the itchiness of my wool dress, squeezing his fingers with excitement. My gloves are itchy, too; people stare at them, but I don't care. I love being here, with Pappa.

Though market day happens every third Friday until winter, I never get to go. I've been a few times, when I was little. I only remember bits and pieces, but I do remember Mamma hating every minute. She had to talk to people without Pappa. Looking people straight in the eye—asking for the best price—too much for her. Accepting whatever they said with a quick nod, she emptied her pockets of coin without a fight. I'm sure it was to save us—save me—from all those eyes. I remember staring at the ground, all pebbly, uneven. Hiding my hands in pockets or mitts.

Today, my eyes take in everything. I can tell Pappa likes the game of it, joking and laughing with each and every person, in awe of what they're selling, even if it's fish he catches himself on the big boats. Each seller puffs themselves up like roosters, so much so, they shake his hand, spilling secrets as if they were his close friends.

"Why, Pieter Aldestaed—it's been weeks, months, even—where have you been? Can you believe that sleet yesterday? And all of it, gone today—strange weather indeed! Care for a pastry?"

"Not today, I'm afraid," he says. "Though it all smells delicious."

They smile and nod, watching as we move away.

"Quite a wee thing, isn't she?"

"Hasn't grown since the last time we saw her."

"Still wearing those gloves, even in summer. Strange."

I suck on my bottom lip. At least with Mamma, people didn't talk like that. They just stared. I'm not sure which I like better, though I am glad for Pappa's solid hand in mine. He squeezes my fingers, and we keep walking.

He leads us to the edge of the market, the part Mor and I never visited. I have always wondered what the other side was like. *And now you can see it, too, dukke.* I skip alongside Far, jumping to see.

The sea is wide open past the path. Two tall ships sit side by side along the water's edge, their sails hanging limp but for the small winds that blow offshore. The path shrinks almost to nothing, the crowd of people gone. We pass by a hunched old lady weaving baskets and rugs and quilts, and an old man carving and whittling driftwood into shapes. Pappa tips his hat but doesn't stop to chat. We follow the winding path up the hill to the very last stall, sitting on the top of the cliff. It is so close to the edge, it's about ready to tumble into the sea.

It is a small tent, unlike all the others; every side is covered, hiding what's inside. The walls are made of patterned rugs, animal hides, and weavings. A colourful banner hangs off a twisted branch, with a painting of a queen sitting on top of a throne. She holds a snake in one hand and a crescent moon in the other. Spirals of red, orange, and green swirl at her feet, fire licking her toes. A chime hangs below the banner—dripping glass, like icicles—tinkling in the wind. A curtain of beads covers the entrance to the tent.

Pappa points at the small opening. "Shall we go inside, birthday girl?"

Yes! Then I hear a jingly noise.

"I would recognize that voice anywhere. Pieter Aldestaed. At last, you have come!" a sing-song voice calls from inside the tent.

I peer up at Pappa, but his arms are already reaching through the curtain. My feet have stopped jumping.

"I am not the one who leaves, Hilde—need I remind you?"

"Of course, blame is easily laid at my wandering feet!"

Pappa grins and takes off his hat. I look around for where the voice is coming from, but all I see are colours and glittering jewels everywhere—on the walls, the floor, the ceiling; every single inch of the tent sparkles and shines, like a treasure chest. I sigh and spin slowly around, wanting to touch as many shiny things as possible.

Far laughs. "What do you think, little *kanin?*"

"It's the most beautiful place in the world, Pappa."

A woman's voice comes from somewhere. "She doesn't look like you, Pieter—but she has your sense of wonder."

"That she does, Hilde. That she does."

"Come here, child—let me see you."

From the corner of the tent, among the many colours of fabric and fur, a woman appears, as if out of thin air. I take a step back. She is wrapped in blue; long skirts drag in the dirt, bare feet poking out from layers. Pappa scoops the tiny woman up into his arms and spins her around. Her laughter joins the tinkling of beads and bells swaying in the wind. He puts her down and steps away, still holding her arms so he can look at her.

"It has been too long, hasn't it?"

She nods and giggles. Then both of them turn, remembering I am there. She waves for me to come closer, her small hands moving slowly, as if she thinks I will run away. I hide my doll behind my back and stay where I am, watching her. Pappa does the same, a funny sparkle in his eye. I wonder how he knows such a woman. I wonder what Mamma would think of her, what she might think of the way Pappa is acting. I squint, trying to see her through different eyes.

She is strange, not like any woman I've ever seen. So different from everyone, including Mamma. She is small, with skin so creamy and warm, it looks like honey. Curvy everywhere: Curves on her hips, curves of her cheeks, curves of her lips, her chest. Even her black hair, wild and loose curls hanging down to her waist. It feels rude to stare, but I can't help it. She searches my face, her eyes black, her mouth red like berries. I grab the side of my apron and shuffle into Far's thigh. He pushes me forward. Her hands reach out to me, every finger ringed, wrists wrapped in rope and leather. Without wanting to, I move toward her.

"Ah, Pieter. She is a beauty, like her mother, I suspect. Though one cannot deny she's of a different sort."

"Like her mother, for sure."

"Like mother, like daughter." She points to my doll. "And who is this? Does she have a name?"

My tongue runs away from me. "Nei, she's just my *dukke*. My mor made her for me."

She fingers the mess of red yarn hair. "Isn't that nice." She says it like it's not nice at all. "And how is that wife of yours?"

"That's why I have come. I need help, Hilde. I fear it's happening."

She lets go of me, searching my face. Something has changed. She grabs my hand and, without warning, rips off my glove. I gasp, try to pull back, but she holds me tight. She doesn't even flinch at my blue skin, tracing the lines on my palm, spreading my fingers. Her thumb rubs in between, where the web has grown back. I snatch my arm away and tuck my fingers into my doll's hair. She hands my glove to Pappa. He balls it up, inside his fist.

"You may be right, Pieter. But what can I do?"

"Nothing too complicated." He clears his throat. "But first, Leidah is here to pick out some fabric for a new dress. A birthday dress."

"Is that so? And how old are you, girl?"

"Almost eight."

I watch as my words sink in. Instead of impressing her, they seem to have the opposite effect. "Oh, Pieter, how did the time pass by so quickly? If the old tales are true, then she *is* running out of time."

Pappa takes off his hat, rubs his hair. "I know it—but I don't know what to do."

She points to the chair in the corner for him to sit. She twists a gemstone at her throat, then bends down on one knee in front of me. Her necklace shifts free, almost floating. It is a black butterfly frozen in glass.

"I have been waiting to meet you, little one. I have something very special for you."

"You do? But how did you know I would come?"

"Because I saw it in the water."

"I look in the water all the time. All I see is sand. Sometimes a fish or two."

She laughs deep from her belly, standing up. "Well, isn't that funny? That's exactly what I see, too." She walks over to the wall of fabric and pulls at one of the veils. "Now, would you like your present?"

My belly does a fish flip, but not in a good way. I don't think I want what she has to give me.

"Go on, it's all right. Hilde is going to give you a birthday gift—isn't that nice?"

"But why, Pappa? She doesn't even know me."

Far gets up. "Apologies, Hilde—she's suspicious, like her mother."

"No, Pieter, she is right to be wary. I'm a stranger to her."

"Go on, Leidah." He nudges me toward the curtained wall. She smiles again. But it's all teeth, not reaching her eyes. My feet feel heavy.

"Wait here, child—I will get it, and then your pappa and I will have a little talk, hmm?"

She disappears behind the hanging fabrics and furs. Pappa winks at me, but I see he is sweating.

"Are you hot, Pappa?"

He wipes his forehead with the back of his hand. "Nei, nei. I'm fine."

I don't believe him. I rock on my heels, looking around. It is then that I see the many pairs of eyes staring out at me, through the folds of material.

"What is that? Why are there eyes everywhere?"

He laughs, kissing my hand. "It's perfectly fine, little one—they're dead."

I wonder what part of their being dead makes it fine.

He points to one set of eyes, high up on a shelf. "You see—a small barn owl—stuffed. Harmless."

I walk over to the wall. A grey-and-brown bird perches on top of a blue silk veil, held by a branch. I let out my breath, a bit relieved.

"Here we are—your special present to take home."

Hilde holds out a tiny wooden cage made out of sticks and twigs. I step closer—I can't help wanting to know. The cage is empty.

"But there's nothing inside . . . is there?"

Her eyes sparkle as she leans toward me, the cage between our faces. "A very good question. But you will have to be patient to find out the answer. You see that tiny cocoon on the branch? You must watch carefully. Very soon, perhaps before your birthday, the most beautiful creature will emerge."

"A butterfly. I see them all the time."

"Leidah!" Far shrugs his shoulders at the lady.

She chuckles. "Oh, it's fine, Pieter. She's clever, that's for certain." She hands me the cage. "You might think you know what this is, but you'll have to wait and see. Maybe it will become a butterfly, or maybe not. Maybe it will become something so mysterious, you can't even imagine it. Now go outside with your gift. Watch carefully for any changes—the magic is already happening inside it."

I stare at the cocoon and wonder how it could be anything but an ordinary butterfly.

"Well, what do you say to Hilde?"

I watch my father. Sweat is trickling down his temple.

"What about the dress, Pappa? For my birthday?"

She claps her hands. "Of course, the reason you came! Look around, dear one—you can have anything you like."

I open my eyes bigger. "Anything?"

She opens her arms. "Anything."

Minutes pass, with me running my hand along the hanging fabrics and furs, long ropes with feathers and beads and stones, all tied up in knots. I pull on one long rope—thirteen knots—the bells jingling as I count.

"Not for children," she says.

I frown, wondering why the bells sound so pretty if it isn't supposed to be rung. Hilde steers me to the other side of the tent, where I put my face into some fluffy fur. She laughs, but pulls me back. Pappa shifts from side to side, crossing his arms. There are so many to choose from; I spin and spin, from one side of the tent to the other, like a bird in a barn. Hilde finally stops me, holding out a soft green fabric.

"What about this? It would bring out the green in your eyes." I wrinkle my nose. She reaches for another. "I'll bet you don't have anything bright like this? Am I right?" She pulls out a red silk, with traces of orange shimmering in the light.

I slide a finger down it. "It's so pretty."

She reaches behind one of the folds of fabric and pulls out a small round mirror, with a white carved handle. She holds it out, draping the red silk on my shoulder. "Look in the mirror, to see what you think."

I stare at the girl inside the glass in wonder. Mamma has a small bubbled bit of glass at home, but everything is blurry inside. This mirror is nicer. A girl with big blue-green eyes stares back at me—eyes that are too big. Too far apart for her small round face. Red makes the girl so white, she's barely there.

I open my mouth to speak, and the girl inside the glass does, too. "Twins," I whisper. I hold my doll up to see, too.

Hilde laughs. "Now, aren't you both pretty?"

I pout, watching my twin pout back. Then I stick out my tongue.

She pulls the mirror away, begins folding the fabric. "A good choice, Leidah—you have an eye for quality. This is raw silk, all the way from the East. You see how it is shot with vermilion, when the light hits it?" She holds it to the sliver of sunshine streaming through the slit in the curtains.

Ver-mil-ee-on. It sounds like a fancy snake. I nod in wonder.

"You are drawn to rare things. Like your pappa." She hands him the material and winks. He smirks. I bite my cheek.

"What do you say, Lei-lee?"

"Tusen takk, Fru Hilde."

"Just Hilde, dear one—I never married. Now out you go. We won't be long, I promise."

She pushes me toward the beaded curtain, and I step through, the sound of tinkling shutting me out. I sit down on a stump beside the corner of the tent. Down the path, the market buzzes with people, but I ignore the sounds and lean toward the tent, the cage on my lap.

"She is so precious, Pieter—a true gift."

"Ja, that she is."

"Too young to be left without a mother."

"I know that. Why do you think I'm here?"

"I don't have it anymore, if that's why you've come. I sold it, like I said I would."

"Good. But that's not why I've come."

"Oh . . . I thought it was time. For you to give it back."

"Nei. I can't do that. I will *not* do that."

"We both knew the day of reckoning would come. It belongs to her, after all—it *is* her, for God's sake."

"Don't. It's the last thing I need from you."

"Then why *are* you here? Surely not to reminisce."

"As much as that appeals these days, I need help saving my marriage."

She laughs. "I can't help you with that. By the gods, if Maeva knew where you were!"

"Don't you think I know that? I'm desperate, Hilde."

"Love is never easy."

"Actually, love is simple. If she loves me, she will choose wisely."

"Choose? Doesn't seem like you are giving her *any* choice."

"God, you sound like Mae. I had some hope that this was all an invention of her mind . . . Maybe the doctor is right—she's hysterical and this is all hallucination."

"Doctor? Oh, Pieter. You can't be that naive or stupid. I knew seven years ago, when you showed up at my tent, wild-eyed, already married to a complete stranger, that this day would come. I thought it was the shipwreck—that you were still delirious somehow and simply couldn't see it. I waited and waited for you to come to your senses. But now I know. It's not that you can't see it. It's that you won't."

"I am not giving up my wife."

"You stubborn fool, you can't give up someone—*something*—you never had. You can't tame the sea, or possess the wild. Being a man of the ocean, I thought you would have figured that out by now. Maeva is not *yours*. She never was. She's between this world and that. You stole *her skin*, Pieter—why would you do such a thing if she truly belonged with you?"

Nei, Pappa would never—

"I didn't steal it! She gave it to me. Of her own free will."

"Then do what I told you to do years ago: give it back, and see what happens. Most likely, nothing. The head is gone anyway, so she can't do much with it. Besides, she has Leidah to think of."

"Leave my daughter out of this."

"Leidah is at the centre of it all. That poor girl—it doesn't take a doctor to see what's going on."

Poor girl? What's wrong with me?

"I said, leave it, Hilde—"

"Open your eyes, Pieter. That girl is *blue*. She's the size of a three-year-old, and she's almost eight."

"She's small-boned, that's all. She'll grow . . . The skin will fade as she gets older."

"That child is bluer than a winter's moon. I wonder who she takes after?"

"Careful, woman." Pappa's voice gets low. "You are on dangerous ground."

"I'm sorry, but it has to be said . . . Has she been showing other signs of strangeness?"

"Like what?"

There is a long pause. "Special abilities. The power to change things. The weather or animal behaviour or . . ."

Pappa snorts. "Now you sound like those gossiping church hens."

"I only know what I know. I've seen women like Maeva. Only once, in the Northern Isles, dancing on the shoreline."

"So?"

"They are mostly tall, slender folk, at least on land. Some believe they change form in the water. But small or white-haired, they are not." She stops. "But then again, neither are you."

I feel the sky spinning, a dizzy whirl above me. I look down at my blue hand without its glove. *Who gave me this skin? This hair?*

"It's time to face the truth."

"Don't say it."

"I should have said it years ago. She doesn't belong to you—"

Pappa's voice cracks. "Of course she belongs to me, she's *my wife*."

"I meant the child." She is quiet. "A foolish thing, to hinge everything on someone—*something*—that isn't yours. Wouldn't you agree?"

Who do I belong to?

His voice drops. "By the gods, Hilde, you don't know what you're talking about. Maeva would never . . ." He stops. "I came here for help. Now help me, damn it. Before I do something drastic."

Like sending us away?

"There is no charm for this, no casting that I can do on such a pure form of magic. My ability pales in comparison. What I *can* do is cast a protective net around Leidah. That cage I gave you will do the trick. It will bind her to you even if Maeva decides to leave. With or without her daughter. But I caution you—weigh this carefully. This will have far-reaching consequences, ones even I cannot foresee. Magic has a price when you call upon it, and I cannot predict how high that cost will be."

Mamma will never leave me. She promised . . .

I stand up quickly. Doll and cage drop from my lap to the grass, hitting the side of the tent. I pick up the cage, making sure the cocoon didn't break. The little bundle is stuck, wrapped tightly around the twig perch, where a bird should be. I stick my finger in. It's soft, like milkweed. I wonder what would happen if I rip it open? Would the thing inside die?

The curtain parts; Pappa's face appears through the beads.

"Leidah, what are you doing?"

"Waiting, Pappa. Like the lady told me to."

"Why don't you go wait on the pier? Watch the boats? We have to go home that way, anyway. I'll meet you by the lighthouse in a few minutes."

But the water is so far away.

"Mor told me not to stray—to stay with you. What will she say? What if I get lost?"

"Oh, Lei-lee, you won't get lost. She doesn't even need to know. You can't possibly miss the lighthouse—we can see it from here." He points toward the harbour, down the hill. Standing tall with red and white stripes, the lighthouse is easy to spot. "Surely you can walk down to the pier by yourself? Think of it as a challenge—your first adventure alone! It's not far down the path. Don't start counting till you reach the water—and don't stop to talk to anyone. I will be there beside you before you can count to one hundred, I promise."

He has a funny smile on his face. All teeth, but not happy.

I nod slowly. He pats my head and is gone.

I hug the tiny cage against my chest, feeling a tightness at the back of my throat. *There is nothing to cry about, silly girl,* I tell myself. I will be fine. It's a short walk. Mamma is fine, Pappa is fine, all of us are fine. I match my moving feet to the march of those words. No one is leaving, least of all Mamma. She is at home, sick in bed. She can't possibly leave. Even if she wanted to. *We are all fine. Together, forever. Always.* If I count the number of steps to the lighthouse, I wonder if it will be more than one hundred? That's more numbers than I know. I start counting. The questions inside my head don't stop. Already they are jumping up and down, stomping on all the numbers.

I pass by an old woman, hunched over. She looks up from her knitting and squints at me. Her eyes are icy blue. Somehow, I know those eyes. I walk by as fast as I can.

"Girl," she croaks like an old toad. I stop and turn. Mamma always says to stay away from strangers, but she isn't a stranger. Her hands hold on to two big pieces of wood, clicking and clacking with wool on them. Clickety-clack, clickety-clack.

Like bones.

She smiles and knits, smiles and knits. She doesn't have any teeth. Her face is all wrinkles and brown spots. She stretches her legs under her skirts, and suddenly I know: It's the old woman, the one without feet. The one who floats above everything. The lady no one else can see.

"What did the *heks* give you, hmm? Come show me, child."

I didn't know she could talk.

She snorts and says, "She doesn't give gifts—only takes, that one. Be careful, *jente*." She shakes a bone in the direction of Hilde's tent. "She likes cages. And trapping things inside."

I back away, almost falling down the path. Her words chase me, sneaking into my hair on the wind. I hear those bones—*clickclack, clickclack*—knitting a song into my ears.

The slope of the hill forces my feet into a run. The wind pushes my legs, collecting the words of the song like leaves. It's as if the old lady is right behind me, whispering so close I can feel her breath on my neck. I keep counting aloud: *Elleve, tolv, tretten* . . . But it's no use; the song swims its way onto my tongue.

> *He found his true love, upon the dark sea*
> *And they fit together, like lock and key*
> *Now his heart is a-bleedin', for evermore*
> *For she was a sharp wind that twisted ashore*
> *And now he is keening, riding the cold waves*
> *For the love he did feel has become his slave*
> *His heart is a-drownin', in sorrow and rage*
> *For the bird he once caught has become his cage . . .*

"Girl! Throw that gift into the sea! *Forstår du?* Toss that cursed thing away!"

I run faster, afraid to stop. Faster and faster, away from the dark lady, from all the shiny objects and dead eyes, from all the vermilion, from all the words I wish I hadn't heard. I stop at the lighthouse, hugging the cage, out of breath. I wipe my tears and snot on my sleeve.

A man glares at me. Quickly I tuck my gloveless hand in my armpit.

He walks over to me, his mouth twisted up. "So you're *her*. The Aldestaed girl. Should have known." His eyes are dark and mean. "Abomination. Freak."

I run right past the lighthouse all the way to the end of the pier, breathing hard. Bent over, I drop the cage beside me, holding my knees and heaving.

Fishermen docking their boats don't see me. They move about, pulling in nets and rope, calling out to one another from boat to boat, swearing and praying in the same breath.

"Jesus and Mary, would you look at that? Now there's a big girl coming in—watch for her on port side, boys, and pray she doesn't take us out."

"She can't take us out, she ain't that big—why, she's no bigger than your wife, and you're still standing after last night."

Big bursts of laughter dance around me.

"Aw, it's only the *Leidah* coming in—she's not so big, boys—we've got room for her, move Aldestaed's girl aside."

What? I back up, unsure how they know who I am or why they need to make room for me.

A tall man in a red hat jumps onto the pier from the moving ship and stands in front of a small boat tied to the edge. He bends down to untie the knot of rope. The other men shake their heads and talk to themselves, but no one moves to help.

"You should keep your hands to yourself, Bjørnsen—you know I don't take too kindly to anyone touching my girl." I turn to see the grin on my father's face. He steps forward to shake the hand of the man in the red cap.

"Pieter Aldestaed, if it isn't my brother in the flesh!" I shrink a bit as the two men crush each other in a bear hug. "It's been months—three at least. Where in the devil have you been hiding?"

Pappa grins. "Easy, Hans, you'll flatten me."

"Actually, that's why I moved your boat—to make room for the big girl here." The man slaps the side of the ship.

"Ja, I saw her from the hill—that's why I came down. That and . . ." He pats me. "To collect my daughter here."

The man squats down to my level, his crooked teeth and scruffy face too close. I hold the cage up between us.

"Now hasn't she grown since the last time I saw her! Leidah, meet *Leidah*." He points to the red letters on the side of the ship that spell out *L-E-I-D-A-H*. But they are so faded, it's more like *I-D-A*.

A boat named after me?

"Ja, Lei-lee, meet the other *Leidah*. Hans has known your mother and me for years. This boat is *his* girl."

"In fact, you could say I saved their lives—that you wouldn't be here if it weren't for me and this ol' girl."

Far nods and claps the man's back. "Much gratitude and many curses to you, my friend."

"Sounds about right, Aldestaed. Welcome to the wonderful world of marriage and domestic bliss. Or so I've heard." They laugh as if they have a secret. The other men move about, dragging nets of fish off boats. The sea air is smelly: worms and fish.

"Ja, you haven't had the pleasure yet—but you will, God willing."

"God's will is to keep me married to that old wife the sea." Hans pulls off his cap. "But enough complaining. Do you have time for some ale, a bit of dinner?"

Pappa shakes his head, pulling me into his hip. "Alas, we must return to my wife." His face gets sad. "Maeva, she's not been well. Another time?"

Hans frowns. "Ja, of course. I understand." He points toward the smaller boat. "You might want to check she's tied up properly—I wouldn't want you to lose her." Pappa nods, and Hans grabs his hand one more time.

Far sucks his breath.

Hans lets go. "Sorry—you all right?"

Pappa rubs his finger. "Just an old injury."

Hans reaches out, turning Pappa's hand over. "Ooh, I know seal finger when I see it. You been around a herd? Some pelts, maybe?"

For a moment, Pappa seems angry. "Only fish." His finger is puffy and red, with a big scabby bump on the knuckle, above his ring. "Let's plan for some ale next time. *Ha det bra, bror.*"

"Yes. Let's do that. Goodbye, brother." They hug one last time.

The man didn't even notice my blue skin. I like him for that.

Pappa holds my hand as we walk away. "Is he really your brother, Pappa?"

"Nei, Lei-lee. But he's more a brother to me than any man. He rescued your mor and me a long time ago."

I walk beside him, wondering what he means. We stop in front of his fishing boat, tied to the pier. "What did he rescue you from?"

Pappa drops my hand as he bends down to check the knot. He runs his hand along the edge of the smooth curve of the boat. I copy him, feeling the softness.

"Drowning. He brought us back to land. My boat crashed against the rocks. If he hadn't come, I don't know what might have happened."

"How come I've never met him before?"

He tucks a stray white hair behind my ear. "Mamma . . . She's never liked visitors." He puts his hand on my shoulders. "She's not herself lately. I'm sure you have noticed. She's a bit sad. And a bit . . ."

"Angry." I say the word quietly, as though Mamma is listening.

He begins rubbing the side of the boat. "Ja. Angry. I'm not sure why exactly. Actually, I do know why, but I'm only trying to help her. You don't have to worry. I will make it better. I will make *her* better. And she will be back to her old self again, I promise." His fingers keep rubbing, as if calming an animal. I let my thumb trace the curve, feeling the smoothness. "Do you understand, child?"

I nod, not wanting him to know that I heard everything, that I know exactly why Mor is angry, that what I'm hoping for is for all of it to go away. I don't want her to change back into her old self. I like the new Mor much more than the old Mor. And I don't want her to get better if it means she will leave us. I pick at the hem of a seam, letting my finger rub the skin of the boat. It is then that I notice there are hundreds of soft, tiny hairs.

"Pappa, why does your boat have so many little . . . hairs?"

"It's a special netting—a sheath to increase the speed and buoyancy of the boat."

"A sheath? What's that?"

"It's kind of like . . . a second skin."

I rub the surface of the sheath with the tip of my finger. The back of my neck gets shivers. "A second *skin*. But how could that make the boat better?"

"It cuts through the waves without any resistance. Smooth as silk—like that new fabric we bought. I catch more fish than I ever did before. I suppose it's my good-luck charm."

I lean in, moving so close to the skin my nose touches the boat. It smells like fish. He pulls me back, clears his throat.

"Lei-lee, let's go home. Mor needs us to take care of her, and we have a long ride. Don't forget the gift from Hilde." Far picks up the cage, taking my hand. "Oh, and your glove, child."

He hands it to me, and I grab it, pulling it on gladly. Then I remember. *Oh, no!*

"Where's my doll, Pappa?"

Pappa's eyes get bigger. "Uh-oh. Did you lose her?"

I feel tears growing, a pain in the back of my throat. Far puts an arm around me. "Don't worry, we'll find her."

We walk away from the boat, and I search the pier and on the path for any sign of red. *Where are you, dukke?* The wind whistles around us, carrying shouts of people and boats. But I don't care what they are saying; I only care about *dukke*. We don't talk on the ride home. I keep my eyes on the road, searching for her, even though I know she's not there. Questions upon questions pile up in my mind, an entire mountain of stones. I hold the cage as the wagon steers toward the sinking sun. The sky eats the light bit by bit, with each clip-clop of the horse's hooves, until there is nothing left of the orange ball but a glow along the top of the mountains.

I am cold by the time Far lifts me down from the wagon. He tells me to check in on Mor while he goes to the barn. Clicking at the horse, he starts to walk away from the cottage path.

I throw myself around his waist, hugging him hard.

"What's all this, Lei-lee? Oh, don't worry." He unwraps my arms and bends down to face me, holding my elbows. "I will find her. Maybe *dukke* stayed with Hilde."

I sniff. "I don't think so." I wipe my nose on my sleeve. "She didn't like that lady very much."

He lifts an eyebrow.

"What if she never comes back, Far?"

He doesn't answer. He brushes a tear away from my chin and puts his forehead on mine, but his eyes are dry. He breathes the same air as me, in and out, at the same time. We stay leaning into each other for a long time.

Then he says, *"Jeg elsker du*, my little *kanin."*

"I know, Pappa. I love you, too."

He tousles my hair.

I feel a little better. "Far?"

"Ja?"

I stop, wondering if I should ask. "What's a freak?"

A Gift

Hilde finds the child's doll, abandoned in the grass. She picks up the ugly toy, aghast at the poorly made thing. Immediately, a surge of intense heat singes her hand. She drops it in pain. *What in the world?* In an instant, she knows what it is. *This is no doll.* She holds it by the hair, carrying it inside the tent. She drops it on the small table, fans out the red mess of yarn, piece by piece, and then slowly draws the flickering candle nearer.

Takk, child.

What Was

I n the dusk light, crows gathered in the yard.

Winter had arrived, and the birds were in full protest, huddling around the cottage for warmth. Maeva sat in the candlelight, hair loose and free. She had been stitching the pink quilt for hours since Pieter left, thoroughly enjoying the stillness of the coming evening. Her rocking chair creaked ever so slightly as she hummed to herself, out of habit; the baby was upstairs, asleep in the cradle. She squinted at the patch. The pieces of the quilt were so small—the needle so tiny, the thread so fine—that it was almost invisible. She pulled at the spindle, stretching and un-winding the spider-silk strand of red: her own hair, carefully collected and saved since Leidah was born.

She moved her fingers to the beat of the clock. The steady rhythm had become a cozy companion; she no longer lay awake at night, her sleep interrupted by it; rather, it helped her to fall asleep. Though time seemed to pass more slowly when Pieter was out fishing, she didn't mind. Sometimes she preferred it, this slow molasses drip of hours and hours of solitude. Something heavy fell away from her body, and the child's; the air changed. Felt lighter somehow. Humming with things unseen. True, Pieter's presence had become a familiar warmth, his bulky body such a comfort beside her in the bed. But on nights like these, when he stayed at sea, she stretched herself out the entire length and breadth of the mattress. Spread her hair across both pillows, taking up as much space as she could. Listening to the wind howl across the sea.

She paused, then closed her eyes. Her thoughts running in circles, to yesterday's events. To the baptism. And the widow's child sobbing in her mother's arms as the Aldestaed wagon flew by. The womenfolk screaming after it. *Heks!*

Maeva had slept fitfully, the venomous accusations playing over and over again in her mind. Pieter refused to play into the dramatics of women and such a scene; he blamed it on jealousy and spite.

"They can't help it, Mae—look at you. They are simply protecting their own."

"From what, goddamn it?"

He snuggled up against her back in the bed, his arm on her hip. He moved his hand to her long braid and twisted it around his fingers. "Your devil-red hair."

His words were meant to make her laugh, to calm her, she knew, but they only stoked uneasiness in her.

His hand dropped to her spine, tracing the star-shaped scar at the base of it.

Unexpectedly, anger sparked inside her. "They said you should have married someone else." She pulled her braid away from him, turning to face him. "Who is Hilde?"

Pieter's eyes registered surprise; then, abruptly, he waved his hand. "No one. A girl long gone. Not even from the village . . . Come now, Mae—there is no woman for me other than the red devil right here, in my bed."

His hands reached for her braid, pulling her toward him.

She had believed him. But now, remembering the shock at the mention of the woman's name, she wondered. *Does he still see her?* Her vision blurred, fingers tensing. She miscalculated, slipping a stitch out of line with the others. *Damn it.*

It was no use; she couldn't see in the dying light. She stopped, balling up the patch, then tucked the needle through the folds. She climbed the ladder to the sewing room, tucking the skin patch into her basket, underneath bits and bobbins and other scraps. *Safe for now.*

A knock downstairs startled her. Leidah whimpered from her cradle. Maeva snuck in to calm her, just as a louder knock rattled again at the door. The baby jumped in her sleep, her little blue hands outstretched.

"Shhh, little one, sleep now." Maeva tucked Leidah's arms back inside the swaddling, picking her up. Eyes still closed, the child settled into the warmth of her mother's chest. Another bang on the door. A shiver passed through Maeva as she made her way downstairs. *Who in the world, at this hour?*

She opened the door to the cold and a circle of women on the porch. Birgit Vebjørnsdatter stood in the centre, holding her daughter's arm out for all to see. Maeva cradled Leidah away from them, pushing the door halfway closed.

"Fru Aldestaed." The widow waited, as if she had asked a question.

Maeva said nothing. Her annoyance obvious.

Birgit continued. "I was showing everyone Unna's burn from yesterday—nasty blistering that is much worse today."

No "Good evening," no apologies for the late hour, Maeva noted. She remained silent, afraid her tongue would betray her.

Birgit lifted the child's arm higher. "Do you see it?"

Margrit Helmsdatter—the innkeeper's wife—spoke up. "Oh, Birgit, how could she miss it? The child's arm might as well have been burned in a fire, it's so red."

The women nodded in agreement.

Birgit dropped Unna's wrist. "You see, ladies, I told you she wouldn't flinch."

"I'm sorry," Maeva said, incredulous. "I don't know what to say."

Birgit put a foot on the threshold, holding the door open. "How about, 'I'm sorry for causing such pain'? How about admitting you cursed my poor girl?" She stepped forward, pushing her way in. Behind her, the rest of the crowd peered into the small cottage. "You and that thing"—she pointed a finger at the baby—"put a rash on my Unna."

Maeva stumbled backwards, shocked. "But I didn't do anything of the sort. How can you blame me?"

Birgit batted her eyes and stuck out her bottom lip. "'Oh, Pastor Knudsen, I'm innocent as a lamb. I would never speak the devil's name, let alone be his consort.'" She sneered. "Unna saw it, you know. Your wolf lover. She saw you follow it into the woods."

Maeva stood as tall as she could. *How dare they?*

"I'm sorry for your pain, Unna—and I'm sorry that you all came such a long way, unannounced, to make false accusations."

Birgit tried to stand taller, but Maeva still towered over her.

"You have some cheek, Fru Aldestaed. Working your way into this town on the heels of tragedy, pretending to be a poor fisherman's wife. Pretending you are one of us. Baptizing that baby in God's temple." Birgit glanced at her flock for support, but they shifted uncomfortably, Birgit's boldness seemingly too much for them. She gestured at them, continuing, "And here we are, delivering food to you, doing our Christian duty, and this is the welcome you give such acts of kindness?"

Maeva felt herself sinking a little. "But you pushed your way in—you accused me of cursing Unna—"

Sensing weakness, Birgit was vehement. "Being a Christian woman, I will forgive you, though I won't forget it." She motioned for the women to place their pots on the table. "My only wish for you is to find Jesus in your heart, Maeva. And for that child to surprise us all and be a better Christian than we expect." She leaned in to scrutinize the baby. "Can I hold it?"

Maeva felt the shape of a curse word rising in her throat. She tightened her grip on Leidah. "She's fussy tonight—I only managed to get her to sleep."

Birgit scoffed. "Yes, well, motherhood has its challenges. Babies aren't all sweet and goodness."

Margrit nodded. "Though we've all managed to raise them, and survived to tell the tale. Thank the Lord."

Birgit looked pointedly at her. "Not all of us."

There was an awkward silence, the spirit of Maren Innesbørg suddenly in the room.

Unna, being twelve, charged into the void. "At least that other witch will hang for it. Right, Mor?" The women ignored her, shuffling toward the fire.

Maeva stuttered, "P-pardon me? What did she say?"

Birgit turned, a smile on her face, the candle casting an eerie light. "Haven't you heard? Nils Innesbørg is searching for something of hers—evidence that will clinch it."

"What evidence?"

"A black book," Birgit threw out casually. "Spells and curses—you know, a book of magic, proving she's a witch. Just what's needed to find her guilty."

"Of witchcraft? But that's ridiculous. What about a trial? What about testimony from—from—"

"You?" Fru Vebjørnsdatter lowered her voice. "That kind of help will be the last nail in the coffin." She waved her daughter ahead of her, then addressed the women. "Spread out—it could be anywhere."

Maeva's mouth fell open as the women dispersed and overturned her cottage: opened cupboards, pulled out drawers, flipped baskets upside down, unfolded and tossed bedding on the floor. Unna climbed the ladder, stomping across the second floor with speed.

"What in God's name are you doing?" Maeva cried.

"Yes, exactly," Birgit said. "We are here in God's name, at the unofficial request of the magistrate."

"But you have no right—I didn't invite you in—"

Margrit Helmsdatter pointed to a large pot. "We are here to drop off soup, of course. You can return the pots the next time we see you at church."

Someone muttered, "Or at the hanging."

Birgit smirked, but tried to hide it. "Witchcraft is still a crime, as is practicing midwifery without a license." She tilted her head in mock sympathy. "We have all used the old woman's services at one time or another, that is true. But this time is different."

Maeva held her tongue, knowing what Birgit was about to say.

"This time, the old hag murdered an innocent babe and a mother. On the same night as this child came into the world. Seems both you and your thing"—she jabbed a finger at the child, an inch away from Leidah's chest—"arrived here in the terrible wake of death." She smoothed her skirt calmly. "Your lies don't fool anyone, least of all me."

Maeva was about to speak, but Birgit held up a hand. "She must be punished by God. And the law. And if we find her black book, she will hang, by order of the state." She paused. "If we fail to find it, officials will come to interview us. Each and every one of us will have something to say, isn't that right, ladies?"

Maeva understood the threat.

She watched further chaos unfold, her mind frantically going over the night of the birth. Did Helgar leave a book behind? No, not possible—she would have found it by now. But Maeva couldn't help feeling a growing sense of dread.

Footsteps stomped again across the upper floor, then Unna's head appeared at the railing. "I've found something strange, Mor." All the women, including Maeva, froze.

Birgit was breathless, her eyes bright. "The book?"

"Nei. This." She held out the beginnings of the pink quilt over the ledge. It was no bigger than a bird, with triangle upon triangle delicately stitched together.

Maeva inhaled sharply.

Margrit reached up, grabbing it from the girl. "What a strange pattern . . . What kind of fabric is this? Certainly can't be warm, it's so thin." She handed it to Birgit, who held it up to the firelight, the glow of which shone right through it.

"Please, it's delicate—" Maeva rushed forward.

Quickly, Birgit pulled her hand away, her pointy elbow jutting squarely into the back of the baby's head. There was a collective gasp, and then a wail of shock from Leidah. The women winced and turned away, unwilling to either watch or condemn. Maeva cupped the tiny head against her lips, shushing softly into the child's ear.

Birgit sniffed dispassionately.

"Delicate?" she taunted, stretching the patch. "Useless, more like it. Do you need to learn some basic sewing from us, Fru Aldestaed? Your baby will freeze if this is what you're wrapping her in." A few stitches tore loose.

Leidah let out another cry. Maeva rocked her as she snatched the sewing from Birgit.

"Are you quite finished, Fru Vebjørnsdatter?"

Birgit met her gaze unflinchingly. The whole room held its breath. The tension about to tip into something more vicious.

Birgit smiled then, clapped her hands, releasing all of them.

"Yes, I do believe we are done here. *God kveld, Fru Aldestaed.* God bless."

Margrit pointed at the rain barrel in the corner. "You might want to put that outside, if you want it to work."

The group tittered in agreement, brushing past Maeva.

Unna stopped. "But wait, Mamma—what about the gift?"

Birgit snapped her fingers. "Yes, of course, Unna, give it to her."

Unna pulled a pair of tiny boots, tied up with an embroidered bit of ribbon, out of her apron pocket. Birgit waved at them, as if they were nothing. "They're from Pastor Knudsen. Meant for Maren's baby. But he has no use for them now, so you might as well have them. He asked us to deliver them, along with the soup." Unna placed them on the table.

Maeva eyed the tiny booties. They were made of leather, with a speckled bit of animal hide on the toes.

Seal.

When Maeva didn't respond, Unna said snidely, "'*Takk*' would be the polite thing to say. You're welcome, Fru Aldestaed."

The flock swooped past Maeva, through the door, onto the porch, and spilled down the steps, muttering. Finding her nerve, Maeva marched outside, slamming the door closed behind her.

Unna pointed to the roof. "Mamma, look at all the crows."

The women stopped and turned in unison. Maeva stepped off the porch. The murder of crows hopped over one another, moving closer to the edge to peer back at the humans. Unna picked up a rock and threw it at them. It bounced off the side of the cabin and landed at Maeva's feet. She bent down to pick it up, trembling in anger. The birds cawed in annoyance, then soared to the sky, a flutter of black wings.

"Odhinn's messengers." Birgit clicked her tongue; then, over her shoulder, "Interesting company you keep." The women climbed into the wagon. The two horses snorted, then trotted away into the dark night.

Leidah nestled into her mother, now serene and still, and Maeva watched the wagon disappear.

Her fingers gripping the rock.

What Is

Hallo, little butterfly. Time to wake up.
*   I haven't been sleeping, girl . . . I've been changing.*
But when will you come out?
Soon, soon.

⌦⌫

I sigh big and loud. I miss *dukke*. I hate waiting. What good is a birthday gift if I can't open it?

I leave the cage on the table and go to the ladder to listen for Mamma to get up and be all better. She will have to wake up soon, won't she? Pappa says she needs time to rest, that sleep and time are the best things for someone who is sick.

But maybe she's not sick.

Maybe she's changing—all the flaky skin falling off her. And when she wakes up, she will be something else.

I hang off the ladder, hooking my legs around the rungs. I lean out and balance off the side rail, opening my arms wide, like wings. *See, Mamma, I can fly.*

The cuckoo bird pops out of the clock to tell the time. Except it doesn't say anything, like always. I wonder why it never has a song. *Poor cuckoo. Can you sing?* I reach to touch it, but it's shy and snaps back inside the little house. I feel the carved wood—pretty windows and flowers and vines all over—and then my finger finds a tiny nub on the side of the clock. I press it, and it moves. Up and down, a switch that clicks. *Chick-chick-chick—*

"What are you doing, child?" Pappa whispers from the top of the ladder.

"Nothing. Waiting for Mor to wake up."

"Go tend the fire. Let Mamma sleep. And you know better—don't touch the clock." His face disappears from the landing.

I flick the switch one more time, just because. Then I climb down from the ladder to watch for a change in the clock.

The minute hand clicks. Then nothing.

I think about what Mamma said. About trying to become something else on purpose so I can learn how to control the magic. I close my eyes and picture the little bird, my mind falling into the tick and tock of the clock. I imagine the wheels inside, grinding against each other on each second, forcing time to go forward, even if it doesn't want to. The wooden wings frozen open but never able to fly . . .

Nothing happens. I open my eyes.

Sorry, cuckoo. I guess we're both stuck.

What Was

Helgar breathed in the fresh air as if it were a glass of cold water. She didn't care that it was from the inside of a witch's cart or that her hands and feet were shackled. The fact that she was finally out in the daylight, after weeks of being in the small cell, was enough to satisfy her.

The cart stank of decay, the metal cage overhead forcing her to hunch into the stink. As far as she could tell, it hadn't been used in over a century, but that hadn't stopped Nils Innesbørg. He hauled it out from the jail cellar, along with the rusted shackles. He told her the story of Jorna Mollesdatter, the last person ever tried in the district for witchcraft.

"She burned at the stake, actually." He stood by, watching as the hired driver hammered nails into the cage. "Which is much more painful than hanging. You should count your blessings."

Helgar had been unofficially convicted that morning; the actual trial was merely a formality, according to the magistrate. The dramatic appearance of the black book sealing her fate. Innesbørg had thrown it in front of her on the cell floor while Pastor Knudsen stood by, nervously fingering his wooden cross. She knew there wasn't any way out of a confession. Especially since black books were forbidden to anyone except holy men.

"You can thank Fru Vebjørnsdatter for this gift."

Birgit. The devil's widow.

"No point in denying ownership—your initials are burned inside the binding."

H.T. Helgar began shaking her head violently. "'Tis true, these initials match my own. But this isn't my book. I swear to God, this belongs to someone else."

The magistrate waved her off. "Swearing to God is useless, and so is your denial. I don't need a confession to convict you."

The pastor gestured to the book. "Perhaps it's simply a record of treatments—I am certain there's no harm in it."

"I am sure Fru Tormundsdatter appreciates your attempt at softening the sentencing . . . Shall I read you a passage?"

Pastor Knudsen protested, but Innesbørg continued.

"Let's see here. A recipe for tempering jealousy. How to drive away unwanted suitors. How to increase a neighbour's generosity. Ah, here's one of interest: how to attract a man who loves another—"

"That's enough, Magistrate."

"Oh, wait—this one is particularly fascinating: a recipe to ensure a barren womb." Innesbørg slammed the book closed, with a smug smile. "Knudsen, if you have anything to help God have mercy on this wretched soul, you are free to offer it."

The pastor began reciting a flurry of prayers while Helgar slumped to the ground.

I surrender, Skuld.

∞

The brown hills and blue sky carried the smell of the sea, the fragrance of seasons changing. She inhaled again, closing her eyes at the exquisiteness of fresh air. When she opened them, she was greeted by the blue expanse of the ocean. The cart moved along the coastal road, past the lighthouse and the harbour. It rounded the bend, following the worn path to the docks. She knew the driver was taking the long route, at the magistrate's orders, to satisfy curious fishermen and villagers.

Most stood and stared, their expressions unreadable. Helgar held their gaze. She had nothing to be ashamed of. Those judging her all had used her services at least once in their lives. And their wives more than that. But no one—except Maeva Aldestaed—had volunteered to vouch for her.

The cart stopped momentarily at a market stall. The driver—a lithe farmer's son, barely twenty—jumped down jauntily, spitting at the ground. Tying up the horse, he grinned at Helgar through a patchy beard of youth.

"No need to rush to the gallows. A man's got to eat."

Helgar was silent, her stomach growling. She watched him move toward the dried-cod stand, her mouth watering.

"Fru Tormundsdatter? Helgar?" Pieter Aldestaed peered through the bars on the other side of the cart. His face registered the state she was in: filthy, smelling of piss.

She spread her arms. "So lovely of you to visit—I'm sorry I can't offer you a place to sit."

She cackled, and he stepped closer, hissing, "What in the devil is happening here? Why—where are you being taken?"

She shushed him, as if he were a baby needing comfort. "No need to fuss, Herr Aldestaed. It's a slight misunderstanding—I'm on my way to greener pastures."

The driver sauntered over, snorted, his mouth full of food. He hit the bars playfully.

"Doubt that—from what I hear, you're as good as hung." He pulled himself up onto the seat.

"What do you mean? She's done nothing wrong."

The driver's whistle was long and drawn out. "If you call murder nothing. Oh, and sorcery. She cast spells on the magistrate's wife—everyone knows she did it for spite—she hates Innesbørg. And they got proof."

"Proof of witchcraft? We're not in the Middle Ages, man."

"They found her black book. *H.T.* burned into the binding."

Pieter's mouth opened, stunned.

"I'm just doing my job. Bring the witch to the provincial magistrate for sentencing, and then I get paid. Whether she lives or dies, it's no matter to me."

Pieter ignored him. "What can I do?" he asked Helgar. "What can Maeva do?"

"Stay away," the old woman hissed. "Let the gods—God—decide."

The driver flicked the reins. "You'd better pray to all of them, *heks*. You're going to need it."

Pieter stood by helplessly.

Helgar rested her forehead on the bars. She placed a finger to her lips, hoping the poor man understood. Hoping he kept his mouth shut.

His family's life depended on it.

Pieter leaped up the steps two at a time, bursting through the door of the cabin. Maeva was on the floor, in front of a low fire. She looked up, eyes red and sunken. He absorbed the disarray of the cottage—as if the wind had blown through—and rushed to kneel in front of her, holding her shoulders.

"What happened, Mae?"

She flung an arm up, her voice high, cracking. "Oh, this? Why, this is Birgit Vebjørnsdatter's way of welcoming our daughter to the world."

"What? How could one woman have done all this?"

She pointed to the table, covered with soup pots and food baskets. "Oh, it wasn't her alone. They all came together, joined by their mutual dislike of me." She laughed; then a sob caught in her throat. "Not sure if we should eat any of it, come to think of it."

She struggled to her feet and picked up the baby boots from a knitting basket, with a mock smile. "A gift—aren't they sweet? Made from a baby seal. How thoughtful." She tried to keep her tone sarcastic, but it came out sad.

Pieter didn't react, knowing it would only fuel his wife's fire. "Where's Leidah?"

"Sleeping in her cradle."

"When did they come? This morning?"

"Nei. Last night. I was too tired to clean it up." She bent down to pick up balls of yarn, plunking them back into a basket beside the rocking chair.

Pieter opened his mouth as if to speak, then stopped himself.

"What? Tell me." Her tone was sharp.

"Nothing, Mae. I'm wondering . . . why?"

"Because they think I cursed Unna. Because I have red hair. Because I don't go to church. Take your pick, Pieter. I told you, but you didn't believe me. Those women are—"

"Widows and wives and young girls, nothing more. A little jealous. That's all."

Maeva started shoving things back into the hutch. "A little?" She forced a drawer closed. "Those women threatened me—and our daughter. They tore our home apart, at the orders of the magistrate. For some book belonging to Helgar."

Pieter pulled at his beard.

She slammed another cupboard door, then stopped. "I know that look. What's wrong? What's happening?"

"It's the midwife. They've already convicted her of witchcraft."

"That's ridiculous. On what evidence? Nothing they found here, that's for certain."

He opened his mouth to answer, but she interrupted, counting on her fingers.

"Oh, I know exactly what they've found: The fact that she's alone and no one can protect her. The fact that she's old. The fact that Birgit Vebjørnsdatter is a scornful wench, and the magistrate is a manipulative, vengeful bastard—"

"Who is grieving his dead wife and child, Mae!" he blurted. "What has gotten into you?"

"Nothing. Everything. This!" She threw her arms up at the upturned cottage. "I'm sorry for the man's misery, truly I am. But to arrest—nay, convict—an innocent woman to make himself feel better . . ." She thrust her chin out. "I have to testify."

"What? You most certainly will not. That woman has sealed her own fate—"

Maeva slammed her hand against the kitchen table. "She birthed your daughter, or have you forgotten? She came at your request, for no coin, in the dead of night. When we needed her, no questions asked. She kept Leidah a secret, for God's sake. The least we can offer her is our gratitude."

"Gratitude? Fine, but it should not equal risking our—your own—reputation—" he stammered, guilt catching in his throat.

"You can't possibly think I could be more damned in this village than I already am? Jesus, Pieter, are you blind?"

His jaw clenched. He scanned the cottage one last time, the nature of his suspicion suddenly clear. "Are you sure they did all this? Or were you . . ."

It only took her a moment to register what he was implying.

She stormed past him, unable to speak.

He spun around, grabbing her arm.

"Let go," she snarled.

He dropped her arm, held out his hand. Inside his palm, a small black stone.

"I found this in Leidah's blanket. After the incident at church." He closed his fist, squeezing the charm in frustration. "To bring this into church? Especially now? Have some bloody sense, Mae. You are testing God. And me." *After everything I've done for you . . .*

He tossed the stone into the fire. The flames licked at the carved lines of the hammer.

"No more, Maeva—I mean it. No more going out on your own, no more trips to market, or the waterfall. Nothing that the villagers can use against you. We need to calm the waters. You have to lie low. Disappear for a while. Understood?"

She said nothing, watching the charm burn.

What Is

I dream of fire. Of *ver-mil-ee-on*.

A red-orange mouth that eats everything in its path: the fields, the grass, even the barn. Our horse pulls a flaming wagon behind it, its tail and mane on fire. I shout into the wind for Mamma to come and save me, but no words come. I run up the steps to the porch, but before I reach the door, the cottage begins to burn on the inside. I can see Pappa sitting in the rocking chair, with *dukke* on his lap. His head is on fire. So is the doll's. They sleep and sleep. I pound on the door, my feet sinking into wet sand that becomes a pool of dark water. I fall down and down, drowning in orange flames.

⁓⧢⁓

I wake up with a jolt. My clothes are soaked, and I am boiling. I pull off a layer, the heat of the dream making me sweat. I fan myself with my apron and walk to the front door, opening it for some night air.

The fresh cold blasts in, making my nose wake up. *Something is burning.* I spin back to the fire to see if something has caught flame by accident. But the coals are charred black, the fire out. I frown, taking another sniff. The smell of smoke is so strong I walk to the ladder and begin to climb, wondering if a candle has spilled in Mor's room. I fall onto the landing but only see darkness, the door slightly open. I peek inside. Pappa is curled around Mor, holding her in his arms, fast asleep. Mor is facing away from him, her body curled around a pillow on the edge of the bed. No one is on fire. But for a second, I think I see a swirl of smoke, lifting off the end of Mor's braid.

What the—

Mamma opens her eyes, and the smoke is gone. She whispers to me, "Leidah." She slides out of bed, putting a pillow in Pappa's arms. He doesn't even stir.

She closes the door carefully, then pulls me into the sewing room, shutting the door and slumping on the stool. I rush to help her, but she waves me off.

"I'm fine. Tired, that's all. What happened today? And what is burning?" Mor whispers, scrunching up her nose. "Do you smell it?"

I nod, and she pulls me toward her, sniffs at my slip in the dark.

"It's charred—did you burn yourself? I knew Pappa was wrong, you are too young to be tending the fire."

"No, Mamma. I had another dream." I am about to tell her about it, and all the new things I saw at the market, but the small wooden cage pops into my mind. *Some woman gave me a birthday gift, Mamma. But I can't even open it.*

I imagine throwing it in a fire, to see it burn.

Mamma frowns. "I need to show you something."

She drops to her knees in front of a large wooden chest in the corner of the small room. Pushing off all the folded fabrics and blankets, she lifts the lid. She pulls out the thing we found at the caves, the thing Pappa almost found earlier today, at the bottom of my wardrobe. Though the room is dark, I can see its face, like a mask, with seaweed tangled on top of the crown, like hair. She holds it up, and I am about to ask what it is, but then she places it on her head, covering her face.

Instantly, she changes; what seemed to be seaweed only moments ago becomes a beautiful mane, shimmering gold and red. I want to fold myself into it and sigh in wonder. She is magic. Better than an angel. Her long hair and seal face, so smooth. Black eyes sparkling.

"I don't understand—what is it, Mamma?"

She holds out her arms. She is all warmth, smelling of the sea. I close my eyes.

She takes me into a place inside our minds, deeper than the deepest cave. Down and down, into our hearts, into our bellies. So deep we must be at the centre of the earth. Except that there is a soft green glow, and we float as one, her long hair wrapping me up into a cocoon. We spin slowly. A dance of dreaming, inside a whirlpool of flowers and salt water, with bubbles tickling my skin and a hint of a song—like the one sung by the old woman at the market—echoing and humming all around us. Except it's sweeter, the notes made of honey and rainwater.

Where once was two, now there is one,
Their love burned strong, till flame was none . . .

We become the sea.

Waves rise and fall, with orange flames that turn into flowers that turn into fish, into seals, into sand. I can only hear the waves lapping at our skin, and the melody of that song, sung over and over . . .

I open my eyes. We are standing in the middle of the sewing closet. Fabrics, blankets, spools of yarn, thread all around us. The mask is on the floor. Mamma has a river of tears running down her cheeks. I reach up and wipe one away and, without thinking, lick it off my finger. "Salt."

She tries to laugh, but it's more like a sob.

I hug her tight. "Don't cry, Mamma."

She hugs me back, then lets go. "The place we went together, just now. Do you understand that it's real? That our spirits actually went there?"

"It's like the places you told me about—the ones that are pockets of magic, that are hidden to everyone else, right?"

"Exactly right. You are such a smart child."

Can Pappa come?

Nei, that's not possible. She tucks a hair behind my ear. *Pappa doesn't know how.*

Can you teach him, like you are doing with me?

I can't. She sees my sad face. "I'm sorry."

I'm so sad, I don't want to talk about it. "Mamma, I think I found it. The other half."

She drops to her knees. "What? Where?"

"I don't know if it's—"

"For love of the gods, where?" She shakes me, and I get scared. I start to cry. She shushes me, pulls me close.

"Today, at the pier. We saw a boat that had the same name as me."

Mamma sits back on her heels, her face whiter than white. "Of course. How very appropriate, Pieter."

I bite my lip. How could she not know where my name came from? "Pappa was checking his own boat and I saw something—or felt it."

"Oh God. It's on the trawler somewhere." She stands and begins to pace.

"It's not *in* the boat. It *is* the boat."

"What do you mean, it *is* the boat?"

"There's a sheet—a skin or something—over the boat. It has little hairs and it's so smooth and—"

"Bastard." Mor spits out the words. She sinks to the floor beside the mask. I wait a minute and then reach down—what would happen if I put it on my own head?

"Nei, child, it is not a toy!" She grabs it back. "Leidah, you must hear me when I say this." She reaches over and holds my hands one more time. "When the time is right, after Mamma retrieves what is rightfully hers off that godforsaken boat"—her eyes close briefly—"then and only then will I wear the mask. Me, not you. *Forstår du?*"

I nod, not understanding at all.

She reaches into her sewing basket. Pushing ribbons and thread aside, she pulls out the pink patchwork quilt. She stretches her arms wide so the quilt is between us. I can see her face through the patches of pink, the stitches all red and raw. She is a ghost.

"This will be your protection, child. It is you and me—your skin, my hair—stitched together. Forever."

Forever. My hand reaches out to touch the ghost Mor on the other side of stitches and skin. The web between my fingers has grown back already. "But why, Mamma? Why do we need protection?"

She pulls back, her hands together like a prayer under her chin, the quilt folding and wrinkling into itself. "Safe passage. It will be your way back to me. Should you ever need to find me, it will carry you from this world to the next."

Prickles slide up and down my spine. The words I had overheard Hilde say to Pappa, ringing in my ears. *She can't stay.*

I sob. "But you promised. Wherever you go, I'm coming with you."

"Oh, Lei-lee . . . I will do my best to keep that promise. But remember what I say: should you need to find me, wrap yourself in this. And pray." She stops, for a moment. "To Odhinn."

She folds the quilt over and over, until it's the size of a loaf of bread.

"But then what, Mamma?"

"I have no idea, child. Perhaps nothing will change. Or . . ."

I hear the rest in my mind.

Everything will change.

The Seventh Knot

S he waited for him to return.

Hilde overheard the market vendors weaving the tale of Helgar Tormundsdatter's trial, passing it from ear to ear as they set up for the day—the terrible news biting its own tail and wrapping around her three times before she had even eaten breakfast.

"Hasn't been a hanging in over seventy years."

"I thought sorcery wasn't a criminal act anymore."

"Ask Martin Luther. I'm sure he would have forgiven her if it weren't for that black book."

"Luther would give her over to the devil himself. That woman is pure evil."

She chewed on a bit of stockfish, washing it down with whisky, ignoring the talk. She swilled the spirits in her mouth. *You will come today.* She said it to herself, over and over, willing it to be true. Though she usually left the coast for the winter months, seeing each other one last time had always been their ritual. Before the snow made the road impassable, she always made a final stop in Ørken, to feel his lips on hers. Now that he was married, circumstances had changed. *But have you?*

She searched the harbour below, holding her breath. *Yes. There.* The red scarf she had made him was tied to the railing of his boat, easy to spot among the grey waves and other colourless vessels. Seeing the flash of red, she felt a flutter inside her pelvis; he had kept her gift, despite his wife. Despite the new baby. *You haven't changed.*

She went inside the tent, then sat on reindeer hides, clutching the bottle of whisky she had been saving for him. She took another sip, savouring the burn in her mouth, unable to contain her excitement. She examined the charm she had made for him: a wishing rope, each knot a prayer for the two of them.

Mind. Heart. Home. Harvest. Spirit. Body. Fortune. Will . . . The breeze picked up outside, swirling around the tent and lifting her hair playfully. *Takk, Skuld.* She breathed upon the last knot—*family*—pulling the rope even tighter, the necessary wind now caught and contained inside each of the nine bindings.

Her mind drifted back to the last time they had made love, over a year ago. *Before her.* He entered her tent in a hot rush, hungry and rooting like a bear, ready to ravage her limb from limb. He didn't speak, his body saying everything. Paws mauling, tearing at her skirts, pulling at her thick tresses. His mouth thirsting for the taste of her. Each new bruise blooming on her skin, a celebration of possession, of ownership. His mark, his territory. She didn't wash for days afterward, reveling in the scent of him.

It was this time that had gotten her pregnant.

It had been six months since the miscarriage. Though she still cried herself to sleep, she couldn't say goodbye to what still grew inside her: hope.

If you'd known about our son, you would have left her.

The flap opened. Pieter was breathless, a bundle in one hand. For a moment, she pretended that time had spun backward. That he wasn't married to another woman. That their baby was still alive inside her . . .

He took a few steps, then glanced at her, hesitant. She waited, relishing his gaze, then stood slowly. Without a word, she passed him to secure the curtain flap, her fingers trembling in the silence. The air hummed with anticipation. With her back to him, she held herself still, her body begging him to embrace her. Suddenly, his arms were around her, pulling her into him. She melted, her body vibrating at his touch. He pressed his face into her neck and inhaled deeply.

She allowed his hands to roam and feed on her body. *I am yours.* When he was about to sink his teeth into her neck, she pulled away from him. "Oh, Pieter. I've missed this."

"Me, too. God, me, too." He took his cap off and rubbed at his beard, embarrassed by his fervour. She smiled smugly, gesturing for him to sit on the deer hide. She pressed against him, wrapping her arm around his waist. Her raven hair spilled over both of them. She gazed into his eyes, the intensity of her attention making him sigh.

"You're here." She paused. "I can only assume—"

"You've heard, then? About the midwife?"

The midwife?

"Sorcery is the charge. They found her black book. With the initials H.T. I'm scared for us. For Maeva. For my baby."

Her eyes widened, disguising her glee. "So you should be. Your family needs protection." Then she leaned into his ear. "Congratulations, Pappa. I heard about the baby. We should celebrate." She reached behind her for the bottle.

Pieter squeezed her hand and smiled. "You always know what I need. It's a girl. Leidah."

She waited for him to drink, sensing he had a story to tell.

"She's . . . very special."

Hilde lifted an eyebrow. "With a father like you, she would have to be."

Pieter's smile faded. "They are saying . . . The villagers are suspicious of Mae. They think she's a witch."

She rolled her eyes. "That's how much these folks know. Fearful. Ignorant. Wouldn't know a real witch if I kissed them on the mouth."

Pieter grimaced. "Yes, but you don't live here. You come and go with the wind. What do people care about market spinsters, Lapps, and Finns?"

She sat up with a pout. "Is that all you think of me, Pieter Aldestaed? After all these years?"

He moved closer. "You know I care more than I can say." He allowed the tip of his nose to lightly brush hers. "When I heard about the black book with those initials—for a moment, I was worried they might think of you. Perhaps you should think about disappearing for a while. To keep safe."

A tiny smirk threatened at the edge of her mouth. *You do care.*

He stared at her lips, a little too long. With pent-up desire, too strong to fight, he kissed her—hard and long, as if she were the last meal of a starving man. He tasted of warm spice. She'd missed his mouth, the way he bit her bottom lip, sucking on it for dear life, his hands grabbing her cheeks, getting lost in her hair and neck. Gorging on her, piece by piece. His beard rubbing her skin raw.

Does she kiss you like this?

Abruptly, he pulled away. "I'm sorry—I shouldn't—I lost myself."

She touched a thumb to her own lip, lingering, teasing. "I know. No harm done. We're old friends, you and I." She reclined, cat-like. "Familiarity is hard to resist. There was a time when I thought you might change your mind." She stopped, tucking her black hair seductively behind one ear.

"Me, too. But we both know being someone's wife doesn't suit you." He watched her hungrily, spinning his wedding ring distractedly. "I wanted more. A wife, a family. And the gods—God—listened. Maeva was sent to me." He scanned her face, searching for a reaction.

She smiled, as if he hadn't mentioned his wife's name. "So, why did you come, if not for our usual . . ."

Pieter became even more serious. "Two reasons. First: I might have to testify. Maeva might have to. I need some protection of some sort."

"Did you not keep the last charm I made you?"

"Of course. I need more . . . assurance."

She turned her head, then stood. She pretended to bustle about the small stall, opening bundles of herbs and sniffing each one, then placing some of them into a sack. Slipping the witch's rope she had already prepared in with them—all too easy.

"Nei—I mean, thank you, a charm would be great, but I need more than that." He scratched his beard. "God, I just chastised my wife for believing in such a thing."

"If not a charm, then what?"

"God forbid, if the worst should ever happen. If Mae and I . . . If we can't take care of Leidah—"

Hilde couldn't hide her shock. "You can't be serious?"

"Hans is her godfather. But he's out at sea half the year, and you don't have anyone. To take care of, I mean."

She flinched. It was almost nothing, but she could tell he saw it. He stood up quickly, then pulled her into his arms, lifting her right off the floor, his hips against hers. Her body slid down the length of him, slowly, until her feet reached the floor. His hands moved dangerously low.

"I need to know you will watch over her. Should the worst happen. Which it won't, I'm certain. But . . . promise me you won't let anyone ever harm my girl."

His heat burned through her skirt. She knew that if she pushed, even a little, she could have him, right here on the dirt floor.

For a split second, she imagined slapping him hard, her open palm stinging against his cheek. She stared into his eyes, controlling the urge. He mistook her gaze for desire, inching his greedy hands around the full curve of her bottom.

I should take you, right now. Moan so loud the entire market will hear. Slap you so hard your mouth will bleed.

Instead, she brushed a wayward hair off his forehead, only a slight tremor in her hand.

"I will always be here for you. You know that."

He dropped his hands, her avoidance of his question obvious. "I know." He kissed her on the cheek, all desire suddenly gone. "*Takk*, old friend."

Hilde pulled away, hurt by the change in him. "And should she ever leave you—"

"She won't."

She stepped back, crossed her arms. *We'll see.* "What's the second thing?"

He paused. "I have something to show you." He reached down for the bundle he had brought with him. "But you have to promise to keep it a secret."

She looked down at the bag, then back at him, flipping her hair off her shoulders. "Secrets are my specialty."

What Is

Even before the clouds roll in, I feel a buzzing between my fingers and toes. *Rain*. I hear Mamma get up before dawn, stoking a fire and boiling water for tea. Soon, the smell of porridge fills the cottage. I go downstairs carrying my pee pot, stomping past the clock. Nothing changed after I pushed that little switch. *Stupid clock*. I place the pot by the back door before going to the fire. I find Mamma standing in the doorway to the porch, the door wide open. I stand beside her, peering out. The rain is coming down in sheets, so much so the field is flooded. The path to the road, a huge puddle.

It is then that I see the cage. It is sitting in the middle of the porch, the tiny twig latch open, as if waiting for something to fly in, or something to fly out. I wonder if Mor put it out here.

She says nothing. I am about to tell her where the cage came from when Pappa calls from upstairs.

"Maeva, what in God's name are you doing? Get back to bed, you will catch your death, woman."

Mamma points to the cage.

"Keep that door open, child. Nothing free should be caged." She walks past me, back inside.

I move to the porch and kneel down. The cocoon split in the night, and something dark is beginning to crawl out. *Finally, you're awake!* I watch as a tiny black leg pokes out of the casing, pawing at the empty air. So thin and tender, the movements slow and careful.

I think about Mamma's words.

If I leave the cage open, won't the thing escape? I may not get to see what's inside. And wasn't it a gift from Far's friend, for *my* birthday?

Pappa calls from inside.

I close the latch.

The rest of the morning, Mamma sleeps, and Pappa paces the floor, waiting for the rain to stop. The more it falls, the more he frets.

"I need to go to town, to talk to the doctor, that's all, child."

Finally, at midday, Mor calls from the bedroom to tell him to go outside and tend to the animals.

He rolls his eyes but then sees me watching him. He smiles and invites me to come, but she stops him.

"Do you want our daughter to catch her death?" Mor has spoken, and Far is on his own. He talks to me and points to the pouch hanging on a hook by the door.

"The material for your new dress is in there, Lei-lee. Happy birthday."

I smile, but only on the outside. "My birthday isn't for a couple days. Besides, Mamma is still sick."

"Hilde's gift is expensive, Lei-lee; you should get the dress started. She thought vermilion was such a fine choice," he whispers, then rubs my cheek. "I'll bet she and *dukke* are having tea right now."

Hilde. "Nei, Pappa. *Dukke's* gone. She died." I don't know how I know this. But it's true.

He looks at me strangely, then leaves for the barn, the door banging behind him.

I open the satchel and pull out the large piece of fabric, soft and warm to the touch. Mor calls from above, telling me to bring the new material—"and some water, child"—so she can start making my dress. I climb the ladder slowly.

The rest of the day is spent watching Mor lay out the fabric on the bed, cutting shapes like a flower to create a pattern. She's almost back to her old self. Except she's so thirsty she drinks so much I have to get another bucket of water from the well.

When I hand her the mug, she gasps, almost dropping it. "Let me see those fingers, child." I hold out my hands, knowing she's going to be upset.

On each hand, the baby finger is fused, the web completely grown back. *One-two-three fingers.* Like a claw. Or a flipper.

"This is Pappa's doing. I knew this would happen—" She stops herself. "Does it hurt?"

"Nei, Mamma, it's fine." *Please don't blame Far.*

I put my fingers around the mug of water and take it from her, to show her how fine I am. "See?"

For the rest of the day, I watch her working, trying to understand how two shapes can become something else, with a needle and thread and Mor's hands, a magic lady at work. By the time the night has fully come, the candlelight gone dim, everything but the sleeves has been stitched.

"Almost there, Leidah. Your dress will be ready by tomorrow, I think. It's truly beautiful fabric, child. I've never seen such craftsmanship. Though an odd colour, a good choice, and so easy to work with—the pieces seem to merge together without me even trying. I've used so few pins." She squints, tying a knot in the thread and snipping it close to the seam. She gulps the last bit of water. "There. Enough of a shell for you to try on. Here, slip it over your nightgown."

I move closer and feel her cold hands shimmy the dress over my thin cotton shift. The new dress hugs me tightly.

"It's perfect. I love it." I smile and do a twirl.

She touches the waist. "It seems a bit tight. Hmm, maybe you've grown? It's hugging your chest a little too much." She tries to slip a finger into the opening under my arm but can't. "I should have sewn a mock-up, but you haven't grown in so long . . ."

I pull the skirt down, trying to make it fit better.

"Where did you and Pappa get the fabric? I've never seen anyone weave such material at the market." She rubs the stitches on the seam at my ribs.

I pick at a hangnail. She asks again.

The third time she asks, I mumble, "Some woman Pappa knows."

Her hands stop.

"Take it off."

I don't move.

She grabs the hem of the dress, ripping it over my head, tearing it at the neck. She balls it up, then tosses the dress to the floor.

As if it were on fire.

What Was

Maeva swallowed her nervousness, steeling herself in front of the tall wooden building. Imagined herself stepping across the threshold of the church. *It's the right thing to do*, she tells herself. Despite Helgar's warning to stay silent.

She checked on Leidah, contentedly asleep, strapped securely on her back. Suddenly, a sharp pain rushed from temple to jaw, down the length of her neck. Must be a storm brewing. She pulled her scarf even tighter. The cold November wind had been an ally this morning, urging her forward, making the journey to Ørken easier than usual. After Pieter left on horseback for the pier, Maeva followed on foot. She couldn't risk her husband discovering what she was about to do. She'd seen the trawler down at the docks, his favourite red scarf waving on the railing. She put her head down, hoping no one, especially Pieter, would notice her.

She pulled the heavy wooden door of the church open, then slipped inside the shadows. The door closed with an ominous thud, the wind giving her one final push. She blinked her eyes to adjust to the darkness. Thankfully, the church was empty, it being a Wednesday.

Odhinn's day.

She tried to push the thought of him away, but images of him swirled about in her mind.

Life would be so different.

She forced herself to focus, forced her feet to move toward the altar. Shame washed over her, the memory of the baptism still fresh.

"Why, Fru Aldestaed, how lovely!" Pastor Knudsen called from behind the altar pillars, startling her, then stepped past the arched threshold. He held a broom in one hand, a black Bible in the other.

"Newest convert, I suppose?" Maeva asked, pointing at the broom.

He seemed confused, then chortled wholeheartedly. "Yes, well, we welcome all walks of life in Ørken, as you know." Maeva tried to hide her discomfort by fussing with the weight of Leidah's sling on her shoulder. He cleared his throat, then stuttered, "I didn't mean to imply—I was only adding to what you—" Taking a breath, he started over. "*God morgen.* How are you feeling, Fru Aldestaed?" He peered at the little bundle on her back. "And baby Leidah, how lovely to see our actual newest convert so soon." He leaned awkwardly to peer closer at the sleeping child.

Maeva couldn't help but smile at his kindness, despite her nerves. "*God morgen.* I have come, first, to thank you in person for the gift." She reached into her satchel to pull out the baby boots. "So thoughtful of you, but we have so many knitted booties, we simply don't need them. Perhaps some other mother could use them."

"It's no trouble at all, please, they are yours now."

She ignored the protest, placing them on the bench. The need to be honest overwhelmed her. "I don't feel right. Knowing they were meant for another child."

His face reddened.

"The other reason I have come today is not so pleasant. I need counsel about . . . Fru Tormundsdatter."

The pastor's open demeanor dropped. He moved to place the Bible on the podium, patting the book twice, then began to sweep the floor in earnest.

"I'm sorry to say I can't help you with that matter. She has been taken by the state." His eyes avoided hers, searching the floor for wayward dust. "The provincial magistrate from Bergen has taken over, and all we can do now is pray. And wait." He moved the broom quickly, the swish of twigs a sharp scraping in the silence of the church.

Maeva wrung her hands. "But surely there must be a chance for testimony of some sort."

"That already happened, yesterday afternoon. Didn't Pieter tell you?"

No, that can't be true. "But why wasn't I asked to attend? Would I not be the natural choice for testimony, given the circumstances?" Her voice echoed in the emptiness.

Pastor Knudsen stopped sweeping. "Oh, Maeva. Pieter stepped in for you, upon my suggestion, since you've been so unwell. The magistrate allowed it, given Pieter's presence at the birth. And since the entire village witnessed how ill you were the day of the baptism, the magistrate granted compassionate exemption." He moved to the bench. Motioned for her to sit. He settled beside her, awkwardly patting her hand. "I'm sure your husband didn't want to tax you any further."

Maeva felt a quiet rage spark inside her. *Pieter.* She pulled her hand away. "And what did my husband say?"

"That Fru Tormundsdatter had only given you tea that night. Leidah was born days later, so there couldn't have been any connection between the Innesbørg tragedy and your child." He pointed to a large book on the side table of the altar. "We have the proof—the date of birth in the registry. Official documents."

The rage made her feverish, her skin itchy. She wiped away drips of perspiration on her upper lip and forehead.

"Are you still unwell, my dear? Do you need a drink of water?"

Maeva stood, then sat again, closing her eyes. *I need an ocean.* She tried to smile at him, but her lips wouldn't cooperate.

He watched her, concern growing. He called to the back of the church. "Unna, dear?"

The girl peered out from the altar interior, candles in each hand. Maeva almost groaned. The girl stepped forward, stopping a few feet away from the two adults. "What is it, Pastor?"

"Let's stop the cleaning for a moment—Fru Aldestaed is feeling faint. Fetch her some water from the well?"

Unna blinked. Stared at Maeva.

"Go, child, do as I ask and be quick about it."

Unna pivoted on her heels, then rushed out.

Pastor Knudsen's tone was apologetic. "There is nothing to be done now, my dear. It is in God's hands."

Maeva bit her cheek to contain her frustration. "I want to testify. I need to speak with the magistrate."

"It is too late, Maeva. What's done is done."

"But what if I have new evidence? Something that could prove Helgar's innocence?" *The fact that she attended my child's birth and my child is perfectly healthy. The fact that she consulted a black book and no harm came of it.*

"My advice to you: go home. This information you speak of, it's not going to help anyone. More testimony will only bring more officials. More interrogations, more needless convictions. Of *innocents*."

He stressed the word, squeezing her hand one last time. His face grave. "You are in no condition to travel, at any rate. The magistrate left early this morning, with Helgar in tow."

A rumbling in her belly, then a churning. She struggled to stand.

"*Takk*, Pastor. I . . . need some air." She rushed out of the church before he could stop her. Tumbling down the steps, she grabbed hold of the nearest tree and spewed her breakfast onto the ground. Leidah began to wail on her mother's back. Maeva leaned her head on the tree, waiting for her stomach to settle.

A hand held a cup in front of her. She looked up: Unna.

Surprised, Maeva accepted the cup, taking a sip. "*Takk*, child."

Unna shrugged, peering at the baby. She held out a finger for Leidah to grasp. Maeva couldn't help but notice the girl's skin, now free of any blistering or redness.

"It's too late, you know. Mamma says so."

Maeva resisted the urge to fling the cup. She shifted to keep Leidah out of Unna's reach, swaying to calm her. "I don't know, actually. Perhaps they need to hear more testimony."

"Nei. The black book Mamma found sealed it." Unna took the cup from Maeva's outstretched hand.

"She found Helgar's book?"

"It had the initials *H.T.* So it must be hers. Stupid to leave it lying about, if you ask me. If I were a witch, I'd hide my spellbook where no one could find it."

This made Maeva pause. *Yes, indeed.* Jiggling to keep Leidah quiet, she casually asked, "Where did she find the book?"

Unna was already climbing the church steps, answering over her shoulder, "Some Finn lady at the market found it."

The door closed behind the girl. Maeva couldn't move.

The wind picked up suddenly, swirling dead leaves around her feet.

The Eighth Knot

The two women sat on stumps, opposite each other, inside the canvas tent. One small, the other tall. Both curious, wary of the other. Who Pieter used to love and who he loved now, a strange sort of reflection in a mirror.

The baby fussed in her mother's arms. Maeva rocked her nervously. The ache in her neck and head suddenly much worse. She shifted the baby to the other shoulder.

Hilde studied her.

Maeva surveyed the tent, taking in all the fabrics and furs. The reindeer skins on the ground and walls. Stuffed dead birds hanging on ribbon. Their sad, lifeless eyes watching her.

After a minute passed, Maeva couldn't stand the silence. "I know who you are."

Hilde nodded slightly. "Likewise."

"I know what you've done."

Hilde motioned to the baby. "Should I say, 'Likewise'?"

Maeva stood abruptly. "What you should say is nothing." She paced one way, then the other. "Or nei, I take that back. How about saying something useful? To the magistrate?"

"And why would I do that?"

"To save an innocent woman's life."

Hilde paused. "Are you so sure of the witch's innocence?"

It was all Maeva needed. "Helgar Tormundsdatter is a midwife, and a damned good one. Nothing more than that. Certainly not a witch." She glowered. Leidah began to cry. She shushed the baby, lowering her voice. "She doesn't deserve to die."

Hilde stood slowly. "And what if that innocent midwife was actually not so good?" She took a step; underfoot, the animal skins buckled. She leaned on the small table between them. "What if she had caused the death of more than one baby in her lifetime? What then?" The words were contained, but Maeva sensed danger. "What punishment would be just, in your opinion, if I told you more?"

Maeva was confused. Could it be that Helgar had made a grave mistake in the delivery of Maren's baby, that she was at fault somehow? And what if Leidah hadn't survived? Could Maeva truly say she would forgive such a terrible tragedy, even if the midwife had done everything in her power to save her?

Maeva's head was pounding. She sat back down, trying to hide her weakness, her bewilderment. "All I know is, my child is well, and I have Helgar to thank for that."

Hilde smiled unkindly, sitting once again. "But I heard that your husband—what's his name? Pieter—yes, that's it. Didn't he deliver your baby?"

Maeva's mouth fell open.

Hilde pressed further, fingers drumming on the table. "I'm sure the magistrate would love to hear of this new fact."

Maeva's eyes narrowed. "You know my husband's name. Don't pretend you don't."

Hilde's fingers stopped for a split second, but she recovered quickly with a smirk. She traced a circle on the wood.

"Yes, I know Pieter." She paused. "I used to know him quite well, in fact."

The air crackled between the two women.

Was that a distant rumble of thunder, far off in the mountains? Perhaps Maeva was hearing things, the headache all-consuming. But even the baby seemed to be listening, holding her breath. It took all of Maeva's strength not to react. To not push for more details of what she feared was between her husband and this other woman.

She cleared her throat, a little too loudly. "What used to be isn't what matters *now*." She looked at Leidah, then glared at Hilde. "The only thing that matters is what *will be*. And you can change that."

Hilde shifted her gaze to the baby once more. Maeva ignored the prickling sensation up her spine.

Hilde balled her hand into a fist, knuckles rapping twice on the table. "But that's where you're wrong, Fru Aldestaed." She pronounced each syllable, as if she had a bad taste in her mouth. "In my experience, what used to be always matters most. Everything is born out of the past. The Norn who snips the thread is inconsequential to the one who spins it. That poor Sister is a slave to circumstance."

Leidah howled again, her face scrunching up as if in pain. Maeva rocked her, trying to calm both the baby and herself.

"Why have you come here, Fru Aldestaed? To beg me to do what, exactly?"

Maeva met her eyes with sincerity. "To do the right thing. To admit that the black book belonged to you."

Hilde stood abruptly, pushing the table with her hip. It bumped against Maeva's elbow, barely missing Leidah.

"That black book has nothing to do with me. Whatever you've heard, it's gossip and lies." Hilde's face darkened. "Besides, that witch deserves to burn in hell, regardless of who owns that damn book."

May you get what you deserve. Maeva shoved her stool back with fury. "I'm done here. I need to find the magistrate. To let him know of my suspicions."

"Please, be my guest, Fru Aldestaed."

"I'd say it was a pleasure meeting you, Hilde, but I pride myself on telling the truth." Maeva moved toward the exit. Leidah's cries escalated into screams.

"Perhaps I should go with you, share that new information you told me about Leidah's birth? *Snip, snip, snip* . . . We're all slaves to circumstance, aren't we, Maeva?"

Maeva paused to touch a rope of knots, hanging at the entrance to the tent. "I'm sure the Bergen officials will be interested in what you are selling in this little tent of yours." She twisted the rope, then let it go. She parted the curtain with a slash of her arm, the fresh air such a relief from the enclosed, stale tent. From the rank conversation.

"Please be sure to give my love to Pieter." Hilde's words chased behind her, a foul wind.

Maeva bit back tears, marching down the hill toward the pier.

Wondering, all the while, how Hilde knew their daughter's name.

Waiting

Hilde waited for Pieter's wife to exit, resisting the urge to reveal everything to the woman. She bent down to lift the deer hides. Under them, his secret, safe and sound.

She had promised him she would sell it. But why get rid of something so valuable?

⌘

Why not hide it somewhere his wife would be sure to find it?

What Was

Maeva threw the rope of knots onto the kitchen table.

"I found *this* in the barn. Remind me, what do people call it? A witch's ladder? A sailor's knot? Or some such *nonsense*?" She paused, letting him feel the sting of being caught. "Oh, no, wait. I remember now. Someone at the market called it a *wishing* rope. I wonder whose wishes are bound inside?"

Pieter blinked but said nothing. He placed his fork on the side of his plate.

She picked up the rope, shaking it in front of his face. "Whose, goddamn it?"

He continued to chew, slowly and methodically, his eyes looking past the woven charm of knots and feathers. Refusing to engage.

She slammed it down, digging her fingers into the last knot to unravel it. The rope seemed almost alive, squirming under her grip, and the knot refused to budge. She balled the rope up in fury. Wheeling away from him, she grabbed a knitting needle from the rocking chair. Stabbed the end into one of the knots, twisting and turning. Still, it held tight, immovable.

A low flame crackled in the hearth.

"No more nonsense." She tossed the rope into the fire. *No more Hilde.*

His silence—not even a word of denial—a confession to her.

The charm caught fire instantly. The flames raged bright yellow, licking at the feathers and beads. A thick snake of smoke spiraled up, slowly. Reluctantly releasing wishes into the rafters.

Maeva put the sleeping baby into her cradle, avoiding eye contact with Pieter. He studied her in silence. Waited for her to lie beside him in the bed. She could feel his need, palpable in the air, thick in the sheets. But the harsh words said by both of them thrashed like a caged animal inside her. She couldn't stop the echo in her head, playing over and over.

When he reached a hand toward her, Maeva bristled.

"Mae, please."

She ignored him, striding toward the ladder.

"Don't walk away from me." His tone a warning.

She snapped back. "I'm not. I'm disappearing." She knew he wouldn't follow her; he wouldn't leave the baby. He knew her enough to know she needed space.

I need air.

She grabbed her cloak and marched out of the cabin. Though she wanted to slam the door, she didn't, for fear of waking Leidah. Her headache had become almost unbearable. The cold air helped; the sky smelled of rain, a contusion of purple clouds smearing across the stars and moon. As she passed the barn, a shooting pain in the back of her skull made her stumble.

The long hike to the pond was suddenly too far.

The water trough. She grabbed the empty feed bucket and dipped it in frantically, soaking her apron. Her arms shook, but she managed to hold the bucket to her lips, gulping as though she hadn't drunk in years. The water was delicious. Coolness slid under her skin. She dropped it with a clang. *By the gods . . . I need more than this.* Overhead, the clouds rumbled in response. The prayer for rain, like a command.

It started as a drizzle, a soft shower on her face. Without a second thought, she stripped off her clothes and basked in the wetness. But she quickly realized even this was not enough. She noted the water level: half full. *This will have to do.* Climbing into the trough, she sank to her shoulders in the frigid water. Thunder boomed. The clouds darkened even more, letting go in a gush.

Yes, this, and more . . . She almost heard her sisters calling under the rainfall. Reminding her of what she had given up. *Come home . . .*

I can't leave her. She fought the voices, but still they came, along with the rain needling into her, unstitching the threads of a buried wound.

Remember how that child came to be . . .

Time was nowhere and everywhere. Looping inside knots and empty spaces, a memory coiled so tightly, it squeezed and suffocated. Defeated, she sank below the surface of the water. *What was*—the scar on her tailbone—suddenly becoming *what is*. Raw. Burning, bleeding . . .

Maeva warms herself on the rocks. The cold sea-spray splashes against her nakedness, her pale skin soaking in the rays of the sun. She relishes the anticipation of him, the heat of what's to come. The last time they met—here, at the shoreline between worlds—torrid. Unstoppable. His mouth on hers, even before a word was uttered. He undid every part of her, with his fingers, his teeth. His tongue. Opening, opening. The width and depth of her, infinite as the stars.

She scans the horizon. In the distance, the brewing storm had passed. The waves, calmer now. The glimmer of the sun on the surf, dazzling.

Where are you, my love?

She passes the time by singing to herself. Arranging seashells, anemones into pleasing patterns. Every second of waiting, excruciatingly slow.

She places a large starfish in the centre of the flat boulder, the five-sided creature completing the puzzle of sea treasures in front of her. Then lifts it off the surface, creating a hole in the arrangement. The shells orbit around emptiness. In a flash, she realizes that his absence—as much as his presence—makes her insatiable. Incessantly craving him. Nothing—no one—else able to fulfil her. *Damn you.* She returns the star to the centre, both soothed and unsettled.

She hears a splash. *Finally.* Sighing out a single note of song, as an invitation.

But he doesn't come. Is he teasing her? She can't believe he's not lunging at her, after all this time apart. *Well, two can play at this game.* She pretends to be unaware that he's there. Leans back on the rocks, sunning herself.

She hears him gasp. Senses his need for her in the air between them. But still, he holds himself back. She rolls on her side, stretching her legs and coyly playing with her hair, attending the seashells beside her. *I can wait, even longer . . .* Finally, when she's tortured him enough, she rounds to face him.

He is backlit by the glaring sun, a dark silhouette of muscle and desire. She squints and holds a hand to shade her eyes. *What's taking so long?* It is then that she notices he's clothed. *And bearded.* He tears off his shirt and balls it up in one hand. Something in her retreats; this new approach, unexpected.

He dives toward the rock. Snatches her grey hide with one quick swipe before she can even move.

But why? Something about this feels different. Dangerous, even. A prickled warning shivers across her flesh.

Her eyes adjust. The sun now fully exposing his face.

It is a stranger's face. *A human face.*

Despite every hair standing on end, Maeva tells herself it's simply not possible, that this stranger couldn't be lunging up on the rocks, didn't just steal her pelt—

This isn't happening. Can't be happening—it must be you, has to be you in disguise—

Then, those human hands—unfamiliar, brutish—force her down onto the rocks.

She holds herself perfectly still. Eyes open.

Birds dip across the blue sky above her. Waves lap at her feet.

I am not here.

Her sealskin mere inches out of reach. The limp mask of whiskers and snout, her only witness. *I am not here. I am not—*

She feels a part of herself leap into the sky. Flying high above the water, confused by the puzzle below.

His body beats against hers, elbows pinning her flat. Hip bones, sharp as the rock and shells beneath her. Beard, a wire brush against her neck. Teeth, shark-like, devouring earlobes, shoulders, breast—*not-here-not-here—*

The sea treasure digs and slices into her skin.

A bloodied trail of shards scarring the very centre of her being.

The outline, deep and permanent, in the shape of a star.

⌾

Time gathered into itself. Threads—tangled fetters, like wings—dragged her back from the deep. She breaks the surface of the water, lungs clawing, feathered fingers retracting, erasing.

"Mae, please. It's freezing out here. Come back inside. The baby needs you."

Pieter stood in front of the horse trough, a blanket in his hand. His voice weakened when he saw her bloated face. "I need you."

Maeva climbed out in a daze. *Where is here?*

Pieter held a blanket up, ready to wrap her inside.

She pushed past him. Her naked body already dry.

Squirrel

The old woman hung limply from a tree limb.

For a stout hag, her body swayed easily, as if she were a child on a swing, watching the ships on the horizon. Her feet dangled in the wind.

It was a fine day for a hanging, the sun shining brightly, the coastal winter winds dancing among the witnesses, playing with tendrils of hair, lifting long skirts and petticoats, blowing hats from men's heads. The entire village had shown up to watch.

He witnessed everything from the top of the tree. He couldn't see faces, but he knew there was only one who shed tears for the old spinster.

Maeva stood apart from the crowd, with the bearded man at her side holding her elbow tightly.

The man—*husband*—didn't cry. But his squirrel sense could tell the man was agitated. Nervous and fearful, trembling.

The rest of them vibrated with something else.

Retribution. Satisfaction.

The words, as if spoken aloud, formed inside his head, though they weren't from him.

He was suddenly aware that he was not alone up here, hidden in the branches of the hanging tree. He turned, knowing even before he saw her that the hag had crossed over. She still wore the noose—like a necklace—around her wrinkled neck.

God morgen, old hag.

She waved. A grin on her face. Her ghost feet kicked playfully.

He nodded to the crowd. *No one grieves you—except her.* He chittered out the words in squirrel speak, his tiny paws gesturing to Maeva.

She shrugged. *'Tis only misplaced guilt she feels.* He sensed this was true. *And fear, for the child. My death protects all of them.*

She held on to the trunk of the tree, floating precariously, inches above the limb, with one leg outstretched, enjoying her newfound freedom from a body.

You have been waiting a long time for her—and the blue one.

He froze, suspicious.

She laughed into the wind, a mere whisper in the leaves. *Don't worry, I won't get in the way.* She held her arms out, balancing.

He scampered to the end of a branch. *Did the Sisters send you?*

I was given a choice. To travel to the next world or stay here for a little longer. She began to fade. *I chose here. I still have work to do.*

The squirrel watched her disappear, uneasy. Then surveyed the crowd below. Wondering if that work had something to do with Maeva.

What Was

Pieter breathed in the frigid sea air, so cold and satisfying. He felt quenched, as though he had swallowed a huge bucket of water after years of thirst.

The wind was good today, enough to propel the trawler into the inlet, between the turquoise-blue waters and the ice floes. The landscape, the palest shades of white and blue, blanketed everything, from sea to mountain. The haul of fish they had caught was enough to feed them for the rest of winter.

It couldn't be more perfect, Pieter mused.

He tried not to let his mind wander outside of the perfection of white. Tried not to think about what had happened with Maeva.

Hans gestured to the clouds hovering over the mountain. "Blizzard's rolling in. This will be the last stop, then home." He eased the boat sideways, dropping anchor. "I'm sure your wife must be missing you."

I'm sure she isn't. Pieter gave a half smile, but said nothing.

The argument they had after the hanging still made him cringe. Her words cutting him deeper than any knife.

You're ashamed of me. Ashamed of our daughter. You want us to disappear . . .

Why didn't you marry someone else? A more willing woman?

Do you still love that market wench? Answer me, goddamn it.

His retorts ugly. Cruel.

My life used to be simple, before I met you. Hilde and I were . . . easier.

We both know you were more than willing.

You want to go back to nothing? Lying on the rocks naked, a prize for any sailor to bed? Be my guest.

The baby screamed and screamed, long into the night. None of Maeva's accusations were true, but she wouldn't listen. Leidah's cries echoed her mother's, hammering at him like a wood splitter. Every word, every wail, driving deeper into him, until he was defeated in splinters. His wife—and daughter—had become unrecognizable to him, unreachable. Inconsolable, pushing his sanity and patience over an edge he didn't even know he had. When he found her outside, unconscious in the water trough, he almost left her there. He hated to admit it, but his wife was destroying him.

So much so, he needed to escape. Some perspective, a bit of time to gather his thoughts. To remember what he was like before Maeva. Before the baby. Before the hanging.

Hans scratched his beard. "She doesn't know you're here. Does she?"

Pieter felt a heat flush his cheeks. Hans patted his back.

"Whatever happened, I'm sure it's just a lovers' spat. A consequence of the baby coming. Perhaps I should come for a visit, break up the tension a bit."

Pieter ignored the suggestion, ashamed to tell Hans how his wife truly felt about him. "Shouldn't we be in parental bliss by now?"

Hans laughed at him. "No such thing, according to my sister."

Pieter grimaced, then allowed himself a smile at his own expense. "Ja, I think she must be right." He paused, then quietly, "The hanging didn't help either."

Hans scoffed. "Unfortunate. Tragic. But not your fault. Leave it behind you."

"If only it were that easy. Mae believes we could have saved her."

"And you would have lost your wife in the process. That's not only foolish, it's short-sighted. Dangerous." He cocked his head. "I could talk to her if you like. Come to see Leidah?"

Pieter heard Maeva's words in his mind—*I don't want him around Leidah. I don't trust him*—and shook his head. "Thanks, but she doesn't even want me in the house."

Hans nodded, then changed the subject. "I suppose you heard about what happened to the old hag's body?"

Pieter felt a shiver up his spine. "Nei. What?"

Hans steered the boat around an ice floe. "Someone chopped off her toes while she still hung from the tree."

"To stop the ghost from haunting the village?"

"Superstitious hypocrites, the lot of them."

An eerie call interrupted them, keening on the wind.

Hans pointed off in the distance: a grey shape lifting its head. "She's calling to her pup."

Pieter swallowed.

"Did you know that mothers and pups recognize each other's calls, even after years apart?" Hans leaned against the rail. "That mother-pup bond, hard to break, I guess."

The words, unsettling to Pieter.

Hans winked, then sprang into action, grabbing the long hook—the hakapik—off the side of the boat. A flash of Maeva hitting her head on it the day of the rescue made Pieter tear up in contrition.

"An unexpected bit of luck, that call. The sea smiles on us today, my friend." Hans threw a pair of gloves at him before jumping onto the floes. "Protect yourself. Those seals are nasty. Wouldn't want you to get *spekk*-finger."

For the first time in his life, Pieter felt seasick.

The lie he'd told—about his whereabouts, what he was doing—growing to monstrous proportions. Maeva was already suspicious of Hans. What his friend was about to do, suddenly unthinkable. Cruel.

"I'm not quite feeling up to it."

Hans nodded once, then shook his head, baffled.

Pieter understood. The seal—its skin, its meat and blubber—was worth three times the small haul of fish they had caught. But how could Pieter tell his friend the truth? About what he had done, about who—what—Maeva was? He waved Hans on. "You go. I'll keep the boat steady."

Hans motioned in the direction of the dropped anchor. "I need you more than the boat does. What if I get caught underneath the ice? Can you dive from here if I go down?"

The blunt end hit square on the seal's forehead. The spike slid through thick blubber like a knife through butter. The ease of the action, so familiar.

It was the colour—that shock of brilliant red trailing behind them as Hans dragged the dead carcass to the boat—that he couldn't stomach. He retched on the ice.

The long smear of blood, soft and feathery, like paint.

Like hair.

What Is

Despite the rain pattering on the roof, the ticking of the clock has grown extraordinarily loud. Maeva stares at the beams above the bed, anxious. The weather might be a sign, she reasons, to wait until morning. *But this may be my only chance.* She eyes her sleeping husband. How innocent he seems. For a moment, Maeva fantasizes about telling him the whole truth while he dreams. *I need to say the words aloud . . .* Pieter's breath changes, deepening into a heavy snuffling snore. *But what if he wakes?* No. She can't risk it. She rolls out of bed, then sneaks out of the room. Gathers what she needs from the sewing room, stuffing scissors into a bag.

She pauses at Leidah's door. *Will she ever forgive me?* Stepping into the room, she tiptoes to her daughter's bedside.

"Leidah. Little one, wake up." The girl rolls over. "Listen, child."

Leidah moans, then rubs her eyes. Still asleep, she curls into her mother. Maeva swaddles her into the coverlet, then stands carefully. The child, light as a bird.

Time to go.

She settles her daughter into the chair on the porch, tucking the blanket around her. The horse will carry both of them easily. But the rain will slow them down. The path is flooded. The road, much worse. *Barely there, under a river.*

The forest, then. She pulls the hood of her cloak around her face, running into the downpour.

By the time she returns with the saddled horse, Leidah is awake, the blanket kicked free. Maeva dismounts and sprints to the porch.

"Mor, what's happening? Why are we—"

"No time for questions." She wraps the blanket around her once more.

"Mamma, you are still sick—it's pouring rain—" Leidah clings to Maeva's neck as her mother picks her up.

She leaps down the steps, then lifts the girl onto the wet saddle. She puts her foot on the stirrup, but can't help herself. *One last look.* The cabin, dark and forlorn.

"Spoon. Chair. Window. Clock." He pointed to each one, enunciating every syllable and sound for her to repeat. "Clock. Try it. *Klokke* . . . You've never seen one?"

She caressed the delicate carvings of vines on the little house, fascinated by the artistry. Everything—the door, the pitch of the roof, the porch—a miniature copy of the cabin.

"My father gave it to my mother on their wedding day . . . Now, I'm giving it to you." His face glowed with pride and anticipation, as though she might clap with glee.

Maeva flicked a finger at the chain, the acorn weight. She wondered at the purpose of such an object. It didn't seem to have one. Why would anyone need a box that ticked?

Unexpectedly, the tiny door flapped open. A tethered bird darted out, its wings caught in mock flight. A grating alarm, repeating over and over and over and—

The box snapped shut, trapping the bird inside.

Pieter grinned. "It sings like that, every hour."

A gurgled wail gets stuck in her throat. She starts to cry. *Come on, Mae . . . Keep moving.* Her foot pushes down into the leather. She throws her other leg over the saddle. But then she remembers the bag she had packed, her most important items in one little sack, sitting on the porch. There is no leaving without it. She slides reluctantly down the horse's flank. Her legs carry her back to the steps, the rest of her wanting desperately to flee. She stops in front of the door. Her hand hovers over the handle. *Can I really disappear without saying a word?* This quiet exit, so violent in its masked civility.

From inside the cabin, a startling sound: the clock chiming the hour.

Cu-ckoo-cu-ckoo-cu-ckoo—

She spins on her heel. Grabs the satchel. Knocking the small wooden cage on its side.

Cuckoocuckoocuckoo—

Instinctively, she flips it upright, the force snapping the twig door clean off.

Then, without a second thought, she flies off the porch.

The canopy of trees shelters them from the deluge. Maeva holds Leidah close in front of her, wrapped in cloak and blanket. Her fingers are cold and stiff, gripping the reins. But the rain feels so good on her dried-up skin. The horse moves slowly but steadily, snorting every once in a while in the dark. Maeva's impatience grows. The thought of finally touching the piece of herself she has been searching for makes her want to kick the horse into a trot. But the uneven muck is too dangerous. *No*, she thinks. *I have waited this long—what's another hour or two?*

Leidah leans into her mother, oddly quiet. Maeva waits for the barrage of questions, but they never come.

Above them, low clouds churn like a boiling pot, bubbling over onto the rolling landscape. No moon, no stars. The night muddied in black and purple fog. Maeva can't help but wonder at the forces at work in such a torrent. *Perhaps we should turn back.*

As she considers turning the horse around, the trees part onto a clearing. She can see the harbour in the distance. *Thank you, Sisters.* The lighthouse sends its beacon into the viscous fog. She clicks at the horse to trot, and the mare whinnies, then speeds up. *Almost home.*

By the time they reach the pier, the rain is even heavier. There is no sign of any human being, only the lonely sound of boats bumping against the dock. Maeva pulls the horse to a stop, then slides down, ties the reins to a post. She lifts her daughter to the ground, then grabs the packed satchel. Leidah's face is wet, stark white.

"Don't worry, girl. We're going to be fine." Leidah's teeth chatter in response. "Now where is Pappa's boat?"

Leidah grabs her hand and walks to the end of the dock, pointing between two bigger vessels. The small trawler rocks in the waves. Maeva wastes no time. She picks up Leidah and boards the boat, placing her daughter under the shelter of the helm. They shift and sway with the vessel's rocking.

"Stay here, out of the rain."

A clap of thunder booms overhead, and Leidah jumps. "Don't leave me, Mamma—" She grabs her mother's cloak.

"I'm right here, child." Leidah hugs her tightly. Maeva tries to pry her off, but fear makes the child cling even more. *Courage, girl.* "How about we light a candle under here, hmm? Then you can see the whole time, and I can find you in the dark."

Leidah nods and lets go. Maeva rustles through the cupboard near the wheel, finding a box of supplies. She pushes aside useless items—a red scarf, an empty bottle of whisky—and then pulls out an oil lantern and a box of matches. She lights the wick and turns it up, filling the helm with a warm glow.

She sets the lantern beside the child. "Don't touch it. I won't be long. I promise."

Maeva takes a deep breath, then climbs back onto the dock with her satchel.

She knows the skin is here; her fingers are buzzing. She walks to the front of the boat, her whole body vibrating. She feels a jolt hit her chest, and she sees it. *Yes! Takk, Sisters.* She nearly collapses with joy. The skin is stretched wide around the bow, its edges looped and tied with a criss-cross of ropes. She chokes back tears as she sees the damage it has sustained, faded by harsh weather, aged by the lick of sun and wind. *I barely recognize you.* But it doesn't matter now, she reasons. *All will return, as it was. As it's supposed to be.*

She pulls her sewing scissors out of the bag, then drops her sack. She begins to snip at the thick rope, slicing through its resistance with determination. Each time a piece snaps, Maeva feels something snap inside her. It's like she is separating into yet another body, the skin she wears molting. When half of the pelt releases off the boat, flapping in the wind, she loses her sense of up and down, and stumbles. The dock spins, as though she is out at sea already, floating on the waves.

I'm coming, my love.

"Maeva!"

No. Her body hardens, solidifies. *No!*

Pieter stands at a distance, his chest heaving, his clothes and boots covered in muck. His hands grip the rope that keeps the vessel tied to the dock. "I can't let you do this." The boat rocks on the incoming waves, about to be unmoored.

Maeva sees the look in his eyes, knows he is past the point of reason. "Pieter, please."

Another thunderous boom in the sky rocks through her.

He shouts into the rain, "Have you even thought this through? What about our daughter, for God's sake?"

She still holds the scissors in one hand. A hand that is shaking with fear. And love. And rage. "I don't have a choice. You are giving me no choice."

"You didn't even say goodbye." His words—his tears—shimmer through the rain. *Oh, Pieter . . .* He sees her softening. He moves to touch her, but the swiftness of his confidence stirs her into action; she wrenches away, the tip of the scissors sharp.

"You always have a choice, Mae. Don't do it. Don't leave us."

Us? "I'm not leaving my daughter. She's coming with me."

He takes a step closer. His voice wavers. "If you leave, you leave alone."

The hell I do. Maeva stands taller, the rain beating between them. "There are things you don't know. About our daughter." Out of the corner of her eye, she sees Leidah hiding, her face peering through the railing in fear.

Pieter is oblivious, struggling to keep the boat steady. He winces again as the rope catches on his hand. The colour drains from his face. Maeva blanches; his fingers are deformed. Swollen and purple. His wedding ring, barely visible. The waves crash against the trawler, smashing it against the dock with vehemence. "I know everything I need to know about my daughter—this is manipulation, wife."

She points to his hand in accusation, spitting out the words. "Jakobsen told me. You have *spekk*-finger." *A condition only a sealer could contract.* A horrifying suspicion washes over her: *he's been hunting.* She flings her arm toward the skin flapping in the wind. "I want to know why, Pieter. Why did you split it in half?" She can feel the scar on her tailbone stinging.

Pieter drops his chin, unable to make eye contact.

She waits. *I want a confession. I deserve one.*

Finally, he mumbles, "I didn't."

She roars in frustration. "You ripped it in two. The head sliced off—" She stops herself. Like a fog lifting off water, she senses the truth, all too clearly.

Hilde.

In her mind, she sees the woman wielding a knife, slashing at her skin. And Pieter watching.

It is a cruel epiphany, to suddenly see someone as he truly is. No artifice, no domestic guile. The stranger she married—a man she thought she had grown to know, to love after all this time—a stranger still. The changes in him—the changes in her—have been a game of pretend and delusion this whole time. *A game of lies.* The years have passed, decaying her mind, her body. This life of contained, complacent routine, so safe, so easy. *So tame.*

But the animal has always been there, lurking.

Without warning, a putrid stench assaults her. Plumes of decay wash over her: rotting fish, the stink of warm algae. Sour, rancid sweat . . . she feels a shard of something—seashell, bone—digging, clawing its way out of her spine.

This man—*this fisherman*—stands before her, casting his net. As he had on that fateful day. The day he caught a wife.

He opens his mouth to speak.

She holds up a hand. "Don't. Don't say another word." It is too much for her to absorb. Too vicious to hear the admission aloud.

He takes another step toward her, his arms reaching. The tumescent thumb, like a claw. Instinctively, she pulls away. The scissors catch his palm, slashing the infectious mound of flesh, splitting it open. The gash oozes red. The shock of open flesh suspending time—

Your grunts were low and heaving. Your breath rank.

The shape of the gods in your mouth, hollow, cavernous, as you emptied yourself inside me. You groaned and sighed, moaned as though this planned savagery were a romantic torment between lovers. You didn't notice me floating away, the blood on my back already a rotten scar. You peeled yourself off me, diving into the water, buoyed by this rescue, you, a saviour—

"Maeva, please . . . I love you." Awkwardly, he shuffles into her. His arms tackling her in a hug. He buries his face into her neck, sobbing. "I'm so sorry."

—I couldn't move. I couldn't speak. You took my mouth, my breasts, my legs, my eyes, my mind. Every last bit of wetness inside me. This body is no longer mine. I scrub and scratch and tear at it, even now. The blame—the shame—bores through me. You slit me down the middle, scooped out my insides, then stuffed me with lies—

*   *   *

She drops the scissors. Pieter's embrace tightens. "I won't let you go."

His hands pull at her hair, her neck, her back, blood smearing across skin. She can taste iron and salt in the air.

—I rolled into the water, numb. I stayed under, watching the blur of you through salt and blood. You held my skin hostage. Using it like a towel, to mop up your sins—

"You told Hilde about me. About our daughter." Her words are monotonous. He pulls his head from her chest, dropping his arms. Her eyes search his, begging for him to deny it. "You let her do unspeakable things—"

"I didn't. Hilde was only trying to help—"

"She sliced me in half." She leans into his ear. He mistakes the gesture, pressing his cheek to hers. "But *you* tore me to pieces."

Then, she speaks the final truth, barely a whisper: three words, the shape of nothing. And everything.

Gutting him from gullet to groin.

❦

He collapses to his knees. The rope forgotten.

Maeva rushes past him. *I'm coming, child.*

The ocean surges, lifting the trawler higher on the next wave. The boat breaks away, unmoored. Pieter scrambles to catch the end of the rope. The force of the vessel pulls him off the dock and into the icy waters. Both man and boat become weightless, inconsequential as sea-grass, as foam.

Maeva lunges, catching the railing in the nick of time. It's slippery, but her dried-out hands are tough, her grip strong. She hurls herself over the edge onto the deck. Another massive swell lifts the boat up, pushing them out to open water.

Leidah is huddled under the wheel. She jumps up. *Mamma!*

The lantern slides across the deck, then back again, like a swaying pendulum.

Maeva stumbles to her feet. She opens her arms wide. *Hurry, Leidah!*

The child leaps into the air.

In one agonizing second—*tick*—she is gone.

❦

Time slows, reverses. Folds into itself, wrinkle upon wrinkle. Furls of desiccated patches. Every moment stitched and torn simultaneously.

A tip of a lantern. A spill of oil. A single spark. Then, a wall of orange and red.

❦

Maeva's arms stretch and stretch, reaching, begging to be filled.

She screams, rushing frantically in circles. "Leidah! Where are you?" The blaze licks everything in its path—bench, wheel, blanket, scarf—spitting and blackening. Surrendering all to ash.

The brutality of nothingness—flakes scattering to the wind—crushes Maeva to her knees. The tip of her long braid sparking. Hissing.

Butterfly

Climbing out of the casing is more challenging than he expects. Never before has he been so delicate a thing. Thinner than paper, weightless, like spider silk. His body, both miraculous and weak, hampered by the fresh wetness of birth. His membrane wings struggling to open; his feet barely able to balance the wide expansiveness of possibility, so finely and carefully attached to his spine.

I am nothing, lighter than wind.

Flight, escape, freedom. The enormity of it all inside the fragility he has become.

The joy of birth—of finally shedding such a hard shell—is tempered by the immediate sensation of precariousness. He can taste, through his sliver-thin feet, that something is amiss. That time has been clipped short somehow, collapsing into swollen layers. What was, what is, what will be, all folding into one burgeoning blanket. Birth, death, and everything in between in this circle of existence spiraling onto itself, in a way he has never felt before. *Is this what time is to such a pathetic winged creature?*

The sticky sweat of birth. The sour taste of death. Synchronously.

Those conniving witches.

The Sisters have tricked him. Allowing him to believe that the end would bring all he desired, that patience would have the ultimate reward. That in the final days, he could become whatever he chooses; that Maeva would be his reward for the sacrifice of time, his sacrifice of godliness. That she would simply find her skin and dive into the sea, with him at her side. Their daughter traversing between worlds, navigating both land and ocean at will.

But inside his miniscule insect heart, he can sense that this is not the case; that Maeva is leaving this world without him, in the same moment he is being born with wings to fly to her. The rain, a mere nuisance to most; to him, certain death. The insignificance of his final form, no doubt an amusing irony for the three Sisters: a god trapped by the illusion of freedom, unable to fly. Powerless to fulfil his strongest desire.

He curses them.

Water must be running down the Great Tree, the well overflowing—another deep groove of destiny on its massive trunk. He imagines the veiled one's knife-like fingernail carving into the bark, snickering. His eagerness, always his downfall. He chose to leap into this forsaken cocoon too quickly, the thought of being so close to Maeva—and their child—blinding his judgement. He sacrificed his eye, his vision, his place among the gods, to become a winged creature with no power, no strength, no words, no magic. He thought he had time on his side, that death never comes to those whose stories have not played out.

How obtuse can you be? Time runs out, then runs over itself. Again and again, the cycle repeats. Even for a god.

Fury fills him. His wings beat with lightning speed.

Wrath is its own source of heat. But so is love.

His lungs suck in the wind of the storm. He imagines inhaling Maeva's entire being, their habitual choreography a dance of survival now. His wings become a blur of flight, a frenzy of flapping. The fire of desperation inside him scorches his miniature heart, the heat so unbearable he falls off the twig he is clinging to.

I am coming, Maeva . . .

What Is

Pieter tries again and again to swim against the incoming tide. To catch the burning trawler. Each time, the waves throw him back more furiously. The distance between the vessel and himself grows bigger with each smack of water. Then, in a final burst of blinding yellow, there is nothing. No burning on the horizon. His boat, his wife—his life—devoured by the monstrous sea. And now, only rain.

His teeth bite into the moving shoreline under him. Grit, salt, sweat, and tears stream down his throat, burying all sound. Washing up on shore, he had found the love of his life in the crash of another storm. His destiny, hiding in seaweed hair.

In these same waters, all is lost.

He rolls on his back, exhausted. What does any of it matter now?

She's not yours.

Three small words. An avalanche. The weight of mountains crumbling, burying him. A single sentence tearing their child—*her* child—away from him. He can't even think about what this means. Who the man is. Who Maeva loved before him. Who Leidah truly belongs to.

Lei-lee . . .

He hears his daughter's name, a scream on the wind.

She's. Not. Yours.

"You are wrong, Mae. She's mine, and always will be." He whispers the words, but the wind smothers them. *Where are you, child? Surely Maeva wouldn't bring you here?* But somehow, he knows she did. He scrambles to his feet, runs across the sand, his feet losing purchase, his eyes scanning both land and sea. He shouts for Leidah, flinging her name to the wind, to the sky, to the rain. *Where is she?*

Running back into the waves, the tide up to his knees, he yells her name one last time, the last syllable dying on his lips. The gales rushing in to obliterate it.

A grey piece of skin, the size of a shawl, skims against his legs. He bends down to pick it up, his hand oozing blood.

It is the last of her. The only thing that remains.

"Maeva!"

Their horse whinnies in response. Pieter holds on to the skin, running toward the mare. He slows down, then murmurs to her, calming the startled animal. Drapes the skin over the saddle. Grabbing the reins, he walks the horse to the pier. Out on the dock, he spies a small bundle. He runs to it, picks it up. Scouring the horizon, he yells Leidah's name again. Feels a tornado spinning inside his chest—a need for drastic action—but his body and mind have turned to wood. He clutches the bag, stumbles back to the horse.

He needs a search party.

He needs Hans.

He needs daylight.

He needs the gods. *Odhinn, bring her back . . .*

He staggers to his knees, his hand clinging to the reins. His other hand clinging to the last part of his wife.

The Last Thread

The ghost flies across the waves, too inconsequential to save anyone. She stands by helplessly as fire and water swallow the boat. She spins in turmoil, up and up, into the centre of the storm.

Why am I here, Skuld? What am I to do?

She sees the husband floundering, sobbing and splashing like a madman. The waves push him back to shore every time. The Fates unrelenting.

She raises a fist at the sky. *At least put them out of their misery. Have some mercy.*

Lightning flashes; the torrential downpour, ruthless. She doesn't feel it, but the electric charge moves through her. *The fury of the gods.*

It is then that she sees it. A white thing flitting inches above the waves. Too small to be a bird. She flies toward it, realizing it's a butterfly. She watches it dance erratically, up and down, its wings slowing, then frantically flapping higher each time it sinks perilously close to the surface of the water.

Hallo, old friend, she thinks, recognizing him finally. *What a terrible choice of shape this time.*

He doesn't respond, exhausted from the flight, from simply trying to survive this shell.

She dissipates into a mist. *Perhaps it's the one thing—the only thing—I can do.* Save this tiny wretch. Her own shape expands, then envelops the butterfly to protect him from the rain. They fly out to sea together. She senses he is about to drop, surrender to the currents. Then, a small mercy: a patch of red seaweed, like an underwater garden in the middle of the sea. *How can such a patch exist in these depths?* She feels the butterfly exhale every fibre of his being, all his will gone. She floats closer, and then understands: Maeva. *This is no small mercy. It is fate.* This is what she has been sent back—here—to do.

Like a sea creature rising from the depths, Maeva lifts her head from the ocean, her copper seaweed hair dancing, buoyant around her body. She doesn't seem to see Helgar, but she doesn't need to.

The old woman releases the butterfly.

He tumbles in the wind, end over end, no strength left.

Maeva opens her mouth, taking one final breath. He lands perfectly, elegantly, on the bed of her tongue.

His last, best transformation.

The Ninth Knot

The knock at the door startles her.

It is past dark, past the time when anyone should be out in such a snowstorm.

Since before she can remember, Pappa always warned her—before tromping out in the cold to the barn—to stay indoors in such frigid temperatures.

"You are much more important than chickens, my little *kanin*. They will survive. Unless the wolves get them." His eyes sparkled. "Wolves are always hungrier in the winter, especially for chickens. But do you know what they love even more?"

"What, Pappa?"

He grinned. "Little girls."

She squealed, bursting into giggles as Pappa nibbled at her neck. He always tucked her in extra tight at bedtime in winter, rolling her up in so many blankets, neither the cold nor the wolves could sink their teeth into her.

It has been several nights since she has been tucked in. Too many nights to count.

Pappa's absences, longer and longer.

She watches him from the window. He mounts their mare each day, then disappears into the trees. He doesn't return until the sun sets. Sometimes, the moon is high before she hears his boots stomping on the porch. Stumbling, smelling of ale or whisky. Sometimes, he doesn't make it inside, letting the cold have its way with him.

Every day brings the same sadness. Every day he leaves her.

She hates being alone, but it isn't his fault. He has to keep searching for Mor.

He has to keep searching for me.

Leidah tries to show him that she's right there, in front of him. She tries and tries, with all her strength, to jump out of what she has become, but nothing ever changes. She wishes with all her might to become a tea-cup, a floorboard, a spoon. To become his Lei-lee so she can wrap her arms around him and say, *I've been here all along.* But it is no use. Something is different. Her specialness, gone. No matter how much she prays—no matter how much she wriggles and writhes and resists—she is stuck. Unable to move or breathe—or become—like she used to.

Thankfully, Pappa held on to the piece of skin for dear life that night, bringing her home to hang in the bedroom window. Perhaps he imagined Mamma was still inside it somewhere, that she needed to feel the sun through the pane of glass. Sometimes, she thinks she hears Mamma calling her name. But she's sure it's wishful thinking. Sometimes, Pappa takes the skin and cradles her ever so tenderly, falling asleep with her nestled into his cheek. She can feel his tears soaking into her. But most days, he simply stares at the skin hanging in the window, for hours upon hours.

The clock stopped. No more tick or tock. Pappa forgot to wind it, and the cabin is so quiet. Only the battering wind sneaks through cracks and crevices, into her mind—*Do I even have a head anymore?* Her prayers for Mamma's safe return, repeating over and over again.

A blizzard batters against the cottage, whipping up a sea of white, hiding the horse's tracks. *He will be back. He has to come home—for where else could he go?* But this certainty doesn't stop the gnawing emptiness inside her, a growing hole that only gets bigger with each passing hour she is alone. The snow piles up until it has made a small mountain below the window, hiding the steps to the porch.

She peers through the darkness. A shadow, barely there.

Is that a knock?

Another bang, this time louder.

A small, hooded figure is below the window, waiting on the porch. Glancing up once in a while to where she hangs, as if sensing she is there.

"Pieter?"

The voice is a woman's. *I know you.*

"I can sense you're in there—please, it's me. I've come back."

Out of the corner of her eye, Leidah feels something hovering inside the room; it is the old woman, the one she has seen her whole life. The ghost shimmers but does not speak.

The wind picks up outside. The hooded woman curses. Then, in the hush, Leidah hears a click. The lock lifting out of its hinge. The door creaks open.

Leidah feels the urge to leap into something—the windowpane, the swirling pattern of frost—but of course, that's not possible anymore. *Bastard in hell.* Even if she could jump, she reasons, she's safe where she hangs.

She can still feel her mother's pulse inside the scrap of skin. The mist of the old ghost disappears, spreading herself to sink beneath the floor.

"Oh, stop your flailing, old ghost," a woman says. "It's none of your business."

Leidah hears the person searching in the dark, pausing every so often to listen.

"I feel you are here . . . But where, where would you hide?"

At the sound of her voice, a shiver passes through Leidah, as if the slightest trace of her mother is resisting the stranger. *Who are you, and what do you want?*

Leidah prays the woman will leave. She hears footsteps pausing, then starting again, then pausing once more. After minutes, the stranger begins climbing the ladder.

Before she can reach the bedroom, the front door opens and slams shut.

Pappa!

"Pieter, is that you? Thank God you are home. It was so cold, I let myself in."

"Hilde? You nearly scared me out of my skin. What in the devil are you doing here?"

Leidah shrivels, a flash of vermilion burning in her mind.

"I . . . I saw you yesterday at the market. You seemed so lost."

He doesn't respond. Then, a shuffling sound, and in an instant, the two of them are inside the bedroom.

Pappa, nei! Leidah strains at the very edges of her mother's skin, screaming through the darkness, but her father cannot hear her. She watches helplessly as the woman takes off her cloak, her dark hair tumbling down her back. Pappa's hands reach out, getting lost in the tangle of black curls.

Leidah squirms in frustration, enough to make the skin move ever so slightly. *I am here, Pappa!* Enough to make him pull back, notice the window.

Hilde follows his gaze. Her tone of voice changes. "Is that hers?"

He nods slowly.

Hilde is quick to move. She snatches the skin from the window and crumples it into a ball.

Every part of Leidah burns in the woman's grip.

"It's time to give this up, Pieter. It's been over a year. Time to move on."

He turns his back.

Hilde wraps her arms around him from behind, holding the skin to Pappa's chest.

Leidah can feel her father's heartbeat, strong and fast. Then, she realizes. *A year? How can that be?* She can feel the woman's fingernails slicing into her, feels the pinch in the centre of her very being.

"You need me—I will get rid of it—then we can talk?"

He pulls away and takes Hilde's hand. Slowly, Leidah feels herself uncurl, draping over the woman's palm. Her father's fingers pause, hovering over the skin.

He sighs, then nods, pulling his hand away abruptly. "There are more of her things. In the sewing . . ." His voice breaks.

Leidah feels herself folded over and over, like the quilt of time itself.

Then, she is tossed carelessly into a sack.

What Remains

The ghost watches as Hilde kneels down, rummaging through the sewing basket. She tosses out scraps of fabric, then dumps the entire pile on the floor, searching. Pieter is downstairs, lost in ale. Unable to witness the last of his family thrown away like trash.

"Come out, come out, wherever you are," Hilde purrs, as if there were a kitten hiding beneath the floor. "Clever witch," she murmurs, picking up Maeva's unused thread, spun by Hilde herself. She pockets the spool and continues to search.

Helgar smirks in the shadows. Maeva could have sealed herself a quicker fate, sewing with that cursed yarn. But somehow, deep down, the young mother must have known.

Hilde picks up a basket and flips it over. She snatches at the delicate caul-skin quilt, stuck to the bottom, and examines the odd material.

The old woman spirals around her in a mist. Hilde waves her away, sensing how the fog is confusing her intuition.

"Shoo, midwife. This isn't your concern."

Ah, but it is. I am here to protect the child.

"You don't protect children, you kill them. Remember?" Hilde's sarcasm hits the mark.

The old woman wafts into the child's bedroom. She slips inside the wardrobe; three small dresses hang like ghost sisters in the darkness. At the bottom of the wardrobe, a bag tossed carelessly aside, forgotten. She brushes a few grains of sand off it, peers inside, and realizes she has found a treasure—the treasure—that will change everything.

The seal head.

She knows what to do. She becomes a slight breeze, rustling the dresses.

Attracted by the sound, Hilde comes and opens the wardrobe, claps her hands. "*Takk*, old woman."

Pieter sits by the fire, watching Hilde pack up her things. "That's it, then?"

"Don't worry. It's all done." Hilde moves to kiss him, but Pieter turns his cheek. Hilde tries to hide her hurt feelings, but the old woman sees. "I can come back tomorrow, to help you clean this house?"

Pieter ignores her, points to the bag that he found abandoned on the pier, the night that he lost everything. "Let me see it. I never had the courage to look inside."

Hilde clutches it closer. "No need to revisit such a painful thing. Don't even think twice—"

Pieter grabs the satchel, tears it open. The seal mask—what Hilde promised to sell years ago—staring up at him.

The witch leaves with a full satchel, but bitterness propels her. The last remnants of mother and daughter shoved on top of each other.

The old woman whispers a song into the witch's ear, an incantation that sounds so much like the wind, Hilde forgets herself, even forgets Pieter for a moment, and begins to sing.

Skin, seal, and sea; what was, what is, will be . . .

The words elicit an irresistible rhythm in Hilde's feet.

She dances all the way to the shoreline.

Becoming Leidah

I can smell the sea. I can hear the crash of waves.

Hilde curses, then throws quilt and mask into the water. I fly through the air, clinging to all the bits of myself and Mamma: skin and web, hair and thread, seal and sea—

We are the map of a thousand oceans, daughters of the sacred deep. Every trace of rock, water, and wind; every island and shoreline carried on our backs. Every battle scar, kiss of harpoon, hungry bite of tooth and talon, a topography of our survival. Velvet tongues, luminescent underbellies; wondrous caves of throat and ear, poems etched into our alabaster bones—

I can hear Mamma's words, our story, echoing in the mouth of wind.

By the time I splash into the water—only one gulp of air, but it feels like forever—I am myself again. A blue girl, with blue fins. Webbing that slices through the waves so easily, I must be a fish.

But I'm not. I'm me.

I can swim, Mamma.

I know I can do even more than that. As much as I can I imagine. *I am more.*

My mother's hair and skin sleep inside me. Her strength, woven and stitched into my eyes, my arms, my legs, my heart, my toes, my fingers, my belly, my blood. My web.

Mamma is the thread between all of the shapes that make up me.

Should you ever need me, wrap this around you, and pray . . .

I float on my back, hearing her voice in the current.

I look up to the night sky. Snowflakes—like stardust—float and dance, tickling my nose. I open my mouth wide. The sky melts on my tongue. *I am the sky.* I kick my feet, stretching my arms on the waves.

It's a long swim, a long dive to find Mamma. *And the blue girls.* I know she's out there—they're out there—playing. Waiting for me.

I twirl in circles, hearing a song on the wind. Inside my bones.

It is a prayer—the lullaby Mamma always sang to me—thrumming, pulsing.

Calling me home.

Epilogue

What Was, What Is, What Will Be

In life, there is death. In death, there is life.

The Sisters greet his spirit at the gate, cackling and howling. He doesn't laugh. Nor does he protest, so exhausted at the futile cycle of time.

All that was, is, and will be. Don't you see?

He doesn't. *You stole my eye. I'm dead. How can I see anything?*

Ah, but this is the best way. Close your other eye.

Wearily, he does what they ask.

Unexpectedly, brilliantly, a pattern is revealed.

So many threads, warping and wefting and winding around one another. Knotted and tied, unfurling, elongating. Then spiraling into new coils. Spinning the most intricate pattern—every creature, every man, every child, every witch and wisewoman, god and demon—integral and absolutely necessary, between all that is and ever was. Changing, transforming, *becoming* all the time, in every moment.

His finale was a miraculous evolution: total dissolution into another. The ultimate sacrifice of all that he was, all that he is. So that she may live. *For Leidah.*

Betwixt and between each of the Nine Worlds, every single filament of him disappears, dissolving on the tongue of Maeva. His spirit shoots into space in every direction. The Great Tree—branches radiating, spreading, collecting—throbbing its drum into the root of Time.

And there, inside the undertow: a red thread tossed in the current, penetrating across realms, to pierce the heart of another. Skin and quilt and creature, mother and daughter—two ends of the same thread. One knot of the truest love, a dance of unravelling. At the beginning and end of everything, they will all find each other. At *shoormal.*

It is Urd, the guardian of What Was, who reminds him: *A god cannot die. Forgotten for a time, perhaps. But perpetually living, waiting for resurrection—*

On shore, he hears the old ghost whisper his name on the wind, feeding an ancient story—his story—into the breath of his daughter, who is swimming, searching . . .

Then the veiled one asks: *Are you ready to be remembered?*

He doesn't have to answer, or even open his remaining eye.

The tug of the red thread, pulling and pulling.

Acknowledgments

First and foremost, much appreciation and gratitude to Laurie Grassi, my incredibly astute and kind editor, who took a chance on an absolute amateur. Her enthusiastic belief in the writing buoyed me up, and her keen eye helped me find the heart of the story. Editing didn't feel like work at all, more like having tea with a dear friend. Thank you to the team at Simon & Schuster, for all the behind-the-scenes, seemingly invisible efforts to bring this to fruition. Credit goes to Elizabeth Whitehead for creating such a beautiful cover, and to my talented friend Cassie McReavy (who is always up for creative adventures) for the playful author photo. Years ago, Karen Connelly (Humber School for Writers) warned me away from red herrings when the story was a tangled mess, and for that I am grateful.

I grew up with stories about my ancestors, most of whom had legendary longevity and fierce faith in God. My great-grandmother Edith was said to have cured herself of gangrene overnight, with only prayer. I like to believe that she and these other incredible women guided my serendipitous stumbling onto just the right book or article, as well as the deep dives into my family tree (thanks to Janet Menard and Linda White for filling in some of these gaps). Kathleen Stokker's *Remedies and Rituals:*

Folk Medicine in Norway and the New Land was such an important read, as was *The Black Books of Elverum,* edited by Mary S. Rustad. These books helped me to imagine what it must have been like for my relatives in rural Norway before they immigrated to Missouri and the Dakotas, finally settling in Saskatchewan.

An abundance of gratitude to my parents, Anna and Wade. Though my mom will never read this, I hope she knows that her constant love and encouragement shaped me into who I am. My dad was a man of few words when I was a kid, and his head was always buried in a book. At seven, I remember thinking, *I need to write a novel.* You made me want to write, Dad; I await your impending criticism. Thanks to my brother, Mike, for all the teasing and truth-telling over the years. And for letting me be "the crazy aunt" to such beautiful kids.

I have been blessed to be surrounded and supported by highly intelligent and talented women my entire life (shout-out to all the wild women whom I love dearly, especially the Lovin' Coven: Rosanne, Kiran, Maggie, Alanna, Charlene, Kim, Francesca, Cheyenne, and all the Estroven ladies). Specifically, my guru, Leslie Godfrey: I can't thank you enough for role modeling who I want to be when I grow up. Having your eyes on the very first draft of this story was much-needed fuel; your unwavering faith in me propelled me to keep creating (book two, here I come). All the members of the Fine Arts department (past and present), this is me, genuflecting; you have been my sustenance, my soul food, my work family. Thank you to all my students (twenty-six years and counting)—keep dancing—and my Arts and English teachers. Jan A., thank you for so many things, but especially Norway. Lesley, Julia, and Sarah, our Bean vacations are the best! (And Group B, you are a treasure in the land of Zoom.)

A special place in my heart is reserved for Jonathon Neville, who leapt into my life years ago, a bit like a barn cat. Somewhere along the way, he shape-shifted into a princely jester, who is currently working on saving the world. Jono, thank you for being such a beautiful man. And for all your tech help (never shaming my digital and social media ignorance). For loving me, even when I'm unlovable. For always asking me to dance.

Lastly—but always first—an ocean of gratitude and love to Taras, the most magical, talented human I know. Writer-painter-beatboxer-musician-composer-traveller-hiker-political-activist-mathmetician-philosopher-comedian-trampoline-jumper-cyclist-etcetera, your intelligence and creativity humbles and inspires me, every single day. Thank you for choosing me as your mom. You are my reason, my world, my everything.

About the Author

MICHELLE GRIERSON is a teacher, writer, dancer, painter, habitual traveller, voracious reader, and enthusiastic mom who has spent a lifetime chasing and channelling ancestral ghosts through her writing, art, and choreography. A firm believer in blood memory, she has been researching her Norwegian and Celtic ancestry for years, and that inspired her debut novel, *Becoming Leidah*. Most days Michelle can be found exploring the woods near her southwestern Ontario home with her son, Taras, and their dogs, Tulla and Bijou. Visit her at **michellegrierson.com**.